"No!" she cried softly just before he leaned forward and touched his mouth to hers.

She could have plucked him up and flattened him on the ground just as he had seen her do to the bennesah, but she did not. Her hands went to his shoulders, gripping him and pushing against him at the same time.

But no sooner had he pressed against her mouth than he was pulling away and looking into her eyes.

"No?" he asked.

Then he moved in and caught her stunned lips against his again, this time deepening the kiss a little. She had every intention of shouting no at the top of her lungs . . . until she actually began to taste him, to draw the flavor of him onto her lips. But just when she was starting to get interested, he pulled back again.

"No?" he asked once more. And this time he did not return. This time he waited for her response. Waited to hear her rebuff him again.

"No," she said. They both immediately knew the difference between the first denial and this last one. This time she was saying no to his no. As in yes. Yes, she wanted him to kiss her again. She didn't know why, but she wanted more. She knew there was something more to be had, and she wanted it.

Books published by Random House are available at quantity discounts on bulk purchases for premium, educational, fund-raising, and special sales use. For details, please call 1-800-733-3000.

CURSED
by
ICE

The
IMMORTAL
BROTHERS

JACQUELYN FRANK

BALLANTINE BOOKS • NEW YORK

A Ballantine Books Mass Market Original

Copyright © 2015 by Jacquelyn Frank

Excerpt from *Bound by Sin* by Jacquelyn Frank copyright © 2015 by Jacquelyn Frank

Published in the United States by Ballantine Books, an imprint of The Random House Publishing Group, a division of Random House LLC, a Penguin Random House Company, New York.

BALLANTINE and the HOUSE colophon are registered trademarks of Random House LLC.

This book contains an excerpt from the forthcoming book *Bound by Sin* by Jacquelyn Frank. This excerpt has been set for this edition only and may not reflect the final content of the forthcoming edition.

ISBN 978-0-553-39341-5

eBook ISBN 978-0-553-39342-2

Cover design: Carolyn Teagle

Cover photograph: © Michael Grecco/ImageBrief.com

Printed in the United States of America

www.ballantinebooks.com

9 8 7 6 5 4 3 2 1

Ballantine Books mass market edition: April 2015

For all my fellow rescuers out there—
your hard work saving lives makes all the difference.
Know that you are very much appreciated for it.

PRONUNCIATIONS

DAVINE (Dah-vēn)
DETHAN (Dē-than)
ISAELLE (Is-ah-el)
JONA (Jō-nah)
SARIELLE (Sah-rē-el)
VINQUA (Vin-kwah)
WRENA (wren-yah)

PROLOGUE

Garreth stumbled and fell for what had to be the thousandth time since this journey had begun. His brothers, each a mighty warrior in his own stead, had been forging the way up the mountain for hours, more determined than ever to reach their goal. But Garreth . . . He was frozen through, and a horrible sense of foreboding had settled on him. Finally he voiced aloud what he had been thinking for the past few hours.

"This mission is cursed," he said, falling to his knees in the deep, hard snow, the painful cracking of his skin ripping around his mouth with every spoken word. His breath clouded hard upon the air, and his moustache and beard were laden with icicles. The air was so thin up on that high mountain point that it was a wonder he could breathe at all. Several of his fingers were turning black, and he had already lost some of his toes. All for what? For the promise of a fantastical prize that could easily not even exist.

His brothers were convinced it existed. They were convinced it was atop this very mountain. They had only a little farther to go, they said. All Garreth knew was that if they didn't find the font of immortality at the top of this mountain, he was going to die upon it. He was already maimed by this frigid venture; his hands had been ruined, and he would never swing a sword again. And since his sword was how he made his way in the world, he didn't know what he would do. He was a fighter. A man of honor who fought for those who could not fight for themselves. He may not be the golden warrior his brothers Maxum and Jaykun were or the great conqueror his eldest brother, Dethan, was, but he held his own in a fight and his sword was highly valued. He did not sell his sword as Maxum did and he did not sit at Dethan's right hand as Jaykun did, but he chose the noblest adventures out there to be found.

This was not a noble venture. It was a selfish one. His brothers were cheating the gods, seeking a shortcut to immortality. They sought the waters of a magical fountain that would give them health and longevity for the rest of time.

He had come with them only after much cajoling, as brothers were wont to do to their youngest sibling. He had thought the mission to be pure folly and had long since been convinced of it. He had been on many noble quests in his young lifetime, but never for his own selfish ends. He should have known better.

"Come, brother. Don't be such a woman. Get up and move on. We are almost there," Dethan said, coming to take his arm and pull him up out of the snow. But Garreth's legs would not work. They were two frozen stumps that he could no longer feel or force to his command.

In the end, the blackness rushed up on him so suddenly that, in spite of Dethan's hands on him, he fell forward, his face planting in the snow as if all that was needed was a spring sun to grow a flowering bush in the spot.

The next thing Garreth was aware of was the feel of being jogged hard against a body, his head hanging in the open air as he swung about. One of his brothers had thrown him over his shoulder. A brother who was now running across the frozen mountaintop. Suddenly Garreth was pitched onto the ground, his body so cold he didn't even feel the ice and snow he was sure was seeping into his clothing. He was sick and dizzy, unable to breathe.

"Look, brother!" Dethan called excitedly. "We have found it! The fountain! It will restore you!" Dethan hurried to take a drinking horn from his pack and filled it with water from a jeweled fountain, which flowed freely in spite of the frigid temperatures. The gems encrusting it were large and fine, glittering in the glaring sun.

Dethan could have drunk from the horn first, but all he was concerned with was Garreth's well-being. It was so very much like his brother, to care for him first, above all others. Dethan had raised him from boyhood to a man after their parents had died, orphaning them all at very young ages. Dethan had always felt responsible for him, often funding his expeditions and ventures of honor.

And yet Garreth questioned the wisdom of what they were doing. He warned his brothers one last time that he had an ill feeling about this. That perhaps it was better to freeze to death on that mountain than to flirt dangerously with the fountain of the gods.

His brothers ignored him.

When Dethan pressed the cup on him, he had no strength to fight him. The water flowed past his cracked lips and onto his tongue. He could not swallow, so Dethan massaged his throat until the water slid down. It was refreshing at the very least. He knew it was of the gods, else it would not flow so freely in the forsaken place, but would it do what his brothers thought and hoped it would do?

He had his answer almost immediately. His body began to warm from the inside out, as if he had drunk a horn of mulled mead. The warmth spread through his veins with a peaceful perfection. There was no pain, as there had been every night by the fire as he had tried to warm his frozen fingers and toes. He had welcomed that pain when it came, knowing it meant there was still life within those digits. It had not come the last time they had camped.

But now feeling was creeping into his fingers and his toes. He could feel the bitterness of the cold—was still frozen by it, he knew—but sensation was returning.

And that was when the pain hit him. He cried out with a bellow of agony, his body jerking into spasms. His brothers could do nothing to help him, for as soon as he had drunk, they had drunk, and now they too were writhing in agony. He knew his body was changing, that he was never going to be the same, but changing into what? How would he be different?

The pain subsided and a wondrous sensation was left in its place. A sensation of being more alive and healthier than he had ever been before. He leapt to his feet, shaking off the remaining cold from his limbs, and laughed.

And then a mighty clap of thunder rocked the mountain, shaking it to its bedrock. Angry lightning streaked the nearly cloudless sky.

That was when the gods appeared to them.

He knew they were gods because they were much bigger than any mortal man might be. And the goddesses were so beautiful it hurt to look upon their faces. At the forefront was a goddess dressed in a warrior's armor, with a breasted chest plate and a golden skirt that reached to her knees and no farther. She stepped forward, a golden spear in her hand and a wey flower tucked into her hair behind her ear.

Weysa, the goddess of conflict. He would have known her anywhere. The statue depictions in her temples were wrong, for they could never truly match the pureness and grandness of her beauty, the fierceness of her posture.

"You dare to steal this reward when you have not deserved it in our eyes?" she said in a deep, booming feminine voice. "You dare to do so without permission, without honor? You will pay for your folly, foolish, arrogant worms. You will pay for your immortality with blood and bone and flesh. We cannot take this gift back, but we can see to it you wish you had never dared to think you could push the hands of the gods to your will and your liking."

And in the next instant his brothers were whisked away, taken from his sight. Suddenly chains sprouted from the icy ground and manacles seized his wrists and ankles, yanking him down to the ice and flat on his back. Hella, the goddess of fate and fortune—a goddess with beautiful blond hair that flowed down her back, her legs, and then onto the ice, where it curled around and around into a golden puddle—moved over to him and bent down to hiss words into his face.

"This is your curse, a curse given to you by the gods. Now you will pay for your insolence, freezing here in this wasteland again and again, within sight of the very fountain that gifted you with immortality. And so your fortune will be until the end of time. I once smiled upon you for your heroic deeds; now I will spit upon you for your hubris."

And then, before he could say a word in his own defense, the gods were gone, leaving him there to do exactly as Hella had said. To freeze.

Again.

And again.

And again.

OVER TWO HUNDRED FULL TURNINGS LATER . . .

Dethan had done it. He had gambled everything and won. He had his mortal life and his beloved wife, and soon they would have their child. He had bargained everything, and now his brother had been freed. Weysa had freed Garreth from his chains on the mountainside, which had seen their folly all those many turnings ago. Now, as Dethan sat in front of the fire, warming the block of ice that was his brother, he tried not to think of the curse that would still follow Garreth for all the rest of his days and to focus instead on the freedom he had been given . . . the reprieve.

He bent over Garreth, rubbing warmth into him briskly, impatient for him to awaken . . . to speak to Dethan for the first time since all this had begun. What would Garreth say to him? Would he hold him responsible? He should. Dethan deserved nothing less than to be held responsible for the entire folly. He was glad Weysa had chosen, out of his three brothers, Garreth to be freed from the bulk of his punishment. Of all of them, Garreth deserved his punishment the least. He deserved his freedom, however piecemeal it might be.

"Garreth . . . speak to me," Dethan urged his brother.

Garreth began to quake and shiver. Shavings of ice became droplets of water. His frozen lashes fluttered. Suddenly his eyelids pried apart and his pupils contracted sharply in the light of the fierce fire they sat near. His teeth began to chatter. Life shook into his body in fierce, quaking trembles.

At last he spoke. "Brother," he said. "Am I free?"

"For the moment," Dethan told him gently. "For the moment."

CHAPTER
ONE

Garreth walked into the command tent and immediately dropped his burden on one of the cross-legged tables within. He wore full armor, so every time he moved the sound of metal striking metal was made. It was a sound he had grown to love over his lifetime. The sound of a man ready for whatever battles might come his way. A sound he once thought he would never hear again.

"Well, little brother, how goes things with the troops?"

Garreth turned to face Dethan. "Well, elder brother," he said with a tight-lipped smile, "they are bored out of their skulls."

"I thought you were sending out hunting parties."

"I did. And we've game aplenty now. But these men have come for a fight and they are itching to do battle. I cannot say I blame them. The summer wears on, and soon you will be returning to your wife and child, taking half our forces back with you to winter. They want to see at least one more glorious battle before they go."

"Outside this tent and a few strides away is that glorious battle to come." Dethan moved to the front of the tent, looking out the opening and toward the city they had chosen to sack in Weysa's name.

That was their part of the bargain, the deal that had freed the two brothers from their torments after they had drunk from the fountain. Dethan, Garreth had learned, had been thrust down into the darkest, hottest pit of the eight hells, cursed to burn to the bone over and over again, just as Garreth had been cursed to freeze. But almost a full turning of the seasons ago, the goddess had freed Dethan.

Weysa needed warriors to fight in her name. She and the other gods had grown weak as the people turned away from their faith and belief in them, for they needed the love and devotion of the people in order to gain power. And now that the twelve gods were at war, split into two factions of six, they desired power more than ever. Weysa's faction consisted of Hella, the goddess of fate and fortune; Meru, the goddess of hearth, home, and harvest; her brother Mordu, the god of hope, love, and dreams; Lothas, the god of day and night; and Framun, the god of peace and tranquility. They warred with the opposing faction of Xaxis, the god of the eight hells; Grimu, the god of the eight heavens; Diathus, the goddess of the land and oceans; Kitari, the goddess of life and death; Jikaro, the god of anger, deception, and storms; and Sabo, the god of pain and suffering.

However, Kitari, the queen of the gods, was being held by Xaxis's faction against her will, a fact they had discovered only last winter, when Dethan had traded away his immortality in order to discover her true intent. It had been a risky proposition, one that could easily have backfired and meant a permanent end to Dethan, but instead it had freed him fully from his curse, made him mortal, and allowed Garreth to be freed from his icy hell as well.

Somewhat.

For every night, between dusk and the juquil's hour, Garreth was cursed to freeze again. A reminder, he thought grimly, of what he had done and of the gods' discontent with him. Weysa had only freed him to fight; she had not been willing to release him entirely from his curse.

But that did not matter. All that mattered was that they and their army perform well. They had Hexis, the city where Dethan's wife ruled with Dethan, and they had conquered one other city already, this past spring, erecting temples to Weysa within its walls and filling their army with more soldiers from that city. Now it was coming on the end of summer and out there, only a short distance away, was the next city.

The city they had conquered in the spring had been easy. Almost too easy. Dissatisfyingly easy. Garreth had wanted a pitched battle, a fight to vent his anger and frustrations on.

Both of which were great and many.

But more than that, he wanted to please the goddess. Not from fear of her, although that was most certainly present, but in the hopes that she would see what powerful warriors the brothers were, what great assets they were . . . and maybe it would compel her to find and release the remaining two brothers from their torments.

Garreth and Dethan fought and conquered just the same, in the hopes that one day their brothers would be free. Yes, most of all, that was what they both fervently prayed for.

Just then a courier ran up to the tent. He handed a pair of dispatches to Dethan.

"Ah! A letter from Selinda!" Dethan said eagerly, moving back into the tent and handing the second dispatch to Garreth, unread. Dethan clearly did not care what was in the other message. The letter from his wife meant more to him than anything else.

Rescuing their brothers was a very close second to that.

"Look! Look how he's grown!" Dethan showed a paper to Garreth excitedly. It was a very skillfully rendered and life-like miniature sketch of Dethan's infant son. The child was nearly five wanings old, and Dethan had been campaigning for three of those wanings. Garreth and the army had conquered their city in the spring alone before Dethan had joined them at the turn of summer, as was agreed by Weysa. Dethan's summers were hers, when he would fight, and the remaining wanings he belonged to his beloved wife, Selinda.

These wanings had been difficult on Dethan, Garreth knew. He had wanted to be with his wife and child, and the separation had often taken its toll on his mood. But Garreth had easily forgiven Dethan his surly moments. He would have felt the same had he a wife like Selinda and a child like Dethan's fine son, Xand.

"She writes that they are both healthy and well. That—" Dethan broke off.

"Yes?" Garreth prompted.

"Well, I cannot repeat this part," Dethan said with a wolfish grin, his eyes bright with delight as he looked up at his brother. "She would never forgive me."

"Say no more, brother," Garreth said, amused by the besotted man.

He was amused, but he did not smile.

He had thought he would never live to see the day his brother was in love. Of all of them, Dethan had never professed to love a woman—even in his youth, when boys tend to be reckless with giving away their hearts. But he was completely around the bend over Selinda, his devotion to her intense.

Garreth envied him that. He envied the warm home and squirming child that awaited his brother once the cold of fall came calling. Garreth would continue the campaign against the new city until it was defeated, however long that took, but Dethan would leave him to it the moment the weather turned cold.

Garreth left his brother to his letter and turned his eyes to the missive in his own hands. The paper was folded neatly and sealed with wax, which had been stamped with the intricate image of a dragon of some sort, its wings broad within the circle of the stamp. The letter was addressed:

To the Beasts at the Gate

Intrigued, Garreth broke the seal and opened the letter.

> *You come upon our small city with aggression and numbers. We do not ask for war, and yet you bring it. We will not stand idly by while you rape our home of its innocence and peace. Consider yourself warned. End your folly against us now and we will let you leave unharmed.*
>   The City of Kith

"Brother, I do believe we have been threatened," Garreth said with thoughtful amusement.

Again, without a smile.

Dethan looked up questioningly as Garreth handed him the missive. He read it quickly and promptly burst out in a rich, raucous laugh.

"Such posturing. They are weak and they know it. Once we lay siege and they begin to starve for lack of fresh game and supplies, they will be welcoming us with open arms. As it is, their mill and butchery are outside the city walls. We have already seized control of them, as well as the farmland and crops, which right now are ripe with growing grain and thick with orchards. They know they are doomed to fall to us. This is mere posturing."

"It has spine, you have to admit."

"It shows fear." Dethan scoffed.

"I think it's just the opposite," Garreth said thoughtfully. "They sound very certain that they are not the ones in danger. Perhaps the more important question is, how did this missive reach us? The city has been locked down against us since we arrived, no one in and no one out."

"There is always a way in or out, whatever the circumstance. There are always some enterprising sorts willing to risk running a blockade. For profit."

"Yes, but the Kithians are violet skinned. Surely we would have noticed one of them in our camp who was not under guard."

There were Kithians in camp, all of them prisoners of the army. Mostly farmers and others who had been caught outside the walls of the city. But as Garreth had said, they were all under guard.

"That is a puzzle, it is true," Dethan said, a frown marring his features. He walked to the tent opening and yelled out, "You! Page! Where did you get this letter?"

The courier who had dropped off the missives stepped into the opening of the tent, leaving the conversation he'd been having with one of the command tent guards.

"A messenger from Hexis brought it only a short while ago," the courier said.

"No, not the one from my wife. The other."

"Other? I handed you only one missive, your most honorable."

"I'm holding both in my hands, page," Dethan said, showing the letters to the man.

"I . . . I only . . . But there was only one," the page insisted, looking flustered and very honestly worried.

"Never mind. Go and get yourself a meal," Dethan

said. Then, once the young man had left, he turned back toward Garreth. "What do we make of this?"

"Altered perception? It must be some kind of magery."

"So it seems. If they have a mage with that kind of power, we will have to be more alert. It was foolish of them to tip their hand though. We will now be on guard against it."

"But what can we do against a mage? Especially one who can alter the mind. Your wife is the only mage we know and she is two weeks' journey away from here."

"My wife will remain home with my son," Dethan said darkly. "We will not even entertain the idea of her coming on a campaign."

"Dethan, she is a magess of fire, one of the most powerful of the mage schools—"

"Enough! We will not discuss it!"

Garreth knew by his brother's terrible tone that it was indeed the end of the conversation. Garreth's sister by marriage, however powerful she might be, would never be allowed from behind the safety of Hexis's walls. Not for anything, and certainly not for war.

"Then how are we to prepare for whatever tricks they have planned? This is clearly a mage of some kind of mindcraft."

"Perhaps. The best way to battle this is by using deception and great numbers. No mage is strong enough to fool an entire army, but they can do damage in small increments. It is most important that they don't know where you and I are. As leaders, we are the ones giving commands and we cannot allow ourselves to be tricked into giving false commands."

"Not an easy ploy considering your armor is black. It rather stands out."

"As does yours with its golden hue. We will have to wear other armor."

"But both of our armors are god made. And you are no longer immortal, brother. I do not wish to see you—"

"I was fighting wars without immortality for a very long time. Do you not trust that I can come away from this alive and well again?"

"Of course I do. I only meant . . . I would not wish to take unnecessary chances. Not when such a valuable tool such as our armor is available to us."

"It is not ideal of course, but it will have to be. I will call a page to find us suits of common armor. You cannot be killed except with a god-made weapon, and since I am the only one with a god-made sword, you have little to worry about."

"I would not say that," Garreth said with a grimace. He moved toward the opening of the tent. "Dusk comes."

Dethan frowned, his clover-green eyes expressing his deep regret, his awareness of what his brother was suffering, and the guilt of knowing it was his folly that had led Garreth to it.

But Garreth had willingly followed Dethan. He had made the choice of his own free will to go on their quest for the fountain. He had been weak and was now paying the price for not being strong against his brothers' cajoling coercions.

"Brother . . ." Dethan began.

"Dusk comes every night," Garreth said quietly. "Will you flagellate yourself every time?"

"Yes," Dethan said simply.

"I wish you would not" was all Garreth could say. Then he left the tent and began to head toward the orchards that stood a little ways away from the encampment. He headed for the section of marjan trees that had turned from a healthy white to a sickly brown, the only trees in the orchards not bearing leaves or fruit. Both had fallen to the ground the day after they had first come to Kith. The day after his first dusk in the orchard.

He stood among those barren trees and slowly removed his armor. Piece by piece, he set it down onto the ground a few feet away from where he eventually stood waiting.

The moment the first touch of darkness bled into the sky, the grasses beneath his feet began to turn white with frost. The frost crept outward in an ever-widening circle, overtaking the dead trees, climbing up the bark and into the branches. Had there been leaves left, they too would have frosted over.

He began to feel the cold seeping into his bones and he could not help but shudder. He tried not to brace against it, tried in vain to just let it come without his body resisting it and causing him even more pain in the long run. But he tensed just the same, his heartbeat racing as his breath began to cloud upon the air.

He dropped to his knees, falling forward onto his hands, as pain screamed through his freezing muscles. His body shuddered again and again in a futile effort to try to warm itself. He felt everything within him turning to solid ice, from bones to sinew to flesh. The insides of his ears, his eyes in his sockets, his scrotum and his penis. Eventually his lungs and heart froze solid and he could no longer breathe. When that happened he fell, a solid block of iced flesh, to the ground.

And after an hour he began to thaw . . .

. . . only to freeze again.

CHAPTER
TWO

They laid siege to the city the very next day.

The city walls had pots of boiling oil atop them, which would be dumped upon the soldiers who tried to scale them. The trick was to ascend where the pots were not; the pots were so large and so heavy that they were fixed into the battlements and could not be moved. Unfortunately the soldiers could learn their placement only by trial and error. When the first wave of soldiers attempted the walls, which Garreth had ordered to be attacked from every quarter at the exact same moment, the pots were dumped immediately upon them, scalding every man the oil touched . . . and showing exactly where the pots were positioned and where they were not.

Garreth then pulled the men back, and the wounded and burned ones were cared for, the camp mems— priestesses who had the ability to heal—making their way through the injured ranks and giving solace wherever they could. Dethan had done likewise on the opposite side of the walled city, looking for weaknesses that could be exploited.

The city of Kith's walls were eight-sided, the octagon large and protective of the inhabitants inside. They rose up at least a hundred feet high, making scaling them a true challenge.

But when the soldiers attacked again that afternoon, they brought in scaffolds, placing them beyond the reach of the oil pots, and began to scale them by tens and by twenties. Archers came into play, shooting from the city battlements down into the climbing men.

Garreth walked up to his best archers, a contingent he had set aside for this one purpose.

"Aim for every archer you see," he instructed them. "Make every shot count and take your time. Let them show themselves and get overconfident. Then pick them off one by one."

"Yes, my lord," they said in unison.

And so they did. Archers began to drop from the walls, their bodies falling into the ranks of the advancing men. Either that or they fell back behind the battlements. In the camp, Garreth watched everything with a steady eye and a magnification scope.

And that was when he first saw her.

She would have been hard to miss, standing openly on top of the city wall facing him. She did not duck and cover, did not dodge the arrows flying all around her. She was dressed in a brilliant jewel-blue, like the blue of a diri's egg. She wore a long scarf, which blew in the wind, trailing behind her like a banner—a magnificent plumage for a brave and fearless bird. Her hair was down, it too blowing in the wild wind, the fiery red of it a color unlike anything he had ever seen—deep and dark in some places, light and coppery in others. And of course there was her lavender skin, marking her as Kithian, if being on their battlements was not proof enough.

Then, like some kind of powerful goddess, she reached her arms up high and wide, tipped her head back, and closed her eyes. She seemed to breathe in the world around her.

That was when a shadow, swift and dark, skimmed over their forces.

Garreth felt himself go cold through the center of his body, as if it were dusk already. He looked up at the sky and there it was, an enormous wyvern, its wingspan massive and magnificent, the scales along its reptilian body gleaming with a blue iridescence. Its dragon's head was immense, the whole entirety of its body so huge it was a wonder it could be airborne, even in spite of its wide, muscular wings.

The men began to cry out in fear and Garreth hardly blamed them. To see such a thing bearing down on them, it was no wonder they began to run.

"Hold steady!" Garreth bellowed, unwilling to lose the ground they had gained. "Archers!"

The archers immediately turned their arrows on the great creature. But they bounced off ineffectively as the wyvern reeled around and began a low-flying pass.

And then it breathed a massive plume of fire down upon the men.

The screams were horrendous, men cooked within their armor, while others fell to the ground, their hair and clothing and weapons on fire. Garreth swore and wondered frantically where his brother was. Dethan was the one with a god-made sword. If anything could penetrate the hide of such a creature, it would be that sword.

As the beast reeled around again, readying for another pass, a banner of blue caught his eye.

The woman.

It could be no coincidence that the beast appeared the moment the woman had. Perhaps she was somehow controlling it, he thought wildly. Perhaps she was the magess they had wondered about and she was using some kind of mindcraft to bond with the creature.

Or perhaps it wasn't even real at all. Perhaps it was all an illusion and she was laying waste to them with merely the power of her mind. Garreth grabbed one of the archers, ripping a crossbow from his back. He began to run, his heavy armor unlike the god-made pieces he usually wore. It weighted him down as he tried to make speed toward her.

He stopped hard in his tracks, raising the crossbow to his shoulder. He aimed at the witch and fired.

The crossbow bolt struck her hard, throwing her off her feet. She disappeared behind the battlements, but he was certain he had struck her in the heart.

The wyvern screamed and stopped its latest fiery run, reeling hard and heading back toward the city, as if in search of its mistress. It perched itself on the wall, its claws digging into the stone, and screamed again. It had turned its back on the advancing army, looking down into the city instead, into the place where the woman had fallen.

Garreth took the opportunity to rally his men, to focus them back where they belonged. It was hard though, because that great beast had cast a pall of fear on them that even the deepest of loyalties could not fight against with ease. The wyvern stayed on the wall, but turned back toward the advancing army, belching fire down at them, even as they made progress. Garreth ordered his men to avoid the fire accordingly.

"Up the scaffolds, men!" Garreth commanded of them.

They were so close to breeching the walls. If they could make it over, then they would have made a great advance.

Garreth nearly shouted with triumph when he saw his

first man climb over the top of the wall. Then another. And another.

It was slow going, one man at a time, but it was happening.

Then the wyvern leapt away from the wall, its scream curdling blood as it sprayed the breeching men with fire. But even as Garreth cursed the thing, he realized that men on both sides were burning. The beast was out of control, perhaps only acting on instinct. The top of the wall was utter pandemonium. Chaos ruled as burning bodies fell to the ground from a hundred feet up.

"Catapults!" Garreth cried, suddenly remembering the best weapon he might have against the beast. The burning balls they usually sent over would not burn the wyvern—it was said that the creatures were immune to fire—but perhaps the impact of the ammunition would be enough. There was no real way of aiming the catapults, but the men did their best and Garreth ordered them to rain hellfire down on the wyvern and the city as a whole.

The beast was actually quite nimble for something so incredibly big. It dodged almost all the projectiles fired from the great catapults. But then one hit it square in the head and the beast went crashing into the city walls, tearing a huge hole in the top of the stone façade.

And so it went, the catapults raining ammunition onto the city and the wyvern until it was clear the buildings beyond the walls were heavily ablaze. The wyvern was clutching a wall, crouched upon it, screaming down at Garreth's forces. Dethan came running up to Garreth a short while later.

"The city will be ours in spite of the beast!" Dethan cried.

"Give me your sword," Garreth demanded of him. "I'm going to scale the walls and kill the thing myself."

"That's madness!" Dethan said fiercely.

"For you maybe," Garreth said, meeting his brother's eyes. "But for me . . . I am immortal. What can it do to me that I cannot heal from?"

Dethan seemed heavily reluctant, but he slowly unbelted his sword and handed it to Garreth.

"Change your armor at least," Dethan said.

"I will. I want them to see the wey flower on my chest," he said, referring to the emblem engraved in the breastplate of his armor, "so they will know I conquer them in the name of Weysa."

He turned and hurried to the command tent, Dethan hot on his heels.

"Its fire will burn you," Dethan warned him. "It will be like no pain you've ever imagined."

Garreth laughed mirthlessly. "Tell me that when you have been frozen to death over and over again."

"I tell you that because it was once my burden, to burn to the bone every night, just as it is yours to freeze. You may think you are prepared for it, but—"

"Let me do this," Garreth snapped at him impatiently, "for I am the only one who can."

Dethan fell silent, then nodded. He moved to help Garreth out of his heavy armor and into the god-made armor Weysa had given him the day she had freed him from that mountaintop. In some respects it galled Garreth to have to fight in the name of the goddess who had seen to his punishment—saw to it even now—but he would do what he must and be grateful for what little freedom she had given him.

When he was ready he strode out of the tent, Dethan once again fast behind him. Dethan followed all the way to the base of the city walls. Then Garreth turned to him.

"Stay here, brother."

Dethan scoffed. "I will not! Do you think to leave me behind like some delicate wife?"

"I think the men need leadership, and if we both fall, the army will be a beast without a head. You must control them from the ground. Continue to batter the city with catapult fire. It is falling. I can feel it. The beast is the only thing that stands in the way. Now go."

Garreth turned away from him and started up the scaffold. He knew it rankled Dethan that he, the younger brother, was now the stronger of the two of them. Although he had been a strong man and powerful warrior in his own right, his brothers had always and would always perceive him as the weakest of them all. He was the baby. He was in need of protection. And he supposed that his performance on the mountaintop had solidified that truth. Another thing that galled him.

But he was not weak now. He was strong. He would fight. He would lay waste to all.

He did exactly that. He flew over the battlements, immediately clashing swords with the opposing army. Three men came at him at once and he cut them down one by one. But while he was dealing with them, a fourth man came up behind him and slid a dagger between the creases of his armor. It went into his left armpit, searing through his flesh. He drew back that arm and crashed his elbow into the man's face, and the man and the dagger fell away from him. The wound smarted as he finished off the original three men.

His goal was easy to see, the massive scaled body gleaming in the midday sun. He surged toward the thing, mowing down man after man who got in his way. He was nearly to it when it saw him coming and breathed fire onto him.

He cooked inside his armor, his flesh burning and bubbling, agony screaming through him. He roared out in pain, falling to his knees, struggling to remain upright. Oh, he had known agony all right, but this was a different torment, just as his brother had warned him.

He could not possibly say which was worse—each was vicious in its own right. But he put the pain aside, grinding his teeth together and forcing himself forward. He held his sword high, lunging for the beast, aiming for the heart of it but knowing it was too far above his striking range as it reared up on those two great legs and spread those massive wings. So he settled for the belly of the beast and sank the mighty sword in deep.

The scream it released was of a different sort this time. It tried to lunge away, but Garreth would not allow it to get away from him. He cut a gash in its hide with the dagger in his left hand and pulled his sword free with the right. As the beast lifted away from the wall, Garreth held on to it with his dagger hand and stabbed into it again with his sword arm.

And then they were flying. He was hanging on to the beast by both of his weapons, but it was in the air and twisting about, skimming over the army below the walls, turning to and fro, trying to shake loose the man on its belly. Finally it caught a wing against the ground and went tumbling head over heels, dislodging Garreth into the dirt and trees. The beast stumbled up onto its feet almost immediately, flopping around like a fish out of water as it struggled to get its wings under itself. Garreth tried to get to his feet, tried to lunge for the thing again, but it gained the air and left him behind. But instead of flying into the city again, it flew off and away, into the mountains, until it was barely a speck in Garreth's sight.

CHAPTER
THREE

Garreth was lying on a cot in the command tent several hours later, his armor having been peeled off him, taking layers of singed skin with it. He had already begun the healing process but knew he would not be restored to health before dusk came and his torment began. That promised to make the experience all the better, he thought wryly.

Dethan was there, and runners came in and out of the tent. The city was falling, far more quickly than they had ever expected, wyverns or otherwise.

"The gates! The gates are opening!"

The cry went out amongst the men and Garreth forced himself to his feet so he could see what the commotion was about. And sure enough, the city gates were opening. Dethan and Garreth moved forward to the edge of the crowd, both with swords in hand, ready for anything, as a small contingent of men came out of the gates carrying a golden litter.

"What's this, then?" Dethan asked.

"I'm rather intrigued myself," Garreth replied.

Garreth stepped forward as the contingent arrived. A small balding man was in the lead, with dark robes of scarlet on his body and a chain of gold around his waist.

He wore many golden and bejeweled rings on his short, stubby fingers. A thin man was beside him in a mage's robes, the scarlet color of them marked with embroidered runic symbols. He had two thin white moustaches, small dark eyes, and hair as white as the driven snow, a huge contrast to his violet skin.

The other men also wore scarlet clothing—pantaloons and vests that only partially covered their bare chests. They were lighter skinned than the short man and the thin man, almost a pale lavender. The short man cleared his throat and then stepped forward.

"Oh, mighty conquerors," he said. "We beg you to leave what remains of our city in peace. We never wished to make war upon you, so why do you make war upon us?" When Garreth made to speak, the man stopped him by raising a hand. "It does not matter why you have come, only that you leave. To that end, we are willing to make a treaty with you. Leave us be and we will give you the most valuable gift in our kingdom." He lifted a hand behind himself, indicating the curtained litter.

"What is it?" Garreth asked, stepping forward. Again the man held up a hand to stay him.

"First, do you accept these terms?"

"No, I do not accept," Garreth said harshly. "You have no bargaining power here. Your city is mine, in Weysa's name. *You* will be held as mine. You will live under my rule. You will be mine in every sense of the word, your valuable gift and treasures included. I have beaten your walls, your city, and your wyvern. That is the end to it. If you wish clemency, you should ask that I do not take you on as my personal slaves."

Garreth had no intention of making slaves of anyone, but this little man irked him. He had some big hanging ones to think he could come there and dictate the way things would be.

The little man had paled at the mention of slavery.

"Please," he said, his voice and hands shaking now. "You can take all the slaves you want." He indicated the lighter-skinned males. "The scourge are yours to do with as you please. But leave the noble Kithians to their lives in peace, I beg of you."

"The scourge?"

"Yes. Our slaves. They are unwashed and unholy. You can see that by their diluted skin."

So the paler-skinned Kithians were slaves to the darker, violet-skinned ones, Garreth thought. And for what reason? What made one so different from the other, besides their skin color?

"I will take it under consideration," Garreth said sternly. "Now, what of this gift you are giving to appease me?"

He moved to the litter and, using his sword, parted the curtains. Inside was a lavender-skinned woman in a jewel blue robe. She was lying back on the pillows of the litter, panting hard for breath, her eyes full of the fire of hatred.

And Garreth's crossbow bolt sticking out of her left shoulder, just above her breast.

He must have missed her heart by mere inches, provided her heart was located in the same place his was. He had seen many strange people in many strange lands over time and not all anatomy was universal.

But her anatomy seemed pretty above standard, he thought as he looked her over from head to toe. She was full of incredible curves, clearly having been well fed for a slave. But why would a slave be carried like royalty?

Unless . . .

"We give you the woman and the wyvern she controls and beg you for mercy."

"Controls?" Garreth met her eyes, seeing the seething emotion there. "How?"

She set her lips stubbornly, breathing hard through her nose.

"She is soulbound to it."

"Soulbound?"

"Her soul and the wyvern's have been meshed together since the wyvern's birth. I will let her tell you the tale of it one day. But she is my slave and now I give her to you. Do with her what you will and please let us live free."

"Why should I let you live free and make her a slave?" he asked, his gaze never leaving the girl's. He saw surprise enter her eyes, though she showed the emotion cautiously. She was in a great deal of pain, and yet she made not a sound.

"B-but she's a-a-a . . ." The man stumbled over his words with his shock. He clearly could not fathom that someone would not be able to see the difference between his own vainglorious self and a simple slave girl like her.

"She's mine now and I will decide what becomes of her," Garreth said to the man. More softly he added, "And she'll be the better for it, no doubt."

She exhaled a soft sound, her jaw set, a world of mistrust in her eyes.

"Get me a mem. Quickly," he said to his page. "Who are you?" he asked the self-important man.

"I am Bento Thoth. Bennesah of Kith." He gave Garreth a slight bow and looked like he expected an introduction in return.

"You have ruled this place?" Garreth asked him.

"Yes. For many turnings now. Ever since the great Bennesah Fortuno left this precious physical world."

"Well, Bennesah, your reign is at an end. Have your people let my men into the city and they will help to put the fires out. I presume you have a castle or fortress of some kind?"

"Th-the keep is the seat of our government a-and my home."

"No longer your home. I will stay there with my brother and my generals from this day until the city is rebuilt and its people understand it is now mine and the goddess Weysa's."

"But where will I—"

Garreth finally looked away from the woman and glared hard at the bennesah. "I don't give a rat's fart where you live. That is not my concern. My only concern is that *you* don't live in the keep and that *I* do." Garreth dropped the curtain. "Bring her into my tent. See to it she is given a cot, some water . . . food if she can stand it, and get a mem to take that bolt out of her shoulder. The girl is suffering."

He looked to the sky.

"Dusk comes soon. Let us be about this quickly," Garreth said.

Garreth walked into his tent some time later and found the girl lying on a cot as he had instructed. However, she was tethered to the tent pole by a chain around her ankle, something he had not requested. When he approached her, those eyes—the fairest blue imaginable— were glaring at him with hatred again.

"Who has done this to you?" he asked, reaching down to close his hand around the manacle at her ankle.

At first he didn't think the stubborn chit was going to answer, but finally she ground out, "Your page. I think he did not appreciate me biting him." She gave Garreth a smug smile.

"You have a lot of fire for a slave," Garreth noted.

"I am no . . . I am slave only to the wyvern . . . and he is slave to me."

"Yes, I am very interested to hear how that works. So

you are not willingly going to stay here with me, where you will be fed, clothed, and healed?" he asked her.

She seemed to think on it a moment. "A comfortable cage is still a cage," she said bitterly.

"This is true. But the cage will not be forever," he promised her. "Only until I understand your connection with the wyvern and can assure myself you will not set it upon me and my men again."

"I make no such promises. You have injured him. You are foul and cruel." Then he saw tears entering her eyes. Whatever she was, whoever she was, she felt deeply for the creature she controlled.

"How is it you can control such a mighty beast when you are so small and fair?"

She seemed taken aback by his description of her for a moment but then had her guard back up a second later. "You would have me tell you my secrets so you can destroy him. I will not do it."

"Where has he gone? I will not have him coming back to attack my camp."

Her bottom lip trembled, tension in her body bowstring-taut. "He will not. You have injured him and you have injured me. We cannot feel each other when we are in so much pain. I cannot control him like this."

"That's good to know. So to ensure the safety of my men I need only see to it you remain in pain?"

She got even more tightly wound in an instant, if that was even possible.

"Do what you must," she said, her chin lifting with stubborn bravery.

Damn but he liked her. He had not seen this much spirit in a woman in all his lifetime. She was beautiful too, with her lavender skin, stunning blue eyes, and mouthwatering curves.

A woman this beautiful had been a slave?

He frowned as he thought of all that could mean for her.

"Tell me. You are the bennesah's slave?"

"Yes," she said shortly.

"What does that entail for you?"

"Whatever he wants it to be," she said bitterly.

Garreth's frown darkened.

"Does he make you a slave in his bed?" he found himself asking before he could stop himself.

She snorted and laughed a hard laugh. "The bennesah would not sully his precious cock on the likes of me, thanks be to all the gods."

Garreth didn't understand why he felt so relieved by that. He was merely glad she wasn't being misused, he told himself.

"What is so different about you?" he asked her, wanting to hear it from her perspective.

"Did you not hear him? We are sullied and unwashed."

"What does that mean?" he asked as he took a seat on the edge of her cot.

"It means that long ago the ancestor of the scourge supposedly made love to Jikaro, the god of anger, deception, and storms, and the scourge was born as a result. We are lies and deceit and the dirt beneath the Kithians' heels, and we deserve no better." She smiled without humor. "Or so the stories go."

"But if you control such a magnificent beast, why not turn it on your captors rather than use it to fight for them?"

"Because it would mean turning it loose on the entire city . . . and there are those I love who would not be protected." She said this last softly and quietly. "And they have used those I love as . . . collateral, to ensure my behavior."

"And who is it you love?"

"As if I would tell you that! So you can use them to control me as well? I think not!"

"Them? So it is more than one."

She took in a small breath and he realized she was cursing herself for the slipup.

"Your family?" he pressed. But she remained tight lipped. "You know I will find out eventually. The bennesah will no doubt tell me."

"Why would he tell you his secrets?" she asked.

Garreth leaned in and gave her a thin smile. "Because I will slit his fat gut if he does not."

"You are a barbarian," she whispered, her eyes wide with fear and disgust.

"And he is better, I suppose? He who makes you a slave and blackmails you for your good behavior?"

"You wish to do the same!"

"Who says I do?" he lobbed back at her.

"But you said . . . you said I am to be locked up until you can hunt the wyvern and kill it."

"When did I say that?" he asked her with a raised brow. "I think you are only hearing what you expect to hear. I merely do not want the wyvern to return and attack my men. If you can guarantee that, then you will be freed."

"You can't mean that. I am the only means you have of controlling him. Everyone wants to be able to control him. To make him fight for their cause. Why should you be any different?"

"As much as I would love to have a wyvern on my side in a battle, I have already proven that I can do just fine without one." He again leaned toward her. "If you choose to stay with me, and your wyvern along with you, that will be solely your decision. Otherwise, once you are healed, you are free to go and take the thing with you."

She stared at him gape mouthed. "Y-you would just let me leave?"

"Yes."

"You are a liar!" she hissed.

"There's one way to find out," he said. "Lie back and heal. When you are well, you will see."

She opened her mouth as if to say something, but then seemed to think better of it and kept her words to herself. He wanted to press her, maybe to make her realize he was being truthful or maybe to simply poke at her and watch the fire inside her eyes rise up in defiance.

He stood up and moved away from her just as a mem was entering the tent.

"There, now," the old woman cackled. "Let's see how you are doing."

The mem walked over to the girl and reached to unbutton the long robe she wore. She slapped the mem's hands away harshly.

"Leave me be!" she said.

"So you wish to remain a slave, then?" Garreth asked archly.

"Wh-what?" she said.

"You are a slave until you heal, remember? Let the woman heal you. The sooner you are well, the sooner you will be on your way."

This time when the mem reached for the buttons, the girl let her do it. They came undone one at a time, each one slipping free to reveal more and more skin beneath the blue fabric. Finally the mem pulled the whole left side of the robe back, baring the girl's full breast to the open air. Hastily the girl covered her breast with her hand to guard it from his sight, but not before he saw the dark violet nipple that tipped it pucker in the cool air.

Garreth was shocked to feel a visceral response ricocheting throughout his body. Looking at the landscape of fair purple skin and that stunningly responsive nipple, he grew stone hard. As he stood there, stewing in the sensation, he found himself wondering what her skin smelled like. Wondering if that berry-colored nipple would taste like a kind of sweet, succulent fruit. She would be powder soft, he thought to himself. Her skin silky and smooth. But that nipple would be hard and stiff.

He broke out of the trance when he heard her hiss in a breath as the mem pulled back the bandage on her shoulder to look at the wound there. The bolt had since been removed and he found he was both pleased with himself for making such a great shot, while in action and at such a distance, and regretting the pain he was causing her because of it.

Then the mem pulled the robe open farther, exposing the girl's slightly rounded belly and her left hipbone. Three horrible wounds were on the girl's belly.

"How were you injured thus?" he demanded to know. Someone had stabbed her cruelly, made a pincushion out of her. And the wounds were fresh, no more than a couple of hours old. Had they punished her because of the wyvern's failures? Had they tried to kill her so he would not gain control of both her and the beast?

She met his eyes in fiery defiance. "You did it."

"You lie! I never touched you with a sword!"

"No, but you tried to slay Koro with one!"

"Koro?" he asked dumbly.

"The wyvern," she hissed.

"Oh dear gods . . . You express the wounds of the wyvern on your own body?"

She gave a short nod of her head. "And he expresses mine on his. So you see, try as you might, *I* will not heal until the *wyvern* is healed. And vice versa."

"That is a terrible thing! What if the wyvern had been killed?" he asked angrily.

"Then I would have died. But it is the wyvern who has the raw end of the deal, for if I die, he dies as well . . . and I am much easier to kill than he is. So now you know. All your problems will be solved if you but take a sword to my neck."

He frowned and moved closer to her, gazing down at her wounded body and her bared skin.

"What is your name?" he asked, suddenly realizing he had not asked it of her.

She went tight lipped again for a moment and he thought she wasn't going to give him what he wanted. She had no control over her situation and her life, and this was one small thing she could try to control. But she surprised him all the same as she reluctantly said, "Sarielle."

It was a beautiful name. Appropriate for a beautiful woman, he thought. And she was that and very much more. His aroused body could attest to that fact.

"Well, Sarielle," he said as he watched the mem button her back up, "you have a very serious problem."

"Do you really think so?" she asked dryly, running her gaze along the length of the chain holding her there.

"Yes. And what I mean to say is, your wyvern was injured by a god-made weapon, Sarielle. His wounds will not mend on their own. Only a mage or mem will be able to provide the healing he needs."

"How stupid do you think I am?" she scoffed. "You are trying to get me to bring him here, out of hiding. Promising him healing when I'm sure once you've lured him here you will capture him for some nefarious purpose or kill him!"

"Sarielle," Garreth said patiently as he met her eyes. "You said yourself all I have to do is kill you in order to kill the wyvern. So why would I bother with luring him here if I can simply cut your pretty little throat?"

He reached down and drew a gentle finger from one side of her throat to the other.

Ah yes. Her skin was just as soft as it had promised to be.

"I cannot bring him here," she said softly, a fine tremor going through her again and again. "He will not come, so don't ask it of me."

"Why won't he come? If you control him—"

"I do not control him like that! He is not a slave to me! He is a magnificent, independent creature who happens to love me, soul to soul, and therefore will do anything to protect me if I ask him to. But my mind does not control his mind. His mind does not control mine. But we . . . I feel him. His pain and confusion. His worry for my safety. His strong dragon's heart is brave, but right now he is frightened and he is hiding. He would not come to me even if I begged him to. I would have to go and find him."

"Go? You can barely get out of bed."

"If you let me go, I promise you I can make it to his side. I will find a way to heal him. Please . . . just let me go and—"

"No," Garreth said with finality.

"Then you are a liar! You have no intention of setting me free at all!"

"I have no intention of letting you run around in the world half healed and weakened. That wyvern is hiding in the Asdar Mountains, some of the rockiest terrain known to man. Just how far do you think you could get in a place like that when you can barely lift your left arm? No. First, we heal what we can of you. The bolt wound is yours and so can be healed, yes?"

"Yes," she answered cautiously, narrowing her eyes on him. Honestly he could not blame her. It sounded like her life gave her little reason to trust anyone.

"So we will heal it first. Then we can talk more. Now,

get some rest. It is almost dusk and I . . . I will return later," he said moving toward the entrance of the tent.

"Your name is Garreth, yes?" she asked suddenly. He turned back to her and nodded. "I heard it from one of your men."

"I see."

"I do not believe you are going to be as benevolent as you say," she said defiantly. "But I will heal since it is in my best interest to do so . . . not because it is in yours."

"I am content with that. Now I must go. You will be taken to the keep later and I will join you there after juquil's hour so we can speak of this further. Perhaps you will find our goals are not so different after all."

"I wish to be taken to my rooms!" she said, making him look back at her with a hard look. "I-in the keep," she explained hastily. "I have my rooms in the keep. You can easily hold me there." She sighed. "It comes equipped with manacles."

The reminder of her enslavement made him frown stormily. "He kept you in shackles?"

"Often," she muttered. "Whenever I misbehaved. Which I am proud to say could be quite often."

That lightened him with amusement. "Why does this not surprise me?" he said to no one in particular. "Very well. Your rooms. I will see it done and see you there later."

With that, he left the tent.

CHAPTER
FOUR

Sarielle was pacing her rooms anxiously. Her entire life was suddenly in turmoil and she didn't know how to navigate this new world with this new man controlling her fate. At least she had learned ways to manipulate the bennesah to her benefit over the turnings.

Well, sometimes anyway. She had learned how to protect herself and the things she held most dear.

The ones she held most dear.

Her sisters Jona and Isaelle.

The twins were being held in the keep, as serving girls in the kitchens, under the tight and watchful eye of the kitchen matron, Soa, who could be a cruel task-mistress. Sarielle should know; she grew up in the kitchens with Soa holding power over her and her mother, who had been a cook. The best cook in the kitchens, it was said. Her mother, Beah, had been lauded by their master, praised and given special considerations for her fantastic meals and the sheer magnificence of her skills. She had been allowed the rare privilege of keeping her children close by as she birthed and raised them.

Then Sarielle's mother had died, soon after their father, whom Beah had loved beyond reason; he had been killed in a horrible wagon accident while getting supplies from a caravan in the mountains. It was believed Beah had suffered from a broken heart. Not even the knowledge that her three daughters would be left behind to fend for themselves had managed to keep her on this physical plane. No. She had much preferred to go to Kitari and the eight heavens with their father than stay with them.

So, that had left Sarielle with the responsibility of caring for her sisters. She had suffered under the cruelty of Soa for turnings as she struggled to become a cook of the same caliber as her mother . . . and failed to do so. But while her cooking did not shine, her efforts did. She was a hard worker and was passionately loyal to her family. She would do anything to better their place in the world.

Anything at all.

Including binding her soul to a deadly wyvern.

It was only a matter of time before this barbarian learned of her small sisters and used them to manipulate her, just as the bennesah had.

Call the wyvern to protect us or I will have your sisters' throats slit right here where we stand.

The barbarian invader was not to be trusted. The destruction in the city alone was proof of that. He had come to conquer and he had done just that. The only small satisfaction to be had was watching the bennesah grovel for his place of comfort in the ruins of his city. He deserved his fall from grace. He deserved everything they did to him, and he deserved to lose everything they stole from him. Now perhaps he would be the slave made to dance to the whims of others.

But petty victories like that did not solve her problems. Her goals were two-pronged and simple: protect her sisters and protect her wyvern.

Koro was the very heart of her. And she was the very heart of him. They had bonded long ago in a way that couldn't be understood by the average layperson. She felt for him as she felt for her beloved sisters. She loved him from the bottom of her soul. And he was out there, somewhere, suffering and in pain.

Because of *him*.

She searched her room, looking for anything she could use as a weapon. But moving around was awkward because she had been shackled to the column that was in the center of her bedchamber. The slack in the chain was designed to give her just enough length to lie down on the bed or sit in the window bench. But there was nothing worth looking at now, darkness having fallen long ago. Juquil's hour came and passed and she waited with bated breath for him to appear. She tried to heft a book in her hands. No. Not heavy enough. She grabbed her hairbrush and smacked it hard against her palm. Yes. That would hurt. But perhaps only enough to enrage him, and if she was going to try to kill him, she needed a better plan than that.

The barbarian talked as though he was an intelligent and reasoning man, but she knew it was all a lie. She had been conned by such mannerisms in the past and she would not be conned again. He would not lull her into thinking he was harmless. Not after what he had done to Koro.

She thought about that for a moment. He had been burned by Koro. She had noticed it along his face and body when she had first seen him at the litter. But by the time he had come into the tent some hours later, he had been much healed. She had never heard of a mem of such great ability as that. His mems must be truly powerful. Truly devout. For it was the devoutness of a mem that allowed her the ability to heal.

It made no sense to Sarielle that the mems of such barbarians would be considered blessed by the gods. But she supposed that depended on which god the mems followed. These mems were of Weysa, the goddess of conflict and war. It would figure that these conquerors would worship such a goddess. They thrived on conflict, on running roughshod over otherwise peaceable cities, claiming them as their own. And for what? Power? Riches? Glory? What was it that drove this man Garreth?

It did not matter, she decided. All that mattered was the safety of her sisters and helping Koro to heal. Koro's wounds were so very deep—she could feel them all the way to her soul. If Garreth had spoken the truth, then Koro could not heal on his own and he would die. What if he got an infection because the wound would not heal? She was not afraid of dying, but she was fearful for her wyvern.

It was nearly an hour past juquil's hour before he entered her rooms. By that time she had worn herself out with her pacing, her wounded body aching and sore, the wounds in her belly raw. She should not be up on her feet, but she could not help herself.

At least the wound on her shoulder was healing well, thanks to Garreth's talented mem. She might be an old crone, but she clearly knew what she was doing. And even though she could not heal the wounds on Sarielle's belly, she had provided an anesthetic cream to apply to the wound to take the edge off the pain. It worked only a little, but it was good enough. Hopefully it translated on Koro's end as well.

He looked different when he entered the room. He was fully out of armor and lacked any accoutrements of war, save the sword and dagger at his belt. The same sword and dagger that had so terribly wounded Koro. She had noticed that the smallest wound on her belly, presumably made from the dagger, was knitting together nicely and starting to heal. She could only assume that the dagger was not god made and therefore

Koro was able to heal from the injury. But the other . . . a gleaming deadly black weapon . . . Yes, indeed it was god made. You could tell just by looking at the thing. It was as though it had a soul of its own.

"I see you are on your feet," he said as he walked up to her. "I will presume that is a good— Whoa!"

He barely had time to catch her when she suddenly fell forward against him. She didn't know what happened. She was fine one minute, and the next everything inside her simply went weak. She pushed at him in frustration, tried to gain her feet, but her body would not behave, would not act in accordance with her wishes.

He bent to put an arm behind her legs and suddenly swept her up into his arms, carrying her to the bed.

"Let me go! I can walk on my own!" she said angrily.

"Clearly you cannot. Will you stop fighting me for one second and take a moment to relax? To rest? Perchance to heal? This cannot be good for you or for Koro."

"Do not talk about him as if you care for his well-being! I know you only want his power for yourself!"

"That is what you keep claiming is my goal," he said as he put a knee on the bed and laid her down on it gently, despite her struggles. "But I have never said that was my intention. Nor have I done anything to support your beliefs."

"Give it time," she snapped, trying to push him away from her.

But suddenly he was encasing her head between his large hands and forcing her to look into his eyes, which were as green as the Faspin Sea.

"I am not your enemy," he said to her intently. "If you would but give me a moment to prove it—"

"Ha! What a joke! Not my enemy! You just laid waste

to the city I call my home! How does that not make you my enemy?"

He seemed to think on that a moment. "A very good point," he conceded. "But I did not lay siege to this place to rape it of its valuables and leave it torn asunder and helpless. I am merely the changing of the guard. I will run this city to my own liking and hopefully to the better benefit of *your* people. There are no slaves where I come from," he said quietly as he held her gaze.

That gave her pause. She could not believe such a claim. No slaves? Who then did the dark and dirty work? How were the nobles supported? How did they gain their luxuries if not on the backs of others?

"So . . . since you are here . . . the scourge are no longer slaves? Is . . . is that what you are trying to tell me?"

"Yes," he said softly.

He was too close to her, she realized in a sudden panic. He had seated himself on the bed facing her, his arm bridged over her, his body leaning toward her, and his face mere inches away from hers.

"I do not believe you," she said.

"You will," he assured her. "But before we worry about that, we need to look after your health. You must tell me where to find the wyvern. If we do not heal him, you could die, and I do not wish to see that happen."

"Why? Why should you care?"

"How could I not care?" he asked her. "I have never seen anything like what you share with this creature. It is an amazing thing. A truly magical connection. One I wish to learn more about. It is blessed by the gods for certain."

She snorted. "The gods had nothing to do with it," she said.

"The gods have everything to do with everything," he promised her.

"The gods aren't even real. That's probably not even a god-made sword. Weaponry like that is just a myth!"

"Oh, the gods are real. I have seen them for myself. And have a care for what you say because you never know which god is listening to you and when."

"Seen them yourself?" She scoffed at him. "Now you make grandiose claims. Why would gods make themselves known to the likes of you?" she asked him.

"You don't really want to know the answer to that question," he said evasively. "Suffice it to say, the gods are real. Weysa is real. And this city has fallen to her glory and will now sing her praises and pray in her temples."

"We have no temples for Weysa here," she said in a hard tone.

"Then we will build them as we rebuild the city." His gaze drifted away from hers and dropped to her mouth. "We will all pay tribute to her."

"Will you lay me out upon the altar? A spoil of war? Offer me up to your killer goddess?"

"Enough!" he said sharply. "Watch your words, Sarielle. You do not wish to incite a god's wrath, believe me."

"Believe you? I do not believe you. Not a word you say."

"How shall I convince you, then?" he asked her, his study of her mouth lasting a long time . . . until she began to get uncomfortable. His intense stare made her feel somehow warm inside. Her belly felt all swirly, and she suddenly felt very aware of her breasts. She swallowed hard, trying to banish the strange sensations through the force of her will. He must be using some kind of sorcery, she thought frantically. But no . . . that wasn't possible . . .

"Let me go. Let me walk off into the darkness, never to be seen again."

"Alone?" he asked with an arched brow. He reached toward her with a single finger, his thumb, letting it settle on her lower lip. It slowly brushed from one side of her mouth to the other.

She hesitated. She cleared her throat.

"You have loved ones here you would not leave behind, I think," he said keenly. "Will you not tell me who they are? Or should I discover this from the bennesah?"

"He holds them even now," she hissed. "You think you control me, but you do not. You have no power over me. He has it and he knows I know it. He has no doubt hidden them away by now, ready to use them against me when the moment is right."

"Which 'them' are we referring to?" he asked.

She growled low in her throat. "My sisters! Twins! Young girls barely ten full turnings old. So, what will you do now? Find them for yourself and ensure your power over me?"

"I have told you before. I am not your enemy and I am not seeking power over you. To prove it I will procure your sisters from the bennesah and bring them to you."

She burst out in wild laughter. "You expect me to believe that?" she said.

"Damn me, woman, but you are stubborn!" he said, taking her shoulders between his hands and giving her a good hard shake. "If I bring them to you, will you believe me then?"

"And only then!" she hissed, her eyes flashing with defiance.

Again his attention fell to her mouth. He frowned deeply, let her go, and pushed himself away. He stood up and stared down hard at her.

"I will bring you your sisters and then you will bring me to the wyvern."

Alarmed, she sat up. "I never said I would!"

"You have no choice," he said, his tone low. "You'll

die if you don't and so will he. I'll bring you the girls and you will trust me to help care for the wyvern."

She lifted her chin. "Fine. I can make the promise because I know the bennesah will never let you have the girls." She bit her lip. "You shouldn't even try. He might . . . I don't want them hurt because you are trying to manipulate me!"

"They will not be hurt. I promise you that."

"Don't make promises you can't keep."

"I can say the same to you," he said. "Rest. Eat something. Try to heal in whatever way you can. I will be back with your sisters before long."

She looked away from him. But he could tell she was nervous. Concerned. She was worried about her siblings. Deeply worried. It was a feeling he could easily identify with.

Garreth turned around and walked out the door, closing and locking it behind him. He paused a moment, his head resting on the solid wood of the door, his eyes closing.

What was wrong with him? For a moment there—for several moments—he had stared at that lush, violet-lipped mouth and all he could think about was kissing the frustrating wench into silence. But that, he had known, would have been a very bad idea and would have destroyed any chance of gaining her trust. And the very last thing he should be thinking of was kissing a woman who amounted to a prisoner of war. A woman who, in her wrath, could call upon the power of a great beast to protect her.

He was fascinated by that connection. How had it come to be? Why had it come to be? And could the bond be broken without killing one or both of them? Would she even want such a thing?

He turned away from the door and strode through

the keep, the page who had been waiting outside the door for him at his side.

"Where is my brother?" he asked, his tone brusque.

"I do not know, Sor Garreth. Although the last I heard of it, he was looking for the treasury."

"Leave it to my brother to be practical." Garreth began to search for Dethan. The keep was convoluted, made of stone and brick, full of twists and turns and far too many dark corners. He finally did catch up to him in the treasury room, which was stone-cold empty.

"Hmm. Either this is the poorest city in the world," he said, picking up a stray gold coin from the floor, "or we've been robbed."

"The bennesah, no doubt. Methinks we'll have to explain a little more clearly to the bennesah how things work. The city was fighting us and he was making off with the gold."

"And other forms of leverage. His offer of the girl and the wyvern came with a small flaw. He controls her by controlling the fate of her sisters."

"Hmm. It seems we need to find our host."

"Where did you put him?"

"I didn't put him anywhere. I thought you . . ."

"Mind tricks," Garreth realized as he swore thoroughly. Somehow they had been tricked into thinking the other was watching over the bennesah.

"The mage. Let's find the bennesah and rout out this mage before we end up putting a knife in each other's backs," Dethan said, scowling.

The first thing they did was scour the castle from top to bottom in search of the bennesah and the girls. Once they were certain the trio were not in the keep, they began to make inquiries. It didn't take long for Dethan's trusted page, Tonkin, to roust up a servant who actually had a clue as to what was going on. The man shivered in his slippers as he was dragged before the unhappy brothers.

"Where is your master?" they asked for what seemed like the hundredth time. They had been interrogating almost everyone in the keep.

"I do not know, milord," he said, his eyes shifting to and fro.

"Brother, methinks we have a bad liar here," Dethan posited.

"Methinks you're correct," Garreth said.

Dethan smiled humorlessly. "My patience is at an end," he growled at the servant. "Where is your master? And while you are at it, where is the mage he uses to confuse us?"

"Y-you can't get to the bennesah. The mage will protect him. He is very powerful."

"Not powerful enough to save this city, you'll notice. Why don't you tell us where they are and let us worry about whether or not we can actually capture the bastard?"

"If h-he hasn't left the city already, he is at his manor house in the lower swells."

"Take us there at once."

The man quailed. "No one crosses the bennesah and his mage. He will put a curse on you!"

"Then point out the way," Garreth said in aggravation. "He need never know you helped us."

Garreth brought out a map of the city, which he had procured upon first arriving, and the servant pointed to a house near where the river ran through the rear of the city.

"Double the guard at the gates," Dethan said to Tonkin. "Mind magery can be fought if you but remain aware. Tell this to the men. Brother, come. Let's see a man about some gold."

"I am more concerned with the young girls," Garreth

said with a frown. "The bennesah is sure to have them with him. If we find him, then we find the girls."

"Strange priorities, brother," Dethan said, lifting a brow. "We have come to conquer a city . . . not one woman."

"This city cannot be safely ours as long as the wyvern is out there," Garreth argued.

"True. Let's go."

Together, and with a contingent of armed men, they descended on the manor house of the bennesah. Dethan walked up and thundered his fist against the door.

There was no answer.

"Enough of this," Garreth said after several minutes of the same. He drew his brother's sword, and with a mighty swing, he cleaved the door down the middle. He and Dethan pushed inside. In the front hallway, a couple of servants were crouched down low in a corner, shivering and quaking with fear.

"Where's your master? And I'm tired of asking the question, so if you know what's good for you, you'll show the way," Garreth said stormily.

"H-he said he was leaving the city," the male said.

"That's a lie!" The female popped upright, shoving her male counterpart over.

"Moyra, don't!" the man cried tremulously.

"He's in the undercity! With the mage! But you'll never capture him now. The mage will trick you! He makes you see things. Terrible, terrible things!"

"And the girls?" Garreth demanded.

"Poor lambs." The woman tsked. "The mage holds them over the wrena . . . only lets her visit with them if she behaves according to his will."

"The *wrena*?" Garreth asked.

"Aye. The woman who controls the wyvern."

"Where's the undercity?" Dethan wanted to know.

"Just as it says. Under the city."

The brothers exchanged looks. They had not been aware there was a city beneath the city they were in the process of conquering.

"Tell me, how do we get past this mage?"

"You can't!" the man cried. "He'll melt away your mind like steel in a forge. Liquefies it and shapes it whatever way he pleases!"

"There must be a way," Garreth said quietly to the woman, meeting her eyes. "I want to bring those girls safely back to the wrena. Tell me how."

She bit her lip and seemed to think on it. "He's weakest when he sleeps."

"You mean he can't hold sway over magic when he sleeps? And I'll bet he can't hold sway when he can't focus either." He patted the woman on her plump little cheek. "There's a good woman. Come to the keep on the morrow; find Tonkin, our head page. He'll find you work if you'd like it."

Garreth turned to his brother. "I have an idea."

"I'm listening."

"First, let's get a feel for this undercity. How do we get to it?" he asked the woman.

"Wherever there's a city gate, there's a door leading to the undercity beside it."

"So all four compass points. We're closest to the south gate right now," Dethan said.

"I don't like the idea of heading underground to a place we know nothing about," Garreth said. He had a very bad feeling about the whole situation. It was almost as though the bennesah had planned for every contingency . . . perhaps including them finding servants and compelling them to divulge the location of their master. It was possible none of these leads were worthwhile and they were simply being led astray again.

"What is this undercity like?" Dethan thought to ask.

"It is the sewer system. Some people they live down there. But mostly it is a place for vermin," the man said.

Garreth looked at his brother. "I might be mistaken," he said slowly, "but did the bennesah strike you as the kind of man who would volunteer to live in a sewer system?"

"With that belly and all those fine gold rings? I think not."

"Then I believe we've been on a wild chase all this time."

"She's telling the truth," Dethan noted.

"I can see that. But it doesn't follow that *he* was truthful with *her*."

"Also true. So, what's your feeling?"

"He's left the city already. As soon as he got the chance," Garreth said.

"Agreed. Let's get our horses and some search parties."

"You think they walked out right under the noses of our army?"

"Yes."

"Then search parties might do us very little good. We need a way to countermand this magic."

"The wrena," the woman said cautiously.

"What of her?" Garreth asked.

"No mind magic can be used on the wrena. The eyes of the wyvern see clear."

"Intriguing," Dethan said.

"I agree. I'll go get her."

"She's wounded," Dethan said with a frown.

"I am well aware!" Garreth called over his shoulder as he hurried away.

CHAPTER
FIVE

When he entered Sarielle's room she sat up quickly in her bed. She also immediately cringed, her hand pressing into her belly in pain.

"Did you find them already?" she asked, guarded hope in her eyes.

"He has escaped the city, walked out right past our army. I'm certain your sisters are with him."

"Vinqua," she spat. At his questioning look, she explained, "The mage. I should have guessed."

"He is laden with the gold from the treasury so he has not gotten far. I know you are unwell, but I am told you are immune to the mage's magic."

She was on her feet in an instant and then she staggered. She was incredibly pale, and he noticed that her bandages had soaked through with blood again and blood was staining her robe.

"Are you well enough for this?" he asked with concern.

"For my sisters' safety and lives? You would have to bury me in the ground first. Besides, if he has my sisters, then that means he plans to come back for me or retake the city while you presumably have no control over me or the wyvern. I do not think you are any better than the bennesah . . . but for now you are my only means of getting my sisters back."

Garreth displayed a small smile at that. "So be it," he said. He knelt down at her feet and unlocked the manacle around her ankle.

"Now, need it be said that you should not try to escape?" he asked sternly.

"Without my sisters' safety guaranteed first? Leaving them behind?"

"I do not know you well enough to assume you have such pure intentions," he pointed out.

She took his offered hand, stepping carefully around the chain on the floor. "I might say the same. But I will pretend to believe you mean what you say and will return my sisters to me without holding them over me. I . . . have little choice but to *hope* you are a better man than the bennesah."

"And I have little choice but to prove it to you. Come. You will ride with me."

"I can ride on my own," she said stubbornly.

"Gods, woman! You can barely stand! You will ride with me and use the support of my body. The last thing I need is for you to fall from a horse!"

She seemed to think on that a moment, then with great reluctance she let him lead her from the room.

She was exhausted before they even made it to the bottom of the stairs. Realizing this, Garreth swung her up into his arms, holding her high against the broad width of his chest. She pushed at his strong shoulders in resistance, but she may as well have been trying to push a cart full of boulders. Eventually she just sighed and relaxed against him, her arms hanging loosely about his neck.

"There, now. Is this so difficult?" he asked her.

"I find it bitterly difficult," she said. But after a moment she did concede, "But thank you just the same."

"You're most welcome."

Before long, they were in the courtyard and a powerful grey stallion was being led up to Garreth. Thinking he would put her down, mount, and then have someone hand her up to him, she made ready to be put on her feet. But to her shock, he barely broke stride before putting his foot in his stirrup and swinging them both into the saddle in one tremendous movement of strength. The next thing she knew he was pulling the skirt of her robe up between her thighs. Feeling his hand between them, his knuckles a hairsbreadth from touching her bare woman's flesh, she cried out and tried to push him away. But he ignored her and threw her leg over the saddle so she was riding astride, her robe bunched up around her. She flushed to find herself in such a position. Women, especially slave women, were not allowed to ride astride. It was commonly thought that it would give a woman ideas of independence their male counterparts would rather they not have. This was doubly the case when it came to slaves. Slave males were allowed to ride, but only sidesaddle, and slave women were not allowed to ride at all. They must be carried in a litter or, more commonly, must walk. Only the most expensive slaves rode in litters.

She was a most expensive slave.

Had been.

She allowed herself to think on the possibility of freedom for a moment. For the likes of her? It was too alien a concept for her to fully grasp. Like riding astride, it was simply one of those things she had never entertained, because to do so meant facing the dissatisfaction of not having it.

She found too much about being in the saddle disconcerting. Riding astride. Being forced to sit upright in spite of the pain in her midsection. The feel of a hard wall of muscle at her back and more muscle on either side of her hips. Her bottom was drawn back on the leather until she was notched into him like a hand would fit inside a glove.

With a single hand he grabbed the reins of the massive horse while his other arm banded beneath her breasts and held her back against him. He was, she realized, very careful not to hold her around her wounded midsection.

He spurred the horse hard and they leapt forward.

"We will ride around the city in ever-widening circles until we track them. Keep your eyes keen to any sign of their trail," he said in her ear.

"It has been a dry summer," she said a bit breathlessly. "There should be tracks leading away from the city. They will be fresh and clear because no one has left the city since it was said you were moving toward us." She gasped at the pain rocketing through her with every stride, but she also laughed.

"What is it?" he asked, bemused.

"Is this what it feels like? I had always wondered!"

"What what feels like?"

"Riding on horseback!" she cried, her delight apparent in every word.

"You've never ridden on horseback before?"

"Never! Slaves are not allowed! Woohoo!!" she cried out, laughing into the wind. She had never felt anything so exhilarating in all her life. Never except once . . .

Garreth was delighted by her in spite of himself. They were not out there to have fun or to be entertained; a great deal was riding on them having success. But just the same, he found himself taking pleasure in her joy. He kicked Draz, his grey stallion, into a hard gallop, sliding himself under her bottom as best he could to alleviate the impact of her rear against the saddle. But she would feel the pain of it when her excitement wore off no matter what he did.

He followed Dethan's lead, watching the ground as it flew by beneath them.

"There! Wagon tracks!" she cried out suddenly. Garreth whistled sharply to Dethan, and his brother reeled around and rode back to them. He looked to where she was pointing but saw nothing except barren ground.

"There's nothing there," he said with a frown.

"There are tracks here," she insisted. "The mage has obfuscated them from you. I can see them plainly."

"Do you see him in the distance?" Garreth asked.

"No. Not yet. But it is too dark."

"Perhaps we should pick this up in daylight," his brother said, looking up at the bright moon. It was so full it was almost as good as daylight, in some respects. Had it been waning, they would not have been able to see.

"No! They will escape by then and I will never see my sisters again!" she said, panic in her voice and in the grip she latched around Garreth's wrist.

"I will not let that happen. Dethan, they cannot be far. They are on a laden wagon while we're on horseback. We can easily catch up to them as long as we can follow the tracks."

"But she's the only one who can see them." Dethan's eyes narrowed on her. "What's to say this isn't all some kind of an elaborate trap?"

Sarielle scoffed. "The mage is wickedly clever, but the bennesah suffers no such affliction. He would not have thought so well in advance of his situation. Now, Vinqua—he is another story. But his downfall will be his hubris. He does not see anyone as a threat to himself or his skills. You should know, however, that he will abandon the bennesah instantly if it comes to a sticking point."

"That is good to know. Now, keep your eyes on those tracks and tell me if you need to stop and rest."

"I won't. Come," she said urgently, trying to spur the horse on herself. "Hurry!"

"We will, little fira, be patient."

"Fira?" she asked as he kicked the horse into a canter.

"It means 'fire' where I come from."

"Where do you come from?" she asked.

From a mountain of ice and snow.

"A long way from here. Across the great Kolla Ocean, a land called Toren. My brothers and I were born there, though I spent very little of my lifetime there."

"Brothers? There are others?"

"Aye," he said, his tone short and hard. She was smart enough to know he didn't wish to discuss it further, and she wasn't much in the mood to press. Her whole body was on fire. Waves of nausea were beginning to roll through her. She swallowed hard, pushing it down inside herself as best she could.

"Have you any sisters?"

"Not anymore," he said. Again, his tone was hard. This strong man harbored pain over the fate of his sisters. A feeling she could understand completely.

"I'm so sorry."

"It was a very long time ago."

"Oh. The tracks go that way," she said, correcting his course.

"Is it just you and your sisters, then?" he asked.

"Yes. My parents died some time ago."

"No brothers?"

"Not anymore," she echoed him.

She expected him to ask her to explain but then realized asking the question would open him up to a similar question in return, and she had a feeling he would rather have a mouthful of sore teeth.

"So . . . have you a sweetheart?" he asked her after a moment.

She snorted at that. "Slaves are not allowed to have sweethearts," she said bitterly.

"But your parents had you. Surely the masters of Kith want slaves to . . . to propagate."

"They do. But they control it. They . . . force it. There is usually no love to be had. The women are forced to take whatever man is directed at them. It is a curse to be healthy. They think if they breed only the healthy ones they will make more healthy ones. Then they can worry less about feeding us, clothing us, and sheltering us. We'll take care of ourselves."

"That's ridiculous. If one were to look on a slave as any beast of burden, one has to put care into it in order to get good work from it. My horse Draz is stabled in a warm, dry stable or a roomy paddock, it's fed good grain, and fresh straw is laid for its bed. If I don't do these things, the horse wears down and becomes ill, perhaps even dies."

"Then you would make a good master," she said, her voice unfeeling.

They rode in silence awhile longer, Sarielle pointing to lead them. Dethan and their outriders remained several lengths behind them, following wherever they went.

"Do you see them yet?" Garreth asked, his breath warm against her ear and the side of her neck as he spoke, sending hot chills skittering down her neck and spine. She was already uncomfortable from her pain, but this was a completely different kind of discomfort. She did not understand it and could not have explained it had she been asked to give it voice. Again she felt that strange heaviness in her breasts, and she felt the need to shift in the saddle.

She shook her head in response to his query, unable to speak for that moment.

It was hard to see far in spite of the moon and it was frustrating her greatly. She wanted to be able to see her sisters more than anything, which was why she said nothing about the pain and nausea that began rolling through her, chasing all other sensations away.

Until her body told the tale for her.

She suddenly vomited over the side of the horse, unable to help herself. Garreth reined in sharply, holding her tightly as she panted for breath and tried to swallow back her pain and sickness. He grabbed her chin in his fingers and pulled her back to see her face.

"I told you to tell me when you needed rest!" he snapped.

"I don't need rest!" she insisted stubbornly. "I'm just not used to being on something that moves so much," she lied. Quite convincingly.

"Are you able to continue?" he asked her.

"Yes! Now, please . . ."

He looked at her hard in the darkness, then finally spurred the horse onward. Relieved, she sat back against his chest with a quiet sigh. Her sisters were counting on her. She had to come through for them. They had no one else in the world. She had to protect them. Even if it meant trusting this odd man. This man who said he did not believe in slaves.

"I see them!" she cried suddenly.

She could. A dark shape in the distance. It had to be them. Who else would be riding in such darkness? Garreth relayed the message to Dethan.

"How are we supposed to fight that which we cannot see?" Dethan asked of them.

"The mage will be counting on that," Sarielle agreed. "However, they must stop to rest eventually. He has to sleep at some point."

"But if we can see them, then they will soon be able to see us. They will know they are being followed," Garreth said.

"Then we dog their steps until they drop," Dethan said.

"No!" Sarielle and Garreth said at the same time. She looked at him in surprise. She knew why she had said no. She was afraid they would use her sisters in some nefarious way if they thought they were trapped. But why had he said no?

"She will not last long enough for that," he said, nodding to her. "She can barely keep the saddle as it is."

He was right. She was finding it nearly impossible to sit upright. But she had thought she was hiding it effectively from him. He was more attuned to her than she had realized.

"I have an idea," Garreth said. "We get ahead of them. Ride around full about them so they are coming up to us and not we to them. They will not think we are traveling from Kith, coming from the other direction. We are faster and lighter than they are. That way we can approach them without them having their guard up until the last possible moment."

"When you're upon them the mage's magic will not be able to hide them any longer. Not when you know to look for them," Sarielle said.

"Then it seems we have a plan. Let's ride!" Dethan said, spurring his horse hard. It leapt forward. The outriders dashed off behind them.

Garreth did not hurry in their wake at first. He looked down at her. "We cannot continue like this at full speed. I am going to turn you around in the saddle so you may put your arms around me and hold on to me. It will allow you to relax against me."

Once again his hand went to her thigh. With a firm grip, he suddenly spun her in the saddle until she was riding astride behind him now. The difference was enormous. She could lay all her weight against him, her arms wrapping around his thick chest to hold herself to him. The instant she was settled, he called to Draz and they lunged forward.

It took all of an hour to maneuver them, undetected, in front of the small caravan that was the bennesah, the mage, and three wagons laden with belongings. Just before they came within true sight of the bennesah's caravan, Garreth handed her off to an outrider, freeing himself up for battle if and when it was necessary. He instructed the outrider to hang back, so Sarielle would not be easily seen as they approached the bennesah.

And sure enough, as they came closer, the caravan magically appeared before their eyes. Like a mirage in the desert, what had once been emptiness was now filled.

Dethan and Garreth rode up on the caravan hard and fast. They plowed into the outriders accompanying it and swords clashed. Sarielle watched Garreth swing his deadly sword with frightening accuracy. Taking off first one head and then another before the outriders finally threw down their weapons. Garreth dismounted and walked to the rear of each wagon, finding the first two full of gold and the third full of a bennesah and two small young girls.

"Why, great conquerors! What a delightful surprise!" the bennesah said as if they had come to visit him in his home unannounced. He held out his hands as if to calm Garreth's wrath. "What can this great bennesah do for you?"

"You can give back the gold you have stolen from your city," Dethan said harshly.

"And more important, these girls," Garreth said, reaching to take first one, then the other from the wagon.

Sarielle threw herself off her horse, hitting the ground hard on her hip and backside. She cried out, but in the next instant was scrambling for her sisters. She hugged and held them, cooed gently to them, but they simply stood against her, faces turned down, eyes fixed on the ground. Their silence in the face of their sister's grateful tears was eerie. Unsettling.

"What have you done to them?" she spat at the bennesah.

"You will watch how you speak to your bennesah, slave," he spat back, all show of benevolence gone from him then. "You. This is all your fault. You and that weakling of a wyvern! It was supposed to be a great protector! A magnificent guardian beast! But in the end, it was nothing! It fell because you fell, you weak, sniveling girl!"

Before Garreth could stop him, the bennesah ran up to her, hand raised, ready to slap her to the ground.

"No!" she cried.

The bennesah went flying.

It was as though something plowed into the bennesah from beneath. He rose to an alarming height and then dropped like a stone to the ground, as if a beast had come and plucked him from the ground, flew away with him, then dropped him from the sky. The impact was so hard that a cloud of dust was kicked up into the darkness.

And that was the end of the bennesah. His brains had burst from his skull on impact and were spilled across the ground, his rotund body lying at odd, broken angles.

Garreth looked at Dethan, then at Sarielle.

"What did you just do? How did you do that?"

But her eyes were wide and fearful. "I-I don't know! I've never . . . I don't know!"

"Maybe it was the mage," Dethan said cautiously. Garreth and Sarielle could tell he did not believe it.

"Where *is* the mage? He's not here," Garreth said.

"He must have slipped away," Sarielle said. "I warned you he would abandon the bennesah if he felt he was in danger. I . . . I'm sorry. I didn't mean to kill him."

Genuine tears were filling her eyes. Garreth did not

think they were necessarily tears for the bennesah. He suspected that she had never taken a life before and now was afraid of whatever it was inside her that had just done what it had done. Garreth didn't blame her. He would be lying if he said he didn't feel some trepidation himself. And he could see the same concern in his brother's eyes.

But all that concern washed away when Sarielle suddenly fell into a dead faint.

CHAPTER
SIX

When Sarielle awoke, it was with a softly indrawn gasp. She was in her room and daylight was streaming through the windows. She immediately looked around, searching for her sisters, and for a moment she thought she had dreamed it all.

And yet . . . there was no shackle on her leg. She could feel her ankle was free of the cuff that she had worn so very often in her turnings as the wrena. Ever since the bennesah and Vinqua had seen her come back from the Asdar Mountains, bearing the mark of the wrena on her body, they had known how valuable she was and had immediately chained her and kept her sisters hidden from view. She touched the mark now, a brand on the back of her shoulder, kept out of sight by her clothing.

If not for the twins, she would never have come back. She would have stayed in Koro's nest with him, let him care for her as she had cared for him. They would have needed only each other and no one else.

But she had gone back for Jona and Isaelle, knowing they had no one else. They were the reason she had ventured out into the mountains, to make their lives better.

She sat up and her body screamed with pain. Her

shoulder was better, but she was weaker overall and she had never known such consuming agony. Koro was suffering and dying. She could feel it down to their connected souls. She had to do something. Not just to save her own life but to save his. He had only tried to help her. Had only done what she had asked of him. What her master had asked of her. Poor Koro.

"I've been waiting for you to awaken."

She gasped and looked to the left. Garreth was standing against the wall, his arms folded over his broad chest, his green eyes intent upon her. He was wearing black breeches, the material so tight against his skin that she could see every muscle. If not for his tunic, she was certain she would have seen far more than his muscles through that gloving material. His tunic was green with lighter green and gold woven throughout and it made his eyes jump out at her. His black hair was damp and curled at the ends, as if he had just come from a bath.

"My sisters?" she asked immediately.

"Sleeping quite soundly, I assure you."

"Why are they not here with me?" she demanded to know.

"Because you are unwell and I did not think you wanted them to see you like this," he said, his tone hard. "Stop expecting the worst of me. It grows tiresome."

She realized then what he had done for her. What he had said he would do for her and had done for her. She would feel better once her sisters were by her side and within her control, but still. He had rescued them from the bennesah for her.

And now he was expecting something in return.

"He is dying," she said softly.

"I know. I can see it in your pallor. Time is short."

"Yes. But I do not know if I can make the journey to him."

"The Asdar Mountains are not all that far away."

"But deep within. In the craggy rocks. There are caves there where the wyverns make their nests."

"Wyverns? Plural? Just how many are there?"

"I don't know. A few. Ten at least . . . last time I was there, anyway. But they don't procreate easily, so it is probably the same."

"Why don't they procreate easily?" he asked, genuinely curious.

"They are loners by nature, so mating is not an imperative to them. And raising young is very hard for them to do overall."

"You know much about this?"

"I know what Koro knows. Just as he knows I am a slave."

"*Was* a slave," he corrected her.

"Was a slave," she echoed. But clearly she still did not believe it. She was still looking for the ulterior motive to his behavior. He could see it in her wary eyes.

"So now you will take me to him?"

"How do I know—"

"You'll just have to trust me again," he said. "But you don't do trust very easily, do you?"

"Why should I?" she asked, closing her eyes, relaxing and sighing through her pain.

"I suppose that's a fair question from your perspective." He pushed away from the wall and moved toward her. She heard the movement and opened her eyes. For a moment she caught her breath and simply watched him. She had never known a man like him before. A man of such strength and stature. His brother was bigger and taller than he was, but it was clear Garreth was the leaner and faster of the two. She had seen it in the way they had battled the outriders for her sisters. He moved definitively and with force. He was a man who always committed to what he was doing, to where he was going, at any given moment.

As he drew closer, she felt his approach on a level that seemed to penetrate her skin. It was . . . it was almost like the feeling she got when Koro was approaching. Her heartbeat grew stronger in her chest, her breath more powerful. She felt everything about him, even at a distance.

It unnerved her.

"Please, don't come any closer," she said before she could help herself.

"I thought we understood that I'm not going to hurt you."

"I-I know. I-I just . . . Please. I need some time to—"

"You're all out of time," he said, pushing past her protests and sitting down on the edge of the bed. "I think you know that."

"Yes," she admitted in a whisper. "I do. I'll . . . I'll take you to him. But only because . . . even if you do want to kill him, he'll die anyway. I have to take the chance that you really do want to help him."

"I really do want to. We will bring our most talented mem with us and she will use her spiritual healing to cure the wyvern." He paused. "What does 'wrena' mean exactly?"

"Well, it just means that I'm one of the wyvern blessed."

"And how does one become wyvern blessed?" he asked, reaching to pull an errant strand of her hair free from the corner of her lips.

"That's . . . a long story," she said, fidgeting to tuck her hair back behind her ear so he wouldn't have a reason to touch it again. But touch it he did. He ran a fingertip along her hairline at the top of her forehead, almost as though he couldn't seem to help himself. She felt his touch sliding against her, felt it echoing into the pulse of her blood.

"I've never seen hair this color before, fira. It's like your head is on fire. It's beautiful, really."

"Thank you," she said on a whisper.

"You're beautiful," he said, his tone dropping deep as his eyes fell to her mouth. He kept doing that! Why? What was so fascinating to him about her lips?

"I'm a slave. We aren't beautiful."

"I've hardly seen a woman fairer than you are," he said. And for some reason that pleased her to no end. She felt herself blushing and cursed the reaction. What kind of game was he playing now, she wondered. What was it that he wanted from her?

And then she realized what it might be.

"No!" she cried softly just before he leaned forward and touched his mouth to hers.

She could have plucked him up and flattened him on the ground just as he had seen her do to the bennesah, but she did not. Her hands went to his shoulders, gripping him and pushing against him at the same time.

But no sooner had he pressed against her mouth than he was pulling away and looking into her eyes.

"No?" he asked.

Then he moved in and caught her stunned lips against his again, this time deepening the kiss a little. She had every intention of shouting no at the top of her lungs . . . until she actually began to taste him, to draw the flavor of him onto her lips. But just when she was starting to get interested, he pulled back again.

"No?" he asked once more. And this time he did not return. This time he waited for her response. Waited to hear her rebuff him again.

"No," she said. They both immediately knew the difference between the first denial and this last one. This time she was saying no to his no. As in yes. Yes, she wanted him to kiss her again. She didn't know why, but she wanted more. She knew there was something more to be had, and she wanted it.

It was crazy. Daring. She didn't know him. Didn't

trust him. But there was something to his strong, handsome features that just drew her in.

This time it was she who moved forward to touch her mouth to his. Suddenly his hands were up and closing around her head, pulling her tightly to him as his mouth slanted fiercely against hers.

She had been kissed before, but it had never felt like this. Stealing kisses with a kitchen lad had never felt like this. Poor Toaw, young boy he had been, had no hope of competing with this man's kiss. Drawing in a deep breath, he coaxed her mouth open with his and introduced his tongue. Shocked, she drew back. He saw her confusion and smiled. It was a warm smile. An expression she had not seen on him before this. It creased across his face and lit humor in his eyes, making him even more compelling.

"Have you never been kissed like that?" he asked her gently.

She shook her head.

"Have you never been kissed?" he thought to ask then.

She nodded. "But please don't tell. I'll get in trouble."

"With whom?" he said, a gentle reminder that she no longer had to worry about the rules of slavery under her Kithian masters. "Why would you get in trouble?"

"We're not allowed . . . unless our master says we can. And the bennesah would never risk me becoming pregnant and dying in childbirth. I was more valuable to him locked up in this room. He kept me here, hid me from his enemies . . . and everyone else."

"Well, that's over now. If you want to kiss me, you can."

"I . . ." She dipped her head and looked at him out of the corner of her eye, a pretty violet blush tingeing her cheeks. "I think I do."

He smiled again and pulled her close once more. She moaned softly at the immediate feel of his mouth, at how good it felt. She had been afforded so few pleasures that this one hit her hard. This time when he touched his tongue to her lips, she opened her mouth for him willingly and without question. And she was glad she did. The way their tongues touched—the erotic, wet warmth of it—was like nothing she'd ever felt before. She followed his lead with ease, his actions slow and purposeful. She felt heat begin to spread throughout her body, in certain places more than others.

When she drew back, she put distance between them, as much as the narrow bed would allow for. He let her go, not forcing her to his will in the least.

"I-I think I'd like to stop now," she said, holding up a hand as if to ward him off.

"Then we will stop," he said simply.

The reaction surprised her and she knew it showed on her face because he said, "What did you think I would do?"

"Become angry," she said honestly.

"No," he said with a shake of his head.

"Oh. Well, thank you."

"For what?" he asked, amusement in his eyes. She liked the way his eyes lightened with the emotion. When he had been kissing her they had gone dark, but now they were the lightest, fairest green. She had never seen eyes that color before. All Kithians, including the scourge, had blue eyes. Differing shades, but all blue.

"For the kiss. And for not becoming angry. But now . . ."

"Yes, now we have to get back to the business at hand," he agreed. "Do you think you can ride again?"

"Do I have a choice?" she asked wryly.

"No, I suppose you don't. We won't find him without you."

"No. And even if you could, he'd run away in fear."

"In *fear*? That big thing would fear *us*?"

"He's still just a baby," she insisted.

"That is a very big baby," he said.

"You should see the other wyverns," she said.

That gave him pause. "How big are they? And will they attack us when we intrude on their nesting area?"

"Not with a wrena with you."

"You were going to explain to me how one becomes a wrena," he said as he stood up and then bent to lift her out of the bed.

"Was I?" she asked. "I don't recall . . ."

"Well, I was hoping you would, anyway," he said, again with that amusement.

She smiled at him for it. "Well . . . you have to tend an egg."

He stopped in his tracks and looked at her. "Tend an egg? Is it that easy?"

"No. You have to find an egg first. And that means invading a wyvern's nest. An act that usually gets people killed. Then you have to lug an egg roughly the size of a twelve-turning-old child somewhere safe. Usually a cave. At least that's what I did. Then you have to—"

"And you did all this?" he interrupted her, aghast.

"Yes. I was . . . desperate."

"Why were you desperate?" he asked as he took her down the stairs.

Her face clouded over. "Because my mother had just died and we were of no value to the bennesah. He was going to sell me and my sisters off to separate buyers. The only thing I could do was make myself invaluable to him."

"So you ventured up into the mountains, stole an egg, raised it in the wilderness, somehow keeping yourself alive, and basically gave birth to a wyvern?" He was incredulous.

"Yes."

"How long did that take?"

"Well . . . I became a wrena the moment the wyvern

was born and the baby recognized me as its mother. That is when the brand appears." She absently touched her shoulder. "No one knows why . . . It just happens. It took only a waning of the moon."

"And how does that bond form?"

"Well, it's like any child's bond to its mother. Only something happens when the wyvern is born that connects its soul to its mother's, the way I am connected to the wyvern."

"And just how far does this relationship go exactly? You can get Koro to do anything for you?"

"Mostly. There are some instinctive things that I can't countermand."

"Such as?"

She flushed again. "The mating instinct. When a wyvern chooses to mate, you'd best not be in the way . . . wrena or no."

He laughed at that. "I can see how that might be," he said.

"What's the joke?" Dethan asked as they entered the common room of the keep.

"No joke," Garreth said dismissively. "She's as ready as she is going to be. There isn't much more time."

"Then let's be off. Tonkin, fetch our horses."

"No, brother. You need to stay here and hold the city," Garreth reminded him. "As long as the mage is out there, we are not safe."

Dethan frowned. "True," he said. "But are you certain? This will be a hazardous journey."

"I am certain. Better to risk only one of us. The city is ours. Soon you can return to your wife and child. Let's just heal the wyvern first."

"I still don't like the idea of this," Dethan said. "Why do we want a healthy wyvern?"

"For the same reason the bennesah did. So it can protect this city when needed." He looked at Sarielle when she tensed in his arms. "Willingly," he added.

She didn't exactly relax, but she felt a little better to hear him say it.

"Very well," Dethan said reluctantly. "But take Tonkin with you. I will feel better if you have a trusted man with you."

Garreth frowned, but he assented with a tilt of his head.

"My sisters?" she asked.

"I'll take you to them. But then we must go."

She nodded and he carried her down the hall. Once they were out of earshot of Dethan, she asked, "Don't you like Tonkin?"

"I like him fine. Why do you ask?"

"You looked unhappy when your brother told you to take him with us."

"Mm. That's more about my elder brother continually thinking I need looking after, when in fact I am stronger than he is right now."

"How so? He is very big."

"Size doesn't always matter," he said. But then a wolfish sort of grin spread over his features. "In some cases it does."

"What cases?"

"Ah. I'll let you find that out for yourself one day."

He stopped at the door to a room just off the kitchens and kicked it open, carrying her inside. Sitting quietly at a table in the center of the room were her sisters, eating jam and bread. Garreth lowered her into a chair and she held out her arms to them eagerly.

"Come, little juquils!"

They got up immediately and went to their sister. Not running but walking slowly. When they reached her, they leaned against her body, again fully silent, their eyes downcast.

"What is it, my loves?" she asked, shooting Garreth a worried look. He didn't blame her. These were not like any ten-turning-old children he had ever seen. There was no energy to them. No gaiety.

They didn't respond.

"I don't understand," she said, looking at Garreth helplessly as she stroked their fiery red hair. Anyone could see the family resemblance by just looking at them.

"If I had to hazard a guess, they've been sorely misused," he said gently. "I am guessing they've been kept captive just like you."

"Yes. They were treated well . . . as far as slaves go . . . I was only allowed to see them every so often. But even so . . . they were still happy children. The bennesah knew he had to keep them well and happy if he was going to control me. The twins depended on each other greatly as friends and playmates. But . . . this is something new. Different."

"I wish I could explain it," he said. And he realized he truly did. He did not like to see her distraught. "Give them time. They will come about."

"I hope so," she said, petting them once more. "Now, my little juquils, I have to go for a while." She took each one's face in her hands in turn and looked them straight in their eyes. "But I will be back. I swear it. And then our days as captive slaves will be done, as they will be done for all Kithian scourge."

"Do not call yourself that," Garreth said with a deep frown. "You are no scourge."

"Yes. Of course," she said, giving the children one last smile before he scooped her back up into his arms. The children immediately returned to their food, as though she had not come at all.

She was still frowning by the time they made it to their horse.

"They will be fine," he said encouragingly. "Just give

them time. All slaves will need time to adjust to their new surroundings and new rules."

"It is a sad day for the slave traders. For they are now out of a job!"

"Indeed they are," he said with a chuckle. "But I am certain they will find other means of employment. This city needs rebuilding and it will take many hands to do it."

He mounted the horse just as he had the last time, without breaking stride and with her in his arms. "Now, shall I put you behind or do you think you can ride up front?"

"We can try up front for a little while," she said. She did feel strong enough, but she had to admit she found it comforting to have his strong arms around her. "But I don't know what we'll do once we get to the crags. You cannot carry me the whole way."

"Can you bring him down to us when we reach the base of the crags?"

"I can try, but when a wyvern is wounded it tends to hide in its nest."

"I can see why they would find that protective."

He spurred his horse and they, Tonkin, the mem, and four outriders began their journey toward the Asdar Mountains.

CHAPTER
SEVEN

She didn't know why, but in spite of her pain, she felt the ride was very peaceful. Maybe it was because she was relieved to be headed toward Koro at last. And now that she felt a little less guarded toward him, she and Garreth spoke a lot—mostly about various cultural things, but it always seemed to come back around to her having been a slave and locked away from the world. Since that was the only life she had known, it made sense.

"So your parents were allowed to marry?"

"Mate. Marrying is for Kithians . . . I mean, the masters," she corrected herself. He had insisted that she too was a Kithian and should refer to herself as such. Whenever she referred to herself or other slaves as the scourge, he'd tense up and correct her on the matter.

"But they looked on each other as exclusive mates, so it was as good as being wed," he pointed out.

"I suppose. But as good as still isn't quite enough," she said with a forlorn little sigh.

"But they broke all the rules. They fell in love first, then asked permission to mate afterward."

"Yes. And then again to have my brother. And again

to have my sisters. I think the bennesah liked the strength of their children."

"I can see why," he said.

The horse went up over an incline of rocks and she hissed in pain. The terrain had grown rockier as they went. They were in the valley now, a narrow canyon that would eventually open up, wide enough for the reeling wings of behemoth wyverns.

"We should be close to your dragon soon," he encouraged her.

"Wyvern. Not dragon."

"What is the difference between them?"

"Size. Dragons are larger. And dragons have four legs. Wyverns have only two, though they do have small claws at the crests of their wings, which they can use to grab things if they like."

"Have you ever seen a dragon?"

"No. Have you?" she asked.

"I have. Four legs, not two," he assured her.

"Where did you see a dragon?"

"The Isle of Thiss is lousy with them," he said.

"Why were you there?"

"A quest of sorts."

"Of sorts?"

"Well, apparently a dragon made off with the king's virgin daughter."

"And you got her back? Alive?"

"Mmm-hmm."

"What would a dragon do with a girl, besides maybe eat her?"

"Oh, these weren't just any dragons. They were were-dragons. They can be dragons or they can be men. Apparently the king's people had been sacrificing virgins for turnings . . . using a lottery to pick which one would go next. As you can imagine, not many women volunteer to go with a dragon."

"I can see why!"

"Ah, but none of them ever wants to come back," he said with a wink.

"Why not?" she asked, her innocence shining through.

"Let's just say . . . were-dragons make legendary lovers."

"Oh!" She flushed that charming shade of violet again.

"Apparently the king's daughter had rigged the lottery so she would be next to go. The king had had her name removed from the start so she would never be picked . . . although he never told her that. So imagine his surprise when they called her name."

"Why did she want to go?"

"Because they make legendary lovers," he said with a chuckle.

"Oh!" She laughed. "It sounds like she was very headstrong."

"She was. Needless to say, she wasn't at all pleased to see me and my men coming for her at her father's behest. And I didn't know any of this when I set out after her. So I thought I was rescuing a poor innocent lass."

"Oh my."

"Yes. I was fighting a dragon and suddenly this girl comes out of nowhere, shoves me onto my backside, and cries out 'Hands off my dragon!' The dragon shifts into a man, drags her into his arms, and kisses her like the world was about to end, and she wasn't exactly kicking and screaming."

"So what happened next?"

"After I made certain she wasn't there against her will, I packed up my men, went back to the king, and told him where he could stick his reward gold. You see, dragons are very rich, and that one paid me quite handsomely to leave them be."

Sarielle giggled. "Well, at least they were happy."

"Oh aye. They were very happy indeed. It's a happiness any man would wish for."

"Including you?" she asked.

"No. I'll never be able to have that."

"Why not?"

"Because I can't," he said shortly.

"Okay," she said with a frown. "Have you ever been married?" Maybe he was pining for a lost love, she thought.

"Yes."

"And you're not now?"

"My wife died a very long time ago," he said.

"And you . . . didn't love her like the dragon loved his lady?"

"Not like that, no."

"But you did love her a little," she realized.

"We were very good friends, she and I. She was a good wife. But we didn't have what my brother and his wife have. The kind of love that blinds you to most everything else in the world."

"He's very fortunate, your brother."

"Yes, he is. And my new sister is very good to him. She just recently gave him a son. He's quite the proud papa."

"I'm sure he's a very handsome boy, like his father and uncles. Where are your other brothers?"

Again that shuttered expression descended on his features.

"I don't know right now. But I hope to one day soon."

"Why don't you know? Don't you write to one another?"

"I cannot get a message to them, nor they to me. What of your brother?" he asked, clearly shifting the topic away from himself.

"He died only a few days after his birth," she said with sadness. "It was so hard on my parents. I think it broke their hearts. Everything seemed to fall apart after that."

"How much farther to the caves?" he asked her.

"Oh, soon." She gnawed her lower lip nervously. "I hope he makes it."

"*He?* I hope *you* make it."

"I'll be all right," she insisted.

His response was just a grunt. He obviously wasn't convinced.

"We'll have to stop soon," he said as he looked at the lowering sun.

"But . . . we can get in at least another hour before it gets dark," she said.

"I don't think you have another hour in you. Or did you think I haven't noticed?"

She sighed. "You're very observant."

"You have to be to survive in this world. You never know when a wyvern might suddenly show up."

"True," she said with a wry smile. "I'm sorry about that."

"Don't be. You weren't given a choice." He reined in and looked back at the others. "We make camp here tonight."

"Yes, Sor Garreth," Tonkin said. "All right, you all heard the man!"

Garreth dismounted and carried her over to where there was an outcropping of rocks. "This will provide some shelter." There was concern in his eyes as he looked at her. "Here, let me see your wounds."

"I'm fine," she said, stopping his hands before they reached her body.

"The more you say that, the more I don't believe you," he said. He shielded her from the others with his big body and untied the laces that went down the front of her robe. Sarielle grabbed his hands, drawing in a startled breath.

"I want to see your wounds," he said softly.

"But I . . ." She flushed. "I am not used to such familiarity from a man," she said.

"I will not be satisfied until I see them, Sarielle."

She bit her lip but then acquiesced, letting go of his hands and allowing him to continue. Garreth parted the material of her robe and looked at her belly. But when he moved the robe aside, his fingertips brushed the bare underside of her breast and she drew in her breath sharply at the sensation. For some reason a wicked flash of heat had bolted through her, and now her nipple was puckered in response.

His gaze darted up to hers, and she could see his eyes dilating and darkening. He looked away from her and down at the wounds on her belly, one of which was healing nicely, two of which were beginning to fester.

"Infection has set in," he said, his voice gruff.

"I—" She paused when his fingers brushed beneath her breast again. This time, she knew, his touch had not been accidental. He was looking her in the eye now, waiting for her to react. "Koro must have an infection," she said a bit breathlessly.

"So it would seem. I am concerned. You feel very warm. Almost feverish." His fingertips drew slowly down over her ribs on the left side.

"Milord, where should we set the fire?"

Garreth jumped at the sound. Tonkin's words broke the spell that had begun to slowly weave between them. Garreth jerked her robe closed quickly so no one else could see her.

"Just here," he said with a nod of his head toward the place he wanted the fire to be. He turned back to her. "I must go for a little while. You will be safe with Tonkin and the others. We will continue this later."

This? Did he mean their conversation or . . . or the touching?

"Where are you going?" she asked.

A frown darkened his features. "Don't worry. I'll be back later."

"These mountains are not safe," she said anxiously. "There are manticores and—"

"I'll be fine," he said firmly, tying the last tie on her robe. "Tonkin, watch her carefully. Mem Vivre, do for her what you can."

"Yes, Sor Garreth," the old woman said.

Garreth walked off, heading deeper into the mountainous region. Sarielle watched him with concern until she couldn't see him any longer.

"Don't worry, my dear," the mem said with a cackling laugh. "He'll be fine."

"I wasn't worried," she lied hastily.

"Mm," the crone said, clearly not convinced. "He's a good man, you know."

"Yes," she replied softly. "I am beginning to see that."

"Your wyvern will be safe. I can assure you of that. Provided we get there in time. These wounds look very ill and you have a fever. I can see it in your eyes."

Sarielle wasn't all that sure the heat in her body was simply from the wounds. She could still feel Garreth's touch against her skin, never mind that the touch had been so light she had barely felt it to begin with. But they both had known he was touching her. It had been very intimate.

"Why has he left?" she asked.

"He does it every night at dusk. No one knows why. We just see him go."

Sarielle craned her head, trying to see him.

"He'll be back. Usually just after the juquil's hour."

"I wonder why."

"Just to be alone is my guess. Sor Garreth is a man of many feelings. He does not wish anyone to know what they are usually, but it is clear he has them just the same."

They fell silent as the mem made busywork for herself, creating some sort of noxious brew in a pot over the fire. The smell combined with the aroma of cooking meat, which Tonkin had spitted and supported above the fire, and both odors made Sarielle nauseous. Exhausted and spent, she lay back in the bedroll Tonkin had arranged for her and soon, in spite of her pain, she fell asleep.

It was fully dark by the time she woke up, and everyone in the camp was asleep . . . save one. Garreth was quietly wending his way around the sleeping bodies. The moon was still very high, so she could see him quite clearly. What was truly odd was that she thought she saw his breath on the air, as if it were a winter day and he was breathing frost into it. But of course even though it was cooler in the mountains, it was still only the end of summer. It would be impossible for her to see what she thought she'd seen.

Tonkin had laid out Garreth's bedroll right next to hers, so she watched his every movement as he sat down upon it. He drew his legs in tightly to his body and she realized he was shivering. She also felt as though the temperature had lowered with his arrival.

It was all very odd.

"Garreth?" she said tentatively.

His head turned with a snap as he looked at her.

"Why are you awake?" he asked. "You should be resting." He spoke his words through his teeth and she took offense.

"I did not plan to awaken. I simply did."

Garreth sighed. She couldn't know that he spoke through his teeth because if he opened them they would begin to chatter. "Are you in any pain?" he asked, using every ounce of willpower to speak normally to her.

Her irritation with him seemed to immediately subside. "Yes. But it is tolerable."

"I suppose that is the best we can hope for," he said.

"Yes, it is," she agreed.

"Try to sleep," he said to her. He wanted to reach out and give her a comforting touch, but he knew his hands would feel like solid ice and he wasn't prepared to explain why.

But to his relief she closed her eyes, rolled over as gingerly as she could, and went back to sleep.

Garreth exhaled on the night air, watching his breath cloud upon it. Soon, he told himself. Soon it would subside and he could try to feel warm again. But warmth was a precious thing in his world, he realized. Rare and hard to find. Just as the warmth of her body was a rare and special thing. She had felt so incredibly warm under the touch of his fingertips. He had wanted to do more than just those teasing, wispy caresses. He had craved the weight of her breast in his hand. Had longed for the point of her nipple beneath his thumb.

Gods, what was he thinking? He was cursed. Cursed to his very soul. He had nothing to offer her. He had come to conquer her city, not to conquer her.

And yet he longed to do just that, he confessed to himself. He had kissed her, but now that he had, he wanted more. So much more. And she, poor little thing, was out of her depth with him. She was innocent and lost. She had no idea what it meant to be wanted by a man. Not really. He had no right, no right at all, to be laying a claim for her in any way. He was simply complicating the matter, making things more difficult than they had to be.

Weysa had brought him from torment for a specific purpose and he must never lose sight of that purpose, must never forget that his brothers were still suffering wherever they were. He must stay focused on his reasons for being out here.

Simply, he did not want her to die. It shouldn't be so important to him, the life of one woman. He killed hundreds of men and women every time he laid siege to a city. He had probably even killed young children like her little sisters.

It was why he had never undertaken his brothers' way of life in the past. He had chosen a nobler path, taking on quests of honor, being the arm of the weak, bringing justice to those who had no other way to find it. He had thrived in that kind of life and he sorely wished he could be doing that now. He could have come to this city on different terms. Freed the enslaved Kithians another way. A way that would not have harmed this innocent woman.

But that was not to be. He had sold his soul at the fountain on Mount Airidara, and now he must pay the price.

But who knew the costs could be so very high? Not he. Certainly not his brothers. But they were all paying for their hubris, and perhaps it was right that they should. They had been selfish, foolish men. Arrogant and conceited.

They deserved nothing less.

CHAPTER
EIGHT

Sarielle could not awaken no matter how bright the daylight around her. Garreth had mounted with her still sleeping and they had ridden with her in blissful unconsciousness. Now she was in a state somewhere between the waking world and the sleeping one. She felt hot and uncomfortable, and the pain she endured was relentless.

"Sarielle. Are we close yet?" Garreth asked her for what she thought might've been the third time in as many minutes.

"Hmm?" she said groggily.

"Sarielle!" He reached down and pinched her thigh. She barely registered the new pain while swimming in the miasma of the old. He gave her cheek a short slap and it brought her closer to the surface. She numbly looked around. Then up.

"They're here," she whispered as she saw, way up in the sky, the reeling and drifting bodies of the wyverns as they flew and played.

"I know. We've been seeing them for a couple of hours now. But you have to tell us where Koro is if we're to help him."

She came awake a little bit more, trying to sense Koro

with that part of herself that was connected to him. But when she did, the pain became excruciating and she cried out. She had not realized just how much she had been trying to distance herself from him until just then.

"Easy," Garreth soothed her. "Tell us where he is."

"He is close. I can feel his pain." Tears seeped into her eyes as she found Garreth's compassionate and troubled gaze. "There's so much pain."

"I know, fira," he said gently. "But you have to bring him to us. I can't get you any closer to him without us climbing upward, and you simply do not have the strength."

"No, I don't," she agreed weakly.

"So call him to us, fira. Come on. Your body is weak right now, but your soul is one of fire. Call him to us. Make him come. Make him understand that we can help him."

"I will try," she said softly.

She closed her eyes and tried once more to focus on her connection with Koro. She cried out again, but this time she held on to the pain, dove into it rather than away from it. Pressed until she broke into a sweat.

Koro, my love . . . Koro . . . you must come to me, Koro. I need you to come.

She panted for breath as she connected with Koro.

"He is weak. He is confused and in such terrible pain." She groaned. "He is afraid."

"It is such a strange concept to me that something so big can be afraid of anything," Garreth said with a shake of his head.

"He can fear *you*," she said sharply. "And rightly so, considering what you have done to him."

"I do not disagree with that. I am merely looking at it from the perspective of a small and insignificant man, versus a great and powerful creature."

She nodded, closed her eyes, and focused on her connection with Koro again.

Koro, do not be afraid. I will not let anything happen to you. We will heal you. We can make the pain go away.

She sighed at last. "He is coming." And then her head lolled back, her eyes shuttering closed.

Concerned, worried that Koro could not sense her if she was unconscious, Garreth tried to reawaken her. He dismounted with her and tried again.

"Fetch me cold water!" he commanded of Tonkin. Tonkin hastened to obey. The other men stood nervously about, their eyes on the sky. The other wyverns were flying so high up that they probably could not even see their group, but the men were not going to rest on that supposition.

Tonkin returned with a flask full of cold water from a nearby stream and Garreth immediately upended it on Sarielle's face. She came to with a gasp of breath, sitting up in his arms too quickly. Pain lanced through her.

"Easy, fira," he soothed her. "He is coming. Hold on to that knowing. He is coming."

"Yes," she breathed, looking up to the sky.

Then, from a point along the stony mountainside, a huge body leapt into the air above them. It reeled and then began to fall. Its movements were awkward, flailing. He was too weak to carry the weight of his own body.

"No!" she cried as she saw Koro plummeting toward the ground.

"Easy. He can make it. Watch," Garreth said, grasping her hand and holding her close to his body for support.

And sure enough, at the last minute, Koro got his wings under him and broke almost all of his descent. He still hit the ground thunderously hard, the impact and slide of his monstrous body kicking up stones and dust all around them.

Sarielle tried to push her way free of Garreth's hold, but she was far too weak to do anything but bat at his hands ineffectually. He gingerly laid her back on the rocks, and grabbing the intimidated mem by the hand, he hurried over to the wyvern. Its body was laboring for breath, each one chuffing out hard. And there, in its belly, were the two festering wounds made by Dethan's sword in Garreth's hands.

The great beast groaned and growled, and Garreth heard Sarielle cry out, "It's all right, my love! He will not hurt you this time."

There was another loud protest, and a talon-tipped wing whipped sharply past Garreth's face. If he hadn't jumped back so quickly, the talon would have opened up his throat.

"Enough!" Sarielle scolded sharply, clearly using the last of her strength. "Please, Koro. Let him help us."

The wyvern settled down, breathing hard, its shiny black eye watching as Garreth moved closer, dragging the frightened mem with him.

"She'll help heal you," he said to the wyvern, hoping it understood since Sarielle had slumped over, her eyes rolling back in her head. The wyvern followed her into unconsciousness shortly after, and the mem was finally persuaded to move up to the large reptilian body. She examined the wound closely.

"It festers like hers does," she said in her high, scratchy voice. "But I believe I can help."

"Then do so. Quickly," Garreth urged her.

It took time for the mem to heal. And during that time Garreth paced the rocky landscape, one hand gripping his sword's pommel and the other on his hip. He kept one eye on the mem and the beast and the other on Sarielle. He was like a man waiting on his wife to give birth. Powerless to do anything but wait and see what the goddess of fate had planned for them. But Hella was a capricious goddess and, it was said, she was a little bit insane. There was never any telling which way she would play her cards.

Nearly three hours went by before he could see anything resembling a good sign. Then he looked at the wyvern and saw that the scales of its hide were now clean, free of the taint of infection . . . although still far from being healed entirely. The iridescent scales shone in the sunlight, and every so often he saw something glittering in them. Gemstones, he realized. The wyvern had gemstones stuck between its scales. It was something he had seen before. On dragons. They often slept upon their hoarded treasures, all things shiny and glittering attracting their attention and making it onto the pile. As they slept, things like coins and gems would work their way in between the scales and make the beast appear to be jewel encrusted.

There seemed to be a lot of red gems in this one's hide. There must be a rich store of the ruby substance somewhere close by.

Garreth stopped his pacing and moved to Sarielle's side. He gently tried to rouse her as he untied the closure of her robe and exposed the wounds on her belly.

Better. They looked better. Much better, he thought with relief.

"Sarielle?" he called to her. But she did not respond until he said, "Fira, your wyvern is healing."

Her lashes fluttered up, her eyes opening.

"Good," she said on an exhalation. "Thank you. So much. I know you didn't have to do this."

"Of course I had to do this," he said. "I wasn't about to let you die. You are innocent in all of this."

"Not so innocent. I made him attack you in the first place."

"As I said, you had little choice in the matter. Now rest and heal. We will be able to go home soon."

She gave him an odd look. "Home? I have no home, now that the bennesah is dead. I do not know what will become of me and my sisters."

"You do have a home. Your sisters too. You will stay in the keep for all your days, if you so wish it. You will have a privileged place as the city's wrena. You will be its protector, if you and Koro wish to do so. But you are free to make that choice at any time."

"Free." She smiled as she said the word. "I am free."

"Yes. You are." He smiled down at her. He understood the value of freedom. He had been a captive on the mountain for hundreds of turnings. He was still a prisoner to it from dusk to juquil's hour, but the rest of the time he was free . . . and he enjoyed that freedom to the fullest he could while also maintaining his agreement with Weysa.

What that meant for him now was that as soon as Kith was fully under their sway, he would move on and leave Sarielle behind. They would leave trusted lieutenants behind to run the city in their and Weysa's names. It would take some time before all that happened of course, but eventually he would move on.

Why was it that the idea of it sat so ill with him? It wasn't that he didn't want to fight. This task of conquering cities wasn't his favorite thing in the world to do, but he would do it as agreed. His freedom for his sword arm. That had been the bargain struck.

So, what was bothering him, he wondered as he watched her drift off to sleep. Something wasn't quite right. He was certain he would figure it out eventually, but for the moment, it was eluding him.

He moved away and let Sarielle sleep.

CHAPTER
NINE

Sarielle awoke to the sensation of a light, drifting touch on her belly. It reminded her of the delicate caresses Garreth had given to her and she opened her eyes expecting . . . no . . . hoping to see him there. But it was the ancient mem who had her hand on Sarielle's belly.

"Well, you look fine, I say." Her old voice sounded more weary than usual and her eyes looked worn and dull. She was exhausted. The mem had used every ounce of skill and strength she had to save Sarielle's Koro. It was a gift Sarielle would never forget.

She took hold of the woman's gnarled hand and squeezed it tightly as she met her eyes. "Thank you," she said with all the sincerity in her heart. "Ask anything of me you will and I will gladly do it in repayment."

"Hmm. I shall have to think on that," the old woman said with a fatigued cackle. "In the meanwhile I wouldn't mind a donation of some of those pretty little gems in his hide . . . in Weysa's name. The mems of Weysa do a great deal of work with those who are displaced by the ravages of war. Your city will have more than enough of those."

"Of course," Sarielle said. "You may have as many as you can carry. He will give them gladly."

There was a chuff of breath from over the woman's shoulder and the wrena found herself looking into the adoring eyes of her wyvern. Koro nudged the old woman out of the way in order to gain access to Sarielle. But a nudge from a wyvern was no small thing, and the old woman toppled over.

"Oh! I'm so sorry!" Sarielle apologized profusely, but the mem waved her off with a chuckle.

"He just longs for you," she said, understanding. "And I long for my bed." With that, the old woman shuffled off to find her bedroll.

The next instant Sarielle had a face full of wyvern head. He nudged her and rubbed against her, knocking her backward and trapping her against the ground. She giggled at his affection and hugged and petted his head as best as her small arms and body allowed.

"Yes, my love. I've missed you too. And I'm glad you are well also," she said. As she petted Koro, she looked around the campsite. It was dark, well past dusk, and the moon was high, but there was no sign of Garreth yet again. Where did he go at night? Why did he go? What was it he felt it was necessary to do so far away from the campsite, where he could be set upon by any manner of creatures? Mountains were known to be favored places for manticore dens. Even now she could hear the sounds of their whistling lullabies, the warbling meant to lure in unsuspecting humans, whose flesh the manticores loved to feast upon.

Koro made a noise and she felt him nudging into her mind.

"No," she said to him with a smile, "it's not necessary for you to find him. I'm sure he will return and is just fine."

She listened then to the urgency in Koro's thoughts and frowned as he made her aware of a new problem.

The other wyverns. He was warning her that they were aware of the campsite . . . and that they were uneasy and unhappy with the humans' presence in the valley.

She patted his head and looked around the campsite again. Everyone was sleeping soundly, but she knew Koro's warning should be heeded as soon as possible. They should pack up and leave before the wyverns got it into their heads to charge at them. She was a wrena, but to only one wyvern. She had no control or communication with the others as far as she knew. She looked up at the moon and judged the time. Almost juquil's hour. If he held true to form, Garreth would be returning shortly.

Feeling better than she had in days, although not quite healed yet, she got to her feet and tried out her legs. She was weak, she realized. And she knew that how she felt was how Koro felt. He would not be strong enough to stave off a wyvern attack if it came down to that.

Where was Garreth?

She took several cautious steps around the people sleeping in the campsite and moved away. Tired as she was, it felt good to move around on her own steam. These last couple of days her movements had been powered mostly by Garreth.

The air had turned cooler and she took in a deep breath. It was brisk and refreshing. Invigorating. She touched the front of her robe and realized the mem had left it open after checking on her. She was about to tie it closed when she heard a rustling sound in the darkness. Thinking it was Garreth, she turned to face the noise.

There was a sudden scream, the sound of an angry wyvern, as Koro suddenly lunged to his feet and belched flames into the air. The sudden and blinding light revealed a creature, its torso that of a large man, like that of a great cat below the waist and its stinger-tipped tail like that of a Bytwyte scorpion whipping in deadly snaps of sound as the head and eyes of a sholet lion stared at her through the darkness. The manticore whistled and hissed, its tail darting forward and stinging Koro.

She felt the pain of it instantly and fell to the ground screaming. Koro screamed as well and his tail thrashed about. The campsite erupted into chaos. A second manticore leapt in from an outcropping above them and Koro reared back.

No! she shouted into his mind, reminding him that, unlike him, the people in the camp were not fireproof. But his flame was his instinctual tool for defense, and she didn't know if she could countermand his craving to protect himself for very long. The other men in the camp were suddenly set upon by now a total of four manticores. Sarielle struggled to gain her feet, but she was too weak from her ordeal these past days and the feel of the manticore sting was phenomenally painful. Poor Koro! He must be in agony!

And then he was stung by a manticore once more. She screamed again, unable to help herself. The snap and burn of the sting was shocking and relentless. The men struggled to get their swords and fight in the darkness.

Then, out of the darkness, his breath clouding upon the cold air, Garreth leapt into the fray. His sword gleamed under the moonlight, the cut of it sharp in sound. It swung straight through the first manticore's neck, sending the head of it flying off into the night. Seeing Garreth, a second manticore swung the stinger of its tail straight into his chest, right over his heart, setting him down into the rocks with a resounding smack of flesh meeting stone.

But Garreth was back on his feet with a single smooth movement in the span of a second. He jumped onto the back of the second manticore, severing the tip of its tail with one sharp swing of his blade, and then stabbed the mighty weapon down into its spine. The manticore fell to the ground, its body writhing in its death throes. By then Koro had regained some control of himself, and with a mighty leap he crashed down onto the third manticore, squashing it under the profound weight of his body. The fourth creature was dispatched by Tonkin and the other men.

When it was over, everyone lay there for a moment panting for breath. Then they began to take stock of one another, to make sure each was all right. Sarielle had moved forward to give Koro a comforting pat, but she stopped dead in her tracks when the firelight lit up Garreth's chest and revealed the gaping hole over his heart, blood seeping out with every beat. She cried out and rushed up against him.

"Garreth! Sit down! Please, you're injured!"

"It's all right," he said soothingly to her.

"It is not! You've been stung in the heart! You're bleeding! Mem! Mem!"

"Sarielle, please," he said, grabbing her head in his hands and forcing her eyes to his. "Listen to me. I'm fine. I'm on my feet and I'll be fine."

She looked at him through tears on her lashes, her disbelieving eyes running over him. "But . . . how? You . . . you should be dead from a hit like that. You should be dead!"

He quieted. "Sarielle, I cannot die."

"Wh-what?" she asked, stupefied.

"I am immortal. The only thing that can kill me is a god or a god-made weapon."

"You . . . you can't die?" she asked, still dumbfounded.

"No."

"But . . . how?"

"That is a long story. One I will tell you as we go. We have worn out our welcome here."

"Koro agrees," she said, trying to catch her breath

from all that had just happened, from all that she had just learned.

"Then if he is well enough, we should go. Will he come with us or go back to his cave?"

She looked at Koro. "He says he will stay in his cave and come see me in a few days. The mem has taken him far enough in his healing; he can do the rest on his own and should heal quickly now."

"All right, then. Let's break camp and journey out of this valley."

Using moonlight to guide them, they carefully picked their way across the rocky floor of the valley. Garreth was back on his horse with Sarielle riding in front of him. He was still bleeding from his chest and she could feel the wetness of it against her. She also noted that he felt very cold. His touch made her shiver.

"I'm sorry," he said. "I'll be warm soon."

"I'm not worried about that," she said. "Tell me how you got to be this way."

"A fool's journey. I was young and arrogant. My brothers and I sought the Fount of Immortality and we found it. But . . . we have paid greatly for taking what did not belong to us."

"So . . . Dethan is like you?"

"No. He was, but . . . no longer. He sacrificed his immortality for me."

"How did he do that?"

"It's a long story," he said with a sigh.

"I believe we have the time," she pointed out.

"Well . . . the short of it? We were punished that day after we drank from the fountain, each in our own way. For Dethan, he was thrust into the deepest pits of the eight hells."

"Oh no," she said, aghast.

"Yes. Because he was immortal, he would burn to death and then resurrect, over and over again. Endlessly. Until the goddess Weysa came and took pity on him, brought him out of the eight hells in order for him to be her champion of the sword. To fight in her name and win followers for her the way he once had when he was a mortal man."

"He's doing that," she said.

"Well, after a fashion. You see, he was supposed to campaign turning-round, create an impetus, an army that would make any city quail to see it on the horizon. But . . ."

"But?" she prompted.

"He fell in love. With Selinda. The grandina of the very first city he was trying to conquer. She became pregnant and could not bear to see him leave her side, so . . . she prayed to Weysa day and night for a way to release him from his vow."

"And . . . you were the way?"

"Aye. He traded his immortality for a normal life with Selinda, and I was chosen to take his place as her champion."

"I see. So how many cities have you won?" she asked.

"Counting Selinda's and this one, fira? Three. In less than one full turning of the seasons."

"That's remarkable," she said, duly impressed. After a quiet moment she added, "You said you were punished. How?"

"I'd really rather not get into it," he said evasively. "It's over now anyway."

"Well, I'm glad it's over. I don't care what you did. You are a good man and do not deserve punishment."

"So your opinion about me has changed?" he asked with amusement.

"You saved me, and more important, you saved Koro. He's still just a baby in so many ways."

"I can't conceive of him being a baby at that size."

"He's only nine. They don't reach full maturity until

they are twenty. And due to his age, he's extremely small for a wyvern. Those others that were flying above us, they are much bigger. I worry for him. Sometimes a wyvern will try to steal a nest from another wyvern. It doesn't happen often, but if a bigger wyvern were to challenge Koro, I'm not certain he would survive. I would much rather he run away than fight."

"I would much rather it too, since every injury he gets will show up on you," he said with a frown as he realized just how vulnerable that left her. "Have you ever thought of leaving here? Taking him with you away from the other wyverns?"

"I've dreamed of it endlessly," she said passionately, reminding him that she had spent all her life a captive.

"Well, now maybe your dream can come true. Seems to me the wyvern has all the money you could possibly need. Gems and gold and more. By the way, why do they collect treasure like that? Do you know?"

"They are attracted to shiny things. They are simply trying to line their nests. The hard stones feel good against their hide when they roll around in them. It also helps them to shed old skin when it's molting season."

"You know quite a lot about wyverns."

"Most of it is from Koro. Some of it is from books. The bennesah allowed me to learn to read and then he gave me everything there was to read about wyverns so I could better understand and utilize Koro to his benefit."

"I have never met a wyvern expert before. Or a wrena." After a pause he said, "That must have been a frightening journey for you. You had to travel into the mountains, face down the possibility of being attacked by manticores, climb all the way up to a wyvern nest, steal and carry a heavy wyvern egg, and then keep it warm and healthy until it hatched, all the while keeping yourself alive in the wilds of that valley. I honestly don't know how you did it. It would have been a challenge even for me. As you have seen, if I had been a normal man, I would have been dead by now."

"Yes. Well, I was very good at hiding. You see, at that point I was also a runaway slave. The bennesah did not take kindly to slaves who ran away, and he hunted them down zealously. I had to hide from outriders. Luckily the manticores and wyverns were enough to keep them out of this valley. They thought I would have been insane to go so far into that kind of territory and they were afraid to follow for the most part."

"It must've been quite an adventure."

"I had to do it. I had to make myself invaluable to the bennesah for the sake of my sisters and to keep us together. By the time I got back, he had already sold them. But . . . needless to say, he brought them back instantly when he saw what I was. He knew he needed them to keep me under his control."

"You were locked away all day?"

"No. I was locked away when I misbehaved. I was locked away at night. I was never allowed to leave the keep, but I was allowed to use the library or walk the walls and courtyard. I could shop the trade wagons that would come and set up in the bailey. I was never given gold, but the bennesah allowed me to buy things now and again. It was . . . it was a better life than most slaves could ever expect. He could have worked me to the bone, as he did his other slaves, but he did not."

"He couldn't treat you badly. You could have called the wyvern to attack the city at any time."

"That was why he kept my sisters under guard. He knew I would do anything for them. That I wouldn't risk them being hurt." She was quiet for a minute, then said, "I am worried about them. Something happened to them during their flight from the city. They are damaged. I don't know what it was. Before this they were such happy children. As happy as they could be as slaves. I . . . I have not seen them for quite a while, nearly ten days . . . The bennesah only let me see them as a reward for my good behavior . . . and when he knew you were coming to attack the city, he kept me firmly locked away for when he would need me most. But I hardly think their treatment would have changed as long as the bennesah sought to control me through them."

"So you wonder why that would have changed just because they were fleeing the city?"

"Exactly. I'm sure he was still of a mind to control me. To perhaps use me later to regain the city. So why would he hurt them?"

"That I cannot say. We will have to speak with them, get them to talk about whatever it is that happened. They will tell us eventually. Perhaps once they realize they are safe now and are no longer slaves."

"Can I ask you . . . if you don't have slaves, how does the unclean work get done?"

"You mean menial work? We pay others to do it. The more important the work, the better the servant's skill, the more they are paid."

"That sounds so . . . fair. And strange. So many of the slaves I know are very good at their labors. They had to be or they would face punishment. But if you don't whip your slav—your people," she corrected herself, "then how do you get your workers to behave properly?"

"They will behave properly if they wish to get paid and keep their jobs. There are many people competing for good positions in the world. They could just as easily be replaced by another if they don't do their jobs adequately."

She tipped her chin up so she could smile at him over her shoulder. "I think I like the world you come from. It makes a great deal of sense. And everyone must be so happy."

"There is a downside to not being a slave," he pointed out. "Slaves are given free room and board. If you are without a position in my world, it is possible you would end up on the street, impoverished and starving. If you are injured and cannot work, the same would happen."

"Injured or crippled slaves are often killed here."

"That is true in other lands as well. There *are* slaves in many lands. But my brother and I do not like the idea of slavery, so we abolish it in whatever city we conquer."

"That is very good of you. I am glad you conquered my city," she said with a definitive nod. "And I am happy to have Koro fight for you to keep it if you like."

"Thank you, fira, but we can keep the city fine by ourselves. You are free to do whatever you like."

She smiled when he used the word "free." It made her exultant, giving her a rush of satisfying joy. And she had him to thank for it.

They were riding in the dark, with only the moonlight to guide them, and the other riders were behind them at a distance. She looked around a moment as an outrageous idea began to creep over her. An idea about how she could express her gratitude. She untied the second and third tie to the front of her robe, creating a small gap. His left hand was resting on his thigh and he was using his right to rein the horse. She reached for his left hand, which he let her take without question, then slowly slid it, with her own hand, into the gap in her robe. She gasped as she felt his touch against her skin. She felt him suddenly tense from head to toe behind her.

"Fira," he hissed in her ear.

"Shh," she soothed him. "Just touch me. I am free to be touched for the first time in my life, and I want you to touch me."

She heard him exhale right next to her ear, his breath

hot against the length of her neck. His fingertips slid along the crease beneath her breast, his palm turning up so he could feel the weight of it filling his hand. He kneaded her gently, his callused palm rubbing across her nipple until it puckered tightly into a delectable point. Sarielle closed her eyes and sighed at the amazing sensation.

Garreth got hard in an instant. Just one touch and he craved more. Craved it all. He flicked his thumb over the tip of her breast, feeling the hardness of it with delight, knowing it was because of his touch that it had happened. Knowing that she wanted it, that she had initiated it, made his whole body harden even more with desire.

"By the sweet gods, your skin is so soft," he whispered in her ear. "I don't think I've ever felt anything so soft in my life."

"You like it?" she asked breathlessly. He took her nipple between his thumb and forefinger and tugged on it.

"Oh yes. I like it." His hand cupped and kneaded her some more, pulling her back into him. Their bodies were pressed together in the saddle, so she could feel every inch of him. She felt something hard against her bottom and she squirmed. His grip on her tightened. "Sit still. You're driving me crazy," he ejected.

"I'm sorry," she said, letting go of his hand and trying to scoot forward.

"No. I only meant . . ." He pulled her back tight again. "It wasn't a bad thing," he said.

"Oh," she said. She sighed as his caresses grew even bolder, covering her ribs and her chest as well as her breast.

"Gods, fira. Give me your mouth."

She tipped her head back, reaching for him with her mouth. He kissed her fiercely, his touch and his mouth combining to melt her body from the inside out. She felt something strange happen, felt her body go wet in the strangest of places. Confused by the sensation, she broke away from his kiss.

"What is it?" he asked, his breathing labored.

"I feel . . . strange," she explained.

"In what way?"

She flushed. "I feel . . . warm and . . . wet. I think something's wrong."

"Sweet gods," he hissed. "No. Everything is right. You're sweet and responsive and so damn right."

"Is something wrong, sor?"

Garreth started when Tonkin's voice came from beside him. He withdrew his hand from Sarielle hastily, holding her robe closed covertly. That was when he realized they had come to a stop.

"No. Everything is . . . Let's go," he said, clicking to the horse and urging it forward. Once they were alone again he said, "Tie your robe closed, sweet fira. We'll continue this another time."

"Do you promise? It felt . . . it felt so good."

"Yes," he said on an exhaling hiss, "it did. And it will only get better. I swear it. Just . . . not here. We can address this again when we are back at the keep. When I can take you to a private room. To a bed."

She blushed again and said, "I've never . . . I mean, I know what you want. But I've never even come close to being in a . . . a bed."

"I know that," he said. "That's why I want to do this right. That is . . . if you want to be in a bed with me."

"I think I do," she said softly. "How does one know something like that?"

"You feel it. Very often it comes with that warm and wet sensation you were talking about. But . . . I'm afraid you don't really understand what you want."

"I'm not sure either," she admitted. "I am . . . I know what happens between a man and a woman. I've seen it."

"When did you see it?" he asked.

"I accidentally stumbled upon two slaves. They were . . . breaking the rules. It was a very dangerous thing to do. I didn't understand why they would risk themselves like that. But . . . feeling the way you make me feel when you touch me, I might have broken the rules too, no matter how dangerous."

"People have risked their lives for less. But your life is no longer at risk. And fira, you don't owe me anything."

"I owe you everything," she argued. "But that's not why I want to . . . to be in a bed with you."

"Mate. Make love," he offered to her. "Have sex. Fuck. It has names. All kinds of names."

"Make love. I like the sound of that one."

"So do I," he said fiercely.

She smiled and snuggled back against him. "I won't distract you anymore," she promised.

"And that's a damn shame. But you're still healing anyway," he reminded her.

"I feel fantastic," she declared, resting her head back on his shoulder.

"All right. I'll take your word for it. Now try to relax. Let's get you back to the keep. We'll talk about the rest there."

"All right," she said with a smile.

She leaned back against him and let him take them home.

CHAPTER
TEN

"So the wyvern is healed and thus the girl. Fine work for a couple of days," Dethan said with a grin.

After over a day of travel, Garreth had just deposited a sleeping Sarielle in bed.

His bed.

He didn't want her to be back in the room where she had been held captive for so long. Dethan had allowed Garreth to take the bennesah's rooms, garishly opulent as they were, while Dethan had taken the mage's. They were not garish, but they were no less opulent. Clearly the mage had had a place of much wealth and importance in the bennesah's household.

And there were perhaps other reasons why he had put her in his bed. He had to meditate on those a little further. She was like a fledgling, testing her wings, wanting to fly. But the trick was to know when the bird was truly ready. He didn't want to push her out of the nest only to have her plummet to the ground in a broken little heap. He didn't want her making snap decisions and regretting them later.

"You seem distracted, brother. Is all well? I see you've been wounded."

"I am immortal so it is of no consequence."

"It still hurts to get injured," Dethan pointed out. "It still weakens you until you heal."

"I am well aware. But the pain of this is nothing compared to . . ." He trailed off and knew he did not need to finish. Instead he told his brother about the wyvern and the fight with the manticores.

"A lot of trouble for one little girl," Dethan mused.

"She is a fine woman," Garreth snapped at him. "Why must you act as if she is not worth the effort?"

Dethan was surprised by his brother's defensive tone. "I'm sorry, brother. I meant no offense."

"She is very special. You do not comprehend what she went through to become a wrena."

"I understand that. But you will make little headway if you become too attached to things in the cities you conquer. We have one purpose here."

"We have many purposes here," Garreth argued. "If you want to keep this city in Weysa's name, then we have to restructure the social order, build a new government, and find trusted men and advisors to run the city after we absent ourselves from it. Sarielle knows what it means to be a slave. And yet she's had power and prestige here as a wrena. I think . . . I think she would make a fine bennesah."

Dethan laughed, sounding shocked. "She's been a slave all her life! How does that qualify her to be a ruler?"

"She has heart," Garreth argued hotly. "She has the spirit that will be needed to rebuild this city. Provided she even wishes to stay. She has freedom now and wealth. She has power in the wyvern. She can do anything she wants. So why not run a city?"

"Why not indeed," Dethan said musingly. "Very well. We can train her if you think she is up for it. But her skin marks her as a slave. Many Kithians of a different color will take offense to the idea of a former slave as a ruler over them. She could face an overthrow at every turn, and we don't want that kind of instability after we are gone from here."

"Then we see to it she has trusted men around her. A strong council of support."

"Well then, I think you should ask the girl what she wants. But don't be surprised if she turns you down. She has freedom for the first time in her life. This may be the very last place she wishes to be."

"I realize that. But she will want stability for her young sisters. So we shall see."

"Indeed we shall. Now, let us talk of this mage. I do not like that he is out and about."

Garreth walked across the room and poured himself a cup of wine, drinking the entire thing in a matter of seconds. It had been a long, hard journey. He was looking forward to his bed . . . and what was in it. But first, dusk was coming. They had made excellent time coming back now that Sarielle was healing, but he had his curse to deal with before he could go back to her.

How had she done it, he wondered. How had she gotten under his skin so quickly? He was not the sort to tumble a girl in every city he seized. In fact, he had not even been with a woman since before his trip to the fountain. He had been true to his wife when she had been alive. He had not been the sort of man to break the vows of his marriage. He had respected Jula. They had been the best of friends. Perhaps, in time, he would have grown to love her. Their marriage had still been new when he had gone off on his folly with his brothers.

But she was long dead. Now he was free to do whatever he wished.

Within the confines of Weysa's demands of him. Within the confines of his curse.

No. Sarielle's life had already been hard enough. He should not drag her down into the mire of his cursed existence. Not even for a little while.

No matter how much he was beginning to crave her.

"Garreth?" Dethan said.

"Hmm?"

"The mage?"

"Oh. Yes," Garreth replied. "With the bennesah, his benefactor, dead, he has no place here. Do you not think he is long gone by now? Moved on to find better things?"

"Perhaps. But I would like to be sure."

"How can we accomplish that?" Garreth asked.

"I don't know. We are going to have to figure that out. Perhaps we should send men out to find him. Bring him back to us so we may question or control him. Perhaps remove him from the equation completely."

"I would much rather let him go and let him live his life in peace as long as he does not wish to disturb our plans to turn this city's attention to Weysa's way. That is what is key. That is where we must keep our focus," Garreth said. It was where he must keep his focus. He did not need to dilute it with the distraction of a beautiful young woman.

"Perhaps. Let us see how things unfold."

"Good. Now I have my curse to contend with. Then, I am weary and would seek my bed."

"Of course. Good night, brother."

"Good night."

Garreth left and headed for the orchard.

After his curse was done for the night, after he had warmed himself significantly, he headed for his bedroom. The path took him through the body of the keep. It seemed the previous ruler liked to survey the majority of his holding on the trip from the main rooms to his private ones. The hallway from one end of the keep to the other was laden with windows that looked out onto the entirety of the city on one side. He paused there, looking down on the sprawling vista. In daylight he would be able to see all the way to the city walls and the main gate. He would be able to see the destruction his siege had wrought. All the fires were long extinguished and overall the damage was not too overwhelming. The city would recover. Eventually.

Just as Sarielle would recover. She would recover and find a whole world of possibilities open to her. He hoped she agreed to become the bennesah. It would give her comfort and power and purpose for the rest of her life. It would ensure a contented life for her sisters.

He walked on, dismissing the city on his left and heading toward . . .

Toward . . .

"Damn you, you cursed fool. Walk away," he hissed to himself, clenching his fists.

He did not. He walked right up to and through his chamber doors. He entered the bedroom and stood in the doorway, just looking at her for a moment. She was asleep on her stomach with her fiery red hair tumbling across the pillow. She was the prettiest shade of lavender he'd ever seen, her skin soft and shadowed and a beautiful pastel. Her violet lips were parted in sleep, her coppery lashes standing out against her skin.

She was still in her ornamental robe, the shapeless thing normally doing nothing to display her figure. But in her sleep it had twisted around her body and was pulled tight to her every lush curve. She was not skinny or frail. Not even slender like Dethan's wife was. She had sumptuous hips, a softly rounded belly, and—he knew from personal experience—the most perfect, bountiful breasts the world had ever seen.

He began to take off his outer clothing—the vest and tunic that were torn and bloody from his encounter with the manticore's tail. Once he was bare chested, he inspected the wound. It was already healing. The tail had just missed his heart—a good thing. Immortal or no, he would have gone down if it had pierced his heart, and he would have stayed down until his body healed itself. As it was, it was still a bad wound. Had he been mortal . . .

But he wasn't mortal, he reminded himself. And that was the key to his present dilemma.

He took off his breeches, which had also absorbed a lot of his blood, then moved to the nightstand, where there was a pitcher of water and a basin. He poured water into the bowl, and using a nearby cloth, he washed the blood from his body and cleaned the wound. Once he was satisfied, he dropped the cloth into the basin and turned toward the wardrobe to get another pair of breeches.

He found himself looking dead into Sarielle's fair blue eyes. She sat up slowly, her eyes never leaving his. They stayed there like that for a whole minute, simply staring at each other. Then she broke away from his eyes and let her gaze fall to his wound. A small frown tugged at the corners of her mouth.

"Does it hurt?"

"No," he lied.

She looked lower.

Her eyes widened.

He grew hard under the touch of her gaze.

"You're so . . . different," she said a bit breathlessly.

"I'll put something on," he said awkwardly, fumbling for the robe that was draped across the bottom of the bed on the opposite side of her. But he had to lean over her to get to it, and when he did, her hands went to the skin on his side and chest.

"No!" she said hastily. "I didn't mean you should hide from me."

"I'm not hiding. I wasn't thinking. I should never have undressed with you here."

"Stop!" She grabbed the robe from his hands before he could come away with it. "I *want* to see you."

He went still. He looked into her eyes as he straightened up once more. "You don't know what you want," he said tightly. "You have a brand new world to discover. You're testing your boundaries. I understand that. But you shouldn't just leap into things you can't fully see."

"I see enough," she said firmly. "I see you."

"No. You don't. You think I'm some kind of noble savior when I'm not. I don't do things like that anymore. Now I'm just a man who creates war in the name of a vindictive goddess. There is nothing noble about that."

"Your heart is what's noble, Garreth," she said softly, moving to put her legs over the edge of the bed, her hands reaching out to touch him on the bare skin of his hard belly. He drew back sharply.

"No. Not anymore. My heart is cursed now."

"Garreth," she said, standing up and following his retreat until his back hit the tapestry hanging on the wall. Her body moved in, her warmth pressing all along his. Her hands rested like two elegant butterflies on his chest. She was so beautiful it hurt to even look at her as she turned soft, accepting eyes up to him. "Whatever you've had done to you, whatever you did that may have deserved censure, it did not change the heart inside you. The heart I see. The heart of a man willing to risk everything just to save a slave girl's life. To save the life of a creature that could have killed you." She bent her head forward and pressed a kiss onto his chest beside the wound he bore.

Garreth closed his eyes, unable to do anything but revel in the sweet sensation of it. It was too good to pass up. Too good to put away from himself. She kissed him again and again, and of its own volition, his hand came up and his fingers threaded into her hair. Her hair was soft like silk, slippery and sweet, the weight of it full bodied like she was.

Then her lips touched his nipple on the right side and he hissed in a soft breath. She must have liked the reaction because her little tongue darted out and licked him there as well. His hand fisted in her hair and he pulled her back, forced her to look up into his eyes.

"I will leave one day," he warned her. "There is no future in this."

"But that day is not here now."

"Sarielle . . ."

"Fira. Call me fira again."

"Fira," he hissed right before he covered her mouth with his and kissed her until neither one of them could draw a full breath. His free hand went to the curve of her lower back and he pulled her up tight to his body, the satiny feel of her robe sliding across his skin. He was hard against her, silk brushing over his engorged penis until he was groaning from the pleasure of it. Of her. Of having her.

Yes. He would have her. Damn his cursed soul, he would have her. She was untried and new, and that made him burn all the hotter for her. Her hands were sliding down his chest as she kissed him with a zeal that took his breath away. Her fingertips rode the ridges of his abdomen one at a time, moving slowly, inexorably downward until by the time her fingers reached the curls at the base of his rod, the tip was weeping in expectation of her.

She wrapped her fingers around him one by one, then slowly skimmed the whole of her hand to the very tip and back again. He growled deep in his chest, his hold on her tightening.

"I long to be inside you," he confessed hotly.

"I know that you do," she said with a smile against

his lips. Her teeth nipped at his lower lip. "You wish to be the first, do you not?"

He groaned. "I would be lying to say otherwise. And you revel in it."

"I do," she agreed. "I am warm and wet again, and I find I like the sensation very much."

"Then we shall have to encourage it most vigorously," he said, catching her mouth in a blistering kiss. He suddenly caught her up, sweeping her legs from the floor and carrying her to his bed. He wanted to throw her down and ravage her body, but he forced himself to move a little more slowly. He laid her out against the sheets, stood back, and looked at her. Then he reached down for the ties of her robe and slowly, one by one, began to unfasten them. His breath quickened with every inch of lavender skin that was revealed, until at last the robe was in two halves from top to bottom and he could slowly sweep the two sides away from the skin they were hiding.

He began to touch every silky inch of her. Across her breasts with their dark nipples, down to her belly, and scraping his strong fingers through her fiery red curls at the apex of her thighs. He used a hand to part her thighs and then dipped his fingers into her cleft. She drew in a soft, delighted breath as he touched her, feeling firsthand that warmth and wetness she had claimed. She parted her legs farther and he was able to see her, to see the darkness of her folds and the way they gleamed from wetness.

She was touching him again as well, her fingertips skimming up and down his length again and again until he thought he would go mad from the gloriousness of it. She gasped softly when he touched her deeply, toyed at the edges of her juicy little clit. It was there like a fat, purple little berry waiting to be devoured and he couldn't keep his appetite for it in check. He lowered his head and brought his mouth against her, his tongue flicking out to taste her.

And she was divine. Utterly divine. The entire remainder of their ride back to the keep after she had let him touch her he had done little else but think about this, think about what she would taste like and feel like and smell like. And all of it came together like the sweetest of aphrodisiacs. He was lost. Stolen away. Gone. And now he wanted to bring her with him. She gasped in short bursts of breath as he worked his mouth over her, stroked his tongue around her, let it writhe over the entrance to her body. He came back to her clit and devoured it, sucking it and loving it until she was crying out from the pleasure of it. Her hands had crept into his hair and were now fisted within it. She held him to her, demanded he make good on the promises his tongue was making to her body. And he did make good on them. He coiled her pleasure like a snake and then released it.

She cried out sounds of ultimate pleasure as she thrust herself against his mouth. But he was not satisfied with one orgasm, no matter how powerful this one had been. No matter that it was the first one she'd ever had. He pushed her sensitized body back to the edge with insistent strokes of his tongue, and she clutched at his hair and went along for the ride. It was like riding astride a horse for the first time. Wild and new and freeing. It meant she was free. Free to do anything. No more restrictions. No more captivity.

She came again, her shouts echoing in the room, filling his ears with the lusty sound of them. Only then did he draw away from her, rise up over her, look down on her. She was passion personified, uninhibited, her head pillowed on a sea of wild red hair that looked like a fiery halo around her. She was, in a word, magnificent.

And she was his. It may only be for a small collection of moments, but she was his. And he was taking her.

He took his eager shaft in his hand, squeezing gently in an attempt to calm the fire within it. Slow, he reminded himself. New.

Vulnerable.

His hands began to shake. He licked his lips, the salty sweet taste of her still upon them. She must have seen the sudden doubt that entered his eyes because she reached out and bracketed his hips with her hands, pulling him down to her, raising her hips so she was sliding herself wetly along the length of his shaft.

It was all he needed. It was everything. It was such a glorious sensation that he wondered how he managed not to come on the spot, before he was even inside her. If she felt this good on the outside, he could only surmise she would be nirvana on the inside.

And he was determined to find out.

He notched himself into her entrance, one hand pressed into the bed by her head, the other gripping her rounded hip and helping her tilt her body to his approach.

"Mordu," he swore heatedly, calling on the god of hope, love and passion. "You feel like everything. Like everything has just become right in my world." He pushed further into her. Then more and more until finally . . . finally he was seated deep inside her body.

He wanted to come almost immediately and it took every ounce of self-control he had to avoid making a silly show of himself. He was a man with a man's passions, not some green boy having a taste of a woman for the first time. And he would show her what it meant to be making love with a man like him. He would show her everything she deserved to see.

"Have I hurt you?" he asked first.

She laughed. "No. Should you have?"

"For some women it hurts. Perhaps that is not the case with Kithians."

"Perhaps," she agreed with a shrug. "And I am glad for it. I wouldn't want pain to mar how wonderful this is."

He smiled down at her, again the rare expression changing the whole of his face into a more carefree version of itself. There must have been a time when he had smiled all the time, she thought.

Well, she was determined to see it happen again. He looked so happy right then, and she wanted the feeling to last for him.

So she tightened her body around him, hugging him with her walls as tightly as she could manage. He hissed in a sharp breath. "By the sweet ever-loving gods," he ground out. "How do you expect me to love you right when you do something like that?"

"Didn't you like it?" she asked, suddenly concerned.

"Like it? I'm about to spill myself without a single stroke!"

"And that's bad?" she asked.

"Mordu!" He thrust into her hard. "I'll give you a detailed explanation later. For now, you're mine! Gods . . . oh my gods . . ."

He pumped into her harder and harder, his speed doubling, his pace frantic and out of control. He knew he was leaving her behind, but there was nothing he could do to stop it.

She moaned at his urgency, felt herself going hot all over. To be wanted in such a way . . . to be needed so desperately, it was all she could have asked for.

He was coming before he knew it, his body jetting out a blinding release. He thrust into her in time to it, dragged himself in and out and in again as he spasmed with pleasure.

When he was done he collapsed against her, drawing

hard for breath, weak and replete and overwhelmed. He had never felt anything like it. Maybe it was because it had been so long for him . . . maybe that was why making love to her had felt so needful and urgent. He couldn't explain it otherwise. Except to say she was perfect. In every way. And by the way she was smiling, she knew the power she had over him. A moment of trepidation crept through him. He could never allow anyone to have power over him. As an immortal man, he could have no weaknesses that others might exploit, using his strength and indestructibility to their own ends.

And then she was kissing him, sweetly and soulfully, and his trepidations evaporated. He rolled off her, removing the press of his considerable weight, and drew her up to rest along the length of his body, her head pillowed on his left shoulder, right above the wound the manticore had given him. It had healed even more in just the time it had taken for them to become lovers. Which, he thought with some consternation, had not been a very long time at all.

"I'm sorry," he said, exhaling a hard breath. "I could have done that better."

"Could you have? What an intriguing thought," she said impishly. "Yes, let's try to do it better." Her hand slid down his belly and closed around his cock, which jumped happily at the prospect, surprising him. He'd always had a reasonably good recovery rate, but this was unexpected.

And delightful.

"Well, you need to give a man some time before—" He broke off when she dipped her head down and licked him just below his navel, her breath coasting warmly over his highly sensitized skin.

He grew hard again at the very idea of where that mouth might end up going. And she did not disappoint. Before he knew it, he was inside her mouth and her tongue was swirling around the tip of his erection. Her hand came up between his legs and cupped the malleable sac she found there. He moaned in pleasure, his fingers diving into her hair.

"Are you sure you've never done this before?" he asked dazedly. It really was a bad thing to do, to question her honesty even in joking, but she simply gave him a lick and a shrug and said, "I'm sure. Why? Am I doing something wrong? Something right?"

"Right. Definitely right. And if you just use a little suction, you can— Mordu!" he cried when she did and did it damn well at that. Before long he was thrusting himself against her tongue, toying with an impending release. But no. Not yet. It wouldn't be like that this time.

He pulled her away from him, drew her up his body until she was sitting astride him.

"Let's try something that's going to feel really good for *you*."

"Okay," she said, but he could see the hesitance in her eyes.

"What?"

"Are we going to . . . like this? Is that allowed? I mean, I thought we had to be the other way." She used her hands to pantomime them flipping over with him being on top.

"No," he assured her. "It doesn't always have to be that way. Take hold of me . . . Yes," he hissed as she wrapped her hand around him quickly and without question. She was so trusting with him, so different from the girl he had first met. He didn't want to ever break that trust, but he was afraid one day he would. "Now hold yourself over me and slowly lower yourself onto me. Gods, you're so wet," he said as she began to do as he instructed. "That's right." He grabbed hold of her hips, and with a single thrust, he put himself all the way inside her.

She gasped when he hilted himself deep, then she rocked herself as she tried to get used to his thickness inside her. By doing that, she introduced herself to the pleasure she could give herself by riding him.

"Oh . . . oh my," she breathed as she moved over him again and again. He watched her ride him, her tousled hair all around her head and shoulders, reminding him of the day he'd seen her on the wall, calling the wyvern to her. Her breasts rose and fell with every writhing curve of her back and bounce of her body. She closed her eyes, getting lost in her own pleasure, but opened them again with a snap when he reached out and put his thumb into her cleft. He stroked her there in time to her movements, and before long she was tensing around him, growing tight with anticipation, her movements becoming more wild. She leaned in, moaning deeply, her hair falling onto his face. He brushed it aside so he could continue to watch the beautiful expressions on her face as pleasure swam through her. She released, throwing her head back, singing out her pleasure like a true siren. Only then did he allow himself to be swept away with her, his own release coming hard and fast. Their pleasured cries combined, echoing in the room around them.

She fell forward over him, her breasts flattened against his chest. She was panting hard for breath and he reached to tip her head back so he could see her face. Her expression and her beauty were both priceless. He had found a very rare little jewel. A treasure in a wyvern's hoard.

And one day he would have to leave it behind with only the wyvern to guard it.

CHAPTER
ELEVEN

Dethan had to say he was shocked. Well and truly shocked. Garreth had never been the sort of man to jump in and out of women's beds. Especially women he barely knew. When Dethan had come down the hall and heard his brother moaning and calling out to Mordu, at first he had thought something was wrong. But when a female voice came into chorus with Garreth's . . . Well, no one needed to explain what was happening. He wasn't that dense. It just bothered him that he hadn't seen it coming. Sure, Garreth had taken on the girl's cause— that was what he had always done. Fought for the underdog. Taken on the impossible quest. But he'd never let himself become a truly personal part of the story. He would save the town from a villain, but he wouldn't want to live there. He would rescue the king's daughter, but he wouldn't want to marry her. He would acquire a precious religious relic, but he wouldn't change his religion because of it.

This had somehow become personal for Garreth, and personal was dangerous for Garreth's well-being. On two levels. One, his emotions might become enmeshed in the situation, and two, Weysa would not take kindly to Garreth being distracted. She had made an exception to her rules once for Dethan. He seriously doubted she would be willing to do so again for Garreth. Weysa was not known for her sentimentality. She was a cold, hard warrior, through and through. Everything she did was calculated to make her victorious.

But perhaps Dethan was getting ahead of himself. His brother had bedded the girl, not wedded her. Perhaps Garreth was simply enjoying what life had to offer, now that he had his life back.

Still, he had been off that mountainside for quite some time now, and as far as Dethan knew, he had not availed himself of a woman before this. Not that he would have announced such a liaison. But Dethan had been on the lookout for it, actually. He had been afraid that Garreth would neglect to live his reclaimed life and focus instead on the unachievable.

Getting their brothers back.

Dethan was no fool. It would be a very cold day in the eight hells before Weysa would free another brother. She didn't even know where one of them was . . . and the other was being kept in an enemy god's territory. Garreth had been working under the assumption that he could do something, anything, to get them back, but Dethan knew the likelihood was beyond remote. So he had hoped Garreth would take the time to find what little pleasure he could in his hobbled life. And until now he hadn't. Over half a turning of the seasons and nothing . . . until today.

Dethan should be relieved. He should be grateful Garreth was showing signs of life, but instead he was overwhelmed by a sense of trepidation. What he needed to do was keep Garreth on task and get him out of the city as soon as possible. They would offer the girl the moon, give her the chance of her lifetime, and then Dethan would go home to be with his wife and son and Garreth would move on to the next city.

But really, he was probably worrying like a mother hen for no reason, Dethan thought. Garreth was nothing if not sensible. He had always been the voice of reason amongst the brothers. Dethan was the eldest, the one who had pushed and pushed; Maxum had been the rake and charmer; Jaykun had been the hellion; and Garreth . . . Garreth had been the peacemaker. He didn't like to rock the boat because his brothers all did such a bang-up job of it. He'd always needed to be the reasonable one.

Yes, Dethan decided. He was worrying for nothing.

Now, he thought with a smile as he closed his bedroom door, it was time to write a very detailed letter to his wife. And thanks to his brother, the perfect mood had been set for it. Oh, she would upbraid him later for writing such things in a missive that could potentially be read by another, but she would get over it . . . once she was done fanning herself with the vellum, that is.

Dethan grinned as he picked up his quill.

The next morning Sarielle snuck out from under Garreth's arm as gingerly as she could. He had fallen asleep after making love to her a third time, but she was not as tired. Besides, she had something very important to do.

She re-dressed herself in her robe, flushing as she realized she was sore and tender in certain interesting places on her body. She had never realized how athletic a mating could be or the toll it could take on a body. The sum total of her experience before Garreth had been some kissing with a boy when she'd barely been a young woman and the time she had nearly walked in on that kitchen wench and the stable hand. They had been going at it with a fair amount of gusto, to be sure, but it had been furtive, filled with the danger of possibly getting caught.

She did not have to live with that fear. Not any longer. But she did have some people to answer to for her actions. She had to go see them right away. They had to know she had not forgotten them, that she wouldn't simply ignore them just because . . .

She snuck out of the room and down the hall. It was surreal to find herself coming out of the bennesah's suite. She had never been allowed to come even close to it, the bennesah always living in fear that the wrena would turn on him, summoning her wyvern to whisk him away, her captive sisters notwithstanding. He had been a paranoid little man, and with good reason. He had made many enemies, holding her and her ability over their heads. He had once had her summon the wyvern to lay fiery waste to one man's fields for not paying his proper taxes. An unintelligent act, if you asked her. How would he pay his taxes without a crop? But the bennesah had thought making the man and his family starve over the winter might make him pay more quickly and thoroughly in the future . . . and he had been right. But she had thought of that family that whole winter and had felt incredibly guilty.

But that was all over with now that Garreth was there. In just a matter of days he had changed everything about her life. Absolutely everything. She was still reeling from it all. She had gone from cloistered prisoner to conqueror's lover as fast as lightning. And it had all been for the better. The only caveat was her sisters. Something had happened to them. So Sarielle was headed down to them to see if showing up alone would help them open up to her about what had happened.

She quietly entered the room the twins had been assigned, expecting to find them playing. Instead she found them sitting in chairs at the table, their hands folded in front of them and their gazes fixed on their hands. It was not normal behavior for her bright sisters and it disturbed her greatly. They did look up when she entered and watched as she approached, but they did not get up and run to her as they usually did.

"Hello, my pets," she greeted them soothingly.

"Hello, sister," they responded in unison.

"What is wrong, my little loves?" she asked as she knelt down beside them. "Why are you not playing? It is a fine day for it."

"We were waiting for you," said Isaelle

"Where have you been?" Jona asked.

"I had to go take care of something. Remember Koro? My wyvern? He was badly injured and I had to go heal him."

"Oh. It's good that you healed him," Jona said.

"Yes, he needs to be healed," Isaelle agreed.

"Well, he is all better now and so am I. But you are not, my flighty little loves. You are sad."

"No, sister," they said in unison.

"We're fine," Jona said.

"We just need to go for a walk," Isaelle said.

"Yes, a walk," Jona said.

"You would like to go for a walk? Well," Sarielle said with a smile, "then we shall go for a walk and you can tell me all your troubles. I must bathe first and change out of my robe. I will put on a walking dress and we will go out and see the last signs of summer."

"We want to see the fields," Isaelle said.

"Yes, the grain is high now," Jona said.

"Well, there is an army in the fields," Sarielle said hesitantly. "But I'm sure some of the grain has been left unmolested," she said quickly when she saw their crest-fallen faces.

"Good. Hurry back," Isaelle said.

"I will."

Sarielle left the room quickly. She went back to her old room and ordered a serving girl to bring her a bathing tub and water. Once she was in the hot water, she scrubbed her body hastily. For a moment she was saddened to wash away the remains of her passion with Garreth, but she had to focus on other things. Her affair with Garreth was delightful and all, but her sisters came first.

She was still damp as she dressed and sat impatiently as the serving girl braided her hair. But as she was finishing, Sarielle's thoughts drifted back to Garreth. What would happen now, she wondered. Would they continue to be lovers or was this a one-time thing for him? He was a soldier on the move, who had an army to lead and cities to conquer. She had no real place in his life. She would simply have to accept that if this were to continue, she was to safeguard herself. It would not do for her to become too attached to him. Her priorities had to be her and her sisters' well-being. Garreth could be a delightful distraction, but nothing more. She would be sure to keep him out of her heart so she would not be affected when it came time for him to leave her behind.

Satisfied with her thoughts and with her hair, she flew back down to her sisters' room. Their governess had dressed them to go out of doors and they were waiting for her at the table, again with their hands folded calmly in front of them. It was as though they weren't even excited to be going out. It truly was strange.

But Sarielle knew they had simply been through a traumatic experience at the hands of the bennesah and the mage. She was glad those awful men were gone from their lives forever. They needed to get back to a normal way of living. The children needed a chance to become children again.

"Let us be off on our walk, my little loves," she said gaily. She swept up their hands and led them out of the room. She chatted with them happily, trying to encourage them to talk to her.

"Why aren't we going to the fields?" Jona asked after they had been walking a few minutes. They were headed toward the city center.

"Because I thought you would like to go to the bazaar first," she said with excitement. She wanted to see the bazaar too. She had spent so little time outside the keep. She and the girls had often imagined what it would be like to visit the bazaar with all its vendors and spices and colorful cloth tents. She could see the tents from the keep, the colors alluring and fascinating.

"We want to see the fields first," Isaelle said. Both girls suddenly drew back, pulling her in the other direction.

"But I thought I would buy you some candy. We've always wanted to try different candies. Remember that one time I was given candy by the bennesah? I shared it with you and we thought it was the most amazing—"

"Maybe later," Jona said. "Can we go please?"

"Well, all right," Sarielle said, puzzled once more by their behavior. But she shrugged it off and they began to walk toward the city gate. Sarielle continued to speak with them, though they gave her minimal answers. But as soon as they had passed the guards at the city gate, they became a little more animated. Sarielle took this as a hopeful sign and her heart soared with relief. The girls pulled her toward the field, eventually breaking away from her and running ahead. The army was to the north, leaving all the western fields untouched. The girls ran toward them and Sarielle had to run to keep up.

They reached the tall huff grasses, the huff grain heavy on its stalks. The girls disappeared in the grass and Sarielle immediately grew concerned. She could hear them giggling, but she could not see them.

"Girls! Come back to me!" she called.

"Come and find us, Sarielle!" she heard them singing out.

She smiled. They were playing and happy, she couldn't have wished for more. Overall she had to say she hadn't been this happy in a long time. As she ran in the grasses, chasing after children she couldn't see, she thought of how else she could express her gratitude to Garreth. It made her smile a secretive smile as her thoughts turned back to him and to their lovemaking.

That was when she ran out into a clearing. To her surprise, there in the middle of the huff field was a covered wagon with two horses hitched up to it. The girls stood beside the wagon, waiting for her.

"What have we here, my little loves?" she asked as she headed toward them.

And suddenly, right before her eyes, both of her sisters disintegrated into nothingness. Sarielle cried out and went to her knees, blinking her disbelieving eyes rapidly.

Then, from around the side of the wagon came a figure in dark robes. She looked up and immediately recognized him.

The mage.

"No!" she cried out, scrambling to get to her feet.

"Yes!" he hissed as he grabbed hold of her.

She fought him for all she was worth. Kicking him and screaming.

"No one can hear you!" he spat at her. "They hear only what I want them to hear! These fools with their simple minds are even easier to control than Kithians!"

"Where are my sisters?! What have you done to them?!"

"Your sisters are safe in the back of my wagon, where they have been all along. And if you want them to remain safe, you will stop fighting me!"

Sarielle quieted at that. "Let me see them!"

"Of course," he said. "But you will let me bind you first."

Sarielle had little choice. She had to know her sisters were all right! She let the mage tie her hands and then he led her to the back of the wagon. He pulled back the hanging tarp and there, bound and gagged, were her frightened little sisters. The real girls, not the doppelgängers she had thought were her sisters. The changelings the mage had used to lure her out there. Now she was under his control again, she realized. A captive once more. And that meant he would control the wyvern through her. Garreth and his brother were in danger! And this time they might not fight the wyvern for fear of hurting her in the process. That is, if they even cared about hurting her. They might not care at all, might think that she was against them, that she had tricked them all along. Tears filled her eyes for her plight and that of her sisters. But also for the danger Garreth was in. The danger Koro was in. In all of an instant, everything had changed.

She had been a fool. She should have known they were changeling children. I fact, she *had* known. She simply had not listened to her instincts.

"There," the mage said. "Now you are more tractable."

"Don't do this, Vinqua. I don't know what you hope to gain from this! You cannot take the city back like this!"

"I do not care about this city," Vinqua snapped. "But if I am to become mage to a new ruler in a new city, I must prove to him that I am the most powerful mage he has ever seen. And for that I will need to be able to call the wyvern. Now, that will be a spectacle! That will ensure me a new position of comfort far away from these invaders. Now get into the wagon! And remember, if you do not behave, I will take it out on your sisters. And I do not think their tender young bodies will accept the whip very well at all."

"I will obey you," Sarielle promised quietly. "You may keep your whip to yourself."

"If it so pleases me. Perhaps I will use it on you as another way of ensuring your behavior. Just keep that in mind as we travel."

He shoved her into the wagon and she hurried to sit beside her sisters. They fell on her, sobbing and trying to hold her, but the way their little hands were bound made it impossible. Vinqua had also bound her hands in such a way that her fingers were wrapped as well and she would not be able to free her sisters' hands if the opportunity presented itself.

"Vinqua! Unbind them please! You have me bound. You do not need them to be tied like this! Please!"

Vinqua seemed to think on it a moment. "No. Do you think me a fool?" He huffed. "Untie them, they untie you. You'll try to escape and we'll just be wasting my time. I warn you, it will not be tolerated. But I will remove their gags. No one will hear your screams anyway . . . and I am not entirely cruel." But his smile belied his claim. He removed the sisters' gags. Then he left the back of the wagon and went up to lead the horses away through the fields.

"My little loves," Sarielle whispered to the girls. "Don't worry. We'll find our way out of this and away from this man."

"Oh, sister!" Jona cried.

"Shh, shh," Sarielle said to her. "I know. But we are together now. It will be all right. We will find a way out of this."

"But how? Vinqua keeps anyone from seeing us. He is so powerful. We were there when he sent you the changelings and when you killed the bennesah. We saw him fly through the air! Did you do that, Sarielle?"

"Vinqua kept us from your sight. When he saw what you did . . ."

"How did you do it, Sarielle?"

"I do not know," she answered honestly. "I wish I did. I would crush Vinqua and take you home to safety."

"We wish you did too. He has been very mean to us."

"We're very hungry. He doesn't feed us very much."

"My poor little loves," Sarielle said, pain filling her heart and tears filling her eyes. She blinked them away. She would not let her sisters see her cry. She would make sure they knew she was strong, that they could take solace from that. "I am here now. I will make sure you are fed and well cared for."

"How will you do that, Sarielle?" Jona asked.

"He needs me for what he wishes to do. I will not cooperate with him if he doesn't care for you properly."

"But he will whip us if you do not cooperate," Isaelle said with tears and a trembling lip.

"Trust me, my little loves. I will not let that happen," she assured them. "Now rest against me. There're my good girls. Do not worry. Back at the keep, there is a man . . . a very good man. He will see I am missing and he will come for us."

"But how? Vinqua will make him not see us."

"I have an idea, but it will take a lot of work. Now hush. Rest. It will all work out in the end. I promise."

"Okay," the twins said in unison.

The little girls hunkered down against her and tried to be quiet, but Sarielle could hear them crying. They did not believe that Sarielle could help them.

And she didn't blame them. She wasn't all that sure she could help them either.

CHAPTER
TWELVE

Garreth awoke shortly before dusk, having slept the entire day away. He sat up sharply, realizing he would have very little time to make it out to the orchard where he suffered his punishment away from any prying eyes. During the time he was frozen, he was helpless. Anyone could walk up to him with a god-made weapon and take his head, and that would be the end of his immortality. The end of his life.

He looked to the bed beside him and saw that Sarielle was not there. He admittedly felt a little consternation about that, even though it was helpful that he would not have to explain a sudden departure to her. If she remained this close to him, eventually she would start to ask questions, would come to realize that there was something going on. But for the moment, he wondered where she was.

Of course he had been asleep all day. He should have no expectations that she would stay there if she were awake when he was not. That was just ridiculous.

So why couldn't he shake this feeling that she should be there with him? Safe, where he could see her. Where he could just drink her in, like a fine mulled cider, sipping and tasting over hours of time. She was a passionate creature, so open and so starved for the smallest bit of affection and life. It was wrong of him to take advantage of that, to take advantage of what was probably more about gratitude than anything else.

But he could not seem to help himself. He could not seem to turn himself off to the idea of being with her. It was a dangerous pastime, to be sure, but it was there nonetheless.

He would search for his new mistress once juquil's hour passed. But he would not go to her immediately. He knew his body remained cold for quite some time after he returned from his curse, and he would not want to bring that to her bed. He did not want to bring anything to do with his curse into their time together.

But the truth was, his curse came attached to him. If he was in her life, then so was the curse.

He hastened to dress and order his horse. He thundered out of the city and he was already beginning to freeze up by the time he tethered the horse and ran to the center of the orchard.

Dethan watched his brother go and could not help the chill that walked his spine. Not too long ago it was Dethan who had raced at dusk to be alone where he would conflagrate and burn to his very bones hour after hour until juquil's hour. But at least it was summer yet, he thought, which meant the time between dusk and juquil's hour was shorter than at any other time of the turning. But already the nights were growing longer, dusk coming all the sooner.

Dethan was writing another letter to his wife, whom he sorely missed. He expressed his concerns about Garreth and his new liaison, expressed his pity for Garreth and his curse, expressed how damn grateful he was to her for helping him break free of that curse. He wrote on and on to her:

I watch my brother suffer every night what I once suffered and it hurts my heart to see it. It hurts me to know there is nothing I can do for him. So perhaps it is wrong of me to question his choice in this woman. If she can bring him even the smallest of comforts, he deserves that. He most of all.

I cannot express the guilt I feel whenever I see him leave at dusk. For it was I who talked him into coming to Mount Airidara with us and I who pushed him forward when he spoke of turning back. I was the one who carried him those last steps and I was the one who put the cup to his lips, cursing him forever. My little juquil, I long for your comforting arms. Though I do not deserve the ease it will bring me, it makes the guilt more bearable. My deepest wish is to find a way to free him, as you once freed me. But I know it is impossible, that Weysa would never willingly give up two of her champions. It would be asking too much and would be a futile hope.

All I can do is help my brother to cope with his curse the best way I possibly can. May the gods guide me in doing that. Perhaps Hella, goddess of fate and wisdom, will guide me and my brother . . .

Not too long after juquil's hour, Dethan saw his brother return. As he watched from the high windows, he could see his brother's breath fogging in the air from the vast temperature difference between them. Garreth threw the reins at a stable hand and walked into the keep.

Dethan knew he should wait, give Garreth time to come down from the pain of his curse, but he was so compelled that he could not seem to help himself. He went to the main hall and stopped his brother there.

"Brother," he greeted him, "how do you fare?"

Garreth gave him a hard look. "You know how I fare," he said bitterly.

"Yes, and for that I will be eternally sorry," Dethan said with a heartfelt frown.

Garreth sighed. "You need not feel guilt, brother," he said. "It does neither of us any good. I came with you voluntarily on that journey. I could have held my ground and stayed behind, but I wanted the adventure as much as you did. I am responsible for my own curse."

"But I—"

"Was there something you wanted?" Garreth interrupted him.

"I wanted to discuss . . . I wanted to be certain you were not becoming unwisely attached to this girl you seem to be championing. First you go to great lengths to save her life, and I can understand why you did—it is in your nature to do the just thing—but now you have made her your lover? What can you possibly be thinking?"

"What I am thinking is that it is none of your business who I bed," Garreth said crossly.

"Garreth . . ."

"No!" Garreth said sharply. "I am not a child, Dethan. I am not your younger brother who is getting into trouble at every turn as we did when we were children. I am a grown man now. I have lived a very long life, just as you have. I am free to make my choices, whether they make sense to you or not. In fact, you never come into the equation . . . nor should you! I shall do what I please whenever I please. Right now there is only one person I must answer to, and she is not you!"

"That's just it! Weysa has hold of you and she does not like to share her champions. She will not want you to lose focus of your goals."

"Bedding a girl will not make me lose focus of my goals!" Garreth snapped. "There was a time when you wenched considerably during your campaigns! And yet you were still able to conquer in Weysa's name! Now, leave me be!"

Garreth pushed his way past his elder brother.

"Garreth—"

"This conversation is over, Dethan," he said.

"Where are you going? To find *her*?"

Garreth rounded on him. "Yes! I'm of a mind for a good fuck to warm me from the cold of my curse! Is that all right with you? Am I to beg your permission for it?"

"No, Garreth," he said quietly. "I just don't wish to see you or the girl hurt."

"As I said, that is not anything within your power. Do not make me repeat myself again."

Garreth turned away and marched out of the hall.

He had thoroughly warmed by the time he finished climbing the tower stairs to Sarielle's chamber, figuring it was as good a place to start searching for her as any . . . although he suspected that after so many turnings of being held captive in that room she might not want to spend much time there at all. Both the hotness of his roiling temper and the vigorous exercise did well toward warming him. When he reached the door he stopped to take a deep breath, trying to cool his temper. Honestly what right did his brother have to question him? To questions his motives and actions? Dethan was way out of line.

But he didn't want to think about his brother anymore. He wanted to focus on the woman beyond the door. He wanted to touch her, to make sure she was real, to steal moments with her that might make him forget all about his brother and his wretched curse.

He pushed open the door, holding in front of him the lantern he'd grabbed, letting the light fall upon her empty bed.

Where could she be?

Her sisters, he thought immediately. She would be with her sisters. He thought about leaving her to them, letting her spend some much desired time with them unmolested. But he could not seem to help himself as he hurried to their room. When he opened the door and let himself in, he moved to the girls' beds.

To say he was surprised to find them empty was a bit of an understatement. Empty not only of Sarielle but of the children too. He quickly strode into the adjoining room and found the woman who had been acting as the children's temporary governess, shaking her awake roughly.

"M-my lord?" she stammered sleepily.

"Where are the children?"

"I . . . the scourge took them this morning."

Garreth grabbed the woman by the front of her dressing gown and pulled her nose-to-nose with him. "Call her that again and I will see you whipped within an inch of your life."

The woman began to shake and tried to pull away.

"I-I don't know where they are! It's bad enough I have to cater to the little . . ." The Kithian woman spat her words but cut herself off from calling them a name that might anger him further. But then she ruined it with her next statements. "Me! Catering to slaves! And those demented little children aren't right! There's something very wrong with them!"

Garreth backed up, dragging the woman with him out of her bed.

"When did she take them?" he demanded of her.

"This morning!"

"And when she didn't return with them you did not think to say something to someone?" he ground out.

"It is not my job to keep watch on a slave woman!"

"In fact," Garreth hissed, "it is not your job to do

anything. You are summarily dismissed from this household!" He shoved her away from himself. "Pack your things and get out this instant!"

"Fine!" she hissed. "I don't care if she is the wrena! She is still a slave!"

Garreth came back up against her with an angry growl. "There are no more slaves in this city. And you . . . Get out of my sight before I have you stripped and pilloried in the middle of the bazaar!"

The woman's eyes went wide and she seemed to suddenly realize she had gone too far.

But Garreth did not give her the opportunity to try to redeem herself in his eyes.

"Where did she say she was going?" he bit out.

"The children wanted to go see the fields," she said. "Sor, if you will forgive me—"

"No, I will not!" Garreth snapped. "Leave, madam. Now!" He turned his back on her and stormed out of the room.

Now he had to go back to Dethan and ask for his help. He was deeply disturbed that Sarielle had not returned to the keep, that she was missing. Where could she have gone? Why would she have disappeared like that?

"Dethan!" His brother was no longer in the hall. That meant Dethan was probably in his rooms. Garreth hurried, a sick feeling twisting low in his gut. Something was not right.

"Dethan!" he cried, pounding on his brother's door.

The door opened and Dethan stood there half dressed, clearly getting ready for bed.

"Sarielle left with the children this morning and has not returned."

To Garreth's frustration, Dethan did not react with any urgency. "Have you checked the entire keep?"

"No! Dethan, something is very wrong here!"

"Garreth, let us search the keep for her before we get ahead of ourselves and worry where worry is not warranted."

Dethan re-dressed himself, much too slowly in Garreth's opinion, and together they set out to rouse the entire keep and begin a search for Sarielle. After over an hour of searching, they came up empty handed.

"She's gone," Garreth fretted.

"Garreth," Dethan said hesitantly, knowing how fractious his brother was at present, "it is possible . . . She is a free woman now, Garreth. Free to go anywhere she wishes. Perhaps she has just taken the children and left. Left to start a new life elsewhere, away from the memories she has of this place."

"No!" Garreth ground out. "She has not left! All of her clothing is still here. As are the twins'. She would not leave with nothing. She would not . . . she would not leave without at least saying good-bye to me."

"Why? Because she bedded with you for a few hours? She does not owe you any—"

Dethan broke off when Garreth's fist crashed into his face. He staggered back in shock and, touching his bloodied lip, stared at his brother.

"What in the eight hells is wrong with you?" he demanded.

"What is wrong with you?" Garreth countered angrily. "If this was your precious Selinda, you would be turning the world on end to find her!"

"Selinda and Sarielle are hardly comparable!"

"Insult her again and I swear to all the gods—"

"I only meant," Dethan said hastily, "that my feelings for Selinda cannot possibly be the same as yours for Sarielle! You've known the girl for only a matter of days!"

"My feelings are not at issue here! The wrena is missing. With her goes the power to call up the wyvern! Is that what you want out there? Possibly able to turn against us?"

He said the words but didn't believe them in the slightest. He was only saying what he thought would most motivate his elder sibling to help him.

"A good point," Dethan said seriously. "But how could she leave unless willingly?"

"We must search the city, question the guards and men. Someone has seen her and we will find out who. Once we do . . . then we can figure out what action to take."

"Perhaps we should wait until daylight," Dethan hedged.

"No. Now. We must find her before too much time has passed. If . . . if we find her and it is as you say, that she is leaving of her own accord and wishes to be let go, then fine. We can leave her be. But . . . until we know for certain, I will not rest."

"Very well," Dethan said. "As you wish."

The brothers began their search.

It was almost two hours later when they found the guards at the gate who had seen her pass and walk out into the huff fields with the children.

"Did it look as though she was set to journey a long distance with them?" Dethan asked.

"No. They looked as though they were . . . playing," the guard said. "But we could not see them after they went into the huff fields. The grasses are too tall."

"So anything could have happened to them," Garreth said. "We must search the fields."

"Brother, this time I have to insist we wait until dawn. We will find nothing in those vast fields in the darkness and we could miss some important signs of their passing if we flounder around."

Garreth had to admit his brother was right this time, though he did not do so with any joy. In fact, he was a cloud of irritability and anger as he paced the hall waiting for daylight. Dethan took the opportunity to gather the men and arrange them into searching groups, then laid a map of the city and the surrounding fields upon a table and organized where each group of men was to search. The fields were vast and the grasses high. It could be painstaking work. It gave Garreth only the smallest amount of comfort to see his brother being proactive.

When dawn came the brothers left the keep and the city behind and began to search the fields. It was quite some time before they found the field they were looking for. In the center of the high grasses was an area that had been trampled down, and there were signs a horse team and a wagon had been there.

"She snuck out into the fields to a wagon and left, as I suspected," Dethan said gingerly, afraid of enraging his brother with the truth. "She must have supplied it over time and—"

"Supplied it how?" Garreth asked. "With what money?"

"You said yourself the wyvern lies on a bed of treasure!"

"And when would she do this? When she was dying? When she was traveling to the wyvern? No. You are only seeing what you want to see," Garreth said.

"I could say the same to you!" Dethan snapped.

"Look, brother!" Garreth snapped, pointing to the ground. "Her footprints . . . but no footprints belonging to the children. In fact, it's as though she came into the field alone. But there are the prints of another adult."

"A lover perhaps? One she is running away wi—"

This time Dethan caught Garreth's wild punch in his hand before it could strike him on his jaw. The brothers struggled, tussled. Dethan finally shoved his youngest sibling away.

"All right!" he said. "Say she left unwillingly! With whom? How? Why? Answer me this!"

The answer came to both brothers at the same time. "The mage!" they cried in unison.

"You see, brother?" Garreth said heatedly. "There is a danger here!"

"But why would she go with him? If the children were not here, he would have no leverage over her."

"Perhaps . . ." Garreth cast about for a reason. "What if somehow he had control over them? Maybe that is why we see no prints. There has to be some kind of explanation."

"Assuming it is the mage, how are we to find him? He can make himself invisible to us at any time."

"I—" Garreth cast about for a response. "I don't know," he said at last.

"What we need is a mage of our own. Surely there is someone in this city who can see through his magic."

"No, my lord," a Kithian guard spoke up. "The mage saw to it his was the only power to be had in the city. Anyone with mage ability was either forced to leave the city or met with an underhanded death by one of the mage's agents or tricks."

"Then we must seek out an answer from other cities," Garreth said. "We will send groups of riders to the cities in search of mages or magesses." He paused. "And I will go back to the wyvern. Surely he can find her."

"No. It would be a fool's errand to go back to that place of danger when the wyvern may no longer be there."

"What else would you have me do?" Garreth railed. "Just sit by and do nothing?"

"You have a city to run, like it or not. We do not yet have a strong enough foothold here. You speak of my wife and child . . . whom I cannot return to until I know you are safely in charge of this city! Now, that may seem selfish to you, but it is also what you promised Weysa you would do and she will not take too kindly to you shirking your responsibilities to her."

Garreth despised it, but his brother was right. He would be mad to risk Weysa's outrage. She could just as easily put him back on that mountaintop, leaving him there to freeze for all time.

And yet it was a struggle for him to care about his own preservation when he knew Sarielle might be out there, a victim to the mage. The gods only knew what he might do to her.

Dejected, Garreth followed his brother back to the Kithian keep. They arranged for search parties to travel both the roads leading out of Kith, in the hopes they might stumble upon the mage when his guard was down and his magic was not in play, and to search other cities for someone to help them find Sarielle.

That left Garreth with nothing to do but wade through the burdens of his day. He struggled to focus on the tasks at hand: the rebuilding of the city, the feeding of his army, the control of the Kithian peoples, and the process of freeing the slaves for good and all. When Sarielle came back, he thought, it would be to the city he had promised her. A city without slavery. A city where she would be free to live for all the rest of her days as an equal to any other Kithian.

Nay. Better than any other Kithian. As their leader, if she would have the position.

To help him feel as if she would be returning soon, he had her things removed from her old rooms and brought into the bennesah's mistress's quarters, which were adjacent to his rooms. The bennesah's mistress, who had gone relatively unnoticed to Garreth before this and who was still in residence, was moved to Sarielle's old room. She did not seem to take great offense, however, which

Garreth might have noticed as being odd had he not been so preoccupied. As it was, the beautiful young woman proved to be a helpful resource when it came to information about the city and its workings ... and most important, in the navigation of its interpersonal relationships. She seemed to have a knack for soothing the many frayed tempers and ruffled and indignant feathers of those close to the government who were being forced to adjust to a life without slaves.

Davine, for that was her name, showed such a usefulness that Garreth and Dethan were willing to overlook the way she was trying for all she was worth to make inroads into Dethan's bed, trying to secure a future for herself with the new power in the city. But the young woman, for all her perfect figure and kempt beauty, was sorely disillusioned if she thought she could hold a candle to his absent wife. It did not matter how long Dethan was away from Selinda; he would never be unfaithful to her. His devotion was pure. Untouchable.

And that is when Davine thought to turn her sights on the other brother. She began by showing great concern for the missing slave girl, offering to help Garreth in any way. She hid her fury when her rooms were taken from her. Showed him only her most pleasant nature. Garreth, preoccupied with other things, completely missed the true nature of her machinations.

"My lord," she said to him in her softest, most concerned voice, "you must take a small amount of respite." She handed him a cup of wine and moved behind him to rub away some of the tension that was knotted in his shoulders. "The riders will be here within days with news of a mage or magess who can do your bidding."

"Days is too long," Garreth said bitterly. "There's no telling what he might do to her in the meanwhile."

"He will not hurt her," she said. "She is too valuable to him."

"Nor will he let her go as long as she is."

"But it is good she has value," Davine said as she leaned her supple body against his back. "For if she were to lose that value, the wrena would be of no use to him."

"Away," he said irritably to her, brushing off her attempts to physically comfort him. "I thank you for your concerns, but I have work to do."

Davine reigned over her temper. She had not gotten where she was by letting her caustic nature show. She was an expert at presenting the image a man wanted to see. If he felt compassion for a slave girl, then so be it. She too would be a slave.

"I'm sorry," she said meekly, putting her head down and standing away from him. "The bennesah always made me do that. I thought . . . I thought you would like it too. Please don't be angry with me."

"I am not angry with you," Garreth said with surprise in his voice. "I simply don't need that kind of comfort."

"Then you will not punish me?" she asked hesitantly, looking at him through her lashes. She squeezed out a tear, letting it drop down her cheek.

"Punish you?" he asked in a hard voice. "Is that what the bennesah did when you did not make him happy?"

"Yes, my lord," she said quietly.

"Well, that will not happen now or ever again. If you wish to help . . . fetch me some more wine, then see about getting some food on my table."

"Oh, I'd be happy to, my lord," she said eagerly. She went to fetch him the wine and brought it to him, taking the opportunity to brush up against him again.

She had been in the rooms adjacent to the bennesah's, and so she had heard a great deal through the door between the rooms. Not the least of which was the passion he had shared with the slave girl. He was most certainly a lusty man, from the sound of it, and with the slave girl out of the picture, he would probably be in need of a woman in his bed. She was determined to be that woman.

And she would be, no matter what it took.

CHAPTER
THIRTEEN

Garreth was mentally and physically exhausted. Dusk had come and gone again, and there was still no sign of Sarielle. Dawn was creeping into the sky, and he had not slept since he had discovered Sarielle was missing. He was out on the walls of the keep, the cool air blowing past him as he looked down on the city.

Where could she be? What else could he possibly do to find her? Once again he thought of going into the Asdar Mountains to search for Koro. He wished he too had some way of calling him.

And that was when a huge, winged creature flew past him, skimming so close and with such a huge wash of air that Garreth nearly tumbled over the wall and onto the rocks below. As he gripped the wall and regained his balance, he looked with shock and a surge of hope as Koro settled, digging his talons into the stone of the keep's walls, his great wings out for balance.

Koro! It was most certainly Koro with those blue iridescent scales that sparkled here and there with the red gemstones stuck between them.

The great beast chuffed out a breath of air and fire, the flames warming Garreth as he stood in awe beneath him. He grinned from ear to ear.

"Koro! She sent you, didn't she? My clever girl!"

Koro simply looked at him. It was as though Koro were expecting something from him.

"Tell her I'm coming for her! I'll do whatever it takes, but I will find her!"

Koro spread his wings, the rising sun showing through their membranes, displaying blood vessels and knobby bones. Then Koro was up again in a great wash of air and circled the keep . . . then the city, then came back again and chuffed fire over Garreth's head.

Garreth got the message instantly.

"Dethan!" he shouted as he went into the keep and ran down the hallways. He got to his brother's room and thundered his fist against the door. "Dethan, get up!!"

A very groggy Dethan opened the door. "Damn you, Garreth, can't it have waited an hour?"

"No! Koro is here!"

That woke Dethan up instantly. "Is he attacking?"

"No! He's waiting! I think he wants us to follow him. I think he wants to lead us to Sarielle!"

"What if he wants to lead us into a trap?" Dethan said with a dark frown.

"I don't give a fuck!" Garreth said explosively. "Whether it's a trap or not, it's leading us toward Sarielle. If he wanted to kill me, he could have picked me off just now. Roasted me like a duck where I stood. I think he wants to lead us to Sarielle so we can help her."

"And suddenly you can read the mind of this thing? You aren't a wrena, you know."

"And you aren't an idiot! Surely you can see what's happening here! Or am I mistaken?"

"No," Dethan said, "I'm not an idiot." He scratched his head. "All right, then. Let me put some armor on. You do the same. Have someone prepare our horses, and get a small group of men together. We'll ride out, follow this thing, and see where it takes us. But I'm warning you. If you get me killed, Selinda's going to take your head off."

"I know. Trust me. I'll do everything I can to keep you alive. Weysa would be just as pissed at me and I can't afford either one of them being mad at me."

"All right. I'll be there in a minute."

He shut the door and Garreth hurried off toward the main hall so he could find some men.

The only person there was Davine. She was sitting in front of a fire, her body lounging on a chaise. It was pretty early in the morning, so he was surprised to see her there.

"Davine, have you seen any of my men?"

"No, but I could go get someone for you," she said helpfully.

Garreth smiled, walked over to her, and touched her chin affectionately. "You're a very good girl," he said. "That would be very helpful, yes."

She smiled brilliantly at him. She was up and out of the room in an instant. As Davine ran from the room, she chuckled to herself. Her plan was working. He was beginning to see her. All she had to do was continue to figure out what he needed, what he liked, and soon he would be completely molded to her hand.

Garreth paced the hall as he waited for his men. He wanted to be gone. He couldn't see Koro from the hall, but he hoped the wyvern understood that he was coming, that he just needed a moment to get his feet beneath him. He had never been so impatient in his life as he was in that moment.

He was going to find her. Koro would bring him right to her—no magician's magic would hide her from her wyvern. He wished he had a mage of his own to counteract the mind magic of this one, but he did not. He would have to do his best and hope that it was enough.

Dethan was there minutes later with Tonkin by his side. He eyed his brother. "No armor?" he asked.

"No," Garreth said. "Unlike you, I don't require armor."

"Damage can still slow you down," Dethan said with a frown.

"And I can move faster without it."

"Very well, brother," Dethan said reluctantly. "Let's follow a wyvern!"

The brothers set out within the hour to follow Koro as he reeled and dipped in the morning sky, apparently very satisfied that they were following him. He kept buzzing them, his great wings flapping and washing air down over them.

"All right, you overgrown bird!" Dethan cried after the tenth time he did it. "You'll blow me off my horse!"

"He's playing with you," Garreth said with a chuckle. "Remember, he's very young yet."

"Which prompts the question, is he really leading us to her or is he just playing?"

"We'll find out soon enough. Now, let's go! They are over a day's travel ahead of us!"

Both brothers urged their mounts faster, following the spike-tailed beast.

In the back of the wagon, Sarielle was sitting with her eyes closed, keeping in touch with her wyvern. Through his mind, she felt Garreth was coming for her, following Koro as Sarielle had hoped he would.

Koro was playing with the men . . . or at least that was the impression he was giving her, that he was having fun. She chuckled to herself as she thought of what that might mean. How exactly does a wyvern play with a human?

Sarielle sat back with a sigh. Communicating with Koro was exhausting sometimes. His thoughts could be

very unfocused, his natural instincts getting the better
of him. But she was pretty sure he was leading the men
from the keep in the right direction. She was assuming
it was Garreth . . . and maybe even his brother Dethan.
But she couldn't be sure. Koro's description of the men
was a little vague: "short" and "tiny" and "shiny metal
skin" could mean just about anything, but it sounded a
lot like men in armor.

Sarielle looked down at her sisters. Her real sisters.
She knew for sure these were not changelings this time.
The changelings had been called forth with the power
of the mage's magic. They were real beings that were
able to take on the appearance of anything they wished.
That was why she hadn't been able to see through the
magic. They had not acted like children because the
mage had controlled the changelings, and his concept
of how a child should behave was distorted. There had
never been children in the bennesah's household. He
had no heirs. His wife had died trying to birth his only
child and the child had followed quickly after. It was
one of the events that had colored him against mating
Sarielle to another slave. As much as he would have
liked to breed the strength of her line, he had not wanted
to risk losing her and the power of the wyvern.

The mage had no idea that men from the city were on
their way. Perhaps if they caught him off guard they
could end this without any of them, her or her sisters,
getting hurt.

She began to sing softly to the girls, always keeping
her mind open to Koro. In the back of her mind she could
feel him swooping and dipping, cutting sharply through
the air and blowing fire. All of these things came so
naturally to him, including his naturally playful person-
ality. Sometimes she wished she could share this with
others, so they could feel the sheer freedom and joy in
the wyvern's heart. His life and needs were simple: food

in his belly, air beneath his wings, gems and shiny things for his nest. When he got older, she supposed he would want a mate. And when that mate laid eggs, he would father the hatchlings. Wyverns in the wild were opposite to humans in that the female came and went as she pleased and the male watched over the nest. In the human world, the men came and went and the women were left to nurse.

She wondered what kind of mother she might be. She had never considered the possibility before. She had never mated before.

Oh! Wait! But she had mated! Did that mean she would get pregnant? Would she bear Garreth a child?

The idea wasn't at all unattractive, but it was a bit frightening . . . a bit concerning. She wasn't stupid. She knew he had no intention of sticking around the city once he had a new government under his control in place. Cities were out there just waiting to be conquered. But . . . perhaps if he had a son . . . perhaps then he would not be in such a rush to leave. Perhaps then he would have reason to return. He could not possibly make war all turning long. The snows would come and the world would become cold and inhospitable. Surely Weysa would not expect him to continue warring in the frozen ice. What man could function appropriately in such weather?

She shivered just thinking about it. Last night had been a cold one and the mage had not seen fit to give them a blanket. They had huddled close for warmth, but the children had wept and been unable to sleep. Now the sun was up, it was late afternoon, and it was warm in the back of the wagon. The girls had finally drifted off to sleep, allowing her to be in constant contact with Koro.

He was close. She could feel it. But he had to remember to fly low or the mage would see him.

Fly low.

She whispered the thought to him and he whispered it back, telling her he remembered.

She went back to singing her lullaby. Her hands hurt her. They were bound in front of her, the rope constantly cutting into her flesh; her wrists were bleeding and raw from it. She didn't complain. As soon as Koro told her they were close . . . she had a plan.

Suddenly she felt his elation. He could see her!

She gasped.

Stop! Don't come yet! Fly low!

"Girls," she whispered. She nudged them until they awakened as the wagon swayed and jounced in the ruts of the ground.

Sarielle got up on unsteady legs and quietly pulled back the tarp. They were crossing a field of some kind with moderately high grasses. It was perfect.

"Jona, Isaelle, you must go out the back of the wagon and hide in the tall grasses. You mustn't let Vinqua see you."

"No! Don't make us leave you!" Isaelle whispered fiercely, her blue eyes growing wide with fear.

"Isaelle, I will never let you leave me again. Koro is here with some men to help us . . . but I need to know you are safe first. Go out, jump into the tall grasses, and hide there until I call for you. I won't lose you. I promise!"

The girls had tears in their eyes and were clearly scared, but Sarielle encouraged them with a smile. She hoped they would not hurt themselves jumping from a moving wagon with their hands tied, but the wagon's progress through the high grasses had slowed it considerably.

Jona, the one who had always been the bravest, helped her sister slip over the back end of the wagon. Sarielle saw Isaelle hit the ground and, after a moment of absorbing the shock, run into the tall grass and disappear.

Vinqua didn't slow down for a second. Facing the other direction and thinking them to be subdued, he wasn't paying attention to what was behind him.

Jona went over next. Sarielle did not get to see her hit the ground because when she leapt, the tarp fell back into place, obscuring Sarielle's view.

She waited.

And waited.

Then she spoke to Koro.

Come now! Come quickly!

She waited.

And waited.

And then she heard it.

The rush of wings.

Vinqua screamed out, and the wagon came to an abrupt halt. Next thing she heard was Vinqua coming toward the back of the wagon. "Stop him! Call him off or I will kill your girls!"

He thrust back the tarp, standing there with a sword in hand, and looked into the back of the wagon.

Sarielle smiled at him. "What girls?" she asked.

"Argh!!" Vinqua shouted. That was when she realized his hair was singed. "Call him off or you're dead!" he cried as he jumped into the back of the wagon.

"My sisters are safe from you! I do not care about the rest! So kill me if you must! And do it quickly because the wyvern is coming back, and this time it won't be your hair he singes!"

"I will kill you!"

"And then he will kill you!"

"I will make us disappear from his sight! I will simply slip away!"

"The wyvern's eyes see through magic! You cannot hide from him! Your only choice is to let me go!"

That was when she heard the thunder of hoofbeats.

"You are outnumbered. You may be able to fool the

eyes of the men coming for you, but the wyvern will see and he will burn you down if you so much as look at me wrong!" she vowed.

Vinqua knew he was beaten. She could see it in his eyes. She heard the beating of mighty wings and he did too. He threw down his sword and raised his hands. "Do not kill me! Please!"

"Untie me now," she demanded of him. "Make sure the men from the city can see us."

Vinqua hastened to do as she asked. As soon as she was free she pushed past Vinqua and leapt out of the wagon. Her eyes burned in the daylight as she hit the ground. She stumbled, her legs weak from sitting so long. But suddenly there was a hand on her, a man grabbing hold of her and jerking her hard against his body. Strong arms wrapped around her and she knew . . . she knew without seeing his face who it was.

"Garreth!"

"Fira!" he breathed into her ear.

"Vinqua! He's in the back of the wagon!"

"My brother has him. All I care about is you."

"I'm fine," she insisted as he enveloped her head in his hands and forced their eyes to meet. She had never seen such a beautiful sight as his fair green eyes!

"Your wrists are damaged. He will pay for that. He will pay for all of this."

"In time. First, the girls!"

"Are they with you?" he asked.

"After a fashion!"

She looked up at the beast in the sky.

The girls are hiding in the tall grasses! You must find them for me!

For Koro, it was like a game and he was intent on winning it. He swooped and reeled and then suddenly she felt his delight. He had found them.

Show the men the way and I will give you such shiny gifts!

She opened her eyes and looked at Garreth. "Koro has found them. They are in the tall grasses, hiding. Can you have the men find them?"

"Of course!"

Garreth ordered his men to follow the wyvern. Before long she had the girls in her arms.

"Good job, my little loves!" she praised them, giving them hugs and kisses. The girls giggled and laughed, so happy to see her and clearly happy to see Vinqua in the custody of the men who had come to save them. "Garreth, these are my real sisters," she introduced them. "Those others were changelings, brought by Vinqua's magic."

"Changelings?"

"Fairy children made to look like a human child."

"But . . . I thought you could see through magic."

"I can. But the changelings themselves are not magic. They are real. And I could see through it; I just didn't know what I was seeing. I let my eyes fool my head. I knew they weren't right . . . just not how they weren't right."

"Well, it's over now. Koro has saved you all. Good boy, Koro!" Garreth shouted up to the sky. The wyvern dipped a wing, then landed close by, kicking up dirt and stones and grass as he skidded to a halt. Sarielle broke away from Garreth and ran over to the wyvern. Garreth followed close behind as she threw herself against his belly, hugging him as best she could with her small, inadequate arms.

My good boy! You did a wonderful job! You are a brilliant boy!

Koro dipped his head and let her feel his gratitude that she was all right. Let her feel how grateful he was that she had been the one to find his egg and be there when he was born.

Sarielle teared up. Garreth saw her sniffling and pulled her into his arms. He kissed the top of her head. "There, now. It's all over. Let's get back to the keep. These sisters of yours look very tired and I suspect they are very hungry. Come along, girls," he said to them brightly. "We have some cheese and bread for anyone who's hungry!"

The girls cried out and ran to the men, who gave them food from their provisions. Jona and Isaelle stuffed the bread into their mouths so fast their cheeks puffed out.

"Chew," Sarielle instructed them as she stroked their hair soothingly. She was so happy. So relieved and happy.

"What shall we do with him?" Garreth asked, pointing to Vinqua.

Sarielle eyed Vinqua for a moment, watching him pale as he realized his fate was entirely in her hands.

"You cannot imprison him. He will use his magic to trick the minds of his keepers and will get free once more."

"I will not let him go for the same reason."

"That leaves us little choice," she said sadly.

"Should we execute him here?"

"No! Wait! I-I-I can be of use to you!" Vinqua insisted. "I-I-I can help you take control of the city! I-i-if you let me be your mage, I can work in your favor. All I have ever wanted was a safe, comfortable position. I could just as easily work for you as anyone. I have very valuable skills. You've seen my talents. Think of the things I could help an invading army accomplish!"

Dethan looked at his brother. "He makes a good argument," he said, a smile touching the corners of his lips.

"You can't be serious!" Garreth said. He looked at his brother as if Dethan had lost his mind.

"Of course I'm not serious," Dethan said with a roll of his eyes. "Clearly there's no choice to be made here. There can never be any trust between us and a man like him."

"Too bad there isn't a way to bind his magic permanently," Garreth said.

"I'm sure there is," Sarielle said with confidence. But then she quieted. "But I don't know how to do something like that."

"Then it's decided," Garreth said, drawing his sword.

Garreth walked up to Vinqua and, grabbing his arm, dragged him around the back of the wagon. Sarielle hastened to follow him. She did not want to see the man meet his demise, but she couldn't risk Vinqua using his magic to trick Garreth into believing he had killed him when he had not. In the end, it was a quick affair. Garreth cut Vinqua's throat and let the man drop to the ground without getting so much as a drop of blood on him. He cleaned off his sword and put it back into his scabbard. Then he walked up to Sarielle.

"I'm sorry you had to see that."

"It's all right," she assured him. "Vinqua had his chance to change loyalties early on. He proved himself time and again to be untrustworthy. And since I am the only one who could not be manipulated . . . there really was no way to take him prisoner. I understand all of this, I assure you."

"Good." It was clear by his expression that he would have happily preferred to not have her watch him kill. She found the attitude endearing. The truth was that he was a killer. A man of war. But she accepted that about him. Understood that about him. It seemed he was afraid that understanding would somehow turn her away from him.

She leaned her body into his and reached for his kiss.

He accepted it with slow amusement. She said nothing, merely smiled at him, then turned and walked back to her sisters.

Garreth instructed the men. "The girls can ride inside and Sarielle will ride with me."

"Sarielle! We don't want to be alone in there!" Jona cried.

Sarielle looked at Garreth, her eyes begging for his understanding. "Don't worry, girls. I'll ride with you."

Garreth smiled softly at her, touching his fingertips to her cheek. "Whatever makes you happy, fira."

"Thank you," she mouthed to him before returning quickly to the wagon.

Dethan mounted his horse and looked down at his brother. "Are you happy now?" he asked with a grin.

"Endlessly," Garreth said. He reached for his own horse and mounted. "Sarielle, keep that tarp pulled back. I want my eyes on you the whole time."

His words made her smile, her amusement shining in her pale blue eyes. "As you wish, Sor Garreth," she said, sketching him a low bow that, as she bent forward, gave him a fine perspective down the front of her dress.

When she looked up at him slyly, he knew she had done it on purpose and just for that reason. He chuckled. Oh, he couldn't wait until they got back to the keep. He would see her sisters safely ensconced with a new and better governess and then he would take the wench to bed, and this time she wouldn't be leaving it without his knowing about it! He was going to keep his eyes on her at all times after this.

They were not going to make it back to the keep before nightfall, so Garreth had them stop and make camp shortly before dusk. Once he had organized where everyone should be, he excused himself from Sarielle's presence and rode off into the wild field grasses. He rode like the demons of the eight hells were on his heels and soon he was completely gone from her sight.

She turned to his brother. "Where does he go?" she asked Dethan without preamble.

"That is not for me to say. It is something he must decide to tell you himself."

"But you do know where he goes?"

"He goes away. But he always returns and that is all that should matter to you."

He didn't have to say it, but she could tell from his tone that he didn't consider her to be a part of their inner circle and she was owed no explanations. For some reason that stung her.

Why? It wasn't as though there was some kind of romantic understanding between them. She had no ties to Garreth, and the reverse was also true. So why did she feel this way?

She pushed the feelings aside. It was probably some nonsense she felt because they had become lovers. But having sex did not make him beholden to her or answerable to her. It was just sex. And she didn't know if it would ever happen again. He might decide that once was enough for him. Once was all he wanted. Had ever wanted. He had made no promises to her. In fact, he had tried to warn her about becoming too attached to him.

But she was not attached, she told herself as she walked back to the wagon and the children. She was free. Free of everything. She could do anything. She could choose any lover. Anyone at all. She could choose one without secrets. One who would stay with her. One who did not go off to fight wars in the name of a vindictive goddess.

Anyone at all.

Except . . . she didn't really want anyone. She wanted Garreth. Oh, she was a foolish girl, she realized. A silly, stupid girl. But it didn't change the way she felt. She wanted him. For what and for how long was not known to her yet, but she would like the opportunity to find out.

And so she sat up that night and waited for juquil's hour.

CHAPTER
FOURTEEN

Garreth returned to camp as soon as he was able, his body still shivering and cold. He tied his horse to the rear of Vinqua's wagon and moved toward the bedroll he had laid out next to his brother. But as he moved a hand came out of the darkness and closed around his biceps.

He started in surprise and turned to look down into pale blue eyes that were lit by the moon. As was her fair lavender skin. She looked almost white in the moonlight, as white as he was . . . as if they weren't from different worlds.

"You're cold," she said with a gasp, her hand tightening on his arm.

"I was riding in the wind," he lied.

"Riding should warm you, and there is not that much wind. Why are you so cold?"

He shrugged her off and turned away. "Shouldn't you be asleep with the girls?"

"I was waiting for you," she said, and he could hear the note of pained confusion in her voice.

"What for?" he asked, knowing he was being a prick to her but unable to control himself. She was getting too close. Far too close. He had fought so hard to bring her back to him, but now that she was there, she was asking for answers he just wasn't willing to give her. About things he would much sooner have her live without the knowledge of.

"To be close to you," she said to him softly. "I . . . I thought you would want that."

He did. He wanted it so badly he could taste it. But the same problems remained. He couldn't really keep her. Not like he might have wanted to. Maybe it would be better if he ended it all now. She had her sisters back. She didn't need him. He would hand her the city and she wouldn't need anyone after that.

So why did that thought make him feel so desolate inside? So alone? He had been alone for decades, but right then he felt it more so than he had while frozen to the Airidara mountainside.

In spite of himself, he turned back to her, lifted his hand to her face, traced the line of her jaw with his fingertips.

"I do want it. More than I should. More than I have a right to," he said passionately.

She exhaled a relieved sigh, her warm breath skimming over his cold hand. "I thought . . . I thought you might have grown weary of me already. Or perhaps I was not very good as a lover."

"What?" he said sharply. "You are an outstanding lover, Sarielle, and do not let anything I do or say change your perception of that!"

"Then why haven't you kissed me by now?"

He wanted to. He could see her full, dark mouth in the moonlight and he wanted to kiss her so badly it just about killed him.

"The girls . . ." he hedged.

"They are asleep. Everyone is asleep." She moved closer to him. Close enough that he could feel her warmth seeping into him. "It is as though we are alone," she said.

"But we are not alone," he said.

"We are," she argued. "There is no one of any importance here save you and me." She rested the front of her body along the length of his and he felt her shiver a little. It made him frown. He lifted a hand to push her away, but his fingers accidentally brushed the rigid point of a nipple, the tip puckered from the chill she had gotten. Instead of putting her away from himself, he let his knuckles brush over that pointed tip once again, listened to the way her breath caught in her throat on the softest little gasp.

Before he knew what he was doing, he turned the full expanse of his palm toward her breast, his free hand going to her waist and drawing her in tight to his body. His fingers found her nipple again, pulling at it . . . tugging at it. It made his mouth water to think of it on his tongue.

That was all it took. The next instant he was kissing her, drinking deeply from her mouth, tasting her on his tongue. He pushed their bodies into the side of the wagon, the wooden wall of it behind her back. His thigh slid between her legs.

He had not worn full metal armor, but he was wearing leather braces and a hard leather vest. Both were suddenly irritating to him, since they interfered with his touching of her. In the next instant he was stripping them away until he was in only a tunic and breeches, the slenderest of fabrics between their bodies. But then there were her skirts, full and voluminous. Thank the gods she didn't wear one of those ridiculous corsets, with its metal boning and constricting ways. It was one of the inventions he had woken up to that utterly baffled him. He would much rather be able to see and feel a woman's natural breasts, ripe and full and soft like hers were. There for the taking at any instant.

He broke from her mouth, his breath coming hard,

his body taut with want. It had taken all of an instant for him to go from not wanting to get close to her to this ravaging need assailing him at that very instant. He grabbed for the front of her dress, pulling it down hard at the neckline, exposing the soft slope of her breast to his mouth. His fingers dipped inside her bodice, pushing her nipple upward until it came free of the fabric and was jutting out into the cool night air. But it did not stay cool for long, because he closed his hot mouth over it, sucked it in deep, almost punishingly so. Punishing her for making him want her so damn much he couldn't think straight, couldn't act the way he should.

She gasped, a sultry, excited sound that sought out his spine and made it tighten the way her nipple tightened against his teeth. He felt her knee, padded in skirts, rising up between his thighs until she was in full contact with him. Had she been able to feel him through all of those skirts, she would have found him hard.

But then she was exploring him with her hands, her fingers shaping him through the soft fabric of his breeches. She molded her hand to him, pressing into him just like he needed her to. It was uncanny, as though she could read his mind. As if it were she and not Vinqua who could manipulate the magic of the mind.

He came back to her mouth, searing her with kisses, savoring the taste and fire of her on his tongue. He forgot they were out in the open. Forgot his brother lay sleeping not five yards away. He began to frantically unlace her top until it sagged open and displayed the bounty of her breasts to his famished eyes. He put his hands to her, kneading her and shaping her, all the while feeling her hand against his cock through the fabric of his breeches. He grew harder and harder, more and more frantic with want of her.

Before he could judge his actions, he had her hips in his hands and was spinning her about, facing her backside toward him, bending her forward as he pulled up her damnable skirts. But then there she was, supple and bare to the night air, her warmth incredible against him as he pushed his hips into hers.

He could hear her breathing quicken, the little gasps and sighs of encouragement she released. She wanted him to unlace the front of his breeches, wanted him to pull himself out into the open air, wanted him to pull her back against him so his stiff rod was running through the wet folds of her core. She gasped again, shifted her hips, caught him at her entrance, and with one easy movement, impaled herself upon him. Garreth groaned from the pleasure of it, from the pristine heat of her core as he punched into her hard. Her skirts were bunched up along her back; her breasts hung loose and full in the open air so he could reach for them and fondle them as he thrust up inside her . . . so he did. He pulled at her nipples in time to his thrusts, then, after a minute of that, he found he couldn't get in deep enough, hard enough, fast enough unless he put both hands on her hips and held her still for his punctuating movements.

He thrust into her again and again, faster and faster, listening to her sounds of pleasure as she tried to bite her own lips and keep from crying out. And crying out was what he wanted to do but did not dare. The only thing protecting them was the cover of darkness and the wooden walls of the wagon. As it was, his hard movements into her were radiating through her and into the wagon, making it creak in time to his thrusts.

He was going to climax. He knew it. Felt it. It was raw and unhinged. Completely out of his control. A wild, animalistic thing. A thing she perhaps did not deserve. Perhaps she deserved better. But for now this was all he had for her, all he could offer her. So he came inside her like any beast that ruts with its mate. He didn't even know if she came with him. Couldn't tell in the wall of the darkness and in the blinding strength of his culmination. He couldn't remember ever coming so hard in his life. The sensation was brutal. Draining. Wonderful.

He drew hard for every breath as he slid away from her and pulled her skirts down to protect her from the night air and any possible prying eyes. It was a little late to think about that, but he almost didn't care. He felt wild and strong, as if he could conquer anything . . . and he had started by conquering this woman. As she turned around in his arms and offered up her mouth, he was content with his spoils. She was everything he could ever have asked for and more, and for now, he was content to just enjoy her.

For now.

Together they leaned back against the wagon, trying to regain their breath, looking into each other's faces in the dark.

"Think of that the next time you question whether or not I want you," he said to her roughly.

"Very well, I will do so," she said. Then she laughed and he had to laugh with her.

"We should go to bed," he said as he lifted a hand to her cheek. She nuzzled it against his palm.

"We should. But we will sleep together," she said firmly.

She would get no arguments from him. All his arguments had vanished in the face of the passion they shared.

"I feel I was ungentle with you," he said with some regret.

"Don't worry. I was just as ungentle with you." She smiled at him.

"That is true. But we will continue this later, when I have a proper bed for you . . . and when I can see your face. Your face is far too expressive to deny me the pleasure of it."

"Then I shall not deprive you of it in the least. Although it is a little difficult for you to see my face when you're . . . behind me."

That made him laugh. "A good point. Perhaps I will have a mirror brought into my rooms."

She smiled again. "That sounds like a lovely idea. Now come." She picked up his hand and pulled him behind her. She brought them to his bedroll and lay down upon it, pulling him with her. Before a moment had passed, she was lying beside him, snuggled up against him, sharing the warmth of her body with him. That was when he realized he wanted her again. Right that very instant. Even though he had only just left her. He exhaled a cooling breath. He had to control the urge. There would be better circumstances for taking her come the morrow when they made it back to the keep. He could control himself until then.

At least he thought he could.

He could be wrong.

No. He would resist her charms for the remainder of this night. He would savor his desire for her until the morrow.

And that was exactly what he did.

Dethan was not sleeping when his brother returned after juquil's hour. He never was. As long as he was within reach of his brother, he could not rest until he knew Garreth was safely delivered back from his curse.

Dethan was beginning to suspect Garreth was in over his head. That he might drown in the pain his liaison with Sarielle could create. This relationship would be like being in the sights of a catapult. The ball was huge and flaming and angry, and there was nowhere you could possibly run to that would keep you from being crushed by it. Garreth was on fire and he didn't even know it. He was in danger and he didn't seem to care.

But Dethan cared. Dethan feared. He would not stand idly by and let Garreth go back to the cursed existence he had finally been rescued from. Not because of some girl.

Once they got back to the keep he would find a way to stop this from going any further than it already had. He could only hope that whatever he did, it would not be too late.

CHAPTER
FIFTEEN

The next day Sarielle managed to convince the girls they should run beside the horses for exercise, picking wildflowers as they saw fit, while she rode astride in the front of Garreth's saddle. Their pace was slow in order to keep even with the children, and neither Sarielle nor Garreth seemed to mind in the least. Dethan minded. The sun was high and he was in armor. That and he was discontented to watch Garreth continually nuzzle and exchange playful smiles with his mistress. His hands were roaming over the girl's body as if he had no control of them. It made Dethan surly to see it. It made him miss his wife.

Summer was ending and it was time for him to go home, but his brother needed to be in good order first. He could not leave Garreth without ensuring his well-being. And in Dethan's opinion his well-being was not attached to Sarielle's.

The wyvern was flying circles around them. First high, then low. He stopped only twice . . . both times to snatch a kloiy from the ground, subsequently devouring the large wild beast and spitting out its horns. Sarielle began to sing. To the children or to the wyvern, Dethan could not tell, but it was loud and joyful. She didn't have a stellar voice, but it was nice and melodic. Certainly able enough for the lullaby she was singing. When Garreth joined in, Dethan rolled his eyes and sighed.

He had never been so grateful to see city walls before. He believed the only thing comparable would be when he finally saw the walls of the city housing his wife and son at present. That would be a glorious day. A day he looked forward to. Hell, he might even sing a lullaby, even though he had a horrid singing voice. Unlike his brother Maxum, who had the voice of a bard and the charm to match. But he would sing to his son. Quietly, so as not to hurt the boy's ears. Just loud enough for him to hear the love in his papa's voice.

When they reached the keep the children, seemingly boundless with energy, went squealing through the hallways. The adults congregated in the main hall.

"I think I liked them better as changelings," Dethan said dryly.

"Be of good cheer, brother," Garreth said with a chuckle. "It is a good day and we are all safe behind walls. Now we can do what you've been begging me to do. We can get to the business of rearranging this city. To that end," he said, turning to Sarielle, "my brother and I have a proposition for you."

"Oh?" Sarielle gave him a look that told him she had a counterproposition.

"What would you say if we told you we wanted you to become bennesah of Kith?"

Sarielle went stock-still, like an animal in the forest that suddenly realizes it is being hunted.

She laughed nervously. "Do not tease me," she said hesitantly.

"I am not teasing you. I am entirely serious. I think the new bennesah of Kith should be a former slave. Only then can the slaves gain the equality they deserve."

"Yes, but . . . the Kithians would never accept the rule of a scourge."

Garreth frowned. "I told you not to call yourself that."

"But I have to!" she snapped at him. "That is what the Kithians will be thinking! You told me what the governess said to you. The way she behaved. That is exactly the way everyone else will behave! There will never be acceptance. The minute you leave, the government would be overthrown, and you would have to conquer this city all over again!"

"Then I will not leave until there is acceptance. I will force acceptance upon the Kithians."

"Garreth, you must do this thing slowly. Too much change will incite rebellion," she counseled soothingly. "Choose a Kithian who is not a scourge. One who favors the abolishment of slavery and one whom you can trust to rule in your stead. There must be a new bennesah, but it cannot be a scourge."

"I wholly disagree," Garreth said. "I think it *has* to be a slave who becomes ruler. I believe it could be you. You could rule here with the twins, ensconced in safety and set in comfort, for the rest of your lives."

"I can see we aren't going to agree on this," Sarielle said anxiously.

For Dethan's part, he was growing more pleased by the second. He may have just found the perfect wedge to drive between his brother and this woman. His brother was an idealist, always expecting more of people than they were usually able to give. In Garreth's world, there was no reason why a slave could not rule. In Garreth's world, slavery could be abolished with just a word. He didn't understand that slavery was a matter that ran deep in people's lives, minds, and hearts. It could not be plucked out like some weed in a garden. Strangely enough it was Sarielle who saw this and understood it. It made Dethan respect her. But respecting her didn't make him change his opinion that she was to be separated from his brother at the first possible chance.

"The twins and I will be fine whatever I choose to do," she assured Garreth. "You need not worry about us. Now, I do not wish to talk about this any further."

"But we *will* talk about it again," Garreth said.

"If you insist," she said, looking troubled once again. She moved away from Garreth with a frown on her lips. She went out of the room, looking for the children.

"I don't understand her," Garreth said to Dethan, frowning as well.

"I know. You would think she would be grateful," Dethan said, purposely baiting his brother.

"Exactly. She would make a very good leader. She has all the qualities. All the strengths."

"I can see what you see in her," Dethan said. "She is not being appreciative of your offer, or of you for that matter. She was a slave. Anything beyond slavery should be viewed as a gift."

"Yes," Garreth said. "I will have to pursue this some more."

"That is, provided she is willing to listen. She seems a little stubborn to me."

"She is simply strong willed. It is one of her most attractive qualities."

"If you say so."

"I do. Now, I am weary from the journey and could use a bath besides. I'll take my leave of you, brother."

"We will continue the business of the city shortly?"

"Of course."

"Good. Because I have a wife to get home to and the season grows short."

"I am aware. I might just have to winter here."

That would be bad, Dethan decided instantly. His brother closed away with that woman for all the winter wanings? Garreth would simply grow more attached to her, and when he had to leave, the pain would be tremendous. No. One of them had to be gone before the winter set in. And Dethan thought he would have a better chance at removing Sarielle and the twins from the equation if he planned it correctly. And soon. She would be less willing to leave as time wore on and she began to realize what a treasure his brother was.

Dethan was well aware of what a good man his brother was. Garreth would make any woman the finest of husbands. But husbanding was not in his brother's future. Not the kind a woman like Sarielle would come to expect. True, Dethan had sought a wife almost immediately after being released from the eight hells, but that had been a matter of wedding to conquer a city. Perhaps in the future his brother would take wives to secure a city, but Garreth could not marry for his heart.

Garreth went to his rooms, unable to shake the feeling of true disappointment that assailed him. He stripped away the majority of his clothing and called for a bath. He was soaking in the tub when there was a knock on the door.

"Come!" he called.

The door opened and admitted Sarielle. She saw him in the tub and immediately went over to him, kneeling beside him. She looked eager to talk, which he found funny because she had just removed herself from conversation a little while earlier.

"You chose a slave," she breathed, her hands going to his bare arm.

Puzzled, he frowned. "I have. I've chosen you."

She looked surprised at that.

"I . . . I meant for the twins' governess. You chose a scourge."

"Moyra. Yes. When I met her a few days ago when we

were looking for the bennesah at his house. She seemed to have a care for the children and I didn't want them being mistreated simply because of prejudices," he said. He met her eyes. "And I feel the same about you. You should not be treated differently than any other intelligent, good woman simply because of the color of your skin. Because as far as I can see, that is the only difference between the scourge and the rest of the Kithians."

"It is enough. Enough to mar the vision of those around us."

"I can see that. It doesn't follow that that is the way it should be."

"You are right," she agreed with a smile. "That is not the way it should be. But it will take time. Time you say you do not have to spend here. So . . . you must do what is best for your purposes, not for what is in your heart."

"I do not think we are going to agree on this," he said with regret.

"No, perhaps not. But it doesn't follow that we can't discuss it calmly and rationally as two intelligent beings."

"Now it is you who is right," he said with a smile.

"I like it when you smile," she said with a smile of her own. "It changes the whole of your face. I insist you do it more often."

"Do you not like my face otherwise?" he teased her.

"Oh, I like it otherwise. I merely like it more with a smile upon it."

"Then perhaps you will put a smile upon it more often."

"Hmm, and how do you propose I go about this?"

He suddenly reached over the side of the tub, lifted her up, and dragged her into the water with him, fully clothed. She cried out and tried to push away from him.

"At least let me undress! My skirts will soak up all the water!"

"Very well, but do so from here," he ordered her.

She hastened to stand in the tub, water sluicing from her clothing, and quickly loosened the ties to her dress, then drew it over her head and dropped it by the side of the tub. She had not been in the tub long enough for her skirts to take on much water, but they still landed with a plop. Garreth grinned at her. Naked and chilled, she quickly lowered herself into his lap and beneath the water, her back settling against his chest.

"Is this a common thing for men and women to do?" she asked.

"It will be a common thing for us to do," he promised her.

She shifted in his lap. "You are awfully lumpy."

"I blame you for that. You are positively delectable naked."

She gave him one of those soft violet blushes. He swept her hair to the side, baring her neck to his kiss. "I don't like it when we argue," he said.

"Neither do I," she said.

"We'll try not to make a habit of it. Agreed?"

She nodded. "I haven't properly thanked you for coming after me and the girls and rescuing us from Vinqua."

"You need not thank me. It was all Koro's doing. Where is he at present, by the way?"

"He has gone back to the Asdar Mountains. But he is close by if he is needed."

"Do you anticipate him being needed?"

"This city has many enemies, thanks to the bennesah."

"Is that so?" Garreth frowned. "I didn't know that."

"He has kept them at bay with the wyvern and Vinqua. You no longer have Vinqua on your side and I suspect you would prefer not to use Koro if it can be avoided."

"Your assumptions are correct. You have told me Koro is young and I have come to realize it takes great effort on your part to corral him."

"But he is very protective of me," she pointed out. "He would fight to the death for me . . . as you have discovered. Wyvern families stay close all throughout their lives. Even if they nest in different areas, they stay in contact telepathically or nest in the same caves together. They share treasure with one another. Actually, sharing treasure is part of the mating dance. Wyverns are attracted to how much sparkle there is in the other's scales. It hints that the wyvern has an excellent hoard. The male brings the female to his nest and gives her gifts; at the same time the female is checking out the male's nest. If it's more glorious than hers, she will most likely choose that male. Then they combine their nests and are a mated pair until one of them dies. The female hunts and the male watches the eggs and hatchlings."

"And neither will mate with another wyvern, for life?"

"Mmm, I didn't say that. I don't really know the answer to that. But I do know that wyverns feel emotions as deeply and passionately as we humans do. Including love and a sense of betrayal. Koro's loyalty to me runs very deep. It would be a challenge to him if I were to ask him to do something that conflicted with what his mate desired. Luckily I don't have to worry about that for a while."

"So they communicate telepathically with one another?"

"Parents do with their children and mates do. Koro tells me he would 'know' his mate when he could talk to her the way he talks to me. So . . . that was my conclusion. Oh, by the way, I owe Koro some shiny things in thanks for his services. He would be happy with armor or cut glass or anything shiny or sparkly."

"I think we should be able to scrounge some stuff up. How much?"

"Not much. Just four or five things should be fine. He already has a very well-lined nest."

"All the more reason you should stay here," Garreth pointed out. "Koro has made a home for himself here. Nests don't travel well and he would probably want to stay close to his mother."

"I can travel without Koro. There will come a time when I have to let him go anyway. He needs to be free to live his own life. To raise his own family and be content and happy, not a slave to a selfish person trying to protect a city by using him. Endangering him."

"Is this bond between you, the one that makes you a wrena—is it forever?"

"Yes. To him I am soulbound. He knows that I took his egg and nursed it until he hatched. I've told him the story many times. But sometimes he doesn't fully understand that I'm not a wyvern. He thinks one day I will change to look like him or he will change to look like me."

"And is it limited to just being able to talk to him? Does the wrena ever manifest other abilities?"

"Just the telepathy and being soulbound. The mystical connection that has us manifesting each other's injuries or health."

"What about what happened to the bennesah?"

"It was Vinqua and not my doing. He told me he had silenced the bennesah so he could not tell us about the changelings once we captured him and began to ask questions."

"I am not fully convinced."

"Well, I am. I have been a wrena for nine turnings. Nearly ten. I have never manifested anything other than my telepathic connection with Koro."

"The twins are barely ten. You became a wrena when they were just babies."

"Our parents were dead. We had no options. My sisters were about to be sold off to an infant slave trader when I left for the mountains. Slave traders buy children cheap, raise them, and sell them when they are of age. I suppose it is an investment in the future." She was quiet a moment. "You must be careful. The bennesah's enemies were many. Once word of his death spreads . . . there will be problems. They will look upon this city as being vulnerable once more. They will test your strength."

"And they will find it inviolable," he promised her. "But you see . . . this is what would make you a good bennesah. You see into the future. You think about what must be done for the sake of the city."

"I would serve better as an advisor to you," she insisted. "Let's not talk about this. I do not want to quarrel with you."

"Very well." He picked up a sponge, and after lathering it up with some soap, he began to wash her arms, taking care to get each of her fingers, around her wrist, and all along the length of her arm. He used slow and methodical strokes. Careful and caring ones. "Tell me of the bennesah's enemies."

"There is one in particular. The Zizo, from a neighboring city only a short distance to the west. The city is called Zandaria, which means 'glittering jewel.' The Zizo are miners. The city sits on rich deposits of many kinds of gems, and it is said the waters there are full of gold."

"And why are they enemies of Kith?"

"The bennesah coveted Zandaria's riches. When his coffers were empty and he could not tax any higher than he already had, he began to plot against Zandaria. Using Vinqua, he made their caravans heading to other cities think they had arrived in those cities and made a good trade for their wares, only to realize later that they had been robbed. Once the Zizo figured out it was the Kithians stealing from them, they started a war. I was asked to bring Koro down on them, and Vinqua worked his magic. The Zizo quickly learned they could not defeat us. But the two cities have been bitter enemies ever since."

"Do you know what god they worship?"

"Diathus, goddess of the land and oceans. That which provides them with their riches."

"Which makes them a part of Xaxis's faction, the faction of gods against Weysa."

"Faction?" Sarielle asked.

"The gods are at war . . . split down the middle." He filled her in on the different factions. "To take worshippers away from one faction and aim them at the other is at the heart of my goals. Tell me . . . this Zandaria . . . You said it is only a short distance away?"

"Yes. Why? You cannot think to lay siege to them!"

"Why not?" he asked as he moved her forward and began to wash her back.

"The rylings, for one."

"Rylings?"

"They are a tribe of fairies who protect the city."

"Hmm. Fairy magic is not to be trifled with," Garreth agreed. "But if we turned away from every city because it would be difficult to conquer, we would never make progress. Every city has its weakness. Yours was your bennesah's hubris—and his dependence on the wyvern and the fear it instilled. Not to mention your inadequately protected walls."

"I know. I became a wrena to ensure the comfort and unity of my family. But it made me a prisoner as well." She sighed as he moved on to her chest, washing the sponge across her breasts, abrading the nipples gently with it. "Will you look for weaknesses in Zandaria's defenses?"

"I will discuss the strategy with my brother. You should not worry about these things."

"It's just that if you do lay siege to the Zizo city . . . since it is so close . . . you can base your attack here. And you can utilize Koro as well."

"I don't want to utilize Koro. I can win a war without a wyvern. I do not want him injured again. Not knowing what it costs you."

"I'm not sure you understand how powerful the rylings can be," she said as she tipped her head back and moaned softly in pleasure and relaxation. The sponge dipped further below the waterline, heading over the softness of her belly and across the thatch of flame-red curls at the crest of her thighs.

"I'm not sure you understand how powerful *we* can be. We are on a search for mages or magesses. Soon we will have them joining the ranks of our army. We will learn what they are capable of and train them and our men in ways to execute their magics in battle."

"But the rylings are—" She broke off with a gasp as his sponge dipped lower and swirled in a circle against a most pleasurable spot. She forgot what she was saying as the sponge continued to caress and clean her, becoming more and more thorough with every swish.

Her head was on his shoulder, her moans and gasps echoing in the large room.

"Like this, do you?" he rumbled into her ear huskily.

"As do you," she said, her hands sliding under her bottom to caress the hard length of him.

"I like to see how responsive you are," he said heatedly. "I love the way you moan low in your throat like that. You and Mordu have a grip on me I cannot give adequate words to."

"Mordu is the god of love and passion and lust . . .

but I am not certain he has anything to do with what you make me feel. I think that is solely your doing."

"Do not forsake the gods," he warned her on a whisper. "They listen and know everything. They are very real and very much a part of everything we do."

"I am not forsaking Mordu. In fact, I consider our passion together to be our tribute to him. The mems of his temple make love to the chosen on the high holidays in tribute to him. Why can this not be seen as the same?"

"I agree. I will make you come for me . . . and for Mordu. I would not share you with anyone, not even Mordu, but I will offer him the sounds and heart of our passion."

"Mmm, I will as well," she breathed as her legs fell open as far as the narrow tub allowed.

The water was growing cool, but they hardly noticed as they stroked each other into a frenzy of pleasure.

"Enough!" Garreth declared roughly, throwing the sponge over the side of the tub and grabbing hold of her hips. He pulled her back, and his swollen shaft slid through her intimate folds. He was at her entrance and then inside her in an instant. She was so hot compared to the cool water that he groaned soulfully upon entering her. The water sloshed over the edges of the tub as he pushed and pulled her, up and down, against his hips. She was gripping the edges of the tub, but the position required him to do most of the work, for she had no traction.

That didn't seem to make a difference. He had strong hands and great motivation to move her on himself with haste and need. Sarielle had never thought that the sexual act could be done in such ways, but as he opened her mind, she began to think of other ways they could share their lust. It made her all the hotter for him in that moment. She began to climax, throwing her head back, the wet tips of her hair falling against him like gentle little whips. He felt her flesh tightening around him as she succumbed to her pleasure, and it heightened his. He began to join her in a sudden surge of sensation, release coming upon him with a fury. He jetted into her, letting her drain him, feeling powerful and weak at the same time. When they were finished she fell back against him, panting for her breath.

"It is hard for me to believe you have never known passion before this," he said breathlessly, "for you have taken to it as though you have done it all your life."

"Do you not believe me, then?"

"No. It is clear you were untouched," he assured her. "The remark is not meant to call you a liar, only to express my wonder at the magnitude of your passion. I feel a very fortunate man."

"And so you should," she said with amusement.

"You are a wretch. And this water is cold." He retrieved the sponge, hastened to finish their bathing, then lifted her from the tub with him. He gathered them together in a warm fur that had been warming by the fire and then settled them down on the fur rug before the fireplace. The rug was the skin of a grismon, a huge six-legged creature that roamed the icy mountains of the northern reaches of the continent. It was known for its thick fur, and so the rug was soft and luxurious beneath them.

There, he made love to her again. And after they dozed a while, he woke her and loved her once more.

CHAPTER
SIXTEEN

~~~~~~~~~~

"Good morning, brother!" Garreth called out brightly as he entered the main hall and found Dethan seated there with a cup of cider and a table set for breaking his fast. The food was just being brought in and Garreth eagerly took a seat. He was starving, having worked up a tremendous appetite with Sarielle—who was now having the morning meal with her sisters in the nursery.

"That depends on whom you ask," his brother said.

"You seem in a foul mood," Garreth observed.

"If I am, I have every reason to be. This city is not under our control. We have spent the better part of the past six days chasing after one thing or another, usually because of that girl. And now I'm afraid you will be far more focused on her than on what you are sworn to do here."

"That is unfair," Garreth said harshly. "That girl is going to be key to the protection of this city."

"If she stays. She may not. As you have pointed out, she is free and independently wealthy. She can go anywhere she likes."

"She will not want to leave Koro," Garreth argued.

"I'm sure there are caves aplenty in other parts of the world."

"Why are you so against her?" Garreth demanded of his brother. "She has done nothing to you."

"She has done something to you," Dethan countered. "She has turned your focus away from where it should be: controlling this city and preparing for the next."

"I'll have you know she has just helped me to focus, as you say, on our next city to be conquered. It will take some research, but I believe the neighboring city of Zandaria will be our next goal. Provided we can gather enough mages to counter the rylings."

"Rylings?"

"Fairies that support the city with their magic. The city worships a god of Xaxis's faction. Should we win it, we will take strength away from that god and bring it to Weysa instead. I will still be keeping to my agreement with Weysa, and I can continue to manage this city throughout the winter as we use it for the base of our attacks."

"You wish to spend the entire winter here?"

Again, Dethan saw no good coming of this. The longer Garreth remained, the more thorough his attachment to the girl would be. No matter how Dethan looked at this, his brother would be hurt. And it all centered on the girl.

"Why not? We have conquered two cities this turning for Weysa. That is more than satisfactory. I will not winter the men in tents if I do not have to. It leads to unnecessary sickness, injury, discomfort, and death."

Unfortunately Dethan could not argue with that logic.

"Very well. But you should spend the winter plotting to take over Zandaria as soon as spring breaks, not fucking with that girl."

"Enough!" Garreth exploded, his fist crashing against

the table as he surged to his feet. "I am not a child in need of your handling! What I do or do not do with this 'girl' is none of your concern, and if you speak of it again, I will cease to be in your company! If you miss your wife so damn much, why don't you go home to her? I am sick to death of you and your overbearing ways! She can have you! I was more than able to take this city and I am more than capable of keeping it!" He pushed away from the table. "I have lost my stomach for breakfast," he said before storming out of the room.

"Fuck!" Dethan spat to the seemingly empty room.

But over in a secluded gathering of furniture by the fire, lying on her usual chaise, was Davine. She stood up, her silk robe fluttering at her feet. It was not diaphanous but nearly so. Her figure and the shading of her nipples could just barely be made out through the rose-colored fabric.

She moved toward Dethan, her gait smooth and graceful. There was a reason why she had been Bento's mistress for so many turnings. She had the beauty, elegance, and cunning it took to keep a man of power on her hook.

"My lord, is there something I can get you for your present relief?" she asked Dethan.

"It is nothing a skilled assassin could not handle," Dethan grumbled.

"If that is truly what you need, I can see about—"

"No. No, of course not," he said. He sighed. "What I need is a way to pry that woman's hooks out of my brother."

"Well . . . perhaps a different set of hooks is what is needed."

"Excuse me?" Dethan asked, his tone sharp.

"Never mind," she said dismissively. She reached to snatch up a piece of fruit, then moved away from Dethan. But her mind was working heavily. It was clear to her the contention between the brothers was due to the wrena. She saw Dethan's concerns and knew that he would prefer the wrena and his brother not have a relationship at all. She found this very interesting because it echoed her desires. She needed to find a position of power in this city or she risked losing the comforts she had grown used to. Sure, she could work her way into the bed and home of another wealthy man of the bennesah's court, but if there was perhaps a way of achieving position and power without having to sell her body . . .

The brothers were young, healthy . . . vital, rich, and powerful. They would no doubt be in charge of this city for many turnings to come. It was also clear they would not be spending much time in the city once they felt it was politically secured for them. If she could install herself as indispensible in this court . . . she would find herself in a particular position of power and security. Security was key. She had come from nothing, had been raised with nothing. If not for her looks and having caught the bennesah's eye, she would still be wallowing in poverty and nothingness. She would not go back to that. She must play her cards as sharply as possible.

And doing something to earn the gratitude of the elder brother seemed a good way to achieve her goals. All she had to do was figure out how to extract Garreth from Sarielle. She could then, on her own terms, parlay Dethan's gratitude into anything she needed.

She returned to her chaise and stared into the fire as she thought.

Sarielle spent the morning playing with the twins. Their trauma seemed to have had little effect on them. They were used to being slaves, their lives dictated by the whims of others, so the experience with the bennesah and the mage had not been as traumatic for them as it could have been. The worst had been the damage to their wrists and fingers from their bindings, but the mems had already seen them mostly healed.

After visiting with the children, Sarielle went down into the main hall to look for Garreth but instead found Dethan there. He was poring over a diagram of some sort that had been roughly drawn on a large plank.

"A map of the city," she said.

"Yes. I've been touring it, finding all the main structures and parts . . . where it is defensible and where it is not. This city fell too easily and will do so again if nothing is done to improve its defenses."

"Your brother said the same thing."

"My brother and I are of the same mind on many things." He looked at her. "Then again, there are things on which we are not."

That had not quite been a veiled remark, she realized. She was beginning to get the sense that Garreth's brother did not like her for some reason. Which was strange since the brothers had offered her control of the entire city the day before.

"This is the bazaar," she said, pointing to a large gap in his map at the center of the city. "The walls surround us. The keep is at the north side, the garrisons at the south and east."

"You know all this from being caged up here?"

"I could see out the windows and from the parapets where I was allowed to walk." She looked back at the map. "How will you better defend the city?"

"By digging a moat around the entire wall. It will be a big project and will take many wanings, but it is possible it can be done before winter sets in if we begin right away and put many men to the task."

"However?" she asked, sensing a caveat. "However," she then answered herself quickly, "you will not be able to rebuild the city if all your laborers are dedicated to the moat. People who have lost their houses will be homeless this winter."

Dethan lifted a brow and gave her a once-over. "Perhaps my brother is right about you. You would make a good leader. You have a good understanding of the needs of the city as a whole and the people as individuals."

"I simply know what it means to be weak, hungry, alone, cold, and afraid. I have been all of those things. I would not wish it on another."

"So which would you choose? Defense of the city or rebuilding it?"

She didn't even need to think. "Rebuilding it. The people must come first. Garrison your army here for the winter, use the men of the city as laborers, and your men to defend the city. Then, when spring comes, move all capable men to the moat project."

"That would mean my brother could not attempt to take Zandaria until the summer wanings."

"He is seriously considering taking Zandaria?"

"It is not a bad idea overall," Dethan said.

"You have no mages here. You must have powerful mages or magesses if you intend to go up against the rylings' magic."

"We have sent for some . . . when we thought we would need them to retrieve you. My men will find the best mages. They will be lured here by the gold I can provide for them. And perhaps when we do preliminary scouting in Zandaria we will find a faction of rylings who are discontented with their lot and will join us in overthrowing the majority government."

"You have done this many times before," Sarielle noted.

"I used to make my living doing this. Now I do it for Weysa. For my brother. In the hopes that one day he will be free of his curse."

"His curse?" she asked.

Dethan's eyes widened. He realized he had said too much and quickly covered. "Being forced to conquer in Weysa's name when, before, he only ever wanted to go on quests that brought peace to others, not war."

"He owes a great debt to Weysa," Sarielle remarked with a frown. "When will this debt ever be repaid? Your brother cannot be killed. I imagine he cannot age. He will be around for a very long time. Will she expect this of him for the rest of his existence?"

"I do not presume to know the mind of a goddess. I only know that she is willful and will not tolerate my brother swaying from his course. You should know that now."

"Why should I know that?" she asked.

But she already knew the answer before he said, "Do not grow too attached to him. He will not stay forever."

"I will do what I see fit to do," she said defiantly. "I am free now and you cannot make dictates to me. As long as your brother wants me and I want him, then we shall be together. I hope you will not interfere with that."

Dethan avoided the query. "Now, what else can you tell me about the city that I do not know?"

"First, which would you do? Rebuild or protect?"

"I would protect. I would dig the moat and let the people find their shelter in what is left of the city. Otherwise, it risks falling again. It is twice as vulnerable now as it was before."

"Then may I make a suggestion?"

"Be my guest."

"Close half of the bazaar. On that land assemble the tents of the army, and use the tents as temporary homes for those without. That way you are shutting down only half of the commerce the city needs for taxes and providing the shelter your taxpayers need to stay alive. The winters are hard here, Sor Dethan."

"You know what? That's not a bad idea," he said, lifting a brow as he looked at her. "But what of my troops? Where will they stay?"

"The garrisons. The city guard is, as you discovered, woefully understaffed because the bennesah depended so heavily on the wyvern to protect the city. That is one reason why we could not properly defend our walls. The barracks were barely a quarter full before your attack on the city; now they are even less so . . . leaving plenty of room for your men to be quartered."

"I had noticed the same thing," Dethan said. Really, it was a shame, he thought. She was a very bright girl, after all. But in the end, Garreth was cursed enough without failing to do as Weysa demanded of him. He did not need to earn her wrath by falling for some girl . . . however clever she might be.

Sarielle took her leave of Garreth's brother and went back to her search for him. In the end, she found him in the second hall, a smaller version of the main hall, though this had no cozy furniture to curl up on; there was only one table and it was not as large as the ones in the main hall.

He was poring over documents from several stacks of them, some of which were a foot high. Sitting in the chair next to him was Davine. The bennesah's mistress was dressed in her usual suggestive clothing and her chestnut hair was thickly woven in a fall down her back. She had put little yellow sumi flowers in her hair and they looked pretty and elegant. Davine always looked pretty and elegant and . . . sexual. All at the same time. And right then she was leaning very close to Garreth, pointing something out to him in the paper he was reading.

Garreth looked up when Sarielle approached the table

and immediately smiled. Davine straightened away from him and smiled as well. Innocently. As if she hadn't just been showing her significant cleavage to Sarielle's . . .

What was he to her exactly? Was she like Davine had been to the bennesah? His mistress? He had put her in the bennesah's mistress's quarters. What did that entitle her to exactly? Exclusivity? Was there a promise that she would be his only focus sexually and . . . and emotionally? Was emotion even involved in this?

For her, the answer was yes and she was shocked to realize it. How had she grown to care for him so quickly? When had it happened exactly? What did it mean? She was a scourge. She had known to never grow attached to anyone or anything because she could be sold on a whim at any moment, tearing her away from everything she loved. The only thing she had refused to give up was her love for her sisters.

But surely she did not love Garreth. She knew better than that.

Didn't she?

Did she even know how to love another?

All of this raced through her head as he rose out of his chair and came around to her. He kissed her quite openly and quite deeply and it soothed her fractious thoughts almost instantly. He was coming to care for her. She was certain of it. Whether that was a good thing or a bad thing she did not know.

"Hello, fira," he said, touching her face in a fond manner that made her smile at him. "Where have you been all day?"

"With the twins mostly. I just saw your brother."

Garreth's face folded into a frown. "What did he say to you?"

"Nothing. We were just sharing thoughts about what to do with the city."

"He was discussing that with you?"

"Yes. Why? Did you not like that he would ask me about such things?"

"No! Not at all. If you are to lead this city, you should have a great deal of say in what happens to it."

"I told you I do not want to—"

"Let's not discuss that right now," he interrupted quickly. "There are many other things to be done."

"Such as?"

"Such as the building of the religious houses for Weysa. This city does not have a single temple to Weysa. It is one of the reasons we chose it. Now . . . we have brought some of Weysa's mems with us to begin the process of opening new temples, but they need temple buildings and grounds. Davine was helping me to find places where that would work. But now that you are here, you can help."

"I don't know how I could possibly help. I spent my days mostly locked away and I was never free to leave the keep. Davine is probably much more familiar with the city and its details. All I know is what I saw from the windows and walls of the keep."

"Well then, come and sit with us anyway. You should be a part of this."

"Yes. Please," Davine said. "Come and join us."

Sarielle was swayed. She moved over to the table and took a seat on Garreth's left while Davine sat at his right. After a moment, Sarielle could smell Davine's perfume. It was a soft and sultry scent. Sarielle did not wear perfume, nor did she use lotions on her skin to make it soft like Davine did. She did not have a wardrobe of soft linens and silks done in the latest fashions. Her only special garments were the ornamental robes of the wrena. Otherwise, she was kept in simple clothing and not much of it. She had only two dresses and two dressing gowns. Both had seen better days. She had petitioned the bennesah for new clothing, but he had not approved the request. And now that he was dead, whom did she go to about such things? Garreth? If he began clothing her like the bennesah clothed Davine, did that make her his mistress? And as for Davine, what was she still doing in the keep? Who would feed and clothe her now? The brothers? Was she going to try to be mistress to one of the brothers? Was that why she was there even now? Was she trying to be Garreth's mistress? If that happened, where would that leave Sarielle?

No, she thought. Garreth did not need another woman. He was content with her. Wasn't he? He seemed satisfied. More than satisfied. But would he stay that way? Was he the kind of man who grew quickly bored with a woman? He did not seem the type, but how was she to know?

And why was she even concerned about these things? For the first time in her life she was free. Free to do anything she wanted! She could be anyone. Go anywhere. Why would she limit herself to one man when she could have any? Or many if she wanted to!

But . . . she didn't want to. For now, she was happy to be with Garreth, and she hoped he felt the same. However, if she wanted him to remain contented with her, she couldn't just be a woman in threadbare dresses and old dressing gowns. She had to . . . she had to be more like Davine.

But she didn't know how to be like Davine. She had spent her days reading and learning things. She had not learned how to be pretty or pampered.

"Actually . . . I was wondering if I could . . . I was wondering who to ask if I wanted to get more clothing for the twins. They are really in need of it. The bennesah did the very least he could to keep them dressed."

"Of course! How remiss of me," Garreth said intently. "I will give you the gold for their clothing, and you should get some as well."

"Thank you for that. The wyvern can give us any riches we need, but I did not think to ask for it and . . . Well, I promised him shiny things and have yet to give them to him because . . . because they are not my things; they are yours."

"I will see to all of that. You only need to tell him to come to us here and we will give shiny things to him. As for your clothing and such, this time it will be me who buys them for you. It is the very least I can do. In fact, I insist you go to the bazaar right this minute and get yourself and the girls some things."

"I will," Sarielle said with a smile. "Do you mind if . . . Well, I have rarely been to the bazaar. I do not know my way around. Davine, would you mind coming with me? Unless you need her still. Of course I can—"

"No! Take her with you. She is always willing to help, I have found. I can meet with her later about this. You two go, and please enjoy yourselves. Tell any merchants to bill me for your goods. Get whatever you want. Without limit."

"I will be frugal," Sarielle said. "There is no need to go wild."

"There is a need if you wish it," he said, raising her from the chair and kissing her softly. "Please yourself. After so much time in captivity, you deserve to be free in this way at the very least."

Sarielle was smiling as she left him. He was so enthusiastic it was infectious. And he gave with all his heart. She didn't think he had a bad bone in his whole body.

She walked out of the room with Davine and together the women exited the keep.

"It still feels strange to be able to come and go from here so freely," Sarielle said.

"No doubt it does," Davine replied, her soft voice just as exotic as the rest of her.

"Can I ask you something?" Sarielle said hesitantly.

"You may ask me anything. You are the conqueror's mistress. You have a position above me now."

"I am not above nor below you," Sarielle said sternly.

"Many people look on me with a jaundiced eye," she said quietly. "They see only the evil bennesah's mistress and think I should be dead too."

"No one thinks that!" Sarielle said.

"Oh, but they do," Davine said, her eyes lowered. "I have heard it said when they did not think I could hear them."

"Well, I don't think that way." Sarielle walked in silence beside her for a moment. "I wanted to ask you how . . . that is, how did you know what the bennesah wanted from you?"

"He wanted what all men want," Davine said with a sly smile. It made Sarielle laugh. "But you mean how I present myself. How I make myself alluring. How I keep a man interested."

"Yes," Sarielle said on a sigh. "All of those things."

Davine laughed gaily. "Do not worry! I will help you to be pretty, yes? For our new bennesah. So he will make you his mistress and keep you."

"Well, I don't know if I want that exactly . . ."

"Then we will make you pretty for you," Davine said. She smiled softly and touched Sarielle's hair. "You need a little work, but there is much we can do for you."

They entered the bazaar a short while later and Sarielle was immediately overwhelmed with the sights and sounds and smells. Many merchants were inside tents, while some were sitting out on rugs with their wares on display. The bazaar was a maze, almost haphazard, but everywhere she turned, there was more to see and feel and even taste. Fruit vendors put pieces of fruit on her tongue and cloth vendors came and touched fabric to her arms as she passed to try to lure her in. Sometimes it worked and she found herself fondling the most sumptuous of fabrics, fabrics like the ones Davine wore. Like she was wearing even then. Although Sarielle wasn't sure she had the nerve to wear some of the things Davine wore. But she did find one fabric, a thick silk one that slid like water through her hands and was the deepest green she had ever seen.

"I like this," she said to the vendor. "May I have enough for a dress, please?"

"What kind of dress will it be?"

"It will be something decadent with long, flowing skirts!" Davine declared with a laugh.

"Yes, mistress lady," the vendor said to Davine. She then cut the fabric, wrapped it in paper, and handed it to Davine.

"Now for a dressmaker," Davine said, grabbing Sarielle's arm and hurrying her through the bazaar. "They will have more fabrics there and you can order as many dresses as you like, for you and the little girls!"

They rounded a bend and there it was, a huge tent in the hub of the bazaar filled with dresses on display. There were wicker mannequins shaped like women and the dresses were upon their reedy bodies. Each dress was more beautiful than the next. Sarielle eagerly followed Davine inside.

"See? Look at them all! Over there is for the children, and over here is for you. Look at this one. You would look delicious in this! He could never resist you!"

Sarielle blushed as she looked at the daring gown. It was completely transparent.

"I could never wear that! No one could!"

"Nonsense. I have two myself. They are for inside the bedroom, not out," Davine whispered to her.

"Oh! Well . . . then I will have to have one," she said with a sly smile. "And I like the blue."

"It should fit you. Let's try it on," Davine said. She

turned to the vendor. "We would like to try on this dress."

"Who would?" the merchant asked, her eyes narrowing on Sarielle. "We don't serve her kind in here."

And just like that, a sharp, bitter coldness was dashed into the face of Sarielle's day.

"I beg your pardon?" Davine said, her voice lowering to an almost threatening level.

"I don't serve the scourge," the woman repeated, biting the words out.

"Let's go," Sarielle whispered.

"No! There is no scourge anymore," Davine defended her to the vendor. "They are all free now."

"Just because an invader comes and says something is true does not make it true to those of us who know what they are. She is filth and she will not try on any of my clothes. I have a clientele to think of. What would they think if they saw the scourge wearing the very dresses they would like to try on for themselves?"

"Davine, please. Let's go," Sarielle said, pulling on the other woman's arm.

"The new ruler will hear of your treatment!" Davine promised her as Sarielle pulled her away. "This will not be the end of it!"

Sarielle had lost all her stomach for shopping, but Davine persisted. "No," she said, "we will not let the ignorance of one woman color our day out together. We will find another merchant. There are simply dozens of them."

Davine chattered on and Sarielle tried to listen, but all she kept thinking about was the vendor's attitude toward her. She had grown up with that attitude all her life, so why had it shocked her now?

Because Garreth had taught her to want more. To expect more. To deserve more. But right then she couldn't decide if that was a good thing or not. He had raised her expectations and now she had been thoroughly disappointed.

"Here. Here is Jugot, my favorite dressmaker. Look at all his lovely things. Jugot, you will serve me and my friend, will you not?"

"But of course, Davine! I thrive on your generous business. Come! Bring your pretty friend. I have had many fine things just waiting for you to see."

"Tell me what you have!" Davine demanded excitedly.

"Froma silk, my love! Froma silk! It came in right before this awful business with the invaders. Who knows what will become of it all! The western half of the bazaar was burned to a crisp! I know many friends who lost their entire livelihood in this terrible war. Some even lost their lives!"

"I am sure it has been hard," Davine said. "But I have it on good authority that these invaders mean to be very fair and have ruled many other cities well."

"They can't do much worse than the bennesah, I'll say. Now, let's see what you have there. Oh, a fine cloth for a day dress, I daresay. Well! Let's get you fitted for the style you like and you can try on anything else in the store."

"Thank you," Sarielle said, her whole heart in the words. She had needed to be accepted and this man was doing just that, as simply as the sun was out. It comforted her a great deal.

She was very grateful to Davine as well. After they bought dresses for her and for the twins, with bundles in their hands, they went shopping for what Davine called "essentials": perfume, lotion, bath salts. Then they spent the rest of the day finding little things like jewelry and shoes. Sarielle's eyes went wide at the sheer cost of things and the freedom with which Davine spent money. It didn't escape her that Davine was choosing things for herself as well and also charging it to Garreth's accounts.

When they got back to the keep, they tumbled inside, arms exhausted from carrying their burdens.

"I must say, I could have used a good slave today!" Davine sang out. Then she stopped and whirled to look at Sarielle. "I didn't mean—!"

"It's all right. The truth is, you are used to using slaves, just as that vendor is unused to serving them."

Davine went up to her. "I do not look at you as a slave. I think I look at you as . . . a compatriot. For, in my way, I too was a slave. The only difference was that people thought I gave myself to the bennesah willingly. They forget that men in power can take whatever they want. He saw me in my father's shop one day and he wanted me. That was the end of my days as a simple girl and the beginning of something different. You have seen the end of your days as a slave, and now is the beginning of something different."

"It will be different for you too. You are free to do whatever you like now."

"Well, we'll see. I'm not sure I know how to do anything else anymore! Now, come. Let's find the children and have them try on their dresses. I cannot wait to see their faces! And the dolls you bought them!"

Davine's excitement was catching and Sarielle eagerly followed her, all thoughts of that vendor forgotten.

CHAPTER
SEVENTEEN

Sarielle had never had a friend before—that much was obvious to Davine. Davine wasn't much for friends either. She had lost everything the day she was elevated to being the bennesah's latest mistress. As such, she had learned there was no such thing as a real friend. If someone tried to make friends with her, it was because they wanted something from her. Or, more precisely, from the bennesah. They knew Davine was guaranteed to have his ear once every few nights . . . if not every night . . . and if they did something for her, she might drop an idea in the bennesah's ear.

Those were the kinds of friendships she had treasured. That was how she had managed to put aside a nest egg for the day when the bennesah would finally grow tired of her. A day that had been rapidly approaching if she'd had to lay bets. But nest egg or not, it wasn't enough for her to live in the comfort she had grown used to. It was bad enough that her slaves had been freed and now she was forced to share serving girls with the rest of the household. Paid serving girls. Who had ever heard of such a thing? Paying for help?

She missed slaves. Her slave Betima had braided her hair perfectly. Her slave Chantro had given the finest massages. When Davine had gone shopping, each had been there to help carry her purchases. When she had said she missed slaves, she had not forgotten whom she was talking to. Just like she had known that vendor would never serve a scourge. But Davine had taken Sarielle there purposely to do two things: one, to remind the upstart of who she really was, and two, to put herself firmly in Sarielle's corner. To bring them together. To make them appear to be *friends*.

So as she lowered herself to braid the slave girl's hair to make her more attractive to Garreth, she reminded herself of the bigger picture. Playing her hand right would bring her comfort for the rest of her days, and all she had to do was drive Garreth and Sarielle apart.

It was going to be incredibly easy, she decided. The girl had been sheltered; for all she had been a slave, protected in a cocoon. Well, now she was out in the big, bad world and she was going to find out just what kind of insidious teeth it had.

"Do you think he'll like it?" Sarielle asked, looking into the looking glass that Bento had had imported from across the Faspin Sea just for Davine, because it was the clearest glass known to man and he had wanted her to be able to see herself completely unblemished. It galled Davine that she now had to watch this slave girl use it as her own, with *her* doing the serving. *Her,* a natural born Kithian! The world had surely come to an end the day these vanquishers had come . . . for all they were handsome, stalwart, and, it appeared, wealthy.

"He will love it," Davine assured her. "Do you not think so?" she asked, purposely baiting the girl.

"Well, I'm not sure. I'm not sure I know what he likes."

Davine laughed at her. "Pussy, darling. He likes pussy. All men do. It's as simple as that. All you have to do is figure out if he's the sort to like just one . . . or if he's the sort who likes a great many different ones at once."

Sarielle was flushing hotly. "How do you know?" she asked.

"Well, they all show their colors eventually. But I must warn you. Finding one who likes just one is nearly impossible. Eventually they almost all stray. The bennesah most certainly did."

"From *you*?" Sarielle was shocked. "Why would any man stray from you? You're perfect!"

"It's not about how perfect we are. They simply cannot help themselves. But I made certain never to complain when I caught him at it. Nothing will get you kicked out of a man's bed faster than telling him what he can and cannot do with his penis."

"But that's terrible." Sarielle then forced herself to brighten. "I am not concerned. Garreth is not the sort to seek out many women."

"You do not know him that well," Davine warned her.

"No. But I have a sense of him. Thank you for all your help. I had fun today. I hope we can do it again sometime."

"Tomorrow at least!" Davine declared, making Sarielle laugh. "Now I'm going to go. I believe I see a light on under your master's door. Good night, Sarielle!"

Davine was off with a flutter of light fabric and gone from the room.

Her master's door? She had no master any longer, Sarielle thought with a frown. Surely it was a habitual word choice. Davine had always referred to the bennesah as her "master," even going so far as to say "Yes, my beloved master" on occasion within Sarielle's earshot. No. She shouldn't really think anything of it.

Sarielle stood up, the diaphanous material of her gown brushing along her body. It was completely transparent, barely what she would call a fabric at all. At first she had been shy to wear it in front of Davine, but the other woman had oohed and aahed over it so much that she had lost her shyness. Now, as she moved to the door she shared with Garreth, she hesitated and suddenly felt shy again. She grabbed the handle of the door and inched it open just so she could peek inside. Garreth was standing there completely naked, his back to her, his fingers reaching around in an attempt to scratch his own back. Apparently he couldn't reach the proper place, although he tried it from all sides.

She eased the door open, blessing the gods for well-oiled hinges, and swept into the room soundlessly.

Garreth was about to give up reaching the bloody itch and was determined to find a good stone wall to scratch against when the light drift of nails coasted down the center of his spine, right where the damn itch was. He sighed as she scratched him gently.

"Ah, harder. Up a little. There's the bloody spot," he ejected happily. "Been trying to reach that thing for an hour."

"Glad I could help," she said with a chuckle.

He reached behind him for her hands, pulling one up under each of his arms until he had both folded across his chest, making her hug him from behind.

"It's been a long day. Most of it spent avoiding a man I can't afford to avoid."

"Who?"

"My brother."

"Why would you want to avoid him?"

He sighed. "It's not important. How about you? How was your day?"

"Well, it was good . . . for the most part."

"For the most part?" He turned in her arms. "What do you mean for the— What in the hells are you wearing?" he choked out once he had come full around and looked at her.

She colored. "You don't like it," she said, covering herself with her arms.

"I-I didn't say that," he said hastily, reaching to take her hands in his and pull her arms away from her reluctant body. "I just . . . I wasn't expecting it. My sweet and loving gods, you look absolutely . . ."

"Ridiculous?"

"Amazing," he corrected. "I didn't think you could get more beautiful, but every time I lay eyes on you, you prove me wrong."

This time she blushed for all the right reasons, reminding herself to thank Davine.

"Now . . . before I devour you top to bottom, I want you to explain to me what you meant by 'for the most part.'"

"There was this one vendor," she said with a dismissive shrug.

"What of him?"

"She . . . would not serve me." There was a distinct beat of her heart.

"What do you mean she would not serve you?" he asked softly, dangerously.

"Please," she begged him, "do not make anything of this. It's just the way things are. I have been trying to tell you this—"

"Which vendor?" he demanded of her.

"Please it doesn't mat—"

"Which goddamn vendor?!" he shouted at her.

"Don't yell at me!" she shouted back.

He reached for her, but she smacked his hands away and backed up. He tracked her all the way across the room, her retreating and him advancing. She slammed into the wall, but his hands had already come about her head and protected it from the stone.

"Stop," he said quietly. "Stop!" he said more strongly when she tried to push him off.

"I won't be yelled at!" she said, fighting back tears. She had come into the room with such different plans. It wasn't supposed to be like this. "I should never have said anything!"

"No. No, you should . . . I'm sorry. You need to promise me that you'll tell me anything you want to tell me. I did not mean to be cross with you. I just don't like it when you tell me you have been mistreated. Those days are over for you. It makes me angry for you, not at you."

"Well, it feels like the same thing when you are yelling at me."

"You are right. And I truly am very sorry. Now please, tell me what happened. I have to understand what is going on in the streets of this city if I am to come up with a way of fixing it."

"It was simple," she said with a nonchalant shrug that wasn't fooling him at all. "The vendor thought I was too dirty to try on her clothing."

Simple? To her that was *simple*? Garreth thought. No. It wasn't that simple to her. He could see in her eyes that it had stung her just as much as it should have stung her, would have stung him had it happened to him. He had been in many lands where as an outsider he had been considered less than good enough, but the difference between him and his fira was that he had never put up with it, and she seemed to think it was her due.

"You fought me so hard when I first came here. Where is that fire now, fira?"

"I fought you because I was afraid. Because I was hurt! I'm not the strong woman you think I am! I am merely a . . . a . . ."

"Do not say slave. Do not dare say slave to me!" he hissed softly at her.

"That is what I am. What I have always been. I don't know how to be anything else except . . . except when I'm here with you."

He drew in a deep breath, exhaled. "I suppose . . . I suppose I am asking much of you. Too much, it would seem. I mean nothing by it except to say that I wish you to see yourself as I see you." He reached and touched a gentling finger to the rise of her cheek. "As something wild and beautiful and *free*."

"Only with you do I fully feel I am those things."

"That is enough for now. Soon, though, I expect it to radiate beyond just you and I. I expect you to demand it of others."

"I will try," she promised him.

"You are the wrena," he said. "The woman who braved a mountain wilderness, lived among manticores and wyverns, climbed up high in order to steal an egg, and somehow carried it safely down. You nursed it to fruition. You have a wyvern at your beck and call. What about any of that screams slave to you? Screams that you are weak or powerless?"

"Nothing," she breathed.

"And now you mold the soul of a conqueror to your hand just as easily," he said, taking her hand with his and bringing it to rest over his heart. "My spirit soars when I am with you, even though it is not mine to give. It is dangerous, I know, but I cannot seem to help myself. My brother sees it. That is the crux of his anger toward me."

"I do not wish to come between you and your brother," she whispered.

"It is this curse that is between us . . . just as it lies between you and I. And with that thought . . . darkness is falling. I must leave you for a little while." He moved away from her and began to dress himself in warmer clothing. It was strange because the nights were not yet quite that cold.

"Where do you go every night?" she asked.

"I would prefer you not ask me that," he said with a frown.

"But I am asking," she pressed as he pulled a jerkin of leather over his head.

"Fira," he warned.

"Why can't you tell me?"

"I have to go," he said, briefly coming past her and pressing a quick kiss on her mouth. Then he was gone, leaving her in his rooms.

Hurt that he would not confide in her, she refused to sleep in his bed . . . at first. She went to her own room and undid her hair of all the frilly curls and braids Davine had put it in. She brushed it out until it settled in soft waves around her shoulders. She was in her own bed shortly after and it felt so alone. So desolate. She realized that after all those turnings of loneliness she didn't want to sleep alone if she didn't have to. She went across the cold stone floor as fast as she could and leapt into Garreth's bed, snuggling down deep under the covers. His bed was close to the fire and was toasty warm, chasing away the small chill in the air that came with living in a cold, often damp building like the keep. Before long she began to grow drowsy and then fell asleep.

Sarielle was dreaming that something—she didn't know what—was chasing after her. It was dark and large, and more than anything, it was cold. Icy cold. She was cold to her sinew and bone.

The walls around her were crackling with frost, and her skin was frozen. Her lips were blue, and suddenly something that felt like ice was pressed against them.

She woke with a shocked gasp to find Garreth kissing

her lightly on her lips. He looked immediately surprised that she had awakened from her slumber. He pulled away, but not before she had felt the cold of his lips. He had been leaning over her, but now moved toward the fire.

"Where have you been?" she asked him.

"I told you not to ask me that."

"Well, I'm sorry if I'm finding the dictate a bit hard to hold on to! Something is going on. Why won't you share it with me?"

"I won't discuss this. If you can't abide by that, then perhaps you should return to your own bed," he said flatly.

Sarielle bit her lip. Something inside her told her that if she left she would be creating a wall between them, which might not be able to be torn down once erected. She didn't want that.

"No. I'll abide by it. For as long as I can. If I see you hurt in any way, I don't know that I can keep that promise."

"I can't be hurt, remember?"

"You know that's not true. You can be hurt very badly. You simply cannot be killed. There is a difference." She paused. "And not all hurts are physical."

He looked at her as he stood by the fire and slowly began to get undressed. "I'm a grown man. I know how to manage my feelings."

"Managing them and feeling them are two different things entirely. I should know. I have kept myself from feeling anything, save the love for my sisters, for so long. And anger. Anger at the bennesah that he would hold them hostage from me in order to control me. I am so tired of people using them to get to me and, through me, Koro."

"I will not use you in such a way," he promised her quietly.

"I know you won't. That is one of the reasons why you find me in your bed when you return from these late night excursions of yours." She held out her hand. "Will you come to bed?"

"In a little while. I want to warm by the fire."

"Is it that cold out?" she asked.

"Getting colder every day," he said. "Dethan will want to leave soon. It looks like I will be wintering the army here." He looked at her. "Would you like that?"

She smiled. "I would love that."

"Then it is settled. We will spend the winter rebuilding what we can in the snow and planning for an attack on Zandaria."

"So you have decided to go forth?"

"Provided we can find mages. I would like to convince Dethan to bring Selinda with him when he returns at the end of spring. She is a fire magess and a very powerful one, as I understand it."

"You've spoken to him about this?"

"A little."

"And what does he say?"

"He cares for his wife deeply. He will not risk her willingly. They have a young son. But that is the beauty of choosing Zandaria. We can base ourselves here. Xand could remain safe and protected here with his nanny, and Selinda and Dethan could come back whenever they needed to be with him."

"It is a good thought. But you will need more than one fire magess to fight the rylings."

"We are working on that. We have the entire winter to gather more mages."

"Good mages are hard to find. Most, like Vinqua, have positions in established political structures. They will not want to leave that comfort and security to go to war."

"I know. That is why we have not found one as yet."

Garreth was standing there before the firelight in just his breeches, the material clinging lovingly to his powerful thighs and other more intimate areas. She could see the definition of him through the fawn-colored fabric. It made a slow hunger for him begin to bubble beneath her surface. He was quite magnificent, bare chested, his arms well shaped and strong, his chest and shoulders broad. She would never tire of looking at the sheer male beauty of him. She loved every inch of him, from the strong column of his throat and neck to his tight belly with the thumbprint navel to his big bare feet with their slightly knobby toes. It always made her smile to see them. Probably because she only got to see them when he was fully naked or close to it.

He stood practically in the fireplace, a huge stone thing that could almost be walked into. The fire had been mild, but now he was loading on wood until it burned bright and hot. She felt the wall of heat and it comforted her. But it looked as though he was having trouble getting warm. He kept rubbing his arms and hands as if to make his blood move and warm.

"Change is hard for anyone to accept. My experiences today only prove that."

Garreth frowned. "I am going to have that vendor thrown in the stocks for her treatment of you. And that will be the punishment for anyone caught doing likewise to any other slave."

"Then you will need to build more stocks," she said with a frown. "You cannot expect people to change overnight."

"No. But they won't change if there are no consequences for their refusal to do so. I will have more stocks built and placed in the center square in the heart of the bazaar. That way everyone can see what happens to those who do not change their attitudes. They will get the message soon enough."

"I suppose. But might I suggest the city guard warn offenders first before they take them to the stocks? You put out a decree to free the slaves, so put one out to announce punishment for segregation and prejudicial behaviors."

"I will see it done tomorrow. Now," he said coming toward her. "I am warmed. Would you like to feel?"

There was something primal in his gaze just then, something with appetite. It made her pulse quicken to see him coming toward her so intently. She sat up as he climbed into bed, but he quickly moved his body over hers, forcing her to recline back again. He hovered above her, his arms taut with the weight of his own body. She exhaled and reached to touch him, finding her fingers eager for the feel of him. Her eyes eager for the look of him. He smelled of the outdoors, crisp and woodsy, and also male and warm and everything virile. There was such life in his body, burning in his eyes, and he looked at her as if he wanted to live that life trying to find the very heart of her.

"So," he said, his voice a low rumble of speculation, "what shall we do tonight? Shall I curl up at your feet like a nice, well-heeled puppy? Or should I nip and bite at you like a naughty one?"

She giggled. "Both sound very attractive in their own right," she said.

"But which do you prefer? Snuggling down for warmth against me or nipping"—he gently bit the cap of her shoulder—"and biting."

"I think I might like a combination of the two. Perhaps one first, then the other."

"Ah. But in which order?"

She could see the amusement in his eyes and the smile at the edges of his lips, and it warmed her to her soul.

"I think I'd prefer the naughty first . . . then the nice."

"I concur," he said on a rich, rumbling growl. She

giggled and squealed when he stripped back the bedding and made as if to devour her in the dead center of her belly. She laughed as he pressed onward, his hands at her ankles and then beneath the hem of her gown before she even realized what he was attempting. By the time she did, his hands were already coasting up the outer edges of her thighs. "And this sinful creation . . . Just as I would punish one dressmaker for insulting you, I would reward another for somehow making you even more desirable than I thought possible. Just when I thought I couldn't possibly want you more, you attend me in this."

The gown slid up past the apex of her thighs and onto her lower belly. The moment her navel was bare he pressed his lips to it, kissing her, his tongue flicking out against her. Then suddenly he was using strong hands to flip her over onto her belly, making her gasp as her backside was bared to the heat of his gaze. His fingers continued to lift her gown until he had shucked it off her completely, letting it slip down off the side of the bed to land in a silky little pile.

With her back to him she could do little more than look toward the wall, or at the forearm braced about a foot from her nose. His skin was tanned a light nut-brown from the sun; small, crisp hair curled along the length of it. He had a mole about midway up his inside forearm and she couldn't help but think how cute it was. Then she rolled her eyes at herself. The man was many things but cute was not one of them.

Now that she was naked, he took the opportunity to run his hands down the full length of her body, from the base of her neck to the backs of her ankles, and then back up again, each time slowing down as he crested over the swells of her backside. On his second trip toward her ankles he shaped her buttocks to his hands, squeezing each firm cheek with his fingers, his thumbs brushing along the center crease. She felt vulnerable, facing away from him, unable to touch him back, unable to see him or his reactions to her. But she supposed he must be enjoying himself or he wouldn't be doing what he was doing. After a moment he lay his body along the back of hers, her bottom nesting into his hips, and she was given hard proof that he was enjoying himself. His breath pooled warmly in her ear.

"How is it possible I want you more now than I did before . . . even before the first time? That should not be possible. And yet it is. The more I learn about you, the more I see and experience you . . . the more I desire everything about you."

"Surely not everything," she argued. "I must have some fatal flaw?"

"You mean besides being irrevocably attached to the physical well-being of a wyvern? No others that I can see."

"My willfulness? My temper?"

"Vexing and charming, I agree, but hardly fatal flaws. Turn over."

She did so slowly, feeling vulnerable again as he watched her with famished eyes. He exhaled a hard breath.

"No. No flaws," he said, touching her shoulder where he had shot her with an arrow before that very first meeting. The healings of the mems had worked and there was little more than a puckered pink spot where the bolt had been. "You were very lucky I did not have poison on my arrows that day. I do not like to use it, but I will when I must. Poison can be a tricky thing though. One careless move and the poisoner finds himself poisoned."

"I am lucky you did not hit my heart."

"It turns out that it was my good fortune to not hit your heart. Else I never would have known this." He bent his head and placed a kiss on her skin. "I was always a lucky man. I usually make my own luck, but I will take it where it is given with ease as well. The bennesah was a fool for putting you out on the wall where you could be seen and targeted. I would have kept you far out of reach of a warmonger's weapons and yet in the open air so you could guide the wyvern."

"Is this really what you wish to talk about just now?" she asked, her eyes light with amusement and fondness.

"No. You are right. There are better things to do with my tongue."

"Oh! That is not what I meant!" she said with a gasp as he boldly tongued her across one of her pointed nipples.

"Shall I stop?"

"No," she sighed.

"What about now?" He took the same nipple between his teeth and tugged gently on it.

"No."

"And now?" He pulled a little harder. She moaned her reply. He then soothed the abused area by closing his mouth over her nipple and sucking at it first gently, then more strongly. She arched her back, feeding him her breast more deeply. She felt him move, felt him working his body in between her knees, his hips driving up between her thighs. She immediately embraced his legs with her own, opening herself up to him, only to be disappointed when she realized he still had his breeches on.

"Why aren't you naked?" she complained.

"Would you like me to be?"

"Yes, very much so."

"Then let me up," he said with amusement.

"Oh!" She untwined their legs, letting him up. He stripped himself of his breeches and came back to her. She had been chilled by his departure; now she delighted in his return.

CURSED BY ICE 215

For an endless amount of minutes, he made love to her with his hands and mouth, moving his body up and down along hers, constantly turning her one way and then another way for her pleasure and for his. He took his time, chased down her every little sigh, every little moan. It was all about her. He refused to let her touch him in return, forced her to enjoy being catered to. She couldn't shake the feeling that his behavior was some kind of apology. Perhaps for not letting her in. For not allowing her to see the part of him he was keeping hidden.

Regardless of his motivations, she lay back and let him pleasure her. She really didn't have much of a choice, it seemed. And when he finally breached her body with his, she had already come for him multiple times. She was almost exhausted by the time he took his first stroke. But the moment he was inside her she revived, coming to life in his arms again. Never once did he change his slow and steady pace, almost to her frustration. But in the end, it seemed he knew best.

Falling asleep in his arms some time later, she couldn't help the feeling crawling over her that told her she was in trouble. That her emotions were now at stake when it came to this man. A man who was not free to give his heart or his full attention to anyone but his warrior goddess. She felt a moment of pure jealousy toward that aggressive woman. Why? Why should Weysa be the only one allowed to have him? Why couldn't she have him for the rest of her life too? She wouldn't get in the way of his goals. In fact, she could travel with him, bringing with her the power of the wyvern. What a mighty weapon that would be for his armies!

But even as she thought it, she knew it was not possible. She would not take Koro from his beloved nest and his home for her own selfish reasons. She could not travel in an army camp with the twins. She would be tethered to one place, probably this place, until the twins were old enough to fend for themselves.

And for some reason the thought brought tears to her eyes.

CHAPTER
EIGHTEEN

"Brother! We are in danger!"

A thundering fist on the door woke Sarielle from an unsettled sleep, then the door to Garreth's room burst open to admit Dethan, who strode up to the bed and thumped his brother on the back. Sarielle, meanwhile, had scooted down under the warm covers, ensuring her naked body was covered and hidden from Dethan's judgmental glare. Garreth was roused with some difficulty, until he saw his brother and registered Dethan's presence in his bedroom. He was up like a shot, his arm crossing protectively over Sarielle.

"What are you doing?" Garreth demanded of his sibling. "Get out!"

"I will as long as you come with me. There is an army at our gates."

"An army?!"

"Yes. Come see for yourself."

Garreth flew out of bed and into his clothes. As soon as the brothers had exited the room, Sarielle bolted into her rooms and did the same.

She raced out of her rooms and after the men, guessing they would go to the upper walls of the keep, which rose above the city walls. She was right. She found them in the chill morning air, looking at the army that had moved into place overnight outside the walls. Thank the gods the men had ordered the city gate closed each night at dusk; the only person allowed to pass was Garreth himself as he came from . . . well, whatever it was he did.

Garreth was watching the army through a telescopic eyepiece. Then he saw Sarielle and handed it to her. "What do you make of them?"

She put the telescope to her eye and looked at the men running around the tents that had been pitched. "Zizo! And rylings," she said. The Zizo were dwarfish creatures, men and women of small stature known for their big noses. The rylings were more fey but just as small as the Zizo. The rylings and the Zizo had worked in concert to build a city and economy of comfort in Zandaria. The bennesah had made enemies of them several times over by refusing to deal with them fairly and insulting them on more than one occasion. "They must have heard the bennesah was dead."

"And thought a newly conquered city would be weak. They are not entirely wrong," Dethan said grimly.

"But the wyvern still protects this city as far as they know. Why would they move against it?" said Garreth.

"Perhaps they are hoping that is no longer the case. Koro was very visibly injured during the attack. Scouts may have taken note of it," Dethan said grimly.

"Very well. They want a war? We will give them one," Garreth said. "We have the whole of a conquering army within these walls. We need only open the gates and we will engage them."

"But the rylings have magic," Sarielle reminded them with a warning tone in her voice.

"And we have mages. Three. They came in last night while you were away," Dethan said to Garreth.

"What sort of mages?"

"I have not had the opportunity to discover this. But I suggest we acquaint ourselves with them with much haste."

"Agreed," Garreth said, taking the spyglass from Sarielle. "Stay inside."

"Perhaps I should call Koro. If they see he is alive and well, they might flee."

"Not a chance I am willing to take," Garreth said. "If Koro were to be injured . . . so would you be too. I will not risk it."

"But . . ."

"I will not argue with you about this," Garreth said harshly. "I have made up my mind about it." He turned on his heel and marched away from her.

Infuriated, she gave him chase. "Don't I get any say in the matter?"

"You do not," Garreth said.

She was shocked that he would be so blunt about his high-handed treatment of her. "Well, can I at least come and interview these mages with you?"

"No. It truly is none of your concern. Please go back inside and remain with the twins. This could be a very long siege or a very short battle. We need time to figure out which approach is best for tackling this."

"A siege would mean a city that starves. We have barely recovered stores from the last one, if indeed we have any at all. Not to mention we now have an army to provide for living behind these walls."

Garreth stopped and looked at her hard. "You think I don't know this? I have made battle in one form or another all my life. Dethan has fought more wars than can be remembered. You have been a cloistered slave for many turnings. You are not qualified to question us on this."

She looked at him aghast. She felt tears welling up in

her eyes. Furious and frustrated, she pushed past him and ran for the stairs.

"Shit," Garreth swore.

"You spoke the truth, brother," Dethan said quietly. "She has no place in this."

"She lives here and therefore has a place in this. She commands a powerful beast that might come in handy if used wisely. And we wanted her to become leader of this city not two days ago. A leader would need to be included in these matters."

"But she turned down that offer. Resoundingly so. She made it clear she doesn't want to be in control of this. She needs to remain inside, safe and out of sight, just as you said. Now, come on. We have much work to do."

The brothers headed down into the main hall and began to send runners for their lieutenants. They called the mages to them. Davine appeared and began to serve the gathering of men wine and smiles and as much helpful information as she could. When Sarielle walked by and saw this, saw her leaning over Garreth with her hand on his back, her anger only intensified.

To her mind, she had every bit as much right to be in that room as Davine did. She could be of use to them. She had control of an enormous fire-breathing beast, for the gods' sake! But she would not go into the room. Her pride demanded she not allow him another opportunity to make her feel small and insignificant.

She racked her brain as to how she could be of help otherwise, but after a while she had to admit that there was little she could offer.

At first.

Then she realized there was something everyone was forgetting. Even she had forgotten it. She hurried into the main hall.

"Magic!" she ejected loudly.

Garreth and Dethan and several of their men looked up at her.

Garreth frowned. "What about it?"

"I'm the only one here who can see through it!" Her tone was triumphant. "You need me where I can see their army at all times, where I can see through any glamours that might be cast. Otherwise, they can trick you. They are fairies. Glamours are their speciality!"

Garreth looked at Dethan. "She has a point."

"Surely the mages can see through that," Dethan said with a frown.

"Not all mages. Mages like Vinqua could," Sarielle said. "But you don't have Vinqua, do you?"

"No. We don't. But that would require you to be within easy visual sight of the battle, which means putting you on the city wall. I don't want you that close to the action. You could be hit by a stray arrow or a purposeful one." The look Garreth gave her was pointed.

"Then put me in armor. I can settle in low where I cannot be seen. I can report everything I see to you. And we can bring Koro to bear as well. I know you do not want to see me hurt," she said quickly, raising a hand to forestall his coming argument, "but I do not wish to see you hurt either . . . and yet you will still be on that wall defending this city. My city. My home."

Garreth was silent a long minute and Sarielle took heart. At least he wasn't ejecting her from the room and shutting her down immediately.

"Very well. But if we use the wyvern, you must call him from atop the keep, not the city wall. And he must not land at any time. If he stays in the air, he cannot be injured. Landing on the city wall allowed him to fall to my blade. It can happen again."

"All right. When he retreats or sets down it will be on the keep, well behind the city walls," Sarielle said.

"Very well. We have decided to attack them immedi-

ately. This city cannot withstand another barrage or a
siege. We must attack while we are at full strength and
before they get the chance to settle in fully. We plan to
do this as soon as the men are armed and ready. These
are our mages." He indicated two men and a woman,
both men wearing light leather jerkins and the female
wearing light leather armor. Nothing too heavy or restricting, since mages often needed to be able to move
their arms in wide gestures to work their magic. "This
is Sona, an earth magess," he said gesturing to the elfin
female. She had a pointed nose and slightly pointed ears,
her entire face narrow and her short shock-white hair
spiking in all manner of directions. "And this is Froom,
another earth mage." He pointed to the old mage, whose
long beard and bent back made him look every bit the
magician. "And Dru, a spirit mage," he said indicating
a strong-looking younger man. He looked to be about
Garreth's age and weight, and was only slightly less handsome to her eyes. He was clean-shaven and had hair as
fiery red as hers. All were white skinned, although Dru
was tanned and Froom was weathered and spotted with
age.

"No mind mages?" Sarielle asked. But she was glad of
it. A mind mage like Vinqua could see through illusions
and having one would mean there was no use for her.
She wanted to be useful. She wanted to be a part of defending her home.

"No. You will be the only one able to see through illusions," Dru said. "I can call up spirits and the dead
and other fortifying spells that can create trickery, but I
cannot see *through* trickery."

"None of us can. You will be crucial," Froom said,
his old voice cracking with age.

"The rylings will be many, but their magic is limited
to illusions and earth magics. So it is fortunate we have

earth mages to counteract that. But there will be three mages against many rylings," Sarielle said with a frown.

"Then we must disrupt their magic whenever we can. We can use the wyvern for that. The fear he instills makes it hard to concentrate, and the fire he breathes can take out many players at one time. But I want him to come from behind the army," Garreth said to her, pointing to the map of the city she had seen Dethan using the day before. "They are focused to the north, beyond the north wall. If Koro comes in from behind them, it will squeeze them up against the army as we come out of the gates."

"We can have Koro come first to lure them into turning their backs on the city. Once they have engaged Koro, we open the gates and send the army out to overwhelm them," Dethan said.

"You earth mages can build walls of earth to the east and west, creating a narrow channel that will force them to fight, leaving them no retreat. Being closed in with no escape tends to make people panic," Garreth said.

Sarielle had to admit she was impressed. The men truly did know what they were doing. If they pulled this off, they would have planned the whole business perfectly.

It seemed plausible in theory, but executing it would be something else entirely. It was possible the rylings would not panic. They would probably be expecting Koro. But by having Koro attack the army from the rear, and not allowing him to fly over the entirety of the enemy forces to approach from the city, the brothers were giving the enemy less opportunity to attack Koro's vulnerable underbelly.

"And what if you win the day?" she heard herself asking. "What then?"

"The day will not be won until they are all dead or running for the Asdar Mountains."

"Not quite the direction of home," Sarielle noted.

"I don't want them to go home. I want them to know they are cut off from their direct route home. I want them to feel the fear that, should we desire it, we could next turn on their home, which they have left abandoned and defenseless."

Dethan was cutthroat, to be sure, and his words only solidified that about him. But she honestly didn't blame him. She took offense at this attack, just as he did, although she had more reason to because this was *her* home. But she supposed the city was the spoils of his war, and to his mind, no man had the right to take that from him.

"Put on your armor, brother. We go to war," Dethan said as he moved to leave the room.

"Surely you're not going to be in the thick of it," Sarielle heard herself saying nervously.

"Surely I am," Garreth said with a small frown. "Why wouldn't I?"

"You are a leader. You must be seen. And if anything should happen to you . . ." The words were tumbling out of her without her control. Her hands twisted together before her as true, unadulterated fear seized her.

He came up to her and settled calming hands on her shoulders. "I cannot be killed," he reminded her in a soft voice so others could not hear him.

"Oh," she said just as softly. "I forgot. B-but . . . you can still be gravely injured. And what if they have a god-made weapon? You said—"

"The odds of that are very slim. The odds of that weapon meeting my neck in the thick of a battle are slimmer still. Do not worry, Sarielle. It is you I am concerned about, not myself. You are not so well protected.

But we will find the armor of a slight man and dress you in it forthwith."

"Actually, there is women's armor in the bazaar," Davine spoke up from Garreth's elbow. "But you will have to get it yourself, for the vendor is like the one who would not serve her."

A thundercloud of anger swept across Garreth's features darkly. "He will serve her or he will answer to me! Sarielle, come! Help me dress in my armor. Then we will see about yours."

She followed Garreth to his rooms, where a squire was already waiting to help him into his armor. Since she knew little about dressing a man for war, the squire stayed and she helped, watched, and learned. She would be able to do this for him next time, she vowed to herself. She would see him protected and ready. She would help to keep him safe.

Once he was ready, with the wey flower etched and then enameled on his armor at the dead center of his chest, she moved into his arms and touched it with trembling fingers. The wey flower was Weysa's flower. It was an enormous bloom with large curved petals that came to points at their tips. It was most often a pink flower, although the one on his chest was a white version of it. A rare version of it. It was said the white wey flower could give a man incredible strength if consumed before a battle.

"She will always have you, and I never will," she said without thinking.

He went still as he looked down at her. "You knew this," he said softly.

"I knew this," she agreed. "But that does not make it any easier."

He reached up and touched a gloved finger to the rise of her cheek, shaping the apple of it slowly. "You have me," he promised her. "I should not allow it, but I cannot help myself. You have me."

She met his eyes, hope unfurling in her chest and tears filling her vision. "What are we to do?" she asked.

"One battle at a time," he said admonishingly. "Let us save this city first, then worry about the rest later."

She nodded and he took her hand, leading her out of the keep and toward the bazaar. In spite of herself, she began to drag her feet. She didn't want to go through this. There was enough to cope with as it was. She didn't need to be reminded that she wasn't deemed good enough by her own people. By Dethan. By Weysa. Not good enough by half.

They found the armorer, and immediately Sarielle saw a woman's breastplate, the metal finely etched with a picture of a powerful archer, an arrow nocked and drawn in her bow, the tip of it flaming. The flame had been enameled in red. It was an archer's armor. Light and strong, the metal brushed so as not to gleam too brightly in the sun, giving away the wearer's position. It made sense since the only women in their armed forces were archers. The bennesah had deemed females little good for anything else, too weak to go hand-to-hand or sword-to-sword in his opinion.

The armor came with a metal skirt that reached to the knees, the metal like the petals of a flower, each piece overlaying another all the way around the waist, keeping the armor flexible and mobile yet thoroughly protective. There were light bracers and gloves and all the necessary padding. And boots. They were made of hard leather with small squares of metal riveted to them, keeping them relatively light and flexible but protected all the same.

"Go on," Garreth urged her forward. "Ask the man if you may try it."

He was purposely baiting the blacksmith to see what

he would do, standing back and letting her do all the interacting. She bit her lip and nervously approached the merchant.

"I would like to try on that armor," she said, pointing to the piece. Garreth was standing in that direction as well, so she hoped the merchant would see him and know better than to behave in a prejudiced manner.

The smith was apparently nearsighted. "That's not for the likes of you."

"Why not?" she heard herself asking sharply, wondering where the sudden rush of temper came from. Apparently the pressure of knowing what Garreth would do next had given her the spine to stand up to the smith. For his own good, really. It was better he deal with her than Garreth.

"You're a scourge," the smith bit out. "I don't serve your kind."

"You will serve my kind," she hissed, grabbing hold of him by his arm. "Or have you not noticed that things around here have changed?"

"They haven't changed for me. Now, get your filthy hands off me before I am forced to have you thrown out on your ass!"

"Do you even know who I am?" she asked, her eyes narrowing wickedly.

"I do not care."

"I am the wrena," she hissed.

That made the smith's eyes widen and he looked at her for the first time.

"I don't believe you," he said.

"Shall I prove it to you?" she asked threateningly. "Shall I bring the wyvern to bear against you?"

The merchant hesitated, looking her over again, head to toe. "Show me proof. Show me the mark."

"I will not. You will allow me access to that armor

and you will pray I never show you proof that I am a wrena."

The merchant was still reluctant, but he begrudgingly took down the armor and handed it to her. Then Garreth stepped forward and helped her to dress in the breastplate, the one piece that might not fit as universally as the others would. The plate was riveted onto strong, hard leather, shaping to her breasts, the archer displayed from the bottoms of her breasts all the way to her lower waist, where the skirt would begin.

"It fits you fine," Garreth murmured in a soft voice. "As if it had been made for you."

"Yes, she looks quite good," the blacksmith was saying in hasty, uncomfortable tones. He had realized who Garreth was and was trying to cover up his earlier behavior with sudden praise. "It is one of my best works for a female. It took me quite some time to perfect it."

"Then it will be doubly generous of you when you give it to her as a gift."

"A-a gift?!" the man spluttered. "B-but the armor cost a small fortune to make!"

"Yes, but think of all the money you will make when she wears this and tells all who see her who the maker is," Garreth said as he stepped up to the man and loomed threateningly over him. "Imagine all the scourge clientele you will suddenly have."

The smithy swallowed noisily, clearly biting back any response to that particular idea. "Yes. Well . . . I suppose I could let it go for a greatly reduced rate of—"

"Free," Garreth said, his tone hard and unyielding.

"F-free," the smithy agreed at last, although through his teeth.

"Good man!" Garreth boomed out, slapping the smith hard on the back, nearly knocking the burly man off his feet. "We'll take the entire suit and padding. And you'll throw in a weapons belt besides. Send the whole of it immediately to the keep. Now come," he said to Sarielle. "I will rest easier once we find you a weapon to go with this."

Garreth helped her remove the breastplate. She needed to put on different clothing before she could don the entire suit in comfort. He took her into the further depths of the bazaar and straight to a weapons maker's tent. A crowd of men was there, inspecting the wares. They were both soldiers from Garreth's army and guards from the city's garrisons.

"Now is not a time for you to be acquiring new weapons," Garreth scolded in a booming voice. "You do not go into battle with an untried weapon! You must practice with it first. Now go. We ready for battle as I speak."

The men abandoned the weapons maker's tent with so much haste it was almost laughable. But Sarielle could not feel humor. Not when she knew Garreth was so close to going into battle.

"But I have never wielded a weapon," she said in a small voice as Garreth began to inspect the inventory.

"Nor do I expect you to. Ah! Here we are." He picked up a beautiful long dagger in a metal sheath, the artwork on it fine and intricate, unlike any kind of detailing she had ever seen before. "A dagger. You are not meant to fight, but I would have you carry a weapon to protect yourself should it come to it." He handed her the dagger.

"I do not think I could use it," she confessed to him, coloring uncomfortably. She didn't want to let him down, didn't want to appear weak. She didn't want him to say she was too cowardly to be a part of the battle. She needed to be there. For him. For her city.

"You will find that when you have no other choice, you will use it," he said intently, holding her eyes the entire time. "I will do all in my power to make certain I keep you safe, but should there be a problem and I cannot get to you . . . I will feel better knowing you have this."

For some reason she found herself melting under the words. No. Not for some reason. For a very clear reason.

He cared. He cared very deeply about her and her safety, and it showed strongly in that moment. There was something very invigorating and strengthening about that knowledge. Something tender and loving in the impression of it.

"Then I will have it," she said, reaching to take the dagger from him. As she held the sheath, he pulled the weapon free of it and inspected the deadly sharp blade. He tested it in a training dummy, which stood in the center of the shop, plunging the dagger deeply into the thing's straw chest and pulling it back out again with ease.

"Yes, this will do very nicely," he said.

He paid the merchant and then quickly urged her back to the keep. By the time they returned, her armor was already in her rooms awaiting her. Garreth went straight to her wardrobe and inspected the choices within it. The wardrobe was still relatively bare, in spite of her shopping trip with Davine. But he grabbed one of her older dresses and a pair of shears from her dressing table. He immediately set the shears to the skirt of the dress.

"What are you doing!" she cried out, trying to stop him.

"The skirt of the armor is short for a reason. So you will be unencumbered by long, thick skirts. You will wear this without any petticoats or other underskirts." He held up the dress with its considerably shortened skirt.

"I will be naked!" she said, her face burning with a blush.

"This coming from the woman who wore practically nothing for me yesterday."

"That was in the privacy of our rooms," she argued as he came around her and began to unlace her dress. "I did it to please you!"

"So do this to please me as well. I confess I am already hard thinking of you in armor, your beautiful legs exposed."

Her blush deepened as he pulled the dress from her body. Poorly banked hunger was in his eyes when he looked at her naked body only minutes later.

"Seems a shame to cover you up again," he murmured as he leaned into her and hotly cupped her breast in his hand. He squeezed the mound of flesh gently . . . then more strongly. She was breathless by the time he bent his head to her, taking her nipple into his mouth and toying with it with his tongue. Sarielle felt herself go immediately wet between her legs, and her body coiled with tension. Her nipple came free of his mouth with a small pop of sound and he stepped back from her. He growled low in his throat. "We will continue this later," he promised her.

"Okay," she said breathily.

"Let's get you dressed."

Before long he had her fully dressed in her new armor and was sliding her dagger into place on her weapons belt. When he was finished, he reviewed her with a critical eye.

"Well done," he said after a moment with a firm nod. "Well done indeed. Now come. Let's begin this battle."

She nodded and went to precede him out the door. But mid step she felt his hand sliding up the back of her thigh beneath her skirt and on to the cheek of her backside. The feel of his leather glove on her skin made her gasp and come to a halt, which brought him directly up against her back.

"Garreth!" she said in a breathless scold.

"I'm sorry," he said, his grin in no way repentant. "I could not help myself."

"Well, try!" she said with a laugh.

"If I must," he said, removing his hand from her body, albeit very slowly.

Together they left the room.

CHAPTER
NINETEEN

Garreth was on his horse, looking at the top of the keep from over his shoulder. Sarielle stood there, just as she had stood on the walls of the city the first time he'd seen her, a proud and beautiful creature. Only this time she was protected, her fiery red hair braided and hidden from sight. It would not be the banner it had been when he had attacked the walls of the city. No one would notice her as being different from anyone else, and that was exactly the way he wanted it to be. The keep was set a little farther back from the city walls, but the top stood above the walls, so Sarielle could easily see the field of battle.

He was about to ride out of the gates and into the thick of the Zizo army. He did not know what he would find when he attacked the rylings and faced down their magic, but he knew that the rylings were mortal and so were the Zizo. That meant they could be killed, and that was what he was there to do.

Garreth led the charge out of the gates, leaving Dethan to the relative safety of the city walls. Dethan would attack with archers from above while Garreth attacked on the ground.

They took the Zizo by surprise when they came pour-

ing from the gate just as the archers let loose on the bulk
of their campsite. The archers had a limited time before
Garreth's army reached the campsite. Once the two
forces engaged, archers could not be used for fear they
would strike their own combatants.

But the archers rained hell down on the enemy while
they could, and the Zizo and rylings found themselves
in chaos. The Zizo commanders tried to rally their men
together, but they were still at a disadvantage by the
time Garreth reached them and pummeled them with
the army's sheer numbers. As Garreth cut down the
small men, he realized that horseback was a disadvantage for him. He had to reach farther down, unbalanc-
ing himself. So he dismounted and rushed into the thick
of it on his feet, calling orders to his men, rallying them
with the sound of his commanding voice.

He thrust his brother's sword into first one, then another, shearing them down. Until he cut one down and
the man dissolved into nothingness. Shocked, he looked
around and saw the same thing happening all throughout the army.

Illusions. The rylings, he realized. They were making
his men work harder to cut down imaginary opponents.
It was impossible to know which combatants were
real and which were illusions. They had to attack them
all, which would quickly wear them out. Garreth might
have more actual soldiers, but with the ryling magic
making these illusions, it was as though the Zizo army
had been doubled. Even tripled. He turned and waved
his sword toward the city walls.

On the walls, Dethan was waiting for the signal.
Quickly he lit the signal fire next to him. It flared to life,
visible to the woman on the keep walls who was waiting
for it.

Sarielle closed her eyes and called to her wyvern, who

had come from behind as the army had surged out onto the field.

Remember, do not fly over them. Simply blow flame at them. Set them on fire from behind.

Sarielle opened her eyes in time to see Koro's large body reeling toward the Zizo army. And with a mighty exhalation, he began to set their rear forces on fire. The screams of men rose above the sounds of war. She heard the echoes of it drifting toward her even from her distant perch on the keep walls. She could see it all. See Koro's attack, Garreth's attack. Then the mages did their part and flung up huge walls of earth on either side of the Zizo army, trapping them inside a bottleneck. The other mage began to call up the spirits of the already slain men, both Zizo and Garreth's, and sent them to attack the rylings. The spirits could not be harmed, since they were already dead, and the rylings did not have the necessary magic to dispel their presence. The fey rylings began to fall, in spite of their illusions and their attempts to countermand the powerful earth mages' abilities.

The Zizo commanders began to call for a retreat . . . but they were blocked off by a fire-breathing wyvern. They took heavy casualties as they tried to run past Koro's attacks. Koro remained out of reach as per Sarielle's constant reminders.

Desperate, the Zizo tried to mow their way past Garreth and his forces, toward the city. Perhaps in the hope of running around the earthen walls blocking them in. It was an act of suicide and desperation. There was no cohesion to their battle plans. Their army was falling apart.

But desperation made an enemy dangerous. Garreth found himself suddenly overrun by Zizo and rylings with their needle-sharp swords. His men were cutting through them with ease, but he was overwhelmed, his arms burning from swinging his sword over and over and over again. He felt a ryling sword pierce through the vulnerable seam of his armor near his armpit, the sword sinking deep into his upper ribs and lung. It was pulled free and Garreth swiftly decapitated its owner. A second ryling sword hacked into his vulnerable neck, but he deflected it before it could do anything more than sever one of the muscles there.

That ended up compromising the swing of his left arm, which held his dagger and had been working in concert with his powerful right sword arm. Two of the Zizo rushed him, taking him out at his legs. He went down.

Garreth fought his way back up to his feet, slaying Zizo and ryling alike, his sword punching through armor, sometimes nearly cleaving bodies in half. Eventually he cleared himself of every enemy, allowing him a moment to see what was happening around him.

The Zizo army had fallen. Given no quarter and with no avenue of escape, they had been forced to face Garreth's greater numbers, their illusions failing them, their numbers decimated.

The Zizo soldiers fell to their knees and put their hands behind their heads in total surrender. The Zizo leader had been slain in the battle, and his second in command was now brought before Garreth.

"I ask mercy for my men," the little man said gruffly.

"You are in no position to ask for anything," Garreth said harshly. "Your army is mine, and before the winter sets in, your city will be mine as well."

"We will surrender to you. There is no one left to defend the city of Zandaria. It is yours already. We were so foolish. We did not . . . We were so foolish."

"You thought we would make an easy target. It was a sound idea overall, but you did not take the time to learn with whom you would be doing battle. Your impulsivity was your undoing."

"Please. I beg you to show mercy to our city. We are not a warring people by nature."

"I will show mercy only when and where it is due. You are prisoners of Kith now. Come passively to our dungeons or die here on the field. It is your choice."

"We will come," he said, his tone as defeated as he was.

On the walls of the keep, Sarielle could see that the battle was finished, but she was not sure which side had been victorious. She could see the overall picture, but the details escaped her.

But after a while it became very clear who had won. The city walls erupted in cheers and she felt her heart leap with relief and joy. They had won!

Koro, do you see Garreth?

At first Koro could not tell the difference between the "shiny" men. She told him to look for the armor with the wey flower emblazoned on the front of it. After a moment Koro came through to her, telling her that he could see him.

Is he all right? Is he moving?

He was, according to Koro.

Koro, come to me!

Koro banked in the sky in the distance and then came rushing toward her. He reached her within a minute and settled down, his clawed feet gripping the keep's walls, his nails digging into the stones. Sarielle hurried up to him.

"Bend your head to me!" she said.

Koro did so and she awkwardly climbed on top of his head, trying to move in the unfamiliar bulk of her armor. She straddled the back of his neck as best she could and gripped one of his scales.

"Take me to him!"

She had flown with Koro only once before. It had been the most terrifying and exhilarating experience of her life. Nothing had ever compared to it . . . until she had met Garreth. It was dangerous for her to ride him like this. The scale she held could come loose or she could slip and fall to the ground, which rushed beneath them, but her desire to find Garreth outweighed her fear of flying with Koro. She closed her eyes tight, so she wouldn't make herself sick watching the ground beneath her, and let Koro lead the way.

Just take it easy! If I fall, that will be the end of me!

Koro heeded her warning, flying very gently from the keep walls to the battlefield. He settled down beside Garreth and lowered his head to the ground so she could dismount.

Garreth could not believe his eyes. Had she just *flown* with that beast?

"Are you mad?" he barked at her. "I told you to stay on the keep walls! What if you had fallen? What if—"

"I didn't! The battle is over and it is safe now. I had to make sure you were all right." She reached to touch his neck where he had been wounded. He was short of breath from his exertions and from his compromised lung, and he was in a considerable amount of pain, but still he jerked away from her.

"Get back to the keep. *Now!*"

"But I—"

"Do not argue with me! It is not safe for you here! Get back to the keep and remain in your rooms for the rest of the night!"

"Are you *banishing* me?" she demanded of him, her shock profound.

"Sarielle, just do it! I cannot have my focus split. I need to know you are safe. Go!"

Sarielle felt the burn of tears threatening her eyes. "I just needed to know you were safe too," she said, her tone thoroughly wounded.

She turned to go from him but he grabbed her wrist

and drew her back. Thinking nothing of doing so in front of his enemies, he gently kissed her on her lips.

"I understand," he said. "Now go. Be safe. Walk through the gate, not on Koro's back. You nearly took my life in your hands when you did so. If anything were to happen to you . . . I do not know what my actions would be."

This mollified her a great deal, and she gave him a wavering smile. She walked away from him, ambling toward Koro's underbelly and giving him a hug.

Thank you. Now go home and be safe.

Koro sent her an impression of utter devotion that made her smile. At least she would always know exactly how he felt about her.

The same could not be said for Garreth.

She was in danger, she realized. She was in danger of falling in love with him. As she walked back to the keep, completely ignorant of her surroundings, she realized the magnitude of what she was thinking. Of what she was feeling.

It was hopeless. To love that man was a hopeless endeavor. He had warned her more than once that he was not free to give himself to her, that she had to be satisfied with what she could get. And she had thought she would be. She had thought she would be happy with the way things were.

But the truth was he would be leaving soon. Perhaps even sooner than she had realized, now that the Zizo army had been destroyed. It had been different when the possibility of them wintering there and battling the Zizo in the spring had been on the table. Now Garreth could walk into Zandaria without any opposition whatsoever. And that meant he would need to find a new city to conquer.

Oh, not right away. She knew that much. It would take time before both cities were strong enough and secure enough to be left on their own. But it would happen eventually.

Before that time came, she would need to leave. Leave him before he could leave her. She would pack up the twins and go. They would spend the winter together, but come the first touch of spring, she would go and never look back. Not too far. She didn't want to leave Koro too far behind her. But far enough. Just far enough.

If such a place even existed. She was afraid that nowhere she went would be far enough to escape the way she felt about him.

She wished she had the strength to leave right away. That very instant. But she didn't. She needed more time with him before they parted for good. She couldn't bear to go otherwise.

Dethan was sitting in the main hall when Davine entered the room on a cloud of soft perfume and wearing a silken gown. She never wore full skirts with layers of petticoats like most women in Kith did. She always wore floor-length gowns of free-flowing silk that most other women would wear in the privacy of their bedrooms, if they even dared to wear them at all.

The truth was that she was a very beautiful woman. Had Dethan not been married and in love with his wife he might have bedded her by then. Might have. There was far too much cunning in the woman. He had considered setting her loose on his brother, but that was beyond the pale even in his desperation. But what was he to do? Weysa would be furious if Garreth did not abide by his agreement with her. And when a goddess grew furious, bad things happened. As much as he respected Sarielle, as much as he did not want to see the girl hurt, Dethan would die before he would see his brother punished again because he failed Garreth once more. He had to find a way to keep them all happy.

It had been ten days since the Zizo had been defeated. Their army was split between the two cities of Zandaria and Kith . . . a position he was none too comfortable with. The mages were all in Zandaria with Garreth and Sarielle, handling any trickery the remaining rylings might come up with. Garreth and Dethan had been taking turns between the cities, but Dethan was growing uncomfortable and impatient. How was he to manage his brother if they were not in the same room with each other?

Fall was closing in and it was high time he was on the road and traveling back to his home and his wife. Selinda was asking for him in their missives to each other and he yearned to go, but he could not in good conscience leave his brother for a multitude of reasons. Sarielle being one. The fact that he was trying to control two cities being another. He did not know which of these two reasons took precedence, but they were equally bad.

"What is it?" he asked Davine shortly.

She smiled in the face of his surly mood.

"Do not fear," she said gently to him, trying to manage him. "Things will work out for the best."

To Davine's mind, she had things well in hand. She had spent the past days making very good friends with Sarielle. The girl was beginning to trust her advice implicitly. Davine had put herself very firmly in Sarielle's corner, and it was helping her to set the girl up for the heart-wrenching betrayal to come. When Davine was through with her, she would never love or trust anyone again.

"It does not seem so from my perspective," Dethan bit out.

"Then you are not looking with proper eyes."

"My patience wears thin, Davine." He cocked a look

at her. "What are you still doing here?" he asked her archly.

The query settled a cold sensation in Davine's stomach. She could not afford to anger this man or outlive her usefulness. She was still young and beautiful and could become mistress to any powerful man if she worked the situation properly, but she did not want to sleep with another odious man like the bennesah, his chubby hands fumbling around on her body. She wanted comfort without having to sell herself in the process. Then she could take whatever lover she desired rather than whatever lover would best serve her.

At first she had thought to coax one of the handsome and manly brothers to her bed, their power and money supreme enough to bring her the comfort she sought . . . and they would clearly know their way around a woman's body. A man could not have that much virility and come up short in the bedroom. They were confident and strong and it gave her delighted chills to imagine one or both in her bed.

But she could be just as happy without one of these brothers, as long as she could buy pretty things, be safe and warm in the luxury of her rooms in the winter, and be catered to by serving girls all throughout the turnings.

And all it would take was destroying the trust of one innocent girl.

"I hope I have made myself useful to you," she hedged.

"You have," Dethan agreed readily, giving her a small sensation of relief. "But I don't see what is in it for you."

"I'm sure I can be helpful to you in many ways," she said. "Ways that you may not yet realize. Keeping me close is purely to your benefit, I assure you. I only ask that my rooms be comfortable and my belly full of food. That is my only aspiration."

"Hmm," he voiced thoughtfully as he took her measure. "Well, you will have your comforts, Davine. You have earned them. See that you continue to be useful and those comforts will continue. There is always a place in a new regime for someone with clever intelligence and the ability to grasp situations quickly. Someone not afraid to take the initiative."

"It is my hope," Davine said softly, "that I can fill those requirements for you."

"Good."

Dethan left the room and the scheming girl behind him, not realizing the flurry of anxiety he had left in his wake. Davine felt time and opportunity were escaping her grasp. She needed to act and to do it quickly.

She took a breath, trying to force patience on herself.

"Easy," she murmured to herself. "Opportunity will come. Then . . . then he will see your true value."

She hoped so.

She was counting on it.

"Sarielle!" Davine cried when her friend came into the hall some hours later. Sarielle ran up to her and the two women hugged each other in delight.

Garreth, who was hot on Sarielle's heels, chuckled. "One would think you have been gone a full cycle of the moon rather than a mere pair of days, the way you two behave. We haven't been in Zandaria that long."

"Do not make fun of my sister," Davine said with a grin as she hugged Sarielle once again. "I will have to defend her if you do."

Garreth held up his hands with a grin. "I am defeated. I will let you two women catch up while I find my brother."

With that, Garreth left the room. Sarielle and Davine hugged again and Davine touched her face warmly.

"You look very happy," Davine noted.

"I am. He grows more wonderful by the day. I think . . ." Sarielle trailed off.

Davine led her to the furniture by the fire and sat her down. "What is it you think?" she encouraged her.

"I think he might be growing to love me a little," she said, turning her face down and coloring softly.

"What's not to love?" Davine asked warmly. "But . . . be careful. He is a man, and men tend to not be as emotionally invested as we women are. Do not mistake his lust for you as love for you."

Sarielle frowned and then bit her lip. "Do you think I am wrong, then?"

"I think you should be cautious. Protect your heart. But"—she smiled brightly—"how can he help but love you? You are beautiful and wonderful!"

The women laughed and hugged once more.

"How are the twins? I do hate to leave them, but I'm comforted that you are watching over them when I am gone," Sarielle said.

"They are well and grow happier by the day. They love to run about in the fields and go to the bazaar. I swear they utterly exhaust me as I try to keep up with them!"

Sarielle laughed. "No doubt! I thank you for watching over them."

"What are friends meant to do?" Davine asked with a warm smile. "I know one day you will return the favor. As it is, you have convinced Garreth to continue to keep me in comfort and for that I am grateful."

"You keep yourself in comfort," Sarielle insisted. "You have proven yourself very valuable to the brothers. Far more valuable than I am."

"Nonsense. You are a wrena. You are invaluable. The defeat of the Zizo proves it. Now, tell me all about Zandaria. I have heard that everything is encrusted with the gems they mine."

Shortly before dusk, Garreth was in the main hall poring over papers that tracked the troop placements in both cities. He was fortunate his army was so large; otherwise, he would be taking an inexcusable risk splitting it between two cities that did not want their encroaching presence. Even so, their army was drawn tightly between the two locations and their lieutenants were being heavily depended on. Luckily he and Dethan trusted the men. Men like the stalwart Tonkin were easy to trust. They were loyal and unshakable regardless of the tasks the brothers set for them. They came through every time. Without these men as leaders, the battle would have been one of dissonance and discord.

Davine entered the room just when he was beginning to think about leaving to attend to his nightly torment. He needed a little bit of lead time to make it to his place in the orchard, assuring he was alone and distanced from anyone who might see him or come to harm because of him. For when he froze, everything around him froze as well.

Davine approached, her hand coming to settle on his back between his shoulders. She often did this; he no longer thought anything of it. She was the sort of being who liked to touch others in whatever way she could, almost as if it were second nature to her. It did not seem as though she were trying to win him into her bed, as he had begun to suspect before she became friends with Sarielle. But he now knew, through Sarielle, the women were close, so he could not suspect Davine would think of betraying her. In fact, Sarielle chattered on about her adventures with Davine almost endlessly, and he was grateful to the other woman for befriending his otherwise friendless Sarielle. She had sorely needed a companion, and Davine fit the bill perfectly.

"You seem weary," Davine observed as she leaned over him and began to read over his shoulder. Again, he thought nothing of it. She had always done this as she helped to advise them on matters of great importance in the city.

"It has been a long day," he confessed.

"Is there anything I might provide for your present relief?" she asked, her hands drifting up to his shoulders, where she began to massage away the tension in his neck. He tensed a moment, finding the intimacy a little disquieting, but then he reminded himself of Davine's nature and of her devotion to Sarielle. He relaxed and allowed her to give him the small comfort.

"What I need you cannot provide," he told her honestly.

What he needed was Sarielle. It was a need that grew more intense with every passing day. And with that need came the desire to find a way to continue to be with her. Oh, it was a dangerous pastime to be sure. He was risking the wrath of a goddess. But surely there was some way he could satisfy both desires—his desire to serve Weysa and his desire to have Sarielle.

He had labored over and over this problem and had yet to find a solution. It was disheartening and frustrating, and on top of trying to manage two cities and his brother's growing dissatisfaction with the situation, it was exhausting. His only solace was Sarielle. And now perhaps a brief massage by Davine.

He closed his eyes and allowed himself a moment of relaxation. Soon enough he would fall under the sway of his curse. He was allowed a brief respite, was he not?

But brief was all it could be. Dusk was almost upon him. After a minute or two he reached up and stopped Davine's thoughtful work on his tension. He took her hand in his and drew her around to his right side so he could see her.

"Thank you, Davine," he said. "You have been a great treasure to me."

And it was true. She had helped him gain control of this city and she had been kind to his Sarielle. She helped care for the twins when he and Sarielle were away and she was thoughtful in every other way.

He stood up and moved around her, leaving the room.

In the entryway on the other side of the hall, standing slightly in shadow, was Sarielle. She was blinking her eyes, trying to absorb what she had just seen. Trying to make sense of it. She had seen the intimacy of Davine's massage and had heard the intimacy of Garreth's words. It was everything she could do to keep herself from jumping to wild conclusions and a feeling of betrayal.

It was not possible that they could deceive her in such a way, she thought firmly. Garreth cared for her and so did Davine. She was reading too much into it.

Deciding that was the way of it, she turned away from the hall and left.

For Davine's part, she had known all along that Sarielle was there, watching them. In fact, she had timed things just so Sarielle would see them. Which was no mean feat. But she had pulled it off.

Now she had an entirely different task to accomplish. When Sarielle had left the entryway, Davine hurried after Garreth. She swept a cloak out of the hands of the serving girl she'd had waiting in the shadows of the hall and put it on, pulling the hood over her head. She had called for a horse to be ready and brought to the side of the keep's bailey. Garreth's horse was in the bailey itself, awaiting its master just as it did every night before dusk. Garreth was out of the keep and onto his horse in a swift display of strength almost seconds after she had gotten herself in her saddle. She was not used to riding, so she felt awkward in the saddle, but she did not care. She needed to find out the nature of Garreth's nightly disappearances. She knew this was a point of contention in Sarielle's relationship with him, and therefore it could be an effective weapon.

She did not think he went to meet a woman. No, if she was reading the situation right, he was definitely devoted to Sarielle. More so every day. But she was at a loss to explain what it was he could possibly be doing every night. She had decided there was only one way to find out and that was to follow him. Doing so with stealth was the only trick. She had to keep a good distance between them, and yet she was afraid of losing sight of him. She was grateful when they reached the orchard because the trees provided a good deal of cover that the open fields had not.

Once they reached the depths of the orchard, she realized he had stopped and dismounted. Some distance away, she did the same and held her horse, keeping it quiet as she watched him pace restlessly in a small circle in amongst the trees.

Was he waiting for someone? Perhaps he was meeting a lover after all. That would be a definitive nail in the coffin of his relationship with Sarielle. However, it would rob Davine of the opportunity to bring about such an end in a way that would make her appear indispensible to Dethan. But she was really good at reading people and she would truly be shocked if infidelity were the case. In fact, she would dare to say that Garreth would rather cut off a limb than do purposeful harm to Sarielle.

The sun dropped below the horizon and Garreth came to a halt. As she stood watching, she saw his breath begin to cloud on the air, which was odd because it was not that cold. Not right away, anyway. But as she stood there, hiding, she felt the temperature drop rapidly. So rapidly she began to shiver with the shock of it. Though at a distance, both horses nickered with discomfort, but if Garreth heard them, he was not visibly reacting to it. Instead he seemed to be focused entirely within himself.

And that was when she heard the first crackle of sound, the sound of creaking wood under strain. Frost began to coat the ground at Garreth's feet, a sheet of white that grew outward in a near perfect circle.

Then everything began to freeze. Sheets of ice began to form on the ground as Garreth shouted out in a sound of pure tormented pain. He fell to his knees as his body shook, and ice crept over him. He froze fast to the ground before Davine's stunned eyes, his hair forming into icicles, his skin a frosted, frozen sheet of ice.

She saw him draw in a last breath before he was frozen into a solid, unmoving block of ice.

Davine did not dare move any closer, the cold of the area surrounding him beating her back, not to mention her pure fear of the situation. So this was his secret, she thought as the hours wore on. This . . . this . . . curse. This happened every night? He suffered this every night? It was beyond cruel. It was, she realized, the work of the gods. That was the only explanation. He was cursed by the gods themselves.

For a moment she was torn between the fear of getting too close to a man so cursed and the sudden sickening feeling that she was so incredibly wrong to be thinking of robbing him of the only solace he had in the face of this. Robbing him of Sarielle.

But his brother had to know all of this. Dethan had to know Garreth was cursed in such a way. He was far too sharp a man for something like this to go unnoticed by him. He knew of this and yet he still wanted to take Sarielle away from his brother.

Perhaps, she thought with a feeling of total dread, it was because Dethan knew something that neither she nor Sarielle was aware of. Regardless of his reasons, they had to be worth heeding. It was unwise to meddle in the affairs of the gods. Davine worried that Sarielle would be caught up in this curse along with Garreth. Perhaps that was Dethan's worry as well.

That was when Davine realized a small part of her had actually grown to care for Sarielle. That, to her increasing shock, she had actually begun to feel like a genuine friend to the wrena. Sarielle was an innocent in all of this. She didn't mean any harm to anyone. She was just a girl in love with a man.

But he was not just any man. He was a cursed soul. It was wrong of him to potentially expose her to such dangers. Very wrong. He knew it himself or he would have already told Sarielle about the curse. And Davine knew he had not told her. She knew that their friendship was one in which Sarielle trusted Davine with even the most intimate of details concerning Garreth. Sarielle would have told her.

Davine did not need to wait to see what would happen next. She needed to get back to Kith long before they closed the gates for the night, long before she would be missed. As she rode hard for the city, she was more determined than ever to drive a wedge between Sarielle and Garreth. And she was afraid she knew exactly how to do it.

CHAPTER
TWENTY

About a week later Sarielle was playing with the twins, but her mind was troubled. She continued to find herself coming around a corner here or there and running into Davine and Garreth, alone, together. It was now happening far too frequently for her to dismiss. She wanted to ask her friend about it, but she was afraid she was mistaken and asking might cost her the only friendship she had.

She was making herself sick over it. Very often she would be sick to her stomach after finding them together in yet another close situation. She also found herself unable to sleep. Her body was weary from head to toe from the lack of it. But then every night he would call her to him and make love to her so fiercely she realized she had to be mistaken. He could not possibly treat her with such ferocious devotion and yet be deceptive at the same time . . . could he? And Davine could not possibly laugh and keep secrets with her and help her learn more ways to seduce her lover each night when she might be trying to seduce him herself . . . could she?

No. It was impossible. She should not suspect either one of them, she thought as she gnawed on her lower lip. All she had to do was remember that very morning . . .

She had been sitting up in bed, watching Garreth sleep, the early morning sunlight spilling over him, turning his tanned skin to a beautiful golden color. He was lightly freckled in all the places the sun touched him. He was on his stomach, one of the thick, down pillows tucked up tightly under his unshaven cheek. His hair was curling softly around his ears and against the back of his neck. As he breathed deeply in sleep, she was amazed at how the sound of his breathing, his signs of life, made her feel so incredibly good and so alive herself. It should be against the laws of nature to feel this good about someone, and perhaps it was. Perhaps it was a very bad idea to be allowing herself to adore him this thoroughly.

"That is very unnerving," he murmured sleepily.

She smiled. "What is?"

He stretched, rolled over onto his back, and smiled. His smile creasing across his face first thing in the morning had to be one of the most beautiful things she had ever seen.

"To awaken because I am being stared at."

She scooted down so she could rest her cheek over his heart. "I cannot help myself. You are simply too beautiful to resist."

"That amuses me because I was going to say the same thing," he murmured against the top of her head.

She smiled again and blushed warmly, emotion blossoming through her like pure happiness. There couldn't possibly be anything bad in the world that she couldn't face when he made her feel like this.

"What else were you going to say?" she asked. "Tell me and I will tell you if I was going to say the same thing."

She knew he was smiling. She heard it in his voice when he said, "I was going to say what a lovely day it is."

"Mmm. Me too," she said, lifting her head and beaming down at him. Their mouths were now scant inches apart.

"I was going to say I have never seen anything as re-markable as your eyes."

"Me too," she said.

His tone lowered significantly. "I was going to say that how much I want to kiss you right now cannot pos-sibly be measured."

"Me too," she breathed, just before he put a hand to the back of her head and drew her down to his mouth in a blistering kiss. He devoured her mouth easily and with great passion, as though he had not kissed her for many days of separation rather than a few hours of sleep.

He drew away from her to add, "And I was going to say how much I wanted to put my mouth on the most intimate areas of your body."

"Me too," she said on a sigh before she realized what she was saying. She did realize it when he chuck-led though. "Oh! Very funny," she said. Then she lifted herself a little, looked down into his eyes, and said silk-ily, "Me too."

"I—" He cut himself off when her hand suddenly slid beneath the warm bedding and wrapped around his thickly rousing penis.

She licked her lips and his cock stiffened almost in-stantly in her hand.

"I was just teasing you," he said, his voice low from more than just being awakened.

"Now so am I, teasing you," she pointed out, her thumb coming to rim the crown of him. He sucked a breath in through his teeth and let it out slowly. His hips shifted, pushing him against her palm.

"And a fine job of it you are doing," he praised her.

"This is merely a fine job," she pointed out. "Wait until I do an excellent job."

She pushed back the bedding, exposing him to the cool morning air. She slid down his body a little and the hand in her hair tightened instinctively. She breathed against him, inhaling the musky, masculine smell of him. The edges of her nails drifted down the length of him and she watched him lift into her touch as though he were a well-heeled pet answering to her every command. It was a powerful thought. A powerful feeling. To have such a man as this—one so strong and virile, so dominant and potent—submissive to her desires, it was beyond compare. And because she enjoyed the feeling so much, she was willing to do everything she could to experience more.

She licked her lips again, and again he twitched.

"Would you like my mouth on you?" she asked in a husky whisper.

"More than you will ever know," he said intensely.

"Well, far be it for me to deny you anything," she said with a sly smile.

"Mordu," he groaned just as her kiss was dropping on the tip of his erection.

She liked it when he invoked the god of love and passion. Of hope and dreams. Every other moment of the day his attention and devotion was to Weysa. But here, with her, it was always Mordu. Surely . . . surely that meant something, she thought as she touched her tongue to him. Surely it meant that he felt something for her. Something he gave to no one else.

He tasted salty on her tongue, musky with sleep and the remnants of their lovemaking the night before. She licked him, down the entire length of him, all the way to the thatch of curls springing up around the base of his hard staff. She licked him all the way back up again, as if she were painting him with her tongue. It was such an erotic idea that she shivered a little. Then he shivered too.

"Gods, woman, you're enough to make a grown man weep for joy."

She smiled at that and decided to reward him by employing the use of her hand. She scraped her nails along the underside of the soft sac beneath his cock and felt him tense. But she knew she had not hurt him in the least, had not come even close to it, and she was pleased she had come so far in her knowledge of her lover's body. In her knowledge of what pleased him. She pleased him, she had come to learn. There was little she could do that was wrong in his eyes, especially when they were in bed together.

She wrapped her hand around the thickness of him, as always quite amazed by the sheer girth of him. Then she placed that girth within her mouth and against her tongue.

He groaned soulfully, his hips lifting once again, pushing himself farther in, past her lips, as his hands came to frame her face. She drew him in deep, then sucked on him as she drew him back out again, eliciting a moan from him. She repeated this, frequently, and got more of the same as her reward. It was nothing bad and everything good. Between his shallowly thrusting hips and her eagerly working mouth, she had him invoking Mordu's name with greater and greater intensity.

"Oh, sweet Sarielle, you're going to be the death of me," he said through clenched teeth.

She hoped so. She worked for it. Worked to taste that sweetly salty fluid she could coax from his body. She touched him along the insides of his thighs, molded the malleable sac, combed through the coarse hair. She touched him every way she could think of as she drew on him with lips, mouth, and tongue.

"Stop, stop, stop," he hissed. "Fira, as good as this is, I want to make love to you too," he said.

She pulled away just long enough to say "No."

Then she doubled her efforts, employed everything she had ever learned about how to make him feel good. She remembered the first time he had coaxed her to do this, explaining to her that it was an ultimate pleasure, just as his mouth on her was an ultimate pleasure. She had been addicted ever since.

But Garreth was not a man to be gainsaid. He grabbed for her, his hands on her hip and thigh jerking her around and across him until she was kneeling on either side of his shoulders, all the while her mouth never leaving him. He spread her thighs wide until she was brought down against his mouth and his tongue was darting out and touching her on her sensitive little nub. His hands curved up her thighs and over her backside, pulling her down tighter. Now he was sucking against her and she was the one moaning, in spite of still having her mouth around him. As his tongue darted and danced, she began to squirm and pull harder on him. Pleasure spiraled through her, in lapping tides that matched the lapping of his tongue.

She couldn't focus on two things at once, she found herself thinking frantically. His mouth was so much magic that she wanted to simply lie back and get lost in the feelings. But then he would win and he would make her stop. She refused to. She wanted to give him this. More than anything. So she redoubled her efforts, wrapping her hand around him and pumping him in time with the sucking of her mouth. His fingers began to dig into her backside and he ground out fierce sounds of pleasure against her.

"Fira! *Fira!*" he cried against her just as his hips lunged upward and he exploded against her tongue. She tasted the heat and seed of him against her tongue, and she swallowed it down with joy and pleasure. She had done it. Made him unravel before he'd had the chance to do the same to her.

But before she had an instant to enjoy her victory, he was throwing her over in the bed so she was flat on her back and resettling himself between her legs. He thrust two fingers inside her and latched his mouth onto her. She cried out from the overpowering sensation of it, finally able to relax back and let herself tumble into it. She burrowed her hands into his hair, gripping and holding him to herself, not that he needed the encouragement. For all she was expecting it, her first orgasm blindsided her, making her weak and free flying. She had only ever known such exhilaration when riding on Koro's neck, and now here, in this bed, with Garreth.

He did not stop. Not even after a second orgasm ripped through her. It was only after the third, when she was begging him, that he finally let her go. Then he flipped her over once more, jerked her up onto her knees, and set the fronts of his thighs against the backs of hers. With a lunging thrust, he put himself deep inside her, proving himself to be just as hard as he had been before she had brought him to pleasure.

Then he pounded himself into her, forcing her to press the heels of her palms into the mattress to keep herself from sliding away from him. He pummeled her hips with his until she was spinning and reeling with pleasure the way Koro reeled and turned in the sky. She came so hard she saw bright lights behind her tightly squeezed eyelids. And then she heard him coming as well, the sound of it so guttural and harsh that it almost sounded like pain.

When he was done, he braced himself against her body, gasping for his every breath, his big body shuddering in fine tremors. She was no different, her whole body shaking from her pleasure.

She felt him fall away from her, rolling onto his back beside her, still dragging for breath. He turned his head and looked at her, a sloppy grin on his mouth.

"It's a good thing I'm immortal," he said. "It's going to take some time before I ever get tired of that."

The words had made her soar. It had been the closest she had ever come to getting him to say he wanted to be with her for longer than just a winter. Oh, she knew it might be a foolish sort of hope to have, but she had not been able to help herself.

"Sarielle! Did you see the new dolls Garreth bought us from the bazaar?" Jona asked, showing her the doll she had gotten. Isaelle showed her hers too.

Sarielle smiled at the girls, but a wave of inexplicable tears came over her. She hastily blinked them away, but they did not go unnoticed by her keen sisters.

"Sarielle, why are you crying?" Isaelle asked. She was the quieter, more introspective of the twins, while Jona was the social butterfly, animated and a little wild.

"Oh, it is nothing, my little love," she said with a smile that did not reach her eyes. If she thought she was fooling the girls, she was sorely misguided.

"Why should you be sad? We are not slaves anymore. Garreth treats us very kindly. He loves you a great deal," Isaelle said.

That got Sarielle's immediate attention. "Why would you say that?" she asked her.

"Oh, we can see it."

"Yes, we can see it," Jona said. "Will you marry him? I should like him for a brother."

"Yes, I should like him too," Isaelle said.

"Oh, I don't think that will happen, my little loves," she said, new tears burning into her eyes.

"Why not?" they asked in unison.

"It is very complicated," she said, wiping her eyes.

"You love him, don't you?" Jona asked.

"Yes. You do," Isaelle answered for her. "And if you

love each other, now that you are no longer a slave, you get married."

It was as simple as that to the girls. Sarielle did not know how to explain it to them. She barely knew how to explain it to herself.

Just then the door to the nursery opened and a serving girl entered the room. She shyly approached Sarielle with a note in her hands.

"I . . . I found this on the table in the hall. I thought it might be yours," she said, holding the note out to her.

Sarielle thanked her and took the note. The girl beat a very hasty retreat. Sarielle read the note.

I want you. I need you. Come to me now.
                                                              —Garreth

Sarielle blushed. She wondered if the girl had read the note. *Of course she has. Don't be silly. How else would she have known it was meant for you?* But why would Garreth leave such a private note where anyone could find it? How was it the message had not made it directly into her hands?

It didn't matter. He wanted her to come to him right away and she would obey him.

"I have to go, my little loves," she said hastily. She gave each a quick kiss and then retreated from the room. She hurried through the hallways, her heart beating hard within her chest. It should not mean so much to her that he wanted her like this, but it did. It meant the world to her that he felt so strongly for her. It was not a declaration of love, it was not a promise that they would be together always, but it was the next best thing.

She entered her rooms and quickly looked in the mirror, tidying a few strands of her hair. She reached for the perfume Davine had talked her into buying— a light, warm scent—and quickly applied it to her skin at her wrists, her neck, and the spot between her breasts that Davine had told her was a must. She straightened her skirts, then laughed at herself. Surely Garreth would not care if her skirts were straight. He usually did not allow them to be on her body for very long once he saw her in private anyway.

She opened the door they shared between their rooms and entered his bedroom, closing the door behind her. As she came farther into the room, she was surprised when she did not see him standing there or sitting waiting for her by the fire, but she did see a body tangled up in the sheets in the bed. At first she was amused that he was already naked and waiting for her.

Until she realized that the person in the bed had deep violet skin and was very much a woman.

Sarielle felt her entire world spin away from her as she realized the reason why the note had not been sent directly into her hands. Because it had not been meant for her.

Davine. It was Davine who was sleeping in Garreth's bed, looking for all the world as though she had been vigorously tumbled within it. Sarielle should know, for she had often looked exactly like that once Garreth had been through with her.

Sarielle reached out to steady herself with the nearest piece of furniture she could grab. It was a chair sitting in front of the fire. Her brain burned with a flash of memory of Garreth sitting naked within the chair, Sarielle straddling his lap as she rode him to orgasm. He had gripped her body then as if he had never wanted to let her go. He had gasped for breath against her neck, his face buried in her hair. Their skin had been damp with the sweat of their exertions.

But now the chair was empty and Garreth's bed was filled with the body of another woman. The note had been sent to Davine.

I want you. I need you. Come to me now.

He had written those words to Davine and Davine had left the note behind by accident. Now she lay sleeping in his bed after . . . after . . .

Tears were not coming. She needed them to come, to blur her vision so she could not see what she was seeing. She heard Davine too. The deep, lusty breaths of a woman well into sleep. Driven there no doubt by exhaustion.

Numbly, Sarielle turned back toward the door she had come through. She walked toward it with deadened, jarring steps, her hands reaching for one piece of furniture and then another, the only way she could keep herself from falling to the floor in a crumbling heap of bones. She made it to the door somehow and fell against it, her hand gripping the doorknob for all she was worth.

Suddenly Koro's thoughts flooded into her mind, swamping her with his concern and sharp worry over her distress.

I am fine. Please . . . please do not worry.

She was begging him. Praying he would believe her.

But he did not.

Sarielle could not bear it. She opened the door and lurched through it. Slamming it shut behind her, she stumbled for the basin beside her dressing table and vomited. She sobbed then, tears finally coming. She crumpled to the floor and began to cry.

But no sooner had her first tears fallen than the door between her room and Garreth's was opening and Davine, wrapped in a sheet from the bed, was coming toward her. Sarielle wanted to scream at the sight, backing away to try to escape her.

"Sarielle! Oh, Sarielle, I'm so sorry! Please! Please forgive me! I-I had no choice! If I didn't . . . I would find myself out on the street with nothing! I-I didn't want to! You are my friend and . . . I tried to warn you this might happen. That this is the way men are. Please . . ." Tears were in her eyes as she dropped to her knees before Sarielle. "Please forgive me. I never meant to hurt you."

Sarielle couldn't manage the jumble that was her emotions. And all the while Koro was in her head, demanding she tell him what was wrong.

Frustrated, he told her he was coming for her.

"Please don't," she whispered aloud. Whether she was speaking to Koro or Davine, she didn't know.

"I . . . I'll go," Davine said softly, her gaze turned away. "I'll go and I won't come back."

"No," Sarielle said numbly. "You can't. You have nowhere to go. I-I'll go. I'll take the twins and . . . Yes. I'll go."

"Where will you go?" Davine asked quietly.

"Anywhere. Anywhere but here."

"But will you be safe?"

"I have Koro to protect us. Please . . . if you ever cared for me . . . help me to go."

"I do care for you. And I'll help you. Just let me get dressed."

The reminder made fresh tears burn into Sarielle's eyes. She wiped them away fiercely. She nodded to Davine. "Where is he?" she asked, her voice, her entire body, trembling.

"He went to Zandaria."

"I should . . . should I tell him?"

"Why? You don't owe him anything. You need to be as far from him as possible. He is cursed and would bring you down with him."

"C-cursed?" she stammered.

"Yes. He told me. That's why he leaves every night at dusk. He is cursed to freeze every night from dusk until juquil's hour."

"He . . . he told you?" The one thing, *the one thing* he

had refused to talk with her about . . . and he had told *her* about it. Shared it with Davine, not her.

A curse. She thought of what he had told her, about his immortality. Thought about all those times after juquil's hour when she had been able to see his breath on the air even when it wasn't cold . . . when his body had been so inexplicably cold, how he always warmed himself by the fire before coming to her . . . and she knew it was the truth.

"Help me," she said to Davine, meeting her friend's troubled blue eyes.

"I will. Wait for me here."

It was an easy request, for Sarielle did not think she would be able to move.

Davine stood up and hurried into Garreth's bedroom. She hastily dressed in her clothing, all the while telling herself that this was for the best. For all involved. Sarielle would be safer away from Garreth. She would suffer a broken heart, but she would heal after a while. It would just take a little time. That was all. Davine would earn her comfortable life and Garreth's brother would be satisfied.

As for Garreth . . . Well, she didn't much care about him. He had endangered her friend knowingly. Brought his curse to her doorstep. Sarielle was an innocent just learning how to be free. She didn't need the weight of Garreth's burdens.

Davine hurried back to Sarielle's side.

Sarielle was numb as she went through the process of packing her things. Luckily Davine was there to help her. She wasn't taking much. Just a change of clothes for herself. She felt Koro coming all the while and knew she needed to meet him on the keep walls or he would tear the place apart looking for her. She sent Davine to fetch the girls as she ran up to the walls and met Koro.

He saw her tears, felt her broken heart. He bristled

in frustration to feel her in such pain, knowing she wouldn't let him help her.

I am going to leave this place for a little while, my love.

He immediately wanted to go with her.

I need to hide, Koro. If you are with me, then I will be found.

A wave of loneliness beat at her. He was afraid to be by himself.

I am always with you and you are always with me. In our minds and in our hearts. We will forever be together. And you can come find me in a little while. Just . . . remain safe in your cave. Now, come close. I need to take some of the shiny things from your scales.

Koro came closer to her and lowered himself down so she could work some of the precious stones free from his scales. They would help buy her escape. She did not know where she was going, but she knew she had to go as quietly as possible; otherwise, Garreth might come after her. Although she didn't see why he would. He had clearly moved on. Away from her. Why would he care if she left?

Koro flew away from her after she had what she needed, heading back to his cave as she had requested. He was such an obedient creature and she was very fortunate to have him. She had never taken being a wrena for granted. She knew how blessed she was.

And cursed.

She gathered up the girls, and Davine quickly found them a conveyance. It was a wagon going to the city of Zandaria. Even though it was going toward where Garreth was, there she could switch to another conveyance and slip away unseen and unknown. She would be lost in the sea of Kithians who had been invading Zandaria since its fall. She simply had to avoid Garreth.

To that end, she waited for dusk to leave, knowing that

his curse would keep him in a fixed place until juquil's hour. By then she would have hoped to have left Zandaria, perhaps as part of a trade caravan, and escaped into the darkness of the night. The Zizo had perfect eyesight in the dark, unlike Kithians and, she assumed, Garreth and Dethan. She and her sisters would easily be able to travel throughout the night if she paid a Zizo driver to leave as soon as possible.

With her plans firmly in place in her mind, she left Kith forever.

Davine sought out Dethan as soon as Sarielle had left the city.

"She is gone."

Dethan looked up from his papers and lifted a brow. "I'm sorry. Who is gone?"

"Sarielle."

Dethan stilled and eyed her for a long moment. "Are you telling me that Sarielle has left Kith . . . for good?"

"Yes. I knew you wanted her gone . . . and now she is. And it is done in such a way that nothing Garreth can say or do will bring her back to him," she promised Dethan.

"How did you do it?" he asked carefully.

"I made her believe he had bedded me," she said quietly as she studied her clasped hands. When all of this had begun she had been looking out for herself, had been selfishly motivated. But now . . . She was not proud of what she had done. She had been seeking comfortable circumstances, but she did not feel comfortable. She did not feel safe and secure. She felt . . . dirty. Like she had done something her soul might never recover from.

"And that is all? All it took?" he asked her.

"Yes," she said quietly. "She loves him. The betrayal . . . It was more than she could stand."

Dethan frowned. Like Davine had said, he had wanted her gone and therefore should be happy with the results she had wrought, with the success of what she had set out to do, but for some reason he felt uneasy and . . . unclean. Even though he had not asked Davine to do this, he had made no secret of his desire to drive them apart. Now this was the result of his selfish desires.

He knew Garreth cared for the girl far more than he ought to, that he perhaps even loved her, despite his claims otherwise. Dethan had never seen his brother so devoted to a woman before. Had never seen Garreth behave with such single-minded loyalty with a woman. He would not easily let this go, Dethan realized. He would no doubt try to hunt her down and bring her back.

"How did she leave? Won't he be able to track her?"

"He won't be able to. We hired a wagon to take her to Zandaria. Once she makes it there, she will switch to another way of travel and he will never be able to track her."

"But no doubt he will try," Dethan said absently.

"I can delay his realization of her escape for a night. If he returns to Kith from Zandaria tonight, I'll send him a note saying she decided to sleep with the twins tonight and perhaps he will not seek her out."

"If he tries to and realizes the twins are gone, he will be after her immediately."

"You must convince him to wait until daylight. That will give her more time."

If Dethan did that, then he would be taking an active part in this. He would be even more responsible for the entire business than he already was. Troubled, he said, "Thank you, Davine."

"This . . . this is what you wanted, is it not?" she

asked uneasily. She felt sick in her soul. She needed to know it was the right thing to do. That it had been for a reason.

"Yes," Dethan said carefully. "Though I did not wish to hurt the girl in the process. She is a good person and did not deserve such pain."

"It was no more pain than she would have suffered had she stayed," Davine said with a lift to her chin.

"What's that supposed to mean?" Dethan asked sharply.

"Separating them was the right thing to do," she said, although she sounded as though she was trying to convince herself even as she was saying it to him. "Your brother is cursed. He would have brought that curse down upon my friend."

"So she is your friend now?"

"Yes," she admitted quietly. "And because she is my friend, I would have her escape him. I would say unscathed, but she is not. She is deeply wounded by this and I must accept my hand in that. But it was to a better purpose."

"You are right. My brother is cursed. And this is for the better where all are concerned."

"I think I will find my bed now. I am very weary," Davine said, her head down.

"Good night, Davine."

She left without ever once asking for compensation for her actions. She no longer cared about that. She no longer wanted a reward for causing such pain to another.

CHAPTER
TWENTY-ONE

It was long past juquil's hour when Garreth returned to the keep at Kith. He was drained from all his traveling and he felt as though his time in the orchard had been particularly brutal that night. He was looking forward to his bed and Sarielle's warm body against his.

When he entered his room and saw she was not in his bed he was surprised. The covers were tossed about, as if someone had been sleeping within them. But he figured she was having one of her restless nights, which she had been having with increasing frequency these past nights. She would not tell him what was troubling her, and he had not pressed her. After all, if she wanted to keep something from him, he had no right to demand she tell him. Not when he was keeping his own secrets and had been so voluble about holding her at a distance regarding that secret.

There was a note on his pillow.

With a furrowed brow, he read it.

Sleeping with the twins tonight. I will see you in the morning.

—Sarielle

The furrow of his brow deepened. Of course it wasn't the first time she had decided to sleep with the twins. She had done so before when Jona had had an unexpected nightmare one night. Perhaps that was the case tonight as well. The girls still had some trauma to deal with in the wake of their kidnapping.

Tapping the small note against his fingertips, he moved to stand in front of the fire, trying to chase away the remaining chill his curse had left behind.

Something wasn't right.

He didn't know what, and he didn't know why he was feeling this way, but something wasn't right and he had always followed his instincts. They had gotten him through more than one tight spot over his lifetime of crusading.

He went into her room and looked around. Nothing seemed out of place at first, until an acrid smell reached his nose. He followed the smell to a basin where someone—he presumed it was Sarielle—had thrown up the contents of their stomach.

Concerned now, he made his way out of the room and headed down the hallway to the twins' rooms. When he opened the door, the bottom fell out of his world.

The beds were empty.

That could mean any number of things, he tried to tell himself. They could be anywhere in the keep. But something was telling him, warning him, that wasn't the case. He went into the room adjoining that of the twins. Inside he found Moyra, asleep in her bed.

"Moyra! Where are the twins?" he asked, roughly shaking her awake.

Looking at him through sleepy eyes she said, "Sarielle came and packed them up. She said they were going to be traveling with you. Are they not with you?"

"No. They are not."

Garreth left the room and tore through the keep,

waking whomever he could on the way to his brother's rooms. When he got there, he thundered on the door, then let himself in.

To his surprise, his brother was awake, sitting in front of a fire and nursing a drink. A hard, blue liquor the Kithians made called gazz.

His brother was not one for hard alcohol. Dethan did not like to dull his senses in any way. The drinking of wine was usually the most he would engage in.

But the understanding was brief in Garreth's mind, his thoughts turned elsewhere and panicked.

"Sarielle is gone! The twins as well."

"I'm sure she's somewhere," Dethan said with a frown as he continued to stare into the fire.

"Dethan!" Garreth went up to his brother and stood in Dethan's line of sight. "Help me find her!"

"Garreth, she'll turn up," Dethan said, taking another swallow from his glass. He then swirled the blue liquor around in the glass, watching the color in the firelight.

"What is wrong with you?" Garreth snapped. "I'm asking for your help here!"

"And you shall have it." Dethan rose to his feet slowly and met his brother's eyes, spreading his arms out wide. "What would you have me do? Run around screaming for her? The servants would be better at that than I."

"You can start by figuring out who wrote this." He held the note up before Dethan's eyes. "I didn't notice it at first, but it is not Sarielle's handwriting."

"How do you know that?"

"Sarielle draws a line beneath her name when she signs something."

"Perhaps she forgot."

"She does it by rote!" Garreth snapped. "Someone has taken Sarielle and the twins! They left this note to delay me! Moyra said she left of her own accord, but I do not believe that."

"And who would take her?"

"Anyone who wants control of the wyvern!"

"Yes, but until you figure out who, there is little we can do about it."

"We can go searching for her!"

"In the dark? The Zizo may be able to see in the pitch of night, but I cannot."

"The Zizo? The Zizo! It must be the Zizo who have taken her! They will try to use the wyvern against us in retaliation for taking their city!"

"The Zizo are defeated. The only ones left of them are the women, the elderly, and the young. All else are dead or imprisoned."

"All the more reason for them to want revenge. We have killed all their men and—"

"So you think it's revenge based, then? Not even a matter of trying to get the city back?"

"Yes!"

"Where is your proof of this? You are engaging in wild speculation."

"Wild . . . ? Dethan, what is wrong with you? Can't you see the danger in this?"

"Of course I can," Dethan said after clearing his throat. "But that may not be the only explanation."

"What else could it possibly be?"

"Perhaps . . . Has it not occurred to you that she may have left of her own accord, as Moyra has told you?"

Garreth's breath froze in his chest as surely as if it were dusk in the orchard.

"What do you know?" he hissed.

"Nothing," his brother lied to him. Garreth knew it was a lie because Dethan would not meet his eyes.

Garreth lost all control. He grabbed Dethan by the front of his shirt, knocking the glass out of his hand. It broke upon the stone floor. He slammed Dethan's back into the stone wall that bracketed the fireplace, following him with the crush of his body and all his strength.

"What have you done?!" he roared.

"I have done nothing," Dethan said, wedging an arm beneath his brother's and shoving Garreth off himself. "I only mean to say she is a free woman of means! She can go anywhere, do anything! And she doesn't have to answer to you for it!"

"No!" Garreth ground out. "Ours is not the kind of relationship in which she would simply vanish without telling me where she was going and why!"

"And just what kind of relationship is it that you have?" Dethan demanded of him. "A close one? A loving one? You know as well as I do that you are not free to give her those things. And perhaps she knows it as well. Have you thought about that? Perhaps she has left you before you could leave her!"

Garreth ground his teeth together as his head spun with thoughts and he tried to make sense of them all, to keep them calm and ordered. Losing his temper would not serve him in finding her, he told himself sternly.

"No. She would not leave me without word."

"So you say. Perhaps word is coming . . . in the morning. When she expects you to miss her."

Garreth held up the note. "Someone else wrote this," he said through his teeth, "and I am going to find out who that someone is. They are going to know what happened to her!" Garreth paced. "Davine!" he said suddenly and with triumph. "They are the best of friends, Dethan! If anyone knows anything about what Sarielle's true thoughts and feelings are, it will be Davine. We will speak to her and you will see . . . you will see she did not go on purpose!"

Garreth bolted out of the room. Dethan turned back

to his decanter of gazz and took a long drink, foregoing the glass this time.

Garreth made it to Davine's rooms in record time. He banged on the door impatiently and incessantly until a sleepy serving girl opened it.

"My mistress is sleeping," she said crankily.

"I am awake," Davine said from behind her. She was pulling a robe on over a fully sheer gown just like the one Sarielle wore to bed. For a moment he could see the entirety of her body. But it meant nothing to him.

"Davine, where is Sarielle?"

"She is not with you?" she asked.

Again he was faced with another person who would not meet his eyes. What was wrong with everyone? Couldn't they appreciate what was happening? Sarielle could be in danger. Or she could have . . . could have run away. Although why she would run away escaped him. Her reasons would not matter. He was getting her back . . . whether he had to rescue her from something or someone or she had run away, whatever it turned out to be, he would lay eyes on her again by the end of the day tomorrow or so help him . . .

"No, she is not with me. If she were with me, I would not be looking for her!"

"Of course," Davine said. She brushed her hair back nervously. "Did she not leave a note for you?"

Now, that was beyond odd. He looked down at the note in his hand, his eyes keen on all the points that made it an obviously feminine script. His eyes began to dart around the room, searching . . . searching . . .

Suddenly he pushed past her and went to the secretary, which stood opposite the fireplace. There were several missives stacked neatly on it and one letter was only partially composed. Pulling a lantern close and turning up its flame, he examined the note in his hand and compared it to the half-completed letter.

"What are you doing?! That's private!" she cried, pushing against him and covering the letter with her hand. He grabbed her wrist and turned the joint painfully against itself. Not brutally, but just enough to get her attention.

"How odd that the hand that wrote this letter is identical to the hand that wrote this note and signed Sarielle's name to it!"

She opened her mouth to say something, but the dangerous look in his eyes must have warned her that she should not push him by denying the truth.

"Very well," she said quietly. "I wrote the note for her."

"To what end?" he demanded to know.

"So you would not go looking for her before dawn," Davine answered honestly.

"Why?"

"Because she did not want you to!"

Garreth took a step back as if she had slapped him. "What are you saying," he asked quietly, dangerously.

Davine swallowed anxiously and, again, answered honestly. "She wanted to leave you without incident. She knew that if she said something, if she tried to say good-bye, you would not let her go easily. She didn't want a confrontation."

"But . . . why would she leave? And in the middle of the night like a Zizo thief?"

"Her reasons are her own," she replied. "But if I had to hazard a guess . . . she would rather leave than be left behind."

"But I . . ." Garreth was at a loss. He couldn't believe it. He simply could not believe it. Just that morning they had made love so intensely and she had seemed so happy. But all the while she was planning this? Planning to leave him? "I wasn't going to leave her."

"Yes. You were," Dethan said from the doorway. "Or

are you saying you would renege on your agreement
with Weysa? Do you know how foolhardy that would
be? There would be no future in it. She would put you
back on that mountainside again and never look back.
Then where would Sarielle be?"

"Shut up," Garreth ground out. "There has to be a
way. I would have found a way."

"Damn you, Garreth, there is no way!" Dethan roared
at him.

"There has to be!" Garreth roared back at him. "I
love her!"

"You don't love her," Dethan scoffed. "If you loved
her, then you would stop being selfish and let her go.
Let her go and be safe far away from you and away
from the notice of the gods!"

"No," Garreth said, shaking his head. "No."

"Yes," Dethan hissed. "What else can you offer her?
A life of war camps and never being in one place long
enough to make a single friend? Dragging those young
girls with you from city to city as you make war upon
many nations? And what if your army should fail to
take a city? If you should lose a war and be taken prisoner? What do you think your enemies would do to the
general's woman? Rape? Murder? Desecration? These
are the things you will open her up to."

"You were going to do it! You took Selinda to wife
and were going to—"

"And it nearly killed her in the process! She was heavy
with child, yet she was on her knees day and night begging Weysa to release me from my vow to her! Do you
think Sarielle would do any less if she were to fall in
love with you? Hell, she probably already has! She's an
innocent young woman who's never known the way of
a man before you came. Of course she's going to fall in
love with you! What do you think she would do if she
learned of your curse?"

"Dethan!" Garreth hissed, casting a sidelong look at Davine.

"What? Like it's a great mystery?" Dethan said acidly. "You leave every night at dusk and don't return for hours. Don't you think she's figured it out?"

"I have," Davine informed them quietly.

That got Garreth's attention. "You have what?" he demanded.

"I have figured out that you are cursed. That every night you suffer to freeze in the orchards. And if I could find out, then no doubt she could too. It may well be what prompted her to leave. No one wants to have a cursed lover."

"No. She wouldn't do that," Garreth said, his voice tight and his hands curling into fists. "She wouldn't care."

"Then why have you never told her?" Dethan wanted to know. "If you believe that, why have you not told her yourself?"

"I . . . that-that means nothing," he said.

"It means something, or you would have told her instead of letting her find out on her own. Or was it just that you did not care about how it might make her feel?" Davine asked.

"We don't even know if she knows!"

"She knows," Davine said. "Women always find out. It's the only reason I can think of why she would want to get away from you as fast enough as she could!"

"No. You're wrong," he said, shaking with his wildly vacillating emotions.

"She loved you. I'm not wrong about that," Davine said. "So what else could make her simply pack up and leave in such a hurry? What else could you have possibly done to her?"

Garreth didn't want to believe it. He didn't want to believe she would so easily give up on him, that she would turn away from him and run because of the trial he had to face every night. Wasn't it bad enough that he had to suffer it forever? Could he not have one small solace? All he had asked for was time in her arms to help him forget about the weight he must carry with him everywhere.

The truth was everything had been fine that morning. He was sure of it. Something had suddenly changed, and just as his brother and Davine were saying, there was only one thing he had not shared with her . . . one thing that might make her run from him of her own accord. Either that or she was trying to avoid watching him leave her come springtime, which he must do.

But Dethan had taken a wife. Why couldn't he? Why couldn't he love Sarielle, come home to her in the winter?

In the next breath, he realized just how selfish that desire was, how unfair it would be to her. Still, wasn't it better to have a love for part of a full turning of seasons than not at all? She was important enough for him to want that. Would she not be able to feel the same? Something rather than nothing? He would take one day with her even if it meant seasons without her would follow. One day would mean more to him than anything else in their world.

But if she had left because of his curse . . . then there was nothing he could do. Perhaps he could explain . . . Perhaps he could beg her to understand. He had to make her comprehend that though he carried this burden, it would not ever harm her or her sisters.

Was that true? He didn't really know, did he? Weysa could be a vindictive goddess when she wanted to be. If she felt their agreement was in threat, would she take it out on the thing she felt was distracting him from his purpose? He honestly did not know. All he could do was vow to the goddess that he would not let his love for Sarielle interfere with his goals and his actions on her behalf.

Oh, how he wished he could do what Dethan had done, wished he could free himself from this terrible burden. But if he were to do the same thing, even if it meant freeing one of his brothers from further torment, he would be burdening that brother with this same untenable agreement. But was it not better than whatever torture his brothers were suffering even now? Jaykun, he knew, was chained to a star, incinerating over and over again in perpetual agony, no relief ever to be found. As for Maxum . . . Not even the other gods knew where he was or what torment he was undergoing. Sabo, the god of pain and suffering, had been put in charge of his punishment and he had not revealed the location or nature of that punishment to anyone else.

All these thoughts went racing through his mind as his brother and Davine stood watching him with cautious expectation. They weren't certain what his next actions would be, only, Garreth knew, that they were going to discourage him from anything to do with retrieving Sarielle.

"She is mine," he hissed at them before he could think to check his own words. "Nothing you can say will change that fact. If Weysa wants to punish me for loving her, then so be it!"

"What if it isn't you Weysa punishes?" Dethan demanded of him. "What if she takes it out on Sarielle?"

Cold dread and horror settled into the pit of Garreth's stomach. Was he so selfish that he would risk her safety? Was he so blind to the possible consequences of his actions?

Frustration burned within him, stinging his eyes and restricting his breath. "I can't do it," he said in a hoarse rasp. "I can't let her go."

"You have to," Dethan said quietly.

Dethan was right. Oh gods, he was right! He could not do anything to harm her. Could not bring her to be hurt in any way.

Unimaginable pain ripped through him, clawing at his heart. He turned from his brother and Davine and lurched down the hallway. He was going to be sick and he didn't want anyone to be witness to it, didn't want anyone to know just how weak with pain he was. He made it out of the keep and into the cold night air just in time. He fell to his knees as his stomach upended itself.

She was gone. And for her sake he had to let her remain gone. Had to let her go to live as full a life as she could, one that was free of the danger he represented. Yes, that was the best thing to do. The unselfish thing to do.

And yet . . . he did not think he could bear it. He had never known love for a woman. Not like this. And what stung the most was that he had held his feelings back from her. He had not told her how hopelessly in love with her he had fallen. Had not told her what a magnificent creature she was in his eyes and in his heart. Had not told her that he had never loved anyone the way he loved her, that she was beyond special. That she was rare and beautiful in his eyes.

Oh, how he wished he had said all of that after they had made love that morning. Maybe if he had she wouldn't have gone and they could have had a few more stolen days together before he would be forced to leave her side forever.

Garreth headed into the dark city streets, the lanterns on the street corners barely enough to make the way visible. But he didn't care. He needed to be where he could feel closest to her. Where he could pray and hope his emotions were delivered somehow to her. She deserved to know how special she was.

He found the temple of Mordu after an hour of searching. The doors were closed to the public for the night, but he pounded on them so hard that a sleepy-eyed mem finally opened the doors and admitted him. Like all mems of Mordu, she was a beautiful woman, one with a lush figure beneath her religious gown. A perfect "bride" for the god of love and passion.

He stumbled to the altar, which sat beneath a statue of the god. Mordu was a truly godly figure of a man, and this statue was uncannily accurate in its depiction, for Garreth had seen the god himself that day at the fountain. The statue's strong warrior's body was clothed in a jerkin and a tunic that reached the tops of his thighs with his bare, powerful legs braced hard apart. His arms were folded across his chest, and his visage was intense as it stared down at his supplicants.

It was said that love was like war, that it required a stout heart and a warrior's soul. That passion required a strong, healthy body, and therefore the god himself reflected these things.

As Garreth fell to his knees, he tilted his head back, so he could stare into that stern countenance, and spread his arms wide, his palms turned upward in supplication.

"Mordu, tell me what to do," he begged of the god. "Tell me how to bear this. How do I love and yet let that love go at the same time? I suffered the torment of the gods, suffer it still, but will it never be enough? Will I never be allowed even the smallest reprieve? Is this my punishment for daring to know happiness in the face of the penance set down for me? Please . . . I beg of you . . . tell me your will. And . . . if she is hurting because of her love for me . . . take that pain from her. I never meant to cause her injury. Give it to me instead. Let my back bear the weight of this. It is not fair that she be set free only to be chained again by emotions too painful to bear."

And so it went. The same prayers over and over again, Garreth begging for guidance . . . begging that Sarielle be released from whatever burdens he may have placed upon her. On and on . . . until dawn lightened the sky and the morning sun began to spill across the altar.

CHAPTER
TWENTY-TWO

Dethan should have been heading home. He should have left over a week ago if he intended to be home before the winter set in. But he could not bring himself to leave while his brother spent every day in a torment far more serious than the one the gods had set down for him. At least when Garreth had been chained to that mountain it had been only his body that had suffered. Now it was his soul that suffered, and Dethan knew the weight of his responsibility in the matter. He had questioned his actions more than once . . . with more and more frequency as the days wore on and his brother grieved.

Every night after Garreth was released from his frozen penance he went to the temple of Mordu and begged for more penance until dawn came. The mems had taken to leaving the door unlocked for him. They had tried to give him guidance and comfort, but he had gently turned them away, taking no succor, thinking he did not deserve it.

And as if this weren't bad enough, Davine had taken to weeping quietly in odd corners of the keep. Dethan had stumbled upon her twice already. She had been making regular pilgrimages to Framun's temple, hoping for the peace and tranquility the god could offer an aggrieved soul. It bothered Dethan because he could have sworn Davine was a selfish soul, that this would not have touched her emotionally. But clearly Sarielle had touched more than just his brother's heart, and Davine, like he, was feeling the burden of what they had done.

Dethan had written to his wife, telling her he needed more time, explaining that his brother needed him without giving details as to why. He realized that was because part of him was a little too ashamed to admit to his loving wife his role in the deception. And it was feelings like these that made him doubt his actions even more. If he truly believed he had done the right thing, wouldn't he want to own his responsibility? Own his part in the whole thing?

No, he told himself. He had done the right thing for all involved. Sarielle was safer elsewhere, and Garreth was safer without her to distract him from his course. Or he would be once he stopped his unceasing prayers to Mordu. Dethan dreaded every day that Weysa would come down on them with thunderous dissatisfaction and take Garreth away, putting him back into his frozen torment once and for all. It was Dethan's fear of this that allowed him to keep his countenance, keep his role in things silent.

All Garreth needed was time, Dethan told himself. After the winter had passed, Garreth would be healed from his pain and move on. His focus would be restored. But . . . if this continued on into the spring, there would be serious trouble. Hells, if Garreth did not keep his head on straight over the winter, he might find himself losing the tenuous grip he had on his newly acquired cities. That would not do at all. That would definitely earn Weysa's attention . . . and outrage.

So Dethan would stay as long as he possibly could to make certain that did not happen.

He sometimes thought things were improving. Garreth was beginning to invest time and attention in the workings of the cities again, but it was clear this was by rote, not because of any passion for it. His passion had left him when Sarielle had left him.

To say his brother was losing sleep was an understatement. Garreth spent his nights in prayer, so it followed he did not spend them sleeping. Then he worked throughout the day in a half-present manner. The mems of Mordu's temple had told Dethan that Garreth sometimes fell asleep on his knees, no doubt out of pure exhaustion, but other than that . . .

Dethan shuffled through papers in front of him but did not really see what he was reading. He suspected his brother was doing the same. Garreth sat across from him, staring at the same page he had been looking at for the better part of half an hour.

"The moat is coming along nicely," Dethan said, for some reason compelled to make small talk, if only to feel that his brother was engaging in life in some way.

"Yes. I saw it when I went to Zandaria yesterday," Garreth said. He went back to looking at his paper.

"I think it will be a particularly bitter winter," Dethan tried again. "Especially here, with the Asdar Mountains so close at hand."

Garreth looked up at him and frowned. "Do you really wish to discuss the weather with me?" he asked almost irritably.

"I wish to discuss anything with you!" Dethan snapped suddenly. "Anything to make me feel you are still alive! It has been well over a moon's turn since she left. How long will you let this go on?"

Garreth's gaze turned glacial. "For as long as it takes," he said.

"I am at a loss," Dethan said, throwing up his hands

in his frustration. "Tell me what to do to make this better for you!"

"Can you bring her back to me?" Garreth asked, his stare hard. They both already knew the answer to that.

"You cannot go to her. She cannot come to you. It is a hopeless business. It is better you set your mind to moving on from this."

Garreth's fists crashed down on the table, making Dethan jump.

"Why are you here?" Garreth demanded of him.

"There is work to be done," he said, indicating the stack of papers in front of him.

"No. I mean, why are you *here*. Why are you not on your way to your wife and son? Your agreement with Weysa says you are to fight for her only during the summer wanings. Fall is near over and winter is coming. If you do not leave, you will be trapped here with me this winter. I cannot imagine that will make your wife happy, so . . . why are you here?"

"Because my brother needs me!"

"I need nothing from you," Garreth said bitterly. "I need nothing from anyone. I will suffer my penance and hold to my agreement with Weysa no matter what it has cost me. What else can I do?"

Dethan clenched his teeth tightly together. It pained him beyond reason to see his brother hurting so. "Garreth . . ."

"Go. Leave tomorrow. I will be fine without you."

"No. You have two cities to run and you cannot do that in your present frame of mind."

"I told you to go! I have good men here to help me run these cities. I will not lose them! Not after what it has cost me!"

Dethan had no reply to that. It made sense, what his brother was saying, but he was still not convinced. He opened his mouth to argue, but what could he possibly say to make this better? What could he possibly do to help Garreth snap out of his overwhelming melancholy? There was nothing. Absolutely nothing. All that Dethan could say had already been said.

"Leave tomorrow," Garreth said.

"No. Another week. There is plenty of time."

"What difference will a week make?" his brother asked.

Dethan did not know. He could only hope that with more time would come more acceptance.

"The moat will be further along. Our positions in both cities further solidified. A week and I will have more than enough time to make it home before the snow falls."

"Very well. A week. But no longer." Garreth moved around the table, heading for the doorway into the hall. He paused at his brother's elbow. "A week, Dethan. After that you will no longer be welcome here."

The words were cold and hard, and Dethan knew he meant every one of them. Garreth would force him out of the city if given the impetus to do so. And while the army they shared was equally loyal to the brothers, he knew Garreth would find a way. His brother was one of the most determined people he had ever known. Garreth had succeeded on his quests and crusades sometimes with only his will to see him through.

Garreth left, no doubt heading for his horse and subsequently the orchard, since dusk was fast approaching. It came earlier now, with the winter season falling on them, the nights growing longer and the days shorter. That meant the hours of his suffering, the hours between dusk and juquil's hour, were longer now.

If indeed Dethan could say his brother's suffering ever came to an end.

Sarielle sat by the window, looking out and watching the twins as they played on the ground outside. It was colder now, so they were wearing wraps, but Sarielle suspected they hardly felt the cold at all. They were more focused on their dolls.

They had arrived in the small city of Moda a few weeks earlier and Sarielle had purchased this little farm shortly after. The house was a strong one, with thick walls and two rooms, a sturdy fireplace positioned between them. One room she slept in with the twins; the other room they used for eating and daily activities.

Sarielle had bought them all new clothes in the Moda fashion so the girls could attend the school on the edges of the farmlands, which taught the farming children in the cold wanings, when the fields had been reaped and there were fewer chores for the children to help with.

Sarielle had also bought a cow for milk and a butchered bosc pig, the pork and bacon salted or smoked for storing in their tiny cellar. They had winter vegetables stored as well and canned fruits, milled sugar, and other staples to get them through the winter. Plus, she had purchased heavy fabrics and was stitching them to make warm quilts for their beds. It was a simple life. A good life. They would hire hands to work the farm come spring, and the money they had gotten from Koro's gems would take them quite far. Moda was many days' journey from the Asdar Mountains and Koro, but the wyvern could fly the distance in no time at all, should she need him for any reason.

But she would not need him. They were safe . . . far from any neighbors, really. Hidden away from prying and curious eyes. To her neighbors, she was a widow taking care of her sisters. She'd had to say she was recently widowed. It was better that way. It explained why she was with child but had no man to be a father to it.

She had discovered she was pregnant within days of leaving Kith. She had been sick with increasing frequency and recognized it had much less to do with her grief and much more to do with being pregnant when a woman saw her throwing up one morning and made a joke of it.

"So when's the child due?" the woman asked with a cackle.

Sarielle paled, all the blood rushing to the bottom of her body, as she realized that was exactly what was wrong with her. It explained why her breasts had grown tender all of a sudden. Why even the smell of food made her sick now. Why she was so incredibly tired all the time. She was going to have Garreth's baby. His son or his daughter.

She had struggled for a full day with the dilemma of whether or not she should tell him of it. Part of her thought he had a right to know; another part of her thought he had lost all rights to know anything about her and what had become of her when he had bedded another woman and betrayed her.

In the end, she had decided it would just be easier to remain completely out of his sphere. He was a very powerful man. He could decide he wanted her child . . . but not her. There had been a time when she wouldn't have thought him capable of something like that, but now . . . now she didn't trust him at all. She didn't know him at all.

She blinked her eyes rapidly as the sting of his betrayal hit her all over again, as it often did when she sat quietly and had nothing to do but think. But the fact of it was that she hurt. She hurt so deeply she couldn't see straight. She called herself a fool for it. He had never made any promises to her. He had warned her not to get too attached to him. Maybe by so visibly bedding Davine he had purposely driven a chasm between them. Maybe it had been his way of forcing a good-bye on her.

And yet despite his betrayal she found she foolishly still yearned for him. She yearned for his smile and laughter. She craved his mouth and his touch on her body. She longed for the smell and feel of him. It was as though a huge chunk of her soul had been torn away from her and was living distantly from her. Not dead, but not alive either.

She touched her cheek and found tears upon it. She felt angry with herself whenever she spilled tears over him, but that didn't stop it from happening again and again. More often rather than less. She had hoped time and distance would help her to heal, but they simply weren't enough.

And as always, when the tears came, Koro's concerned thoughts followed. He wanted to know why she was so sad. Wanted to understand her pain and the reasons why he was not able to fix it for her.

Do not worry, Koro. I will get better.

But she did not believe it herself, so it was difficult to convince him. And then, in the next moment, he asked when his sister would be born.

Sarielle sat up straight.

Your sister? she asked hesitantly.

Yes, he said. The one inside her. The one whose thoughts he could hear.

Sarielle was shocked. He could hear the baby? But . . . how? It didn't even have any thoughts yet . . . did it?

Did *she?*

A girl. Koro thought it was a girl. And he was probably right. Sarielle couldn't question the wyvern's power. They were creatures of great magic. Magic that grew stronger as they aged. Koro was still just a baby in so many ways. He had not yet come into all his power. But she had heard of wyverns that could disappear from one place and appear in another. Others that could use the power of their thoughts to move things.

What . . . what does she say? Sarielle asked hesitantly.

She did not say very much apparently. She was very

quiet. It took some explaining as to why she was inside Sarielle, as opposed to being in an egg, but eventually Koro seemed to understand

Sarielle could feel his curiosity and his sudden excitement. He wanted a "sister." And she understood why. If not for her, he would be all alone in the world. She couldn't imagine Koro doing well by himself, with no touchstone whatsoever. And she didn't even remember what it had been like for her before she had had him nestled securely in her mind at all times.

She took a deep breath and exhaled shakily. She had to be careful. If Koro thought for even a moment that Garreth had caused her pain, there was no telling what he might do in retaliation. And the last thing she wanted to do was sic a wyvern on Garreth. No matter how hurt and angry she was, he did not deserve that. And she could not bear the idea of anything happening to him. Even after all her pain . . .

She still loved him.

CHAPTER
TWENTY-THREE

Mordu sighed.
    If a god could get a headache, then he most certainly had one. And he knew what it was from.

Weysa's champion.

As an immortal being, Garreth had some of the power of a god inside him, and that made him able to connect with whatever god he chose to connect with at the time. It used to be Weysa this man connected to, sending her prayers and bringing her glory. His army was marching across the world, gaining power for him and, more important, Weysa.

Really it had been a stroke of genius on Weysa's part, freeing these little men and using them to help her gain power. Mordu was part of Weysa's faction. So her gain was for all intents and purposes his gain. He hadn't been so sure these men had deserved freedom from their torments, but they had proven themselves worthy warriors and they had devoted themselves to the task of winning Weysa the followers she needed to grow stronger.

But now one of them was calling to *him* incessantly, the pain of the man's broken heart almost too much to be borne. Mordu had rarely seen such pain as this, except in cases in which souls had been meant for each other, the bond so profound that it was nigh unbreakable. But it was uncommon for two such souls to really find each other. Hella, the goddess of fate, could be cruel like that, keeping destined souls just out of reach of each other. She was a mercurial witch sometimes. Some days she delighted in toying with mortal fates, laughing at the torment she could bring to them, and other days she grew soft and loving and was eager to see two such souls find each other.

In this case, she had done both. She had thrown two destined souls together . . . and then made it their fate to be driven apart.

Truly, she was a cold-hearted bitch at times.

But he was only saying that because she was his wife.

And because it was true.

So as a result of her fickle ways, Mordu was now being bombarded with the grief of this warrior of Weysa's. At first Mordu had been able to ignore it. He had thousands upon thousands of people coming to him, begging him for the love of this one or that one. Occasionally it amused him to have a hand in how things worked out, but mostly he basked in the power of what his wife, fate, had wrought in the way of love.

But this . . . this was ceaseless, this begging for his help. And . . . what was most vexing about it was that the man wasn't wishing for his love . . . but instead wished his love would not feel pain over her love for him. Wished Mordu would lighten her burden.

At least that was what he prayed for aloud. But deep in the soul of this man were the true cravings of his heart: To be reunited with his love. To be able to keep her and treasure her for all time. And yet he would not wish his cursed state to be within her sphere for fear of it doing her any harm.

In a nutshell, the warrior couldn't make up his mind what he wanted. Oh, Mordu could see what was at the heart of it, but he could also see the dilemma for what it was.

So he was driven to find a solution . . . if for no other reason than to hush the man up and give himself a moment's peace in the process. To that end, he had called Weysa and Hella for a meeting of their godly minds.

"What is it?" Hella asked impatiently.

At present, Mordu was not one of Hella's favorite gods to be around. Oh sure, they were married . . . but that didn't mean they always got along. At present his beloved wife was peeved at him for some such thing or other. He honestly didn't know what it was this time. Just like he didn't know what had possessed her to throw two soul mates together and then drive them apart the next instant.

"It's a little matter of the warrior Garreth."

Weysa sat up in her chair, then pushed to her feet, her body language erect and tight. "What of him?"

Mordu sighed. This wasn't going to be easy. "I want to shut the man up."

"You cannot kill him," Weysa said harshly. "He is mine. And he is doing a very good job at what he's been asked to do."

"I do not wish to kill the man," Mordu said impatiently. "I merely want to give him some form of ease."

"What did you have in mind exactly?" Hella asked, narrowing her eyes on him. His wife did not like it when he meddled in her affairs. Nor did Weysa.

"Is there not some way we can bring them together rather than drive them apart? My love," he coaxed his wife, "you are so good at warm reunions."

She preened. Mordu had always known how to manipulate Hella. All it required was going straight for her ego and giving it a good brushup.

"No," Weysa said flatly. "You cannot give him the woman. I forbid it."

Mordu deflated. "Why in the eight hells not?" he demanded of her.

"Because she will distract him from his true course! He and his brother have won me four cities in a single turning! I will not lose him to the simpering love of a mortal woman. I already lost his brother before him."

"Yet that brother still battles in your name," Mordu pointed out. "Wife and child and still he helped to capture those four cities."

Weysa turned up her nose. "That is only because Garreth was a driving force. Dethan's focus is squarely on his wife, not on me."

"I only mean to point out that he can have a wife and still win cities in your name."

"You will be doing her no favors," Weysa said harshly. "To bring her to her love only to have her watch him leave time and again."

"There has to be a solution. One that will satisfy all involved," Mordu said with frustration.

"Well, I have a suggestion," Hella said, her fingertips drifting over to touch Mordu on his thigh. A flirtatious gesture. Mordu was surprised. Hella had been angry with him for quite some time.

"Please," he invited her, taking the opportunity to pick up her hand and press a forgiving kiss to the back of it. "What do you suggest?"

"Why, another brother of course. There are four of them. Why not take one to replace the second one."

"And let this one off free and clear? I do not like it," Weysa said. "How do I know the new brother is a worthy soldier? How do I know he will win the cities and followers I need? We need."

"He will," Mordu assured her. "And we will not set

this brother as you say 'free and clear.' There will be a task for him and his love . . . working for me. I find your idea of having a human battle for your cause and bring the name of the gods back onto the lips of the people to be a very keen one. So give me this warrior, let him fight for followers in my name now. You may have your new soldier, and if this one gains me followers, it is all the same to our faction."

What Mordu did not say was that he had been watching Weysa grow stronger as the brothers battled in her name and he wanted that strength for himself.

"The brothers can still fight side by side . . . winning the cities in your name . . . but the flip side of war is love, and there is nothing wrong with bringing that to their conquered cities as well as your name."

Weysa seemed to mull that over a moment. "There is only one problem with that. One of the other brothers is chained to a star . . . that's Grimu's territory. Enemy territory. It would take quite a lot to free him. And the fourth brother . . . we don't even know where he is. Sabo took him away, no doubt to a territory of his own. Again, enemy territory. So what do you suggest? That we risk ourselves in battle just to free a soul from torment that, in my opinion, does not truly deserve release?"

"Weysa, please," Mordu said gently. "I feel as you do, that they needed punishment for their audacity in trying to force the hands of the gods, but it has been hundreds of turnings now. Surely a reprieve is not such a reaching idea."

"Perhaps not," Weysa said speculatively. "I must admit I never expected them to succeed as famously as they have. They are of a true warrior breed."

"So we have two dilemmas," Mordu said. "One, how to free the one called Garreth from his curse, and two, how to free another brother. I am thinking it would be best to go for the one chained to the star. At least we know where he is. It would take a great deal of effort to find the other."

"Well, I can solve one of those problems. He was cursed by cruel fate." Hella chuckled. "Planting him within reach of that fountain was really a stroke of genius on my part. The irony of it amuses me still."

"Yes, it really was quite good," Weysa agreed with a smile. "But now . . . will you withdraw it?"

"I will . . . but only if we manage to free the third brother from Grimu's territory. I am willing to forgive him his crime if all of you are willing as well."

"I am," Weysa said with a nod.

"Good," Mordu said with satisfaction. "Now, let us see about freeing this other brother."

"Actually, it will be quite simple," Weysa said. "We will begin a battle with Grimu as our target, drawing him away from his territory, and one of us will stay behind to sneak in and free the brother."

"Do you think the others will agree to this?"

"I believe so," Weysa said. "I have grown very strong, thanks to these brothers. I can attack Grimu with ease."

"Then I will free the other brother from his torment on the star. However, like his brothers before him, he will suffer that torment again every night from dusk to juquil's hour."

"This time, Hella, do not toy with my warrior," Weysa said. "No more falling in love, Mordu."

"Don't worry. What is the likelihood of three brothers in a row falling under the sway of love? These are men not prone to loving," Hella said.

"And yet they have," Weysa said, her look at Mordu almost accusatory.

"I did not plan this," Mordu said, holding up his hands. "Speak to my wife, who enjoys toying with fate."

Hella laughed. "Do not place all the blame on me. I merely turn fate, I do not decree who should love another. That is your doing."

"I assure you this happened all on its own. I have had nothing to do with it," Mordu said.

"And yet you are meddling now," Weysa pointed out.

"I've been given no choice! He is all but screaming for my attention. I cannot bear to see a soul suffer from love, no matter what his crimes in the past."

Hella smiled and leaned into Mordu. "You see? You are simply soft at the heart of you."

He clucked his tongue at her but did not push her away. He had missed his wife, he realized.

And after all, nothing went together better than fate and love.

Garreth was on his knees in Mordu's temple a week later, just as he had been every night since Sarielle had abandoned him. Only tonight he asked for nothing. He was numb from asking. He was empty of pleas and full of heartache. What else was there for him to do? What else could he do?

He heard a sound behind him and turned disinterestedly toward it. It was another one of the curvaceous mems, her beauty on display as her gown flowed freely against her body. And yet he did not register her beauty. Just like everything he saw, she appeared pale. Just like everything he tasted was bland and everything he touched was numbed.

He had never known so much pain. Not even when he was being frozen fast to the ground.

"Can I get you something, my lord?" she asked, her voice dulcet.

"No. I thank you."

She moved closer to him, so close he could feel her body's warmth and smell its gentle perfume.

Again, it made no impact on him.

She reached out and touched his hair, her hand drifting through it intimately. He drew back and gave her a hard look.

"Do not do that again."

"But why?" she asked softly. "You are in the temple of the god of love. Perhaps your prayers would be better heard and answered if you were to use the power of passion to propel them to the heavens." She stepped up to him and leaned the whole of her body against him, her hand cradling his head to her breasts.

He lurched away from her with a resounding "No!" Gaining his feet, he put distance between them. "I know you are trying to help," he said, "but I would rather find another way."

"There is no other way," she said. "Mordu demands you make this sacrifice if you want your love."

Garreth went still and narrowed his eyes on her. "And you know this how?"

"I am his priestess. One of the most powerful mems you will find in any of his temples. I know Mordu's ways. He insists on you using love to regain love."

"Where did you come from?" he asked, still suspicious of her and growing more so by the second. "I have not seen you here before."

"But I have seen you. Night after endless night. Praying for your love. Now I am standing here, telling you the way to have your prayers heard. Lie with me in passion and you will have your prayers answered."

She reached for him again but he caught her hands.

"No! I am sorry, but . . . if that is what I must do to get my prayers answered . . . I cannot do it. It would be a betrayal to the one I love and I cannot betray her."

"Not even to gain her?"

"I would gain her and lose her again all in the same instant. I know Sarielle. It would cause a wound in her that might be impossible to repair and I will not hurt her."

"But how do you know this? She has left you of her own accord because you are cursed. What makes an inconstant woman deserve such devotion?"

A part of Garreth went icy cold.

"Who told you I was cursed?" he hissed at her.

She hesitated. "I heard your prayers to Mordu. You said it yourself."

"I said no such thing. I spoke of penance and torment; I said nothing of being cursed. Who are you?" he demanded of her, grabbing hold of her wrist.

"You would abuse the handmaiden of the god you beg favors from?" she asked fiercely.

"If you are a handmaiden of the god of love, then I am not cursed," he spat at her. *"Who are you?"*

She pulled away with an incredible show of strength, taking the warrior by surprise. As she pulled back, her body grew in stature and her soft, feminine looks fell away. In their place stood the mighty figure of a god. A god he had seen once before.

Sabo.

"You have called me to you only to deny me?" Sabo thundered roughly.

"I never called you!" Garreth said even as his stomach quailed and churned. It was never a good thing to make a god angry.

"You have called me every moment of these days past, your pain and your suffering so loud as to garner my full attention!"

"I want nothing from you. You have nothing to give me," Garreth said.

"What if I said I did? What if I could give you something you want very much?"

Garreth narrowed distrusting eyes on him. "Like what?" he asked carefully.

"Your brother."

His brother. Maxum. Sabo was the only one who knew what had become of him. For the first time in weeks Garreth's attention shifted away from his grief. If there was one thing he wanted as much as he wanted Sarielle, it was his brothers' freedom from their respective torments.

"Where is he?"

"I could tell you. But you must make a pact with me first. You must promise to keep yourself away from this woman you crave for all the rest of your days in this world . . . which is a very long time since you are immortal for all intents and purposes."

"Why would you want me to make a promise like that?" It was strange, but as things stood it would be an easy promise to make. He would not wish himself on Sarielle. She was better off far from him and his wretched existence.

"Because I enjoy your pain and suffering. It feeds me just as your warring ways feed Weysa."

Now Garreth truly hesitated. He had been brought back to this world to serve Weysa and her faction. Sabo was now saying that Garreth was, in fact, feeding him and Xaxis's faction? That had not been his intention. And yet there he was, standing before a god grown strong because of his agony and torment. He could not knowingly defy Weysa by making a pact with this god in the face of his pact with her.

Nor could he cure the source of his pain. He was damned either way.

So be it. If he was going to be damned regardless, he

may as well use it to discover the whereabouts of his brother.

"Where is my brother?" he asked quietly.

"Do you so swear? To never set eyes on that girl again?"

"I . . ."

What was wrong with him? He wasn't going to see her anyway. Why didn't he just say yes and be done with it?

But he couldn't do it. He couldn't bear the idea of saying definitively that he would never wish to see her again. And he could not bring himself to defy Weysa. To do so might bring her wrath down upon Dethan. He didn't care what happened to him, but he would not rob Selinda of her love the way Garreth had been robbed of his.

"Leave me be and enjoy my pain from afar," he said quietly. "I make no pact with you."

"You are a fool! You'll never see her again anyway! Don't you want to know what hole I have buried your brother in?"

That got Garreth's swift attention.

"Buried? He is buried alive?"

Sabo roared out in fury, realizing he had given away information he had not wanted to. "It doesn't matter!" he growled. "You will never be able to find him! He is buried so deep the world would have to split apart in order to free him!"

"Yes, but at least I now know his fate," Garreth said grimly. "And for now, that is enough."

Sabo roared in anger once more. "Kneel before me! I will show you pain and suffering like you have never known!"

"There is nothing you can do to me that will touch the suffering I already endure," Garreth bit out.

Sabo lifted a hand high and a bright, brilliant light filled his palm. "Shall we see if that is actually true?"

He pulled his arm back and Garreth tensed for the coming strike.

To his shock, there was an explosion and Sabo went flying across the temple and into the far wall. He hit it so hard that the thick marble stones cracked down the center. Garreth's head whipped about and he saw that two other gods had come into the temple. Hella and Mordu. He would have recognized them anywhere.

Hella put her hands together and a darkness swelled between them, the darkness and power of the unknown, of the abyss of the world if there were no fate or future. The black bolt shot free of her hands and slammed into Sabo once again. She was a beautiful virago, a force to be reckoned with. Mordu put his hands together as well and a light so bright formed between them that Garreth had to look away. The light of pure love and hope—that which everyone prayed for and longed to see, but they often flinched in the face of it.

Sabo didn't have a chance. The powers of both the gods thrashed him thoroughly. He wasn't able to get a single shot off before he roared in rage and disappeared from the temple.

"And good riddance, I say!" Hella said with a huff. She turned to Garreth, who was still holding a hand up to protect his eyes from the brightness of the powers being thrown about. "Well. Now, look at this one. Darling, I must say I am impressed with him."

Mordu nodded. "He is most loyal."

Garreth suddenly realized he was standing in front of gods and quickly dropped to his knees and bowed his head to Weysa's compatriots.

"I beg your forgiveness," he said quickly. "It was never my intention to feed Sabo's power."

"Nonsense," Mordu said in his booming voice. "The fault is mine for not finding a solution to your pain sooner."

"A . . . a solution?" Garreth asked hesitantly.

"Yes, yes. I almost forgot! Here!" Hella snapped her fingers and suddenly a large body was falling against Garreth. He instinctively reached out and caught it as it collapsed. It was burned black, barely more than a skeleton, but it was clearly a man.

"I do not understand," Garreth said as he laid the body on the floor as gently as he could. But as soon as he did, the body gasped in a breath and the man's eyelids opened, revealing a set of dark green eyes Garreth had known all his life. "Jaykun!"

"Yes, it's your brother!" Hella said with a delighted laugh and clap of her hands. "Now, tell me. Is fate not kind to you?"

Garreth was speechless, his eyes welling at the sight of his brother and the horrible state of Jaykun's body. Jaykun could not speak, could not move, but he held Garreth's gaze with what must've been every ounce of energy in his body.

"I . . . I don't understand," Garreth choked out as his tears blurred his vision.

"It's simple. Jaykun is to take your place. You are to bring the name of Mordu into the cities your brothers will dominate," Hella said sternly. "This is your fate now."

"I . . ." Garreth was speechless.

"What she means to say," Mordu said as he touched his wife's hair fondly, "is that you are released from your curse. You have a new bargain if you choose it."

"My curse? I am released of my curse?" he said numbly.

"Yes. But now it is your brother who will suffer his own curse. He will fight turning-round in Weysa's name, and you . . . you can go find that little thing you've been wailing about for the past moon's waning and give her child a father," Hella said.

"*Child?!*"

"Yes. You will find she is with child," Mordu said. "Your child, to be clear. And you will find she is just as miserable without you as you are without her."

"But . . ."

Garreth simply could not process what he was seeing and hearing. It was all too much at once. Luckily Hella found his speechlessness amusing, not offensive. She tittered like a girl and leaned her body flirtatiously into her husband's.

"Is this not fun?" she asked him. "I would like to do this more often."

"Whatever you wish, my love," Mordu said to her warmly.

"I thank you," Garreth blurted out at last. "I am . . . I am so grateful. There are no words! I beg you to forgive me for not having the right words!"

"We are merely pleased that you are pleased . . . and that you will not be wailing about in my temple any longer," Mordu said, his tone turning stern at the end.

"No! I swear I will not! How can I? You have . . . you have given me everything!"

"Not everything. You must win her heart back on your own."

"Do you know where she is?" Garreth asked.

"Of course we do. But surely you don't expect us to give you that too?" Mordu said with a hard look.

"No! This is more than enough! I will find her myself! Thank you. I . . . Please, at any time tell me how I might thank you!"

"I am sure you will think of something. Now, remember your pact."

"I will. I will bring the name of Mordu wherever I go!"

"Very good. Now come, my love," Mordu said to his wife, touching her cheek fondly. "Let us bring more fated loves together, shall we?"

"Oh yes! Let's!"

And just like that, both gods were gone.

Garreth was breathing hard, which brought the acrid smell of flesh burnt to cinders to his nose. He cradled his brother closer and looked about wildly. He saw a stunned mem standing in the corner of the altar room.

"Get my brother!" When she did not move fast enough he roared, *"Now!"*

Dethan watched as his brother paced and prepared saddle bags. Garreth's energy was frenetic, his plans clear.

"Once she hears the curse is removed she will come back to me. She will want to come back to me," he kept saying aloud, although Dethan was pretty sure he was talking to himself rather than talking to Dethan. But his words filled Dethan with dread and he knew he needed to speak up, to come clean about what Davine had done.

"Garreth . . ." he began. Then, quailing in the face of his guilt, he said, "How can you possibly find her after all this time?"

"She isn't far. She would never leave Koro too far behind. So, that is the fastest way to her."

"What is?"

"Koro. I am going to find him."

"Are you mad? You can't go into the wyvern's den by yourself!"

"Why not?" Garreth wanted to know. "Have you got a better idea?"

"We can send runners out to all the nearby cities and search—"

"That will take too long! With winter setting in . . . I want my child and my wife with me! Not wintering in a strange place far from my side!"

"Your wife? She's not your wife!"

"Not yet by law but in all ways that matter."

"You can't be certain . . . She may not accept you," Dethan said uncomfortably.

"Why? Davine says Sarielle loves me. I have to believe she will take me back once she knows there is nothing standing between us. I don't fully understand why she felt the need to leave . . . I can only assume it was fear. But all the cause for fear has been removed." Garreth stopped and looked at his brother, a grin a mile wide on his lips as he thumped Dethan hard on the shoulder. "Free!" he said with pure joy. "I am free of that wretched curse and can now live a normal life!"

"Albeit an immortal one," Dethan muttered.

"Don't be jealous because you had to give up your immortality," Garreth teased him.

"I am not jealous. I would much rather grow old with Selinda than watch her grow old without me. Have you not thought of that?"

That gave Garreth pause, but only for a second. "I don't care. And neither will she. I will love her until the day she dies and that's all that will matter."

"Garreth . . . I have to tell you . . ."

"What?" Garreth said absently as he began to look around himself for other things that needed packing.

"She may not . . . forgive you."

"Forgive me? What is there to forgive?"

Dethan swallowed hard. "She may not forgive you for sleeping with Davine."

"Davine?" He laughed. "I've never slept with—" Garreth broke off when he saw the guilt stamped across his brother's features. Suddenly everything seemed to rush in on him, seemed to make sense.

"What . . . what did you do?" he asked his brother quietly. Then more strongly, *"What did you do?"*

"Sarielle thinks . . . that you slept with Davine."

Garreth felt his entire body go cold. "Why would she think that?" he demanded of his brother.

"Because . . . Davine made her think it."

There was a heartbeat. Two. And suddenly Garreth punched his brother square on the jaw, knocking Dethan back into a table.

"You knew? You knew this and yet you said nothing!"

Dethan fended off his brother's next attack, this time prepared for the rage being vented toward him. And why not? It was certainly his due.

The brothers wrestled, the two almost evenly matched. But Dethan had always been bigger and stronger than his brother, immortality or no immortality, so he was able to leverage his raging sibling into a wall.

"Stop! I know! I know it was wrong. I know it *now*. But then . . . I didn't want you to lose sight of your pact with Weysa. I feared the repercussions if you did!"

"This is why she ran from me? Davine sent her headlong into the world thinking I betrayed her?! And you let it happen!"

"I'm sorry!" Dethan cried, battling for control of the situation. "I was only trying to keep you safe. That's always been my responsibility. One I failed to accomplish the day I dragged you up that mountain!"

"You failed me then and you've failed me now," Garreth hissed in his brother's face. "At least I can blame myself for following you on that trip, but this . . . this is no fault of mine! And you made me think otherwise!"

"Please! I know! Please forgive me, brother!"

Garreth finally shoved him off with a tremendous heave. Dethan staggered back and caught himself against a table. Garreth was immediately in his face.

"I will forgive you the day she becomes my wife and not a second sooner! And I'll not have you under the same roof as her, so be ready to leave the moment I return!"

He turned and grabbed the saddlebags he'd packed and stormed off down the hallway. Dethan was hot on his heels.

"You need me to run these cities!"

"Only while I'm gone. Jaykun and I can run them without you once I return."

"Jaykun is barely conscious!"

"He will be healed by the time I return. We both know this."

"Garreth—"

"I mean it, Dethan. The moment I bring her back you are to get on your horse and go home to your wife!"

"Garreth, wait!"

Garreth finally came to a halt, and with a clenched jaw, he turned to face his brother. He took a breath and exhaled slowly. "Dethan . . . just let me do this. You and I . . . we are brothers, and as much as I want to kill you right now, that will never change. I just . . . I need to find her. We'll deal with the rest later."

"All right," Dethan said with a measure of relief. He didn't know if he could bear his brother's anger toward him. But this was Garreth they were talking about. Garreth didn't have a hateful bone in his body. "Is there anything I can do to help?"

"Yes. You can get that lying whore out of my house before I bring my wife back here. I don't want Sarielle to have to see her face."

"Do not be too hard on Davine. She . . . I think she feels the weight of what she has done." Dethan swallowed. "She is alone in the world. She was just trying to survive."

"And now Sarielle is alone in the world and trying to

survive when she should be here with me. By the gods, man, she's *with child*!"

"I know. I'm sorry," Dethan said, his contrition boundless.

"Stop saying that. Just . . . I have to go."

He turned his back on his brother and left. This time, Dethan let him go.

CHAPTER
TWENTY-FOUR

Sarielle stood in the doorway of the small house, letting the cold air wash over her. For some reason her body had been burning hotly these past minutes, as if she were standing before a raging fire. The cold of the coming winter felt good against her body.

Behind her the girls sat before the fire, quietly doing their schoolwork. They had never had schooling before and were enjoying learning to read. They were sometimes frustrated because so many of the children seemed to know more than they did, but there were others who were at their same level and that caused them to not feel so bad. The whole business made Sarielle a little sad for them. They had missed out on so much. At least she'd had books to read when she had been idle as a wrena. The bennesah had allowed her them for reasons she hadn't entirely understood. But she had been grateful for them. Perhaps that had been his entire motivation. To make her grateful and therefore more malleable.

As she took another breath, she felt the strangest sensation wash over her. It was familiar, in a way, but at first blush she couldn't place it.

Then, when she felt a tremendous wash of air blast over her, she realized what it was.

"Koro!" she cried as the wyvern spun hard in the sky and buzzed the cottage once more.

What are you doing here, my love? she wanted to know.

As delighted as she was to see him, his big body in the air would soon draw attention. Attention she did not want. Attention she did not want Koro to have focused on him. People would fear a large, fire-breathing creature like the wyvern. It was possible they did not have a wrena here, that they wouldn't understand what was attracting him here. And she didn't want them to understand. She didn't want them to know she was a wrena. If they knew . . . there was always someone out there who would try to exploit her for her ability to control the wyvern.

Koro immediately let her know he had a gift for her. Sarielle could not help but laugh. Koro was clearly delighted with himself and this gift he had brought her.

"Very well. Let me see this gift!"

"That would be me, I believe."

Sarielle gasped and whirled about, shocked to find herself staring into Garreth's sea-green eyes.

The bottom dropped out of her world.

Garreth moved just fast enough to catch her before she sank to the ground. She didn't lose consciousness, but her eyes did roll back for a moment and she exhaled in a rush.

"Easy," he soothed her as he jogged her weight against himself. Then he scooped her up into his arms and stepped into the warm little cottage.

"Garreth!" the twins cried in unison.

They rushed him and he tried to accept their hugs while bringing their sister to a bed in the next room. There were two beds, one on either side of the room, bracketing the fireplace. He chose one and settled her down onto it.

"Fetch Sarielle some water," he instructed the girls.

"I can go to the well all by myself!" Jona cried.

"I will help!" chimed in Isaelle, much to Jona's consternation.

"Well then, it won't be by myself," she complained.

"But I want to help," Isaelle said with a frown.

"Why don't you both go to the well, but Jona can fill the glass," Garreth suggested.

"That's a good idea!" Jona said. Both girls ran off to the well in a burst of energy.

Garreth turned his attention to Sarielle. She was breathing shallowly, her eyes fixed on him now, her hand pressing against his chest as if to push him away.

"No," she said softly, breathily. "Please. I don't want you here."

"I know," he said just as softly. "But . . . I would like you to hear me out just the same."

To his infinite agony, tears filled her eyes as she shook her head.

"No. It hurts too much," she said, a sob catching in her throat.

"I know that too," he said grimly. "But please . . . you have to know . . . Davine lied to you. I never took Davine to my bed. She created that fiction to chase you away from me."

"But . . . I saw the note. I found her in your bed."

"I never wrote that note. And I was in Zandaria long before she entered my bed. There was no way I could have come back and bedded Davine and then gone again to Zandaria. There would be no sense to it: No sense at all. Especially when you take into consideration that I was, and always have been, in love with you."

"In . . . in love with me?" she asked.

"Yes, my sweet fira. In love with you."

"But . . . you told her. About your curse. You told her and not me."

"I never told her. She figured it out for herself. I don't know how. Either Dethan told her or she followed me and found out. I never told her. The only one I ever discussed it with was Dethan. Only Dethan. I did not wish to burden you with it. I feared that if you knew, it would put you in some kind of danger. That it might anger Weysa somehow or . . . or . . . I don't know what. All I knew was that I wanted to protect you. I never wanted you to be hurt. But I guess I hurt you anyway."

"Yes," she said softly. Then more tears fell from her lashes. "It hurt so much."

"I'm so sorry, fira," he said softly. Fiercely. "I want to kill Davine for making you think that I would do such a thing to you. I will see to it you never have to lay eyes on her again."

"But . . . I thought she was my friend. I thought . . ."

"I'm sorry. She lied to you, Sarielle. I never touched her."

Sarielle sobbed once more and then began to cry in earnest. He hushed her gently and pulled her into his embrace. He hushed her again.

"It's going to be all right," he murmured. "Hella has freed me from my curse. Weysa has amended her agreement with me. I am yours, fira, if you want me. All we need do is bring the name of the god of love to the people and we will be free to love for ourselves. I will leave you for short times in order to do so, but only for short times. Other than that . . . I am yours. I will be here for you and our child."

Sarielle gasped. "How did you . . . ?"

"Mordu told me. Or was it Hella?"

"The *gods* told you?"

"Yes, fira. The gods told me that you are carrying my child. That and perhaps the fact that I notice you're a wee bit bustier than I recall. And you're getting thick in the middle."

"Thick!" she cried in outrage.

"Just a little!" he amended with a laugh.

"This isn't funny! I . . . I'm still very angry!"

"Yes, but does it follow you're mad at *me*, wife?"

"I . . . I don't know. I'm still a little confu— Did you say 'wife'?"

"As a matter of fact I did."

"I . . ." She blinked away fresh tears. Tears of a completely different emotion.

She suddenly felt a burst of delight in her mind, and a great shadow whipped over the cottage.

"Oh! Koro! He's going to frighten the neighbors!"

"Then send him back home before they put together a raiding party or something. I'll bring you and the twins home."

"Home?"

"Unless you'd rather stay here?" he teased her. "It's a nice place, by the by, but . . . it'll be hard to make love to you with the twins in the next bed."

Sarielle blushed as the twins tumbled in the front door with a bucket held between them, water sloshing everywhere.

"I'll get the glass!" Jona cried.

"I'll help!" Isaelle said.

"You're not supposed to help!"

"But I can!"

"Girls!" Sarielle called out.

"Sorry, Sari!" they chorused.

Sarielle looked into Garreth's eyes and saw the broad smile on his lips. "A-Are you sure? We . . . we come all together," she said hesitantly.

"I've known that all along," he said.

"And . . . you want me?"

"I do."

"And you'll never sleep with Davine or any other woman again?"

He laughed. "I never slept with Davine."

"I know. I'm just checking."

"I'll never sleep with another woman as long as you are alive," he vowed to her.

"Well . . . that could be a very long time."

"I hope so," he said.

"No. I mean . . . a very long time. I-I'm a wrena."

"I know," he said, although he said it carefully because he had a feeling he was missing something.

"It means I will live in perfect health as long as the wyvern lives in perfect health. Barring any more injuries on either side . . . well, you realize wyverns live hundreds of turnings, don't you?"

"I . . . I do. I just didn't realize . . ." He laughed, amazed. "And Dethan was worried about me being immortal while you were mortal!"

"Yes, well . . . I didn't learn about the longevity factor until after I became a wrena."

"Would you have still done it if you'd known?"

"Yes," she said after a minute. "I needed to save the twins at any cost. It makes me sad to think I will watch them grow old and die, but at the same time . . . there will be something beautiful about it. About seeing the whole of their lives from beginning to end."

"And what about . . . ?" He touched her belly.

"I don't know. Koro says he can talk to her already. I didn't know that was possible. I've never heard of a wrena having children before this. I suppose we can research it."

"Does Koro know?"

"I suppose he can find out. He can ask one of the senior wyverns. They've been around for ages. They would probably know."

"Did you say . . . did you say *her*?"

Sarielle smiled. "I did."

"It's a girl?" His smile bloomed wildly across his face. "A daughter!"

Sarielle laughed softly. "I would have thought you would want a son. A warrior like yourself."

"I do. I will. When the time comes. But for now, a daughter is perfect." He kissed her forehead warmly. Then the tip of her nose. Then he gently kissed her lips.

"Water!" Jona announced, shoving the glass between their bodies, forcing them apart.

"Thank you, Jona," Sarielle said with barely repressed amusement. She accepted the glass and took a sip.

"So your sister is going to marry me," Garreth announced to the twins, who squealed with joy. And then just as quickly there were sounds of dismay.

"Are you leaving us?" Jona suddenly thought to ask, her bottom lip trembling in fear.

"I would never leave you, my little loves!" Sarielle swore to them.

"You're all coming back home with me!" Garreth announced.

The girls began to tear through the house, squealing and laughing.

"I'd say they are quite happy," Sarielle said with a smile.

"And you? Are you happy? I know I'm pushing you around, but . . . I have no choice. I have to have you and I'll do anything to keep you."

"Well, when you put it that way . . . I have to have you too."

Garreth grinned and a sudden lecherous gleam entered his expression. "And it's been far too long since I've had you," he said.

"Yes, well . . . the twins," she said with a pretty blush on her fair lavender cheeks.

"They have to go to sleep sometime," he said with a raised brow and a chuckle.

"Garreth!"

"Sarielle, come with me," he said earnestly. "I would bend worlds to have you ... live through any curse. And I have. Come home with me."

"Yes," she said softly. "I'll come home with you."

EPILOGUE

Sarielle was redecorating the mistress's rooms she had once lived in. They were going to be the nursery for their child.

There had never been such a thing as a coruler in the city of Kith, but they had done away with that notion and now both she and Garreth had taken on the role of joint bennesahs, ruling together.

The people of Kith did not know the wrena and the bennesah were going to be so long lived, but they would figure it out eventually. For now, the rulers were going to focus on other things.

Like decorating a nursery.

The crib had been handmade by some of the best woodcrafters known to man. In a corner of the room was a small statue of Framun, the god of peace and tranquility. Weysa outside their walls was one thing, but the goddess of conflict would understand why they did not wish to bring her nature into their child's room. Still, Framun was of Weysa's faction, so she would be pleased overall.

The floor had been covered with a thick-piled rug— a place for the baby to crawl. The outer room had been fitted with a bed for the child's nanny. But the care of the child would gladly fall upon the parents' shoulders. They were not interested in a wet nurse. Sarielle wanted to feed her child herself. She would not share that experience with anyone.

She was afraid of childbirth. She worried for her safety and, through her, Koro's.

But Sarielle tried to push all of that aside as she focused on directing her laborers in what way she desired things. There was a shelf being installed. A series of them, really. They were to hold the numerous toys the child's father was constantly buying in anticipation of his daughter using them . . . even though some of them would not be able to be used until she was much older.

Her aunts had been just as bad, using their pocket money to buy her dolls and clothes. They looked forward to her birth. No doubt so they would have a live doll to play with. They had even put a little more attention to their needlework, a task they normally found tedious, as they made her special little things like a mismatched quilt and a slightly lumpy little pillow. Sarielle had secretly undone the stitching on one edge of the pillow and filled it properly with down. That way the baby could use it and the twins could see her using it . . . never the wiser to the change that had been made.

"Sarielle!"

Sarielle turned as Davine hurried into the room. She had a little dress in her hands. "Isn't it divine?" she asked in a breathy rush. "I saw it in the dressmaker's store and I simply had to buy it."

"Davine, you don't need to do that."

"Yes, I do. If I am to be this child's nanny, I wish to do the job right."

"I am simply glad you wish to do it at all. Moyra could just as easily play nanny as she does governess for the girls. You know you don't have to. Your comfort here is secure."

"I want to do it," Davine said with feeling.

"You don't owe me anything," Sarielle said quietly. "I have long forgiven you."

"I do owe you," Davine insisted. "Forgiveness or no, I owe you for your kindnesses and generosity. For giving me a home when I did not deserve one . . . and for being my friend when I was such a bad friend to you."

"You know I don't blame you for it," Sarielle said. "What you did was wrong, but your heart was in the right place in the end. You were trying to protect me. Yourself as well. I can't fault you for that."

"Well," Davine said with a lift of her chin, "regardless, I am caring for this child. She will mean the world to me . . . just as her mother does."

Sarielle reached out and hugged Davine, who hugged her back desperately. If there was one thing Sarielle was sure of when it came to Davine, it was her contrition.

She believed Davine. Without question. The two had become fast friends once more after there had been apologies and forgiveness. Garreth had not fully understood, but Sarielle had repeatedly pointed out that he had forgiven his brother. Garreth had insisted that was different because Dethan was his brother. Brothers forgave. That was just the way it should be. Davine was not blood. Her fate, he had thought, should not matter to either of them.

But Sarielle had convinced him otherwise. Now he was accepting of the idea of Davine as their child's nanny . . . and as his wife's fast friend.

"I will put these with the others," Davine said with a smile. She hurried over to the chest that held all the baby's clothes.

"Oh my. Koro's here." Sarielle bit her lip in concern. Koro didn't usually come to her for no reason. She hurried as fast as she could to the castle wall, out into the blustery cold, and saw Koro there.

Why are you here, my love? she asked him.

Sarielle watched as he dropped a suit of armor from his claw to the snow at her feet. She jumped back when she realized there was a man inside the armor. A dead man.

Oh no! You didn't kill him, did you?

Apparently he had. The man had come on a quest to kill a dragon. So Koro had dispatched him . . . and was now giving the shiny suit of armor as a gift to her baby.

Oh. Well . . . thank you. She gave him a patient smile and a pat on his scales. She would have Garreth take care of this particular problem later. *I'm glad you kept him from hurting you, but in the future, I think the baby would prefer very small shiny things. She is very small, after all.*

Koro seemed to think on that a moment. To him, the man in the armor *was* small. But . . . whatever made Sarielle happy made him happy. So the next time he would pick something even smaller . . . like maybe a cow . . .

Meanwhile, he could use the shiny armor in his nest.

Koro grabbed the suit of armor and immediately launched into the air. He looked magnificent as always, but she could swear he had gotten a little bigger. He was growing. Aging. Soon he would not be a child anymore. She did not know what that would mean for their relationship, but she hoped it would not change too much. A little more maturity wouldn't be such a bad thing.

Sarielle went back inside the keep. It was brutally cold, the winter being a particularly hard one. She was shivering when she got back inside.

She hurried to her and Garreth's room and immediately crossed to the fireplace, trying to warm herself.

"What did you do?"

She turned at her husband's stern voice. He crossed over to her and put his arms around her, holding her close to the warmth of his body. "I saw Koro. Did you go out in this weather to see him?"

"Yes," she said with chattering teeth.

"Sarielle!" he scolded. "You have to be more careful of your health! What if you got sick? Damn!"

"S-stop. I'm fine. J-just chilled." She gave him a sly smile. "You can warm me, if you like."

Garreth elevated one brow. He smiled just as slyly and reached a hand to cover her distended belly.

"Are you certain? With the child . . . ?"

"I've fallen asleep on you every night for quite some time," she said, reaching to kiss his warm lips with her cool ones. "I miss you."

"Hmm," he growled softly. "I miss you as well. But I do not mind that you fall asleep. I know the child wearies you."

"Well, I mind." She turned in his arms so she was fully facing him and wrapped her arms around his neck. She pulled him down to her mouth and kissed him slowly and deeply, enjoying the familiar heat it stirred inside her body. "Come," she beckoned him on a soft, wispy breath. "Come inside my body."

This time the growl he released was more ferocious. He swung her up into his arms, and after moving to shut the door with his foot, he carried her over to their bed. It was covered in furs for the winter, keeping the chill from their bodies as they slept. Now they enveloped her softly as he set her down. He followed after her immediately, his body looming over hers.

"I long to take you fiercely," he said to her. He kissed her deeply, until she couldn't breathe. "But I fear my daughter is in the way."

Sarielle smiled as his hand went to her belly and stroked it lovingly.

"Well, you could always approach me from a direction where our child will not be in the way."

He grinned at that. "I could. Perhaps I will later. But for now, I will take you more tenderly . . . facing me . . . so that I may look into your eyes and see your beautiful face. See the full beauty of your body."

His words warmed both her body and her heart. "Well, I think then you should be my stallion," she said, her hand drifting down the center of his body until she was stroking him firmly between his legs. "And I should ride you to victory."

He closed his eyes briefly and groaned. "That is a fine solution," he said roughly, his eyes opening and looking down at her with a fierce green fire. His hand went to the lacing of her loose gown, pulling it free and exposing her chest and shoulders. "Whatever will I do without you when I must go?" he asked, bending his head to kiss her breastbone.

"No!" she said suddenly, pulling his head back up and forcing him to meet her eyes. "Do not say anything that might be viewed as dissatisfaction by the gods. I will not have them thinking we are ungrateful for all they have given us!"

"Of course," he said, touching her face soothingly. "You know I feel the same. I only meant to say that I will miss you."

"Well, at least you will not have to leave until after the birth," she said.

Both his hand and hers went to her belly. Spring was still some time away and the birth a full cycle of the moon after that.

"I am infinitely grateful for that. We must be certain to plan the timing exactly the same with our next child as well."

"I will do my best," she said with a laugh. "Now, enough talk of children. She will be here soon enough and consume all our time. Make love to me," she said beckoning to him.

He smiled at her, his heart feeling beyond light and his body hot with need for his wife. As he made love to her, turning her body every way he could, making sure to love every part of her, he thought of how very fortunate he was. He had never known such happiness. It eclipsed the memories of the curse he had left behind. He would never quite forget his curse though, and like Sarielle, he would always remember the lessons of it. But he was free of it.

The same could not be said for Jaykun.

Sometime later, after his wife had fallen asleep in the afterglow of their passion, he went looking for his brother. He found him where he usually could find him: Zandaria.

He would have preferred Jaykun stay with him in Kith . . . He had been separated from him for long enough. But Jaykun had wanted very little to do with his brother since his return. In fact, he had not appeared to have much in the way of feelings about anything. Except maybe bitterness and anger.

That was to be expected, Dethan had said. Although neither Garreth nor Dethan had responded to their freedom in such a way, Jaykun had been the brooding sort even before his punishment. As Dethan's second in command, he had taken the business of war very seriously. Now he must be the leader of their armies, Dethan and Garreth playing second to him, his task even more serious.

But . . . Jaykun would not be able to handle his curse without letting his brothers in. Not that he was fragile in any way. Like his brothers, he was a formidable warrior in his own right. But Garreth felt that being able to confide in Dethan had made his curse a little more bearable.

Garreth entered the main hall of the castle of the former rulers of Zandaria and found Jaykun immediately.

He was sitting on the throne at one end of the room. The throne had been made for a man of much smaller stature, so his significant height didn't exactly fit well on it. Still, he was reclined on the chair, one leg thrown over the arm of it. He was turning something over in his hands repeatedly. He glanced up when Garreth entered the hall.

"What are you doing here?" Jaykun asked, his tone unwelcoming.

"I came to see how you are."

"I am the same today as I was yesterday. Still, both days were infinitely better than those of the past seasons."

Garreth frowned. "I am glad you appreciate your change in circumstances."

"Am I supposed to thank you for it?"

"I . . . No. I do not expect gratitude."

"Good."

"What is wrong with you?" Garreth asked him.

"You mean besides the fact that I am incinerated for hours every night? Besides the fact that both my brothers are free to love and live? Besides the fact that my wife, the woman I loved, and my children are all long dead?"

"Jaykun . . ."

Jaykun sighed and held up a hand. "I'm sorry. That is unfair of me. I was the one who dragged you up that mountain. You did not deserve the punishment you received."

"I do not hold you responsible. It was my own choice."

"You don't?" He was honestly surprised. His posture straightened. "I thought surely you would. I know I blame myself. For all of it. I was the one who discovered the location of the fountain."

"Jaykun, I was a man in charge of my own destiny. The choice was mine."

"But you tried to turn us back several times. We did not listen."

"It makes no sense to cast blame for the past. It is the past and should remain there. You have a future now. You must look to it."

"I will try, brother. But . . . it will be hard. I loved Casiria . . . no matter what else happened."

His wife, Garreth thought. He was grieving the loss of his wife. Jaykun had loved Casiria beyond all reason. He had been devoted to her and his children. Garreth had never thought Casiria was deserving of his brother's affections, but Jaykun had been blind when it came to the woman. And he had loved his children with all the devotion Garreth would have for his daughter when she was born. He thought of what it would feel like to suddenly be without Sarielle and his child, and he understood why his brother was grieving.

"Your mind should turn toward your pact with Weysa," Garreth said, trying to be helpful. "Leave the past behind and embrace your future as Weysa's warrior."

Jaykun nodded. "I will, but it will take some time. I will be ready by the break of spring. I promise."

"Come back to Kith with me. Eat at my table. Be with us."

"No. Thank you, brother, but I cannot watch you be with your loving family." Jaykun looked at him apologetically. "In time I will, perhaps. But for now . . . I am too jealous of your life and your love."

"I understand. But my door is open, should you change your mind."

Jaykun nodded to him and Garreth headed back out of the castle.

Garreth once again found himself counting his blessings. He was grateful to have two of his three brothers free of the majority of their torment. He was grateful for his release from his own curse. He was grateful for his life of comfort and his home.

But more than anything, he was grateful for his wife. Sarielle meant everything to him. She meant the world and then some. He was lucky to have her and to know the true measure of love with her.

He went back to his home, back to his wife, and climbed into bed with her. He pulled her sleeping body close, tucking her into the bend of his body. He brushed her hair back, baring her sleeping face to him. He settled his hand on her belly.

His curse was over. He was free. Free to love.

And never again would he do anything that he felt in his soul was wrong. He would never risk losing her.

Never.

Garreth snuggled in with his wife and fell asleep.

Read on for an exciting sneak peek
of the next book in

The IMMORTAL BROTHERS series

BOUND BY SIN
BY JACQUELYN FRANK

By the time Jaykun awoke, the battle was over.
And dusk was approaching.

He sat up and a sharp pain lanced through him, taking his breath away. Still, he was much better off than he had been. And he had felt much worse before. Much worse. Garreth and Dethan were both missing from the tent, as was Shey. Tonkin was sitting close by however. No doubt keeping an eye on him.

"Where are my brothers?" he asked with a groan as he threw his legs over the side of the cot. Tonkin hastened to his feet and reached to help him, but Jaykun fended him off with a raised hand.

"They are helping bring the wounded off the field."

"And the battle?"

"Won. All that's left now is the city walls to breach. But I don't imagine it will be much of a fight since they sent most of their men into the field."

"Wise rulers would have held at least some for defending the walls. But in the face of an army as massive as ours, they would have been much better served to open their gates and let us in peacefully. Now there is death on their doorstep and women without husbands and sons. Even some daughters."

"People think fighting for their way of life is more important than their lives themselves."

Jaykun straightened to his full height, although it took some doing. His whole body ached, as well as his throbbing chest. But his heart was beating and the bleeding had stopped. It was an improvement over hours earlier.

"Sor, where are you going?" Tonkin asked hesitantly. He knew that questioning Jaykun wasn't a wise idea, but the brothers had told him to keep Jaykun down as long as possible.

"It is dusk. I have business elsewhere."

Tonkin nodded. He had been around the brothers long enough to know what came with dusk. He stepped back and let Jaykun pass.

Jaykun walked out of the tent and into the camp. The whole of it was active, but it was a weary sort of activity. The bustle of men coming back from battle, tired and bloodied and some deeply wounded. But their day would not end until darkness forced it upon them. They were good men, dedicated soldiers. Jaykun was completely committed to them, as they were committed to him.

He didn't have time to find his brothers, and there was no reason for him to. They would know what had happened to him.

He walked through the camp as quickly as his abused body allowed for. He had chosen a spot for this when they had encamped four days earlier. He had come there every night at dusk for each of those four nights . . . and would for every night following.

It was along a not-too-distant beach. Far enough away from the battlefield and the encampment to ensure he would not be seen. The beach was littered with seals, their large, sleek bodies sprawled out in the late-day sun, catching the last of its light on their shining fur. There were natural jetties bracketing the sheltered cove and they, too, were full of seals. There were even some morari to be found, their bodies just as sleek, if not on a much larger and bewhiskered scale, tusks long and ivory as they jutted out beneath their lips.

Jaykun had found a cove . . . a cave really, not too far down that beach and he headed right for it. The floor of the shale cave was submerged and that was fine. It didn't matter. He walked to the rear of the shallow cave and slowly disrobed, placing all of his clothing on a shale outcropping. Once he was fully nude, he sat down in the water. Upon being seated, the water came up to the bottom of his ribs and lapped there quietly.

From there he watched the sinking sun in the west. When the first touch of dusk came, he began to feel it. Sometimes he thought this was the worst of it . . . when he went from feeling fully normal to . . .

It always started in his hands. It felt like a stinging sensation, and then it intensified. He put them under the water, as if it might somehow delay what was coming.

It did not.

In the center of his palm his skin began to blacken. Then, like the sharpest burning cinder, the center of his hands began to glow. That was because it *was* cinders. His entire body was burning from the inside out and even the water could not douse the ferocious burn. He began to glow hotly, like a star caught on land, and agony clawed through him again and again. But he gritted his teeth together and refused to shout out, even though it took everything that he was to keep from doing so.

The water around him began to steam and boil, hissing as it lapped up against his fiercely burning body. The burn overtook him completely, every molecule of his body on fire. The water did not help or soothe.

Nothing could help.

This was his punishment and he must see it through, every night from dusk to juquil's hour. There was nothing he could do to change it. Would never be able to change it. He must suffer it alone, far away from anyone who might be accidentally harmed by what he became.

But what he didn't know was that he wasn't alone. Curious eyes were watching him, growing wide as they watched him burn and the water around him bubble.

But Jaykun was far too overwhelmed with his pain to realize it.

At juquil's hour the burning stopped. His body still glowed like the hottest ember in the fire, but now the water was able to douse those embers. It was still steaming hot around him, but it was better than the temperature of his body so he laid down in the water and let it cool and soothe him.

He began to heal almost as soon as the fire was out. It would not be an instantaneous process, but it would happen quickly. As soon as his vision had healed enough to allow for it, he got up, stumbled, and waded out into the colder, deeper water. The salt of it burned even as the cold of it soothed. He could hear the hoarse barking of the seals, even though he could not make them out in the darkness, other than to see dark round shapes lumped out on the rocks.

Slipping into the ocean, swimming into the calm waters of the cove, he let the water cool him completely.

The dead, burned skin sloughed off of his body and within an hour freshly healed muscle and pink skin could be seen in odd patches on his flesh. By the time two hours had passed there was no more blackened skin, only the scarring of the healing burns. Given several more hours, that scarring would disappear almost completely as well.

Jaykun swam back to the mouth of the cave and waded into it, looking for his clothes. He was nearly dressed when he thought he heard a splash that was somehow out of place in the rhythmic lapping of the waves. Probably a seal, he thought. But he was on his guard just the same. The last thing he needed was to be ambushed by a stray enemy contingent. Especially since he had foolishly left his weapons behind. But he had not been thinking very straight when he had left the camp. Still, the lapse was inexcusable.

He moved to the shore, stepping around the shale outcroppings with sure footing, the darkness meaning very little to him. He could not see in the dark any better than any man as a rule, but he did have a keener eyesight and sense than most and so was able to navigate pretty easily. It helped that the moon was coming full in a few days, so it shed a fairly bright light upon the beach.

Jaykun stepped from the sand and into the low, scrubby vegetation, picking his way back toward the camp. That was when he heard the shuffle of sound. The sound of brush being disturbed . . . but not by him. He turned about in the darkness, his eyes narrowing. He could sense that he wasn't alone.

"Get him!"

The shout preceded the launch of dark bodies from out of the vegetation. They had been crouched down low, indiscernible from the shale rocks and long grasses. Three men in dark clothing. Moonlight gleamed off a

raised sword and Jaykun had to move swiftly to get out
of its damage path. As it was the tip of it nicked his already abused skin, leaving a thin cut on his cheek in its
wake.

But that was the last lucky shot they were going to get,
he thought with rising anger. But even though his temper began to bubble, his movements were sure and calm,
almost rote. He caught the hand wielding that sword
and jerked on it, throwing the wielder onto the rushing
rise of his knee. His enemy grunted as Jaykun belted the
breath out of his body, and then Jaykun disarmed him,
arming himself in that same fluid movement.

The sword he had acquired was heavy in the pommel,
making it poorly balanced, but it was just right for
smacking the butt of it into the temple of the second
man. The third man rushed in, tackling Jaykun to the
rocky sand. Jaykun rolled with the weight of the man
until his enemy was beneath him. Jaykun straddled his
chest and brought the pommel of the sword down hard
on his nose, breaking it and stunning him all at once.
Then Jaykun jammed the heel of his free palm up under
the man's chin, pushing his head back and opening his
neck to the swipe of his blade.

Blood erupted from the man's cut throat and splashed
against Jaykun's clothing. Not that he cared. He was
more concerned with the two remaining men who had
since thrown off the effects of his stunning blows and
were now rushing him as a single force, tackling him
back into the sand. He felt his shoulder wrench under the
impact, but literally shrugged the sensation of it off. His
heavy-bottomed sword, however, went flying from his
hand. He was wrestling for control of the situation, trying to throw off the weight of two heavy bodies sitting on
his chest and legs. He arched his back hard, twisted every
way he could think of, but the fact was he was wrung
out. After being run through the heart and then suffering

his nightly torment, there was almost nothing left inside of him. Oh, he was immortal, but he felt every single second of that immortality in one way or another. Tonight it was in the injuries he had been forced to sustain. They weakened him, made him vulnerable. And gods help him if by some rare chance one of these men was wielding a god-made weapon. All it would take was a simple beheading by one such weapon and that would be the end of him. Although, sometimes—some very low times—he wondered if that wouldn't be for the better. It would certainly end the torment he suffered night after night. But who was to say he would be spared an entirely new torment if he should end up in the eight hells? At least alive there was some reprieve.

And so he fought. Oh, how he fought. He kicked and snarled, throwing both men off of himself, but they quickly pinned him down again. Still, he did not go down easy. The two men were panting hard for breath as they held him down, their faces battered from where he had managed to punch them, their bodies bruised likewise.

"Stay down *trega*!" the one nearest his head snarled at him, calling him what the Krizans had called the invaders to their lands. The Krizan on Jaykun's chest was built for sheer brute strength. There was no grace to him, merely muscle and ferocity. His bottom canine teeth, like all Krizans, tusked up over his upper lip. They were capped in a silvery metal that gleamed in the moonlight. The Krizans liked to adorn their prominent teeth in all manner of ways, but the warriors preferred to keep them sharp or make them somehow more vicious. A Krizan was not above biting his enemy.

His nose was flat, his nostrils wide. He looked a great deal like one of the morari Jaykun had seen on the jetty. He had on a sealskin hat, the floppy ends of it hanging over his ears.

"So, *trega,* you fall to Lukan! You are perhaps not so formidable after all!" he said in his guttural, heavily accented voice. There was a common language that most people on the trade routes spoke, but not all spoke it well or clearly.

"I presume you are Lukan?" Jaykun said dryly. He had relaxed, saving his strength for the opening when it came.

"Lukan! Greatest of all the mighty Krizan warriors!"

"Your mighty warriors looked more like sleepy women out on that battlefield today," Jaykun said.

The Krizan roared in outrage, spittle flying from his lips.

"The demon *trega* leaders use sorcery to win their battles! Evil trickery!"

"I hate to break it to you, but we don't have any mages with us at present. The most dangerous thing we have along those lines are the mem healers. Not very dangerous at all I'm afraid."

"You are a liar, *trega*! All *trega* are liars and demons!" He hissed past his over plump lips. "Now we will disembowel you and cut you into little pieces, painting a picture with you on the beach for the other *trega* to find in the morning."

So, they didn't realize he was the *trega* leader. That was perhaps a good thing, Jaykun thought. Otherwise they would have tried to kill him immediately, using him as some sort of trophy or whatever it was that the Krizans liked to do to the leaders of an enemy force.

"Why don't you all just give up already? We're going to come over your walls tomorrow, whether you like it or not. No one else has to die if you simply open the gates."

"We would rather die than let *trega* like you into our cities where you will kill our children and defile our women."

"Trust me, we don't want anything to do with your women," Jaykun said. To be blunt, Krizan women were twice as ugly as their hideous male counterparts.

"Again he lies," the second warrior said. "Who wouldn't want the beauty of a Krizan warrior woman? Kill him. His words irritate my ears."

"Yes, do get on with it," Jaykun said with a sigh.

His blasé tone enraged the Krizan warrior. He balled up his fist and punched it dead on into Jaykun's face. And it hurt. There was no two ways about it. Krizan warriors were definitely strong, if not exactly bright.

The Krizan pulled a dagger from his boot and reared back to plunge it into Jaykun's chest.

Oh no. Not that again, Jaykun vowed to himself. He freed a hand and reached to catch the downward plunge, his hand grabbing the meaty forearm of the warrior and stopping the dagger dead in the air. The warrior seemed as though he couldn't believe his eyes for a second, couldn't believe that Jaykun had the strength to countermand his strike.

The two struggled for several long moments, the warrior pushing down, Jaykun staving off.

Then the softest little sound slid through the air. Like a musical note, only gentler and more beautiful. The Krizan warriors froze and to Jaykun's surprise all the strength behind the dagger was gone. Instead they were suddenly tripping over themselves to withdraw.

"*Prava!*" one said to the other, their eyes wide. Both men scrambled off of Jaykun, turned and ran. They were trying to run so fast that they fell more than once.

Jaykun sat up, at a complete loss to explain what had just happened.

Then he heard it again. That soft, lilting note. Like a laugh. The sweetest most singsongy laugh he'd ever heard.

He got to his feet and peered out into the darkness.

That was when he saw a figure standing there in the moonlight . . . a woman. She was slight of build, tall but slim. She had long hair that rustled around her body in the ocean breeze. He could not tell what color it was, only that it was dark. It fell all the way to the backs of her knees. It could have covered her entire body, he found himself thinking. And a good thing too, for she was completely naked.

She was dark skinned, again, an undetermined color, but it appeared to be an even and beautiful tone in the moonlight. She had small breasts, curvy hips and long legs. And though he couldn't make out her features perfectly, he knew she was quite beautiful. Not a Krizan woman—she was too tall, too lithe, too pretty.

She came closer and became increasingly more beautiful as she drew to within five feet of him. She was smiling softly, her eyes running down the length of him, no doubt sizing him up just as he was judging her. She seemed . . . fascinated. She reached out as if to touch him and he jerked back. Her hand lowered.

"I won't hurt you," she said, her voice musical and sweet.

"Who are you?" Jaykun demanded of her.

"I saw you. Saw you burn. Saw the waters boil. How did you do that? Why would you do that? Do you enjoy it? Does it not hurt? Do you do that often?"

She barely paused between questions, leaving him the moment he needed to get over the shock of knowing he'd been watched. He supposed it would have to happen some time, but he had not seen anyone. He could have sworn he was alone.

"Did the Krizan hurt your tongue? Can you not answer? Is the moon not beautiful tonight?" She turned her face up toward it, closed her eyes and drew in a deep breath. She opened her eyes and looked at him and he saw they were silvery light in color under the moon-light.

"Who are you?" Jaykun asked again.

"Jileana. Who are you?"

"Jaykun," he answered in turn. "Where did you come from?"

"From the beach," she said. "Can you show me how to make the water bubble again? I want to learn how to do it."

"No, I can't, and trust me, you don't want to know how."

She frowned at him in consternation. "Very well. If you don't wish to share. Let's go back to the beach. It's safer there."

"I would much rather go back to my encampment." He eyed her nude state. "You shouldn't be out here . . . unprotected."

"Yes, it is not safe. Men make war."

"I am one of those men," he told her baldly.

She took a hesitant step back. "Are you going to make war with me and my family?"

"I . . . I don't know who your family is. But I don't make war on just anyone. In fact, I prefer not to make war. When I first go to a city, I see who it is they wor-ship, then try to convince them to let mems of my god-dess set up temples there. If they refuse, I become more . . . forceful, in my request."

"But my family worships Diathus. We have always worshipped Diathus."

"The goddess of land and oceans. That would make sense, coming from . . . well, I assume you are from around here. On a coastline. But everyone should wor-ship Weysa as well. For without conflict there can be no peace—of the mind, the body, or the soul. We must be conflicted from time to time, so that we may make the best choices and judgments, making us stronger and more sure."

Jaykun couldn't believe he was in the grass philosophizing with a naked woman, but it didn't stop him from doing so.

"You make a very good point. I shall have you speak to my father one day. He is quite learned and enjoys such debates. My mother as well."

She turned her head suddenly, and looked back toward the beach.

"I have to go now. Will you come back tomorrow night?" she asked.

"You can be certain of it," Jaykun said wryly.

"Very well, I will see you then! Goodbye!" She waved at him and hurried off. She was fast, moving sleekly into the darkness. All Jaykun could do was watch the line of her bare body until she disappeared into the cove he had come from. Odd, there was nothing down that stretch of beach. It was the very reason he had chosen it. Where could she possibly be going?

Jaykun didn't have time to dawdle over the matter. It was late and there was the danger of another enemy patrol coming by. Although, he suspected this raggedy band had been soldiers that had fled the thick of the battle, waiting for darkness to hide their presence so they could perhaps escape or, as they had done, cause trouble.

Jaykun went back to their encampment without any further molestation. Which was a good thing because he found himself completely preoccupied by the appearance of Jileana. Not just the baffling question of where she had come from, but so much more. Why had she been naked? There were dangerous men from both armies encamped just a short distance away. It was madness for her to be out and about at all, never mind in such a vulnerable way.

She had been really quite beautiful. As Jaykun thought about it, he could not recall having seen any woman to compare. All the more reason for her to be more cautious. Beauty could be a curse for a woman, drawing unwanted attention. Dangerous attention. And if he had to confess it, he himself had been incredibly drawn to her. Had she actually touched him . . . there was no telling what his reaction might have been.

No. Not true. He would not have had any reaction, Jaykun told himself sternly. She was just another woman who happened to be pretty. No more no less. And he had no place in his life for women, pretty or otherwise.

He made it back to the command tent, the encampment quiet now in comparison to the activity of earlier. When he entered the tent he found both of his brothers pacing anxiously, still fully dressed in their armor.

"At last!" Dethan cried when he saw Jaykun. "What took you so long?"

"You know why I must go."

"Yes of course we do," Garreth said with a manner of impatience. "But you are usually back— Have you been in a fight?" he asked abruptly.

"That is why I was delayed. I was waylaid on the way back."

"Oh. I see you made it out in one piece," Dethan said.

"Don't I always?"

"You know, it is not a given that you will make it back with all your limbs or head attached. You cannot be killed unless you are beheaded with a god-made weapon, but you can still be beheaded by a normal sword and be left on the ground and unable to heal until your body parts are reunited."

"Yes," Garreth said. "It is very hard to find one's head with one's body when the body cannot see the head for lack of eyes."

"This is all a moot topic. I am fine," Jaykun said, impatient with his brothers' worrying. He did not like to be coddled. He was perfectly capable of handling himself in any situation. "If you wish to discuss something, then let us discuss how we will approach the city walls tomorrow."

"I was thinking we would send a messenger, offering them one last chance to open their gates peacefully to us. Their army, such as it was, has been decimated. Our taking of the city is only a matter of time. Surely they must realize this at this point."

"They might. It does not follow they will behave wisely. Would you risk the life of a messenger?"

"Better one life than the lives of many as we embark on this last attempt at the walls."

"Yes, but the Krizans are very dishonorable," Jaykun pointed out. "They will be very unlikely to respect parlay."

"So we don't try at all?"

"I think not. If they want to parlay or surrender all they have to do is open the gates. They know this. We have already sent messages that we will not harm the citizens of the city if they but lay down their weapons. The rest is up to them. We will take this city one way or another and we will earn the fleet of ships in their harbor. I want those ships. If we are to move on the Isle of Moroun, and then to Shintu we will need those ships."

"It is said Moroun is heavily protected by the goddess Diathus," Garreth hedged. "If you plan to lay siege to an island that is protected by a god of Xaxis's faction— It is unwise. Especially when we are more able as a land army rather than a seafaring one. "

The gods were at war. There were twelve gods in all, and they had been split into two factions. One was lead by their goddess, the goddess of conflict and war, Weysa. The other was lead by Xaxis, the god of the eight hells. Meddling in the affairs of the gods was never a wise thing for a man to do, but they had been sworn by Weysa to do exactly that, for the power of the gods came from the multitude of their worshippers. The more they were worshipped, the more powerful they became. Every temple the brothers raised in Weysa's name made her and her faction more powerful. Every city they stole from Xaxis's faction made his weaker.

The only thing that protected them from the wrath of Xaxis at this point was their goddess's protection. But she only gave that protection if the brothers honored the agreement she had foisted upon them. An agreement they must honor no matter what, else they enrage the goddess and find themselves . . . well, all three brothers had learned firsthand of the vindictive nature of the gods. They would not court it again for any reason.

"One step at a time. I am not certain I will try to take Moroun. First let us take this city. Then we will worry about the next. Now, I don't know about you, but I am weary." He began to take off his clothes, revealing the burn scarring and damage that had been done to him that day. His brothers watched him with troubled eyes for a long moment, but then finally began to follow suit. They were each in their cots shortly after, sleeping the troubled sleep of men at war.